WNR

Contents

To the Reader

Most countries have their own particular heroes: Switzerland has William Tell and the United States of America has George Washington. Can you think of any other national heroes? In England one of our heroes is Alfred the Great. When you have read this book you must decide for yourself why we have made him a hero.

In writing this book my greatest difficulty has been to discover the true Alfred and distinguish him from the imaginary one who burnt the cakes and did all sorts of other unlikely things. I have tried to put into the main part of this book only facts about Alfred which I think are *authentic*. At the end of it you can read about the sources from which I took these facts and also about some of the *legends* of Alfred. I hope you will find the real Alfred even more interesting than the imaginary one.

Words printed in *italics* are explained in the Glossary on page 78.

1 *Kings of Wessex*

The south part of England is the country of the chalk downs – long, bare ridges of hills that seem to race along the sky. You can lie on the fine, short turf on top of the downs and watch the wind sweeping through the grasses, while the blue cloud-shadows slide over the fields below. On a clear day you can see a very long way – on one side, over the sweeping ridges of the downs, and, on the other, out over the lowlands beneath. Up there the ground is dry and the grass is short; there are few trees, hedges or walls to stop you galloping away like the wind. If your enemies were prowling, they could swoop on you quickly across the downs, but you, too, could chase them fast. Down in the lowland valleys you and your enemies could hide from each other more easily, but you would move much more slowly through thick woods and marshes.

Long ago much of the downland formed a kingdom by itself – the Kingdom of Wessex. It belonged to the West Saxons who had fought for hundreds of years to win it for themselves. They were a branch of the Anglo-Saxon or English people who had invaded Britain from the continent. The West Saxons had pushed back the Britons into Cornwall and into Wales. Then they had followed the West Welsh into Cornwall and conquered them there.

Perhaps the West Saxons hoped that there would be no more enemies to fight and that they could settle down to farm in peace. If so, they were wrong.

In the reign of good King Beortric, in the year 787, the people of Wessex were scattered all over the countryside peacefully ploughing their fields when suddenly men by the sea-coast saw three strange ships on the skyline. They were long and curved and swift. As they came swooping towards the shore, people saw that they were warships filled with fierce men. Everyone fled in terror. The King's *Reeve* came galloping down to the shore. He thought there was a chance that they might be peaceful merchants, so he shouted across the water, commanding them to come with him to the King. The only answer he got was from fierce fighters who leapt from the boats and killed him and all his men. Then in all the country round about they burnt and killed and

Viking ship on a carved stone in Gotland. Count the warriors in it. What does the prow look like?

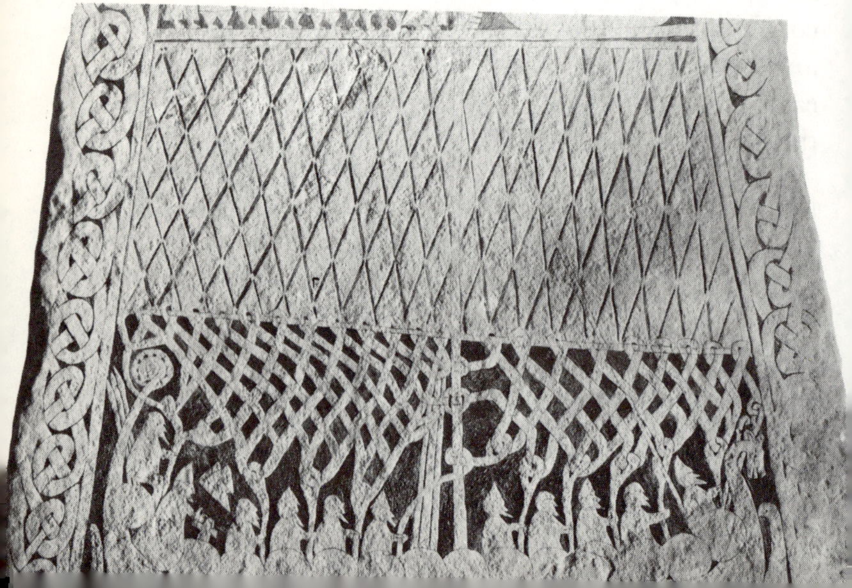

plundered, sailing swiftly away in their ships before anybody could catch them. These were the first ships of the Northmen that came to the land of England.

Soon the people of Wessex heard of these long, terrible ships swooping down on other parts of the English coast. They belonged to sea-faring men from Scandinavia whom the English called Northmen or Vikings. People living by the sea kept watch in dread and fled when they saw the fierce dragonheads which the Northmen carved on the *prows* of their boats cutting through the waves towards them.

Nearly fifty years after the first raid there was a great king of Wessex named Egbert who was determined to fight the Northmen. In the year 835 Egbert faced thirty-five of these ships as they drove ashore at Carhampton and all their crews swarmed on land. There he fought bravely and made a great slaughter of the Vikings, but two of his chief men (called *ealdormen*) were killed and the raiders stood to their ground. Look at the map inside the front cover to find Carhampton and the other places where the Anglo-Saxons fought the Northmen. Two years later they came again in many ships and this time King Egbert put them to flight. Alas – the next year he died, worn out by much fighting.

Still the Northmen came on, like packs of hungry wolves. Almost every year men watching anxiously on the coast would see the dreaded sails racing in and would go galloping off to warn the folk that the Northmen were coming. In the churches men and women prayed: 'From the fury of the Northmen, Good Lord deliver us!' But still they came. Against them fought King Ethelwulf, Egbert's son, and with him fought many brave ealdormen.

Later, as we shall hear, men wrote a 'Chronicle' of these terrible and exciting days. It was a chronicle with nothing in it for these years but battles:

> 840. In this year Ealdorman Wulfheard fought at Southampton against the crews of 33 ships and made a great slaughter there and had the victory.
> 841. In this year Ealdorman Herebert was killed by *heathen* men and many men with him in Romney Marsh, and later in the same year many men in Lindsey, East Anglia and Kent were killed by the enemy.
> 842. In this year there was a great slaughter in London and in Rochester.
> 843. In this year King Ethelwulf fought against the crews of 35 ships at Carhampton and the Danes had possession of the battlefield.
> 845. In this year Ealdorman Eanwulf with the people of Somerset and Ealdorman Osric with the people of Dorset fought against the Danish army at the mouth of the Parret river and there made a great slaughter and had the victory.
> 851. In this year Ealdorman Ceorl with the men of Devon fought against the heathen army and the English made a great slaughter and had the victory. And for the first time heathen men stayed through the winter on Thanet. And the same year 350 ships came into the mouth of the Thames and stormed Canterbury and London and put to flight the King of the *Mercians* with his army and went south across the Thames into Surrey. And King Ethelwulf with the army of the West Saxons fought against them and there inflicted on them the greatest slaughter we have ever heard of and had the victory there.

Did you notice in how many different parts of England the enemy landed? As you can see from the map inside the front cover, East Anglia and Mercia were separate kingdoms, like Wessex.

Did you count up the score of victories and defeats for the English?

Stem post at the front of the Viking ship. You can see this in the British Museum, London

2 The Birth of Alfred

Just in these terrible years, probably in 848, a little boy was born at Wantage under the Berkshire downs. His father was King Ethelwulf and his mother Queen Osburgh. He had three elder brothers – Ethelbald, Ethelbert and Ethelred – and his own name was Alfred. On the smooth slope of the downs above Wantage there was a strange shape of an animal cut out in the white chalk by men who lived long before Alfred. Perhaps one of the earliest things Alfred could remember was this strange beast, rather like a horse. (You can see another one like it on page 71.) When he was very little, too, he must have seen frightened messengers rushing in to his father. Then for the first time he would find out that there was a great enemy. He would be told that so far the heathen Northmen had only landed on the sea-coasts and ridden a little way inland. They had never yet got near the centre of Wessex to places like Wantage, or to Winchester which was the King's capital. They usually dashed in during the summer, raided as far as they dared and sailed home before wintertime. Did you notice where the 'Chronicle' said:

> And for the first time heathen men stayed through the winter on Thanet.

 How old was Alfred then? Thanet was some distance

from Wessex but it was bad news to hear that the heathen men had come to stay. King Ethelwulf and his ealdormen looked more and more anxious, and as Alfred grew from a baby to a little boy he began to understand why.

The court of King Ethelwulf moved about from one royal village in Wessex to another, and the small Alfred probably went with it. He learnt to ride a horse and gallop swiftly over the downs. Hunting was the great sport of all the King's court and soon Alfred was eagerly learning all the skills of hunting the deer through thick

An exciting hunt drawn in an Anglo-Saxon book

woods, of chasing fox and hare, of winging his hawk after game-birds. It was exciting sport to follow the chase all day and then return – horse and rider dog-tired – to the King's great hall, to a roaring fire and a huge meal of *venison* and, later, to sound sleep on a hard bench by the fire.

During the long evenings in the King's hall Alfred probably enjoyed most the songs of the *minstrels*. When the great steaming joints of ox, venison and wild boar had been eaten down to the bone and the drinking horns were going round the tables, the minstrel would start strumming on his harp. Then he would sing story-poems, in the Saxon language which Alfred spoke, about great heroes and their adventures, about battles and wanderings and strange monsters. They were long poems, but everyone listened, while the great logs blazed on the hearth and torches flickered round the walls. Night after night Alfred listened to the same poems until he knew them by heart and could recite the great deeds of his *ancestors* himself.

Perhaps he heard the story of the great lord Beowulf who slew the monster Grendel and then killed Grendel's mother, rescuing people from the terror of these two hideous dragons.

Osburgh, Alfred's mother, was a kind and noble queen and I think Alfred was very fond of her. Later on, one of Alfred's friends, Bishop Asser, told a story about Alfred and his mother. One day she showed her four sons a book of Saxon poetry. It was a beautiful book in which the first (or *initial*) letters were decorated with patterns in bright colours, like the one opposite.

Queen Osburgh said: 'I will give this book to whichever of you can learn it most quickly.' Alfred loved the brilliant first page and said eagerly, before any of his elder brothers could get in a word: 'Will you really give this book to the one of us who can soonest understand and repeat it to you?' She, smiling, said again: 'To him will I give it.' Then Alfred – without giving his brothers a chance – seized the book and ran off with it to his master, who read it to him. And when he had read it right through. Alfred went back to his mother and repeated it all to her. So he got his book of poems.

 You can see that Alfred was fond of books as well as

of hunting and that he learnt by heart very quickly. You can also see that he was a favourite with his mother. Bishop Asser says that he was the most handsome, pleasant and good-tempered of all the four brothers and so he was everybody's favourite. Besides wanting to be good at all sports, Alfred longed for wisdom and learning. It was not easy to get these, for there were no schools and Bishop Asser thought that Alfred's private *tutors* did not teach him nearly enough, so that he could not read till after he was twelve. Bishop Asser makes him seem rather a prig, but the good bishop never saw Alfred as a boy. He thought he was a wonderful king, so he made out that he had been a perfect little boy. Probably Alfred behaved much like other little boys, and yet perhaps in a special way he wanted to be wise, good and strong all at the same time.

One very exciting thing happened to Alfred when he was only four years old. His father, King Ethelwulf, wanted to ask the Pope in Rome, who was then head of all the Christians in the West, to pray that God would save Wessex from the Northmen. So he sent his precious possession, the small Alfred, away over the sea and over the mountains on the long journey to Rome. Of course a great many people went with him, bishops and great *thegns* as well as ordinary servants, and one of them must have carried the small child on his horse. For remember, there were no aeroplanes or trains: they had to ride for many days on horseback with dangers from robbers and wolves during much of the way.

When Alfred reached Rome he saw churches and palaces far grander than anything in his father's kingdom. He saw the great Pope, and at a most solemn ceremony the Pope placed on him a special robe and a fine decorated belt. Perhaps the little boy was quite bewildered and did not understand at all what was happening, but I wonder if he remembered it afterwards and pictured to himself the bishops in grand robes and rich *mitres* standing round the Pope at this solemn moment?

Alfred got safely home again through all the dangers of the roads, but two years later set out on the same long journey, this time with his father. King Ethelwulf took rich presents of gold and silver candlesticks to the Pope and gave money to the poor people in Rome. This time they stayed a whole year before turning back again over the Alps, through France, over the Channel to far-off Wessex.

Perhaps Ethelwulf had been worn out by the journey. Perhaps he was depressed because, in spite of the visits to Rome, the terrible Vikings still kept coming. Anyway he died very soon, in the year 858. Now Alfred and his brothers were left to fight alone.

3 *Four brothers against the Danes*

When King Ethelwulf died, he divided his kingdom between his two elder sons: Ethelbald had Wessex, while Ethelbert had Kent, Surrey, Sussex and Essex. They had their two younger brothers, Ethelred and Alfred, to help them. So there were three strong young men and the boy Alfred to hold back the Danes. The most important thing was that they should not quarrel with each other, because this would give the Danes just the chance they wanted. Perhaps Ethelbald was bad-tempered and did quarrel, for when he died, after reigning only a few years, the people decided it was better to have only one king. So Ethelbert became king and there were no more quarrels, for the two young princes, Ethelred and Alfred, were loyal and faithful to him. They never tried to get kingdoms for themselves, and it was fortunate that they did not, for very soon the terrible heathen enemy came sweeping down on them once more. This time a great many of the Northmen came from Denmark and so were known as Danes.

A great fleet of ships swarmed up Southampton Water, and their crews, seizing all the horses they could find, galloped inland and pounced on Winchester, the capital of all Wessex. This was terrible! Always before, the Northmen had attacked further away – in Kent, in the west, or in the north – but now they were striking at the very heart of Wessex itself. When the news came, two of the King's faithful ealdormen, Osric and Ethelwulf, raised an army of all the men of Hampshire and Berkshire. On their horses they went thundering over the downs until they caught the Danes and did battle with them and put them all to flight. This was a splendid victory, but the next news was bad: the heathen army had camped on the Isle of Thanet and the people of Kent had given them money and made peace with them. When the Danes had got all they could out of the Kentish people, they had stolen away inland, taking advantage of the peace, to burn and destroy all the farms they could find.

After reigning only five years poor Ethelbert died too. Fighting the Danes was a task to wear out any king. Now there were only two brothers left to save Wessex. Ethelred became king and the young Alfred was now second in command. Like great thunder-clouds the danger of the heathen enemy grew blacker every year. Now they had stopped their grab-and-go raids and had come to stay – a great army that moved like a plague of *locusts* over the country. The very year that Ethelred was made king of the West Saxons a new Danish army, the biggest ever, landed and wintered in the east part of England called East Anglia. Like the men of Kent, the East Anglians were afraid to fight, so they made peace and gave the Danes horses. The next year the Danes crossed the Humber into the kingdom of Northumbria and swooped on the city of York. Alas for the people of York! They were quarrelling as to who should be king and so no one was ready for the enemy. Too late the people of Northumbria rallied against the
 Danes with a great army and there was a terrible

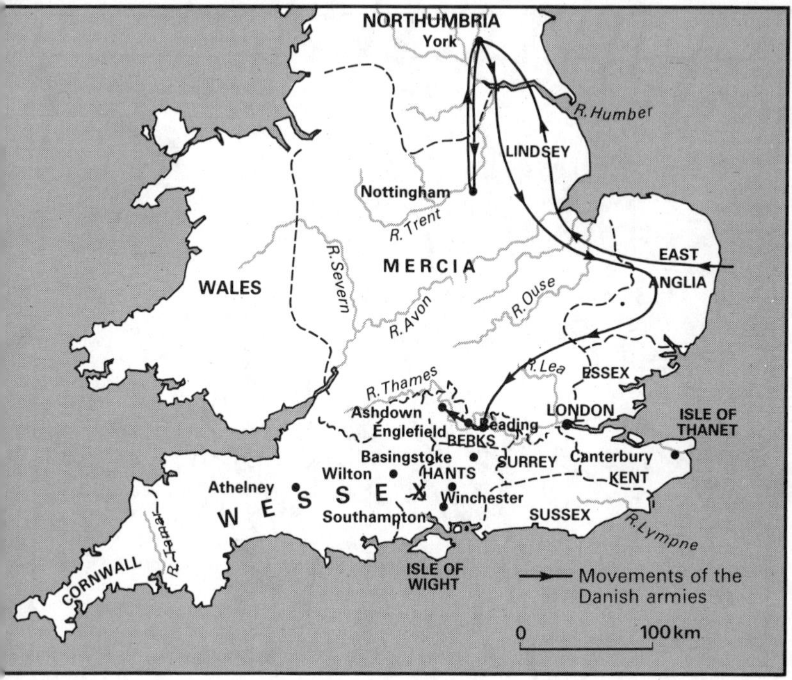

Movements of the Danish army, 865–871

slaughter of both heathen and Christian through the streets of York, and those that were left of the Northumbrians made peace with the Danes.

Ethelred must have listened anxiously to news of this disaster, and when he and his brother heard next year that the great army had moved south to Nottingham in Mercia, their fear grew. The thunderclouds were gathering close. The King of Mercia sent to ask their help, so Ethelred and Alfred rode north with an army of West Saxons. This is the first time the 'Chronicle' actually tells us of Alfred riding to battle. They were not very successful. The Danes were safe, inside the strong fortress of Nottingham, and the English army tried in

A king with his army. What weapons do the soldiers carry?

vain to break the walls. Perhaps the Mercians were half-hearted – anyway, they made peace with the heathen army and the two brothers rode back to Wessex knowing that a strong and unconquered enemy lay at their back.

Have you noticed how sometimes inky-black thunderclouds will pile up in the sky, and just when you think the storm is going to break right over your head, they seem to move away, always muttering in the distance and circling round but not quite reaching you?

Then, just when you think the storm is going to miss you, it comes rushing back, and bang! you are in the midst of it.

It was rather like that with Ethelred and Alfred. The heathen army did not follow them south from Nottingham as they feared. It went back to York and stayed there a whole year. Then it rode across Mercia, killed the King of East Anglia and conquered all that part. Still, East Anglia was some distance from Wessex, and perhaps Ethelbert and Alfred were just congratulating themselves that the storm had passed them when it broke with a great clap right on top of them. This is what the 'Chronicle' says:

> 871. In this year the heathen army came into Wessex to Reading and three days later two Danish *earls* rode farther inland.

At Reading on the River Thames the kings of Wessex had a royal hall. Southwards into Berkshire and Hampshire the long ridges of the downs made easy roads into the midst of the kingdom. Reading was a key place and if the Danes held it they could swarm all over Wessex.

It was time for urgent action. Messengers hurried over the downs to summon all the fighting men of Wessex. The first to get there was Ealdorman Ethelwulf with the men of Berkshire. He caught part of the enemy at Englefield and fought against them there and had the victory. Then, four days later, King Ethelred and his brother Alfred led a great army to Reading and fought there, with a great slaughter on both sides. But the brave Ealdorman Ethelwulf was killed and the Danes held the battlefield, for the West Saxons could not by any means dislodge them.

Ethelred and Alfred, however, were determined not to give up and make peace like the other kings. In four days' time they were back again fighting the whole heathen army at Ashdown. They knew this might be a fateful day, so they prayed to God before the battle. Bishop Asser tells us that the Danes started to attack while King Ethelred was still praying, and that, when he refused to stop, Alfred began the battle alone. This may be a true story, or Asser may have told it just to make his hero Alfred seem braver than his brother.

It was a fierce battle. The Danes were in two divisions and they managed to get on the top of the down so that they could charge down the slope on to the West Saxons. They looked terrible and bright as they came, with gaudy painted shields and flashing gold bracelets and gleaming *byrnies*. Ethelred fought against one army and Alfred against the other. Alfred drew his men close together, so that their shields made a wall in front of them, and charged up the hill like a wild boar. In the midst of the battlefield there was a great thorn-bush and round this the fighting was fiercest. Men slipped on the steep slope as they slashed and thrust at each other, but fighting never stopped until darkness came. Then many of the Danish earls lay dead on the short turf, with thousands of their followers, and the two heathen armies fled away into the night.

Yet Ethelred and Alfred dared not rest. Enough of the heathen army was left to move southwards into Wessex. After them went the two brothers and a fortnight later fought them at Basingstoke. Perhaps the West Saxons were very weary, for this time the Danes had the victory and began to plunder and burn right in the middle of Wessex. It took time to gather yet another army against

Another army from an Anglo-Saxon book. How do the soldiers protect themselves? Have they any armour?

them, for messengers had to be sent to the furthest corners of Wessex to call for men to fight.

Two months later Ethelred and Alfred at last caught the Danes again. This time the two brothers were victorious, but so many of their men were killed that they had to break away from the fight.

One of the terrors of the Danes was a banner which they carried in front of them when going into battle. On the banner there was a great black raven. The West Saxons told each other a story that the raven beat its wings when the Danes were going to win. But when the Danes were going to be defeated, the raven dropped down as if dead. You can imagine how eagerly the West

Saxons would look for the raven-banner as they advanced to battle. Perhaps at this time they never saw the raven dead, for the Danes were never utterly defeated.

Just when Alfred must have been almost despairing, two disasters happened. His brother Ethelred died, and news came that a great new summer army of Danes had reached Reading.

Now only Alfred, aged twenty-two, was left to fight the Danes. There was no time for an elaborate coronation. A month after he became king Alfred had gathered together a tiny army to meet the whole Danish host at Wilton. His tiny force fought stubbornly, and far on in the day put the Danes to flight. But once again the West Saxons were not strong enough to win a real victory over the enemy. For the moment Alfred's fighting strength was at an end, so the King of Wessex did what the kings of Kent, East Anglia, Northumbria and Mercia had long since done – he made peace with the Danes and paid them to go away.

So the year 871 ended. What a year it had been! Alfred and his brother had fought nine big battles with the Danes, besides many little skirmishes. They had killed nine Danish earls and one king, but they had not driven the Danes out of Wessex. That task was left for Alfred.

4 *Battle for Wessex*

By good luck King Alfred got a breathing-space. The great army moved out of Wessex and wintered in London. Then it moved northwards and drove the King of the Mercians across the seas and conquered all that land. In the year 875 the Danish host split up. One part, under King Halfdene, conquered Northumbria and settled down to live there. The other part, under the great leader Guthrum, looked round for lands to conquer and began to think of Wessex again.

At the moment Alfred was looking for enemies in another direction, for his scouts had sighted a Danish fleet off the south coast. It got a great surprise. The 'Chronicle' says:

> That summer King Alfred went out to sea with a navy and fought against the crews of seven ships and captured one ship and put the rest to flight.

So far as we know, no English king before had thought of going out to fight the Danes on the sea. Where did King Alfred learn to fight sea-battles with ships? We do not know. Perhaps in the breathing-space, when the heathen army had gone away up north, he was busy building his ships and training the crews. He was determined to fight the enemy every way he could – by sea as well as land. Look at the map on page 30 to see where

An Anglo-Saxon picture of Noah building the Ark. Alfred's boat-builders would use a tool like this but build a lower ship

the Danes went and where Alfred fought against them.

It was very hard that just after King Alfred had won this victory at sea over one enemy, another enemy struck him in the back. Guthrum the Dane was cunning and quick-moving. While Alfred was busy with his fleet on the south coast, the Danes in the north swept down. They dodged the West Saxon scouts, galloped right across Wessex, and got into the strongly fortified town of Wareham in the year 876. Alfred knew it was hopeless to try and get them out. So once again, he had to make peace with the enemy. He knew how often they broke their promises, but tried to get a specially solemn promise that they would speedily leave his kingdom. They took a particularly solemn oath sworn on a holy ring, yet still they did not keep the promise. Secretly by night they mounted their horses and stole away past the English army camped outside Wareham. Then they made a dash for Exeter.

 The fight with the Danes was now almost like a game

of 'touch'. Riding as hard as they could, Alfred and his army tore after the enemy, but could not catch them before they were safely 'home' in the fortress of Exeter. Once again peace was made with solemn oaths, and this time the enemy kept it – for a little while. It was now harvest-time in 877 and the Danes all trooped back to Mercia, where they settled down, while Alfred's weary men went back to their homes. There they reaped their corn and hoped the heathen men would never return.

But the next trick they played was worst of all. In those days armies did not usually move about during the long, dark winters, but stayed snugly in winter quarters. So Alfred probably did not think it necessary to keep many scouts out at Christmas-time. In his great hall the fire blazed and the Christmas feast was celebrated with joy and song, while all over Wessex his people sat at home, keeping Christmas. Then the heathen army slipped out of their winter quarters and, riding swiftly, came stealthily into the middle of Wessex and pounced on the royal town of Chippenham at Christmas 877.

You can imagine the terror and confusion when doors were suddenly burst open and the Northmen swarmed out of the black night into the cheerful halls. There was no time to snatch down swords and fight. The people of Chippenham gave in at once: there was nothing else to do. Then the Danes spread over most of the land of Wessex and settled down there. They seized farms and drove many people away from their homes. Others they forced to work for them. They seized everything they wanted and destroyed the rest. It looked as if the Danes had finally conquered Wessex. The 'Chronicle' says that all the people submitted to them, 'except King Alfred'.

Alfred seemed to have lost his kingdom. He had no army, for all his men had been scattered in their homes when the Danes had swept down. He seemed to have lost most of his lands and treasures too. But away to the west, guarded by the thick forest of Selwood, there was a part of Wessex the Danes had not reached. Here Alfred had many royal villages and many good friends. So, with a few faithful men, he began to ride secretly towards Selwood. It was dangerous going, for the Danes might have captured him many times. This time he did not go riding along the ridges of the downs where horsemen would be easily spotted, but pushed his way stealthily through the woods and marshes of the valleys.

Beyond Selwood, in Somerset, lay a great stretch of marshland with the Isle of Athelney standing up in its midst. Unless you knew the secret tracks through the wide beds of reeds, it was difficult to reach the island. For some time Alfred and his men wandered miserably among the marshes with little food or shelter. Then guides took them over to the island. Once in Athelney, they turned it into a stronghold where the Danes could never surprise them.

But Alfred never intended to sit tight in Athelney and do nothing. Backwards and forwards across the marshes went his messengers and scouts, seeking out Alfred's faithful ealdormen, urging them to gather armed men together secretly and be ready for the signal, telling people everywhere that the King was coming back. When the scouts returned to Athelney, they could report that the ealdormen were loyal to King Alfred and people were ready to fight whenever he called them.

Alfred waited until the winter was over and Easter past. Then he gave the signal and rode out, across the marshes and through Selwood, until he came to a high ridge with a great stone called Egbert's Stone, after his grandfather. Then all the armed men of Somerset and of Wiltshire and of Hampshire came to meet him there. Bishop Asser says: 'And when they saw the King they received him like one risen from the dead, after so great troubles, and they were filled with great joy.' Can you picture them crowding round the king they thought they had lost?

But there was no time for rejoicing. Alfred and his army must move secretly and swiftly in order to catch the enemy unawares. They camped one night above Warminster, then on they rode over the downs, looking for Guthrum and his army. Scouts galloped back to tell Alfred that the Danish host lay just underneath the steep edge of the downs. Coming hard over the top, Alfred and the men of Wessex charged down the grassy slopes and with a great shout pounced on the Danes at Ethandun (or Edington, as it is now).

There in the year 878 a mighty battle was fought which saved Wessex. Perhaps on this day the West Saxons imagined they saw the black raven dead, for at the end of it Alfred and his men put the whole Danish host to flight and chased them back to Chippenham. There Alfred stayed a fortnight to arrange a peace.

King Guthrum knew he had been defeated in a great battle. Perhaps he was a generous fighter who could admire this brave Alfred and his men. Anyway, he made the most solemn promises ('swore great oaths', the Chronicle says) to leave the kingdom of Wessex and gave Alfred some of his most important men as hostages. Never before had the Northmen been willing to make such a peace. Three weeks later, King Guthrum and thirty of his chiefs visited Alfred at the little village of Aller, near Athelney, and there an astonishing thing happened. For Guthrum, the heathen Northman, became a Christian and was baptized in the small church at Aller. King Alfred was his godfather. This font, which still stands in the church, may have been the very one used.

It must have been strange to see all these fierce, tough fighters crowding into the tiny church to see the christening.

In those days a newly baptized person wore for eight days afterwards a white robe with a white band round his head where the holy oil (or *chrism*) had been placed.

So you might have seen King Guthrum feasting with King Alfred in his hall still wearing his white baptismal robes. How different from the terrible Northman armed with helmet, sword and shield! On the eighth day, at Wedmore, there was another solemn service, called 'the unbinding of the chrism' in which King Alfred helped to take off the white robes. Guthrum stayed twelve days after this; when he went away, Alfred gave fine gifts to the Dane and his companions to do them honour.

This time the Northmen really did keep their promises for quite a long time. Guthrum and his army moved out of Wessex and finally settled in the eastern parts of England. They stopped fighting and became farmers and seemed much less terrifying.

Still, it was difficult for Danes and West Saxons not to quarrel and so begin fighting again. Alfred, above all, wanted them to settle down peaceably and learn to live side by side. So a few years later he made a special peace with Guthrum in which the two kings tried to stop quarrels. First, they drew a firm boundary between the Danish part of England (called the *Danelaw*) and the English part. Then they agreed on the sum of money which had to be paid by the English when a Dane was killed, and by the Danes when an Englishman was killed. Alfred was generous about this and let the Danes have a high price compared with the English. They also made rules to try and stop people going across the frontier to steal horses or oxen from the other side.

Never again did a large heathen army get right into the middle of Wessex. Of course this did not mean that Alfred was free from trouble. There were so many different bands of Northmen wandering over the seas that at any moment the dreaded boats with dragon prows might swoop in somewhere. Sometimes Alfred put out to sea and fought them with his ships. Once he hurried over to Kent to turn another band out of England. But for some time no big army attacked Wessex. Guthrum kept his promises and the other big armies of the Northmen were busy raiding and burning in northern France.

Alfred's fight against the Danes, 875–895

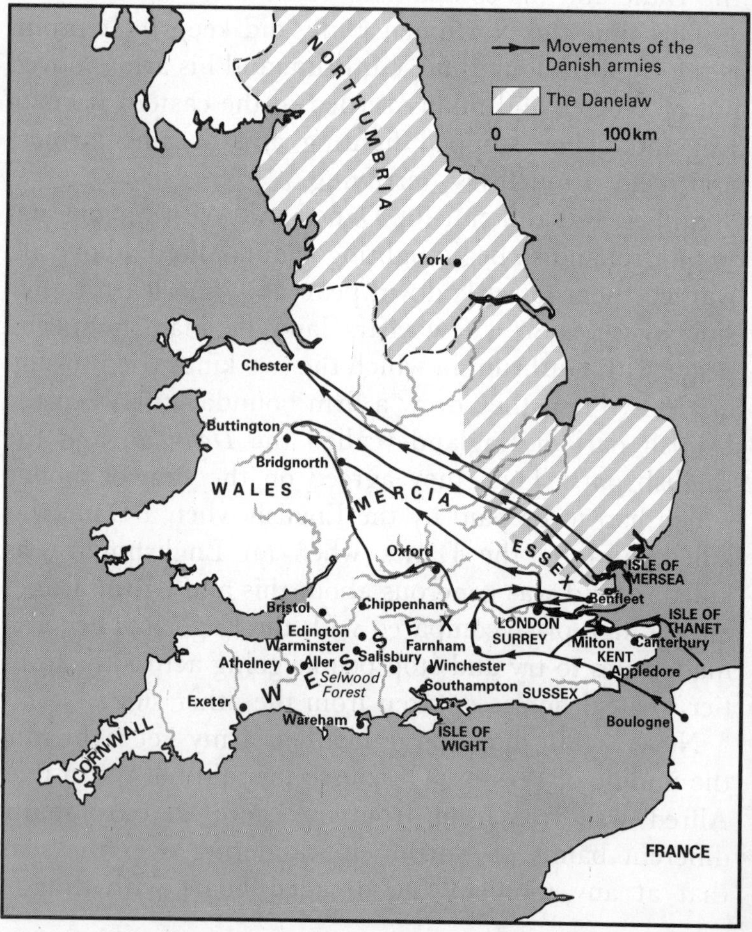

5 *King Alfred and his people*

No one painted a picture of Alfred while he was living, so we do not really know what he looked like, except what we can guess from a silver penny on which his head was engraved. This is a drawing from the penny:

Below left is a picture of an Anglo-Saxon king to show you how he probably dressed. His cloak would be fastened with a jewelled brooch.

His Queen, named Ealhswith, came from Mercia, the land just north of Wessex. Again, we have no picture of her but she probably looked like this noble Anglo-Saxon lady on the right above. Her long dress was usually woven of wool which was dyed to rich colours. The Queen and her women would probably spin, weave and dye the cloth themselves.

Alfred had several children. The eldest was a girl named Ethelfleda. When she grew up, she married an ealdorman of Mercia and was called the Lady of the Mercians. We shall hear more about her later. Alfred's eldest son, named Edward, became king after his father. Elgiva, the second daughter, became a nun and later was the *Abbess* of the *nunnery* which Alfred built at Shaftesbury. Elftryth, a third daughter, came next. Ethelweard, the youngest son, was bookish and chose to be a scholar. What do you notice about these children's names?

You remember that Alfred succeeded his brother as king. Now his brother had left two young sons and these might have made trouble for Alfred by trying to get the kingdom for themselves. But Alfred was very kind to them – he did not try to have them put out of the way, as some kings have done with young rivals – so they worked for him loyally and never rebelled or plotted against him. When Alfred made his will, he left them some land to show his gratitude to them.

All these children probably grew up together in Alfred's court. They had nurses and masters who brought them up carefully, teaching them to obey their father and be polite to everyone. They were never allowed to slack, and, as we shall see later, were made to go to school. But the court was an exciting place for children and all around them were Alfred's fighting men and faithful ealdormen. When they were not away fighting the Danes, there would be good hunting after the deer or wild boars or even wolves. In the evenings there would be stories of great deeds and adventures or long poems sung by the minstrels. I do not think these children would ever find life dull. Messengers would come galloping in to report about the enemy, and strange visitors from overseas, in outlandish clothes, would appear suddenly.

Alfred was fortunate in having loyal followers.

Perhaps it was because he was so faithful and hard-working himself that he found such good servants. There were men of all ages in his court. His ealdormen were the most trusted and experienced warriors. Here is a picture of one promising to be loyal to the King.

Each of the *shires* into which Wessex was divided had an ealdorman at the head of it to see that all the fighters were ready and to lead the army when the King called it out. Part of the time the ealdormen spent in their own shires and part with the King, helping and advising him.

Next there were the King's thegns, noblemen who

served the King in all sorts of ways, but especially in fighting. All the King's people had to fight, if need be, but the thegns were more warlike and had better weapons than the ordinary folk. They would fight in battle close round the King, and they knew that if he were surrounded they would have to fight with him until they were all dead. Luckily this never happened to King Alfred, but there is a story of one King of Wessex whose thegns all died with him in battle. In Alfred's court, too, there were many young noblemen, sons of his ealdormen and thegns, all eager to become warriors and to fight the Danes. There were also some special servants who looked after the King's household, with curious titles like dish-thegn, robe-thegn, bower-thegn. Can you work out what their duties were?

Besides all these, there were many bishops and priests at the court of King Alfred. He felt that his bishops were often wiser than he himself and so he asked their advice about many things. Some of the priests were his secretaries, doing all his writing, for they were almost the only people who could write at that time. One of Alfred's bishops became very famous. His name was Asser and he was a Welshman whom King Alfred invited to his court because he was very learned. The West Saxons probably found him rather strange at first, for he spoke with a Welsh accent and perhaps hardly understood the Wessex language. Asser felt he ought to go back to his own people in Wales sometimes, but in the end he stayed with Alfred a large part of his time, for he admired the King greatly. We shall hear later how he helped Alfred, and about the life which he wrote of his hero-king.

Asser tells us that Alfred loved all those who served

him 'with a wonderful affection'. He had their sons brought up with his own children and he himself used to teach them their letters. He arranged service in the royal household most sensibly, dividing his servants into three groups, so that each had a month on duty at court and two months off at home.

Imagine yourself visiting the court of King Alfred on a great night of feasting, perhaps the one celebrating the victory over the Danes at Ethandun. The great hall is built of wood with huge timbers rising into a high, pointed roof, rather like this old barn.

It is lighted by flaring torches stuck into the walls, but above their glow the roof climbs mysteriously into black shadows with only little glints of light on carved figures touched with gold. Blue smoke goes straight up to a hole in the roof from an enormous roaring fire in the middle of the hall. At one end the King sits in a carved chair in the middle of the high table. The Queen sits beside him. Everyone else sits on long benches.

On either side of the high table you can see grey-bearded ealdormen, solemn bishops, strong thegns. Perhaps the young princes are there, too, and some eager young noblemen who long to be as famous as the tough warriors around them.

For drink there are huge *pitchers* of *mead*, a very strong drink brewed from honey. Instead of glasses they use drinking horns. Some are beautifully decorated like this very old one.

Now from the far end, where the kitchens are, the servers come in procession with the food: great steaming hunks of venison, roasted wild boars' heads, with the tusks still on, a lovely roasted swan all in its feathers, dish after dish of meat and hundreds of little birds roasted on skewers. There are no spoons and forks. Everyone seizes a joint and tears the meat off with his own knife, fingers and teeth. They eat a great deal of meat.

The feasters get more and more excited as they raise their horns high and drink in triumph over the Danes. They begin to tell stories and to boast about their own or other people's brave deeds; the shouting gets louder and louder. But when the King calls his minstrel, everyone grows quiet. The minstrel strikes a long, wavering chord with his hand across the string of his harp.

Then he begins to sing a long poem about the great dangers and deeds of heroes in the past. Sometimes he sings sadly of their troubles, sometimes gladly of their victories. Men think of their own dangers and hope they will be as brave as these great warriors of the past. When the minstrel stops, King Alfred perhaps speaks to his own fighters, praising their loyalty and urging them to stand steady against the enemy, or perhaps he takes the harp and plays with the other minstrels. At last, full of food and drink, men begin to sleep where they sit. Then they tumble off the benches and settle down among the rushes on the floor for a good night's sleep. The King and his family go to their own separate room, called the *bower*. The great fire dies down and the torches flicker out: all you can see in the dim red glow are sleeping men lying all over the place.

King Alfred and his court never stayed long in one place. The King had several palaces, of which the most important was at Winchester. In each palace there was a great hall where the whole court could feast on special occasions, but the rest was not very much like a palace – just a collection of little wooden houses for various purposes. Scattered all over Wessex there were royal villages which the King liked to visit. He would probably sleep in a very humble wooden house, while some of his servants might have to put up with tents. The people in these villages had the duty of feeding the King and his court for a set time, perhaps one or three nights. They must have meat and corn and cheese and honey and perhaps special delicacies (eels, or a good goose or a salmon) all ready for the King when he came. So, when he was not fighting battles, Alfred moved round from village to village, sending a messenger in front to warn the villagers that he was coming.

At each village the King would be met by his Reeve, the servant who looked after all the King's property in that place. The King would hear all about the crops and the cattle and the work on the farm. He would probably ask a lot of questions about the people: whether they have enough to eat, if there are any thieves about, if people are doing their duties and paying their taxes properly, if anyone is refusing to obey the laws. The King liked to know as much as possible in order to govern his people well.

The ordinary people, many of whom were called *churls*, had to work hard in order to live, ploughing and sowing the crops, reaping the harvests, rearing sheep and cattle and pigs. Before they could start to farm they had to cut down trees and bushes and clear the land, for much of the country was still wild and uncultivated. This is what one ploughman said about his work:

> Oh sir, I work very hard. I go out in the dawning, driving the oxen to the field and I yoke them to the plough. Be the winter never so *stark*, I dare not stay at home for fear of my lord, but every day I must plough a full acre or more. I have a boy who drives the oxen and with a *goad* and he gets hoarse from cold and shouting. Yes, indeed it is very hard work.

The churls had to work hard to grow enough food for themselves, for the King, and for his ealdormen and thegns.

Famine was their great fear, for if the crops failed or the cattle died of *plague*, people just starved to death. Besides farming, all the men must be ready to fight in the King's army when they were called out and therefore must keep their spears, bows and arrows in good order. They also had to build bridges and fortified places at the King's command. Meanwhile, the women were working hard as well. Besides cooking, baking and brewing, they must spin and weave all the woollen cloth needed by the family and make it into cloaks, tunics and dresses for everybody.

As he rode round Wessex watching people at work, Alfred came to see that everyone's work was valuable and important, the poorest churl's as well as the greatest ealdorman's. He saw that a strong king needed workers of all kinds – priests to pray and churls to plough, as well as thegns to fight. Once he wrote this thought down in a book:

> A king must have many men for his service: men to pray and men to fight, men to labour with their hands, men he can trust as his friends.

If the king needed all these kinds of people, he thought, then he must look after them all properly. So Alfred saw that his own particular task was to govern all his folk well and to give them good laws.

6 *How King Alfred Governed Wessex*

Alfred would not make his laws in a hurry or just out of his own head. He collected all the laws he could find that had been made by earlier kings; he listened to people's complaints; finally, he called together a great council of all his wisest men – bishops, ealdormen and thegns. This council, or *Witenagemot*, as it was called, held a solemn discussion on all the laws. When everyone was agreed, King Alfred's priests wrote out his new laws. At the beginning he told them to write these words:

> Then I, King Alfred, collected these laws together and ordered to be written many which our *forefathers* kept, which I liked; and many of those which I did not like I rejected with the advice of my councillors. But I dared not presume to set in writing many laws of my own, because it was unknown to me what would please those who should come after us. But those just ones which I found anywhere, either of the time of my *kinsman* King Ine, or of Offa of the Mercians or of Ethelbert, I collected here. Then I, Alfred, king of the West Saxons, showed these to all my councillors and they then said that they were all pleased to observe them.

Here are some of the laws which Alfred made:

1. Let each man carefully keep any promise which he makes.
2. If anyone plots against the King's life, he is liable *to forfeit* his life and all he owns.
3. Whoever steals on Sunday or at Christmas or Easter, he is to pay double *compensation* for his theft.
4. If any man burns or cuts down trees belonging to someone else, he is to pay 5 shillings for every large tree.
5. If a dog bites a man to death, the owner is to pay 6 shillings for the first offence, 12 shillings for the second and 30 shillings for the third.
6. If anyone with a band of men kills an innocent man whose *wergild* (or price) is 200 shillings, each man in the band is to pay 30 shillings and the slayer the whole wergild. If the man slain has a wergild of 1200 shillings each man in the band is to pay 120 shillings and the slayer the whole wergild.
7. If anyone, for an insult, cuts off a man's beard, he is to pay 20 shillings compensation.
8. If anyone disturbs a *folk-moot* (or meeting) by drawing his sword, he is to pay 120 shillings to the ealdorman as a fine.
9. The fine for breaking into the King's house shall be 120 shillings.
10. We command that the man who knows his enemy to be at home is not to fight before he has asked him to do justice.

You can tell from these laws the kind of crimes men

did in those days. Look carefully at the punishments and think whether we should give ones like these. What do you think of the penalties for numbers 5 and 7? Do you notice that nearly all the crimes can be paid for in money, even killing a man? Do you think this is right? But one crime in these laws cannot be paid for by a fine. Which one is it?

Alfred sent his messengers to carry copies of the laws to every shire, for it was most important that the laws should be kept and criminals should be punished. Once a month all the people in one district met together in a folk-moot. This was usually held in a royal village.

The King's ealdorman or reeve was the chairman, but all the folk took part in accusing and judging the criminals. This was a very solemn meeting. As you saw in the laws, if two people got angry and started to fight in the middle of the folk-moot, they had to pay a heavy fine. In the moot men would stand up one after another and make accusations. One would declare that a certain neighbour had stolen his cow; another would show that he had had two teeth knocked out in a fight; a third might say he had been robbed on the road; others might accuse people of breaking into their houses or burning their hayricks.

The great problem in these law-courts was how to prove if the accused man was really guilty or not. The people in the court decided how the matter was to be proved. If it was a question of stolen cattle, they ordered the accused to find a man who had seen him buy the beasts, or a man who could swear that they were calves from his own cows. If he could not find a man to do this, then he was declared guilty of having stolen the cows. Sometimes, if the accused declared solemnly that he had never done the crime, the court would order him to find six or twelve friends who, in their turn, would declare solemnly that they believed he was telling the truth. These friends were called oath-helpers. It sounds an easy way out, but people believed that if you told a lie when you made this solemn oath, God might strike you dead. So generally the oath-helpers were honest in their oath and if the accused person could find enough people to take the oath, he got off. Do you think this was a good way of trying to find the truth?

If a man was accused of a serious crime like killing someone, the court ordered him to go to the *ordeal.*

There were several sorts of ordeal. For the ordeal of hot iron, the accused man had to carry a red-hot bar of iron for a certain distance in his bare hand. Then the hand was bound up for so many days. If it healed quickly, then the man was thought to be innocent. If it festered, he was guilty. In the ordeal by water, the accused man was tied up and thrown into a pond or river. If he sank, he was proved innocent and, no doubt, pulled out quickly. If he floated, he was guilty. In each case the people thought that God gave a sign in this certain way, so that really God was the judge. You will notice that there was no jury such we have today.

In those days families, or *kindreds*, as they were called, stuck closely together. If your brother or uncle or cousin lost an eye or arm or got killed in a fight, you marched along to the folk-moot with all your kindred and demanded justice from the kindred of the man who had done the injury. There was a time, much earlier than Alfred's, when you did not stop to go to the moot but got down your weapons at once and galloped off to put out an eye or chop off an arm or kill a man in the other family. It did not much matter whether you caught the real culprit; anybody in the family would do. This was called a *blood-feud*. But by Alfred's time people had agreed not to be so bloodthirsty. Before starting a blood-feud, they agreed to come to the folk-moot and demand that the other kindred should pay the proper compensation for the injury. Each man had a price, or wergild: the ordinary folk were two-hundred-shilling men, and the nobles were twelve-hundred-shilling men. How much more valuable was a noble than an ordinary man? If you killed a man, your kindred had to see that you

 paid the full wergild. If you knocked out a tooth or cut

off an ear, you had to pay the proper price according to a kind of scale: of course a noble's tooth or ear cost more than an ordinary man's.

This worked quite well so long as the other kindred agreed to pay, but sometimes families got tough and would not come to the court or obey its orders. They would *barricade* themselves in their houses and defy everyone, for their wooden houses could be fortified quite strongly. King Alfred was anxious to punish these lawless people and make them obey the courts, but he wanted this done, if possible, without a fight. That is why he made law 10 in the list which I gave you. The man of the family that was injured must first call the enemy to justice; then, if he refused, some of the chief thegns must ride with the injured family to try and persuade the wrong-doer to come to court. If he remained obstinate, the other party must sit down outside the barricaded house. If after several days the enemy still refused to come to justice, the house must be besieged and the wrong-doers punished. But this usually meant a bloody battle and started up a terrible family feud. King Alfred wanted to stop blood-feuds if he could, so he tried hard to persuade people to settle their quarrels peaceably in the courts.

Sometimes, however, the folk-moot was not very fair in its judgments. Perhaps the people were afraid to anger a very powerful man, or the ealdorman was obstinate and wrong-headed. The King wished everyone, rich and poor, to have a fair deal, so he allowed men to come directly to him to complain if they thought they had got bad justice. He was especially anxious to help the poor, for they had few other helpers. Although he was always busy, he would hear them patiently and try to put things right, for, says Asser, 'he was a careful searcher out of truth in judgments.' Once he heard someone's complaint and gave his judgment while washing his hands before dinner.

You can see that King Alfred wanted good peace in his country. There was a special King's Peace, and special punishments for breaking it. If you killed a King's Messenger or ambushed your enemy on the King's highway, or fought with him in the King's presence, or broke into the King's house, you had to pay a heavy fine to the King, besides all the other penalties. And gradually the King's Peace was becoming more and more important.

So long as the Danes stayed away, Alfred could give his people good peace in which to cultivate their farms and live quietly. But he was not so stupid as to think that the Danes would never trouble him again. Guthrum had settled down in peace, but there were other fierce Northmen fighting in France, and Alfred knew that one day they would turn back to swoop on Wessex again. So he tried to prepare for them.

He did three things. First, he built more ships and bigger ships ready to dash out when enemy boats were sighted off the coast. Secondly, he built little fortified towns, or *burhs*, as they were called, at good places on the coast and inland, so that, if the enemy landed, people could gather in a strong place and fight them better. Thirdly, he tried to arrange the army in a better way. Everyone had the duty of fighting, as you know, but the farmers hated being called away to fight just when the hay or corn was fit to harvest. The Danes so often came in summer time – the most inconvenient time for farmers. Alfred divided the army in two: half would be fighting, while the other half was farming, and then they would change over. So Alfred would have half an army of willing men, instead of a whole army of unwilling men. What do you think of Alfred's three ideas for fighting the Danes?

The great difficulty was to get people to work hard enough against the return of the Danes. When the King's ealdormen went round, they found burhs only half-built and people beginning to slack. You will hear what happened when the Danes did return.

7 *A king who loved books*

In those days kings who were good at fighting battles were not usually good at books as well. Indeed, they usually could not read or write at all themselves. Alfred was unusual. He did not shirk fighting and he loved sports, yet he was always hoping to have more time for books. When he looked around, however, there seemed to be very few books and very few scholars in Wessex. Books, of course, were not printed then but written slowly by hand, mostly by monks in monasteries. The Northmen – alas – had burnt some monasteries and others had been deserted by monks who fled in terror from the enemy. Many books had been burnt or lost and it was not easy for scholars to sit down calmly to write new ones when the Northmen might appear at any moment. So there were few monasteries, monks or books left in Wessex.

Alfred was determined to get them back again. He sent messengers to Mercia and to Wales and across the Channel to France and Germany, asking scholars to come to his court. These messengers were rather like bees sent out from the hive to bring back honey. They found Werferth, Bishop of Worcester, and Plegmund of Mercia; in France they searched out Grimbald, a learned man and an excellent singer, and from Germany they brought John the Old Saxon, who was cunning and skilful in many things. And especially there was Asser the Welshman, about whom you have heard already.

Perhaps Alfred made a special friend of Bishop Asser, for Asser tells us a great deal about all that Alfred wanted to do. First of all, he wanted to read and understand Latin. This Asser helped him to do. At first he used to read aloud to the King, and Alfred would soon repeat from memory whole pieces of the books he heard. Then one day, when the two of them were sitting in Alfred's own room talking of many things, Alfred suddenly pulled out a little book from under his cloak and showed it to Asser. In it the King had written with his own hand many of his favourite pieces from the books they had read together. So Asser discovered that Alfred could read and write Latin for himself. After that they always kept the little book handy to write down quotations. When one book was full, they started another one. So Alfred, in the midst of all his worries about the Danes and all the business of government, managed to sit down with a calm and quiet mind to his lessons with Asser.

The second thing Alfred wanted to do was to start a palace school. He thought that all the people important in government ought to be able to read and write, so he wanted his ealdormen and thegns to go to school, just as he himself was doing. This they found very hard to do, for many of them despised books: reading was priest's work, not the job for good, tough warriors. Yet when they got tangled up in the law or gave wrong judgments which the King had to straighten out, some of them began to feel perhaps Alfred was right. He would say to them: 'You judge badly because you pretend to be wise, but really you are very ignorant. Unless you go to school and learn wisdom, you must give up being a judge.' Then the terrified ealdorman would go away and try hard to learn his alphabet. It was stiff going, for he found it much easier to kill a raging wild boar than to learn to read. If he really was too old or stupid to learn, he would groan and say to his sons: '*You* must learn to read instead, and then you must read aloud to me.' Asser says that these stupid old ealdormen used to sigh deeply wishing they had learnt their letters when young.

A schoolmaster teaching boys

At any rate, Alfred insisted that all the sons of ealdormen and thegns should go to the Palace School with his own children. I expect that some of these boys, too, wanted to play truant: they would rather have learnt to master a horse or throw a spear accurately than master their letters or learn to write straight. But the King himself encouraged them to learn to write straight. The King's children, who seem to have loved books like their father, helped to make the school a success. The masters, who were priests, taught them to read both Latin and Saxon books. The King's children loved Saxon poems especially. Asser often saw them reading books, but the real bookworm among them was the youngest, Ethelweard. If King Alfred was not successful with all, he was with some. Do you think he was right to say that book-learning was as important as skill in fighting?

The third thing Alfred wanted to do was to write books in the Saxon language himself. It was difficult enough to persuade many of his thegns to read at all, and Latin was certainly too difficult for them. So Alfred decided to translate some of the important Latin books into Saxon. Asser helped him with this work, and some of the translations were done by other scholars, but Alfred did a great deal himself. I wonder whether, after a long day riding through the villages and settling disputes, Alfred sat with Asser and tried to translate one more chapter, and whether he sometimes fell asleep over the work?

He chose first to translate a book by Pope Gregory, called the 'Pastoral Care,' especially to help the priests, for even they were bad at Latin and found Saxon books easier. At the beginning of it he wrote:

> I turned it into English. And to every bishop in my kingdom will I send one, and in each copy there is a pointer, and in God's name I command that no man remove the pointer from the book.

Many people now think that the beautiful Alfred Jewel, which was dug up in Somerset, is the head of one of those pointers. You can see it and read more about it on pages 69–70.

For himself and his thegns, Alfred chose history and geography. He loved the story of how the first Christian missionaries came to England and of all their adventures, so one of the books translated was the history of these early times written by the famous monk Bede. Alfred was also curious about all the strange and wonderful things in the world, so he translated a history and geography of the world written by a Roman named Orosius. Whenever foreigners came to court he would ask many questions about their country and then add his own information to Orosius' geography. Once a sailor from the far north named Othere came to visit him and told a strange and exciting story of his adventures in that terrible frozen region. Alfred listened eagerly, wrote it all down and put it in his geography-book. This is the story:

> Othere told his lord King Alfred that he dwelt northmost of all the Northmen. He said that the land was very long north from thence and that once upon a time he desired very much to see how far that country extended due north or whether anyone lived north of the wasteland. So he sailed due north for three days along the coast, leaving always the waste land on the right and the wide sea on the left. Then he was as far north as the whale-hunters go at the farthest. Then he sailed still due north, as far as he could sail in another three days. Then the land there turned due east and he there waited for a west wind

> and thence sailed eastward as far as he could sail in four days. Then the land turned south and he had to wait for a wind from due north. He then sailed five days along the coast due south and came to the mouth of a great river. He dared not go any further for fear of hostile people called Beormians who lived beyond. (So far all the land had been deserted.) But by this time Othere had done the two things he wished – discovered new land and caught *horse-whales* on account of their beautiful bone teeth. So he turned home again. Othere gave King Alfred some of these whale teeth, but told him that the best hunting for big whales was in his own seas. There the whales were 48 or 50 *ells* long. He once killed 60 in two days! He told Alfred that he himself owned 600 reindeer, 20 horned cattle, 20 sheep and 20 swine.

Othere's men probably grew afraid as, day after day, they sailed beyond the farthest point to which the whale-hunters had ventured. See if you can work out on a map of northern Europe where Othere went. What winds did he need to blow him home again?

Alfred particularly wanted his people to know their own history, so he commanded some of his scholars to write the 'Anglo-Saxon Chronicle,' the story of the West Saxons and all other Anglo-Saxon peoples in this country. The writers collected old stories and songs and everything that had been told from one generation to another. They wrote down many exciting tales in the 'Chronicle': how the first bands of Anglo-Saxon warriors had come across the seas and landed on the coast of Britain, how their great heroes had fought hard battles

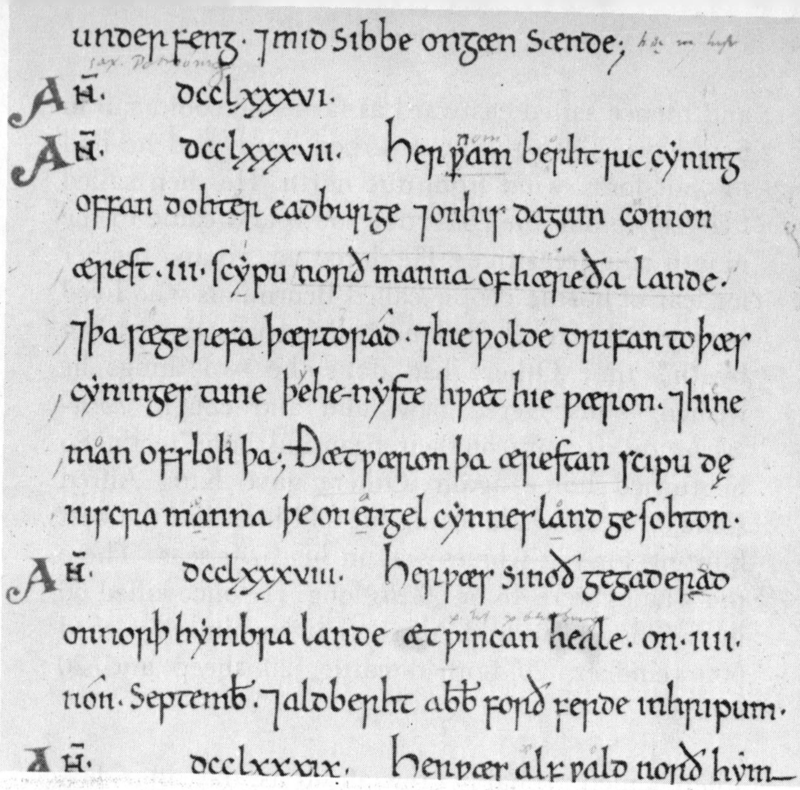
underfeng. & mid sibbe ongæn sende;
An. dcclxxxvi.
An. dcclxxxvii. Her nam beorhtric cyning offan dohter eadburge. & on his dagum comon ærest .iii. scypu norð manna of hæreða lande. & þa se gerefa þærto rad. & hie wolde drifan to þæs cyninges tune þe he nyste hwæt hie wæron. & hine man ofsloh þa; Ðæt wæron þa ærestan scipu deniscra manna þe on engel cynnes land gesohton.
An. dcclxxxviii. Her wæs sinoð gegaderad on norþhymbra lande æt pincan heale. on .iiii. non. Septemb. & aldberht abb forð ferde in hripum.
An. dcclxxxix. Her wæs ælfwald norð hym—

A piece of the Anglo-Saxon Chronicle. AN means year: find out the date (in Roman figures)

with the Britons, how they had gradually conquered the land and settled down. They told the tale of all their kings right down to Alfred himself, and then, of course, they wrote all about the fight with the Danes. On page 8 you read a piece from the 'Chronicle'. Here they were not putting down old tales which might be all wrong, but writing about things they knew. So when we read in the 'Chronicle' about Alfred's battles, we can be fairly sure that this is near the truth. The King himself would make the writers tell the truth. When Alfred and his thegns read about all the mighty heroes and deeds of the past, they longed, perhaps, to have great names in history too. But Alfred would never let the chroniclers make his victories sound greater than they really were; they must write it all in a plain, straightforward way, without any exaggeration.

If Alfred had lived today he would probably have been a great traveller. But in those days he dare not leave England for fear of the Danes. He did, indeed, see Rome and France when he was very young, but for the rest, he had to satisfy his curiosity by receiving visitors from far countries. All sorts of strangers came to see him, for Alfred was a king worth visiting. There were Frisians and men in large fur caps from the Baltic, wild Irish men, Franks and Gauls and splendid ambassadors from eastern lands in purple cloaks and tall golden caps. They brought him curious presents, and to all he gave rich gifts and letters to carry back to their masters. One day ambassadors came from Elias, the *Patriarch* of Jerusalem, and Alfred asked many questions about the Holy Land of Palestine which he longed to see. He sent back gifts and asked Elias to tell him some good medicines, for he knew there were wise doctors in the east. Elias wrote again telling Alfred all sorts of remedies. He said that petroleum was good to drink as medicine! This was one piece of his advice:

> The sick man should not let the wind blow on him, but go to his bath and sit in it till he sweat; then let him take a cup of warm water and treacle and drink it and then let him go to bed and wrap himself up warm and so lie till he sweat well.

For what illness would you say that was the cure? Alfred's family and courtiers must have grown quite accustomed to entertaining strange visitors who perhaps could not speak the Saxon language at all. They themselves went travelling, too, for Alfred sent his own ambassadors with letters and presents to the Pope at Rome, to the King of France and to other foreign rulers.

Alfred was interested in so many things that he perhaps could hardly find time for them all. He knew how to look after his beautiful hunting-dogs and *falcons*, and used to teach his dog-keepers and *falconers* their jobs. He liked to slip away to the *forge*, and hammer out beautiful things in gold which he designed himself. His goldsmiths were important people at his court, for they

A man working at a forge. What do you think he is making?

made fine brooches and clasps to wear on cloaks and rich ornaments for the churches. You will find out about the one very famous ornament, called the Alfred Jewel, a little further on.

Alfred also had builders who set to work, at the King's command, to pull down some of the old, wooden palaces and build fine, new stone ones instead.

Have you ever thought of inventing a clock? In those days there were no clocks except sundials, which were no help in the night or in cloudy weather. Now Alfred particularly wanted to mark the hours of day and night because he had vowed to give one-quarter of his time to God. So when he had thought about the problem for some time, he experimented with candles until he found out exactly how long they burned. Then he ordered six large wax candles to be made, each twelve inches high and of the right thickness to make the six, burning one after the other, last exactly twenty-four hours. But then he met a difficulty: if the candles stood in a draught, they burnt away more quickly and did not tell the time properly. Even Alfred's palaces were terribly draughty places where great winds blew through the windows and the chinks in the walls. So Alfred thought again and then ordered a lantern to be made of wood, with windows of ox-horn which could be split into very thin sheets as clear as glass. Inside the lantern the candles burnt steadily; as each one finished, another was lighted, and so Alfred counted the hours. Do you think this was a good idea for a clock?

Whether he was fighting, hunting, studying books, governing, inventing things or praying, Alfred wished to use his time, his riches and himself properly. That was why he invented the clock – to divide out his time carefully. In the same way he wished to divide his wealth carefully. So he commanded his servants each year to divide his income into two equal parts. Then he took one half and divided it again into three: one third he paid to his thegns who fought for him and served him; with the second third he paid the wages of all the craftsmen – goldsmiths, builders and the like – who came to him from many places; the third he gave to all the wayfaring men and strangers who came to him from every nation, near or far. The whole of the second half of his wealth he gave to God, and this he divided into four parts. The first quarter he gave to the poor. The second quarter went to two monastic houses which he founded – a *monastery* on the island of Athelney (where he had taken refuge) and a *nunnery* at Shaftesbury. The third quarter he gave to the Palace School, and the fourth he divided among other monasteries and churches in various places.

With his riches Alfred offered himself to serve God with a good heart.

8 *The last fight against the Danes*

For some years after Guthrum had been beaten Alfred did not have much trouble with the Danes. There were a few skirmishes and in the year 886 Alfred was able to capture London from the Danes. By this time Alfred was really King not just of the West Saxons, but of all the English who did not live in the Danelaw.

From the other side of the Channel there came terrible stories of great heathen armies storming Paris and destroying France, but for a while they let England alone. Then suddenly, in 892, the thunderstorm burst on England again. The great Danish army turned westward and came to Boulogne. There they seized 200 ships, and in one journey, horses and all, they crossed to Kent and sailed into the mouth of the River Lympne.

Have you noticed how often – even when you expect a thunderstorm – no one gets the raincoats ready until you are caught? Alfred had been warning his people that the Danes would come back; he had ordered them to build burhs and be ready. Yet four miles up the Lympne the Danish army caught a miserable band of peasants all unprepared in a half-built burh. Of course they captured it easily. That was bad enough, but immediately afterwards another leader, named Hasten, sailed up the Thames estuary with eighty ships and made himself a fort at Milton, while the first army dug itself in at Appledore. (Look at the map on page 30.)

So King Alfred had two armies to fight. He tried to prepare for battle by making the Danes already settled in the Danelaw promise not to help the fresh invaders. It was no use: they were always ready to promise, but they always broke their promises and joined in the raids which the new armies were making. At last Alfred collected an army and marched to a place where he could watch both enemy forts at once. You will remember that he had divided his army into two halves, serving 'turn about'. Now, with the half whose turn it was to serve, he sat down to wait until the enemy came out of their forts. It was most aggravating. They were too cunning to come out in a large force, but time after time, in small mounted bands, they slipped through the thick forest, between the English sentries, and went off raiding. At last, however, the Danes grew tired of being cooped up, so the whole force made a dash for open country. They collected much booty which they wished to carry north across the Thames, but at Farnham Alfred's son Edward caught them and with his army put them to flight and recovered all the booty. Then all the Danes plunged across the Thames through deep water and fled upstream until they took refuge on an island and there the English besieged them.

The Danes were in grave danger. Their leader was wounded and their food was running out; in a short time they would have surrendered. But at this moment the English had some bad luck. The army with Prince Edward which was besieging the Danes came to the end of its time of service and finished its food supplies. The men wanted to get back to their farms, so they started for home while King Alfred was marching up with a fresh part of the army to take their places. But while he

Defending a fort (burh). What weapons are the defenders using?

was hurrying there, he heard bad news – that the Danes who had settled in the Danelaw had broken out again; they had collected several hundred ships and, sailing round the coast, were besieging Exeter and destroying Devon. Alfred wheeled his army westward and went dashing off down to Devon to meet this new threat. So the besieged Danes were able to escape from the island. Then all the pieces of the great Danish army gathered together under Hasten and fortified themselves at Benfleet in Essex.

Now Alfred had left behind some of his trusted men, and Alfred's ealdormen would always do things on their own, if they saw a chance. They collected a small army, added some more men from London, and went to spy on the Danes at Benfleet. To their joy they found Hasten away on a raid, so they pounced in quickly, captured the fort and brought back to London all the booty and women and children, including Hasten's wife and two sons. Better still, they captured many ships.

This was good news to Alfred, who was not having much success down in Devon. But he would not keep Hasten's family captive, because the two boys had been baptized as Christians and Alfred himself was the godfather of one. So he sent them back to Hasten with rich gifts, reminding Hasten that he had once promised not to fight in Alfred's kingdom. Alfred hoped to shame Hasten by kindness, but Hasten kept no promises. The next news was that he had collected together once more all the bits of his army, and got large reinforcements from the Danelaw, and was off again up the Thames, burning and capturing all he could find.

Then three of Alfred's ealdormen, Ethelred, Ethelhelm and Ethelnoth, made a mighty effort. They sent messages to all the King's thegns in all the burhs all over Wessex, both west and east of Selwood. They sent also to the Mercians and to the Welsh. From all parts brave warriors rode in and when the army was assembled the ealdormen followed the Danes up the Thames and then up the Severn, until they overtook them at Buttington on the bank of the Severn. There they camped on both banks of the river and besieged the fortress on every side.

For many weeks the Danes held out, until they had eaten all their horses and were near starvation. Then, once more, they made a dash, but without horses they could not get away. There was terrible fighting and many of Alfred's thegns were killed, but the Saxons had the victory and only part of the Danish army escaped the slaughter and fled.

Yet still there was no rest for the West Saxons. The
 Danes were never beaten. When the remnant got back

to Essex they put their women and booty in a safe place, collected more horses and men, and were off again, galloping continuously until they reached the ancient Roman fort of Chester (then a deserted place). They went so fast that the English could not catch them before they were safe inside. Alfred's men could only grind their teeth with fury and burn all the corn and cattle outside. In the end it was hunger that drove the Danes out; they slipped past the English into Wales and then doubled back across England with all their captured booty. How hard it was to catch this slippery enemy! They got right back to Essex and safely on to an island, called Mersea, just off the coast. The English never caught up with them at all.

It had taken Alfred a long time to get rid of the Danish navy that was plundering Devon, but at last it sailed away and he could come to the help of his ealdormen. The Danish army had now been two years dashing all over England and raiding wherever it chose. In the winter of 894 the Danes moved from Mersea and rowed their ships up the Thames and then up the River Lea where they made a fortress twenty miles above London. This was very bad for the Londoners and the next summer they all marched out against the Danish host. Alas – they were beaten. Now at last King Alfred came. He camped outside London, to protect the people reaping their corn outside the city, and considered how to conquer the unconquerable Danes.

One day he rode up the bank of the River Lea to spy out the land and there he saw a place where the river could be blocked below the Danish camp. So at this spot the English started to build two forts, one on each bank of the river. When the Danes saw that their precious ships were bottled up and could not be got out, they abandoned them and made another dash across England to Bridgnorth on the River Severn. The English were very triumphant as they brought all the Danish ships back to London, but Alfred wondered what the enemy would do next.

If you have ever put your finger on a ball of quicksilver, you know that it splits up into many little balls. This is finally what happened to the great Danish host. After Alfred's finger had come down heavily on it on the River Lea, it soon broke up. Some bits remained rolling round the east and north of England, and a great nuisance they were, though not very dangerous. The rest managed to seize some ships and sail away to France. So the great Danish army disappeared and did not come back in Alfred's lifetime.

Alfred had one more effort to make, when he sent out his new ships against Danish raiders. He was proud of these ships – they were nearly twice as long as the Danish ships and swifter and steadier as well. Some had more than sixty oars. Nine of the new ships were sent against a Danish fleet that was doing great damage in the Isle of Wight. Alfred's ships blockaded them in Southampton Water and captured two ships. But, as you may know, tides are tricky there, and, just at the crucial moment, the English ships ran aground, six on one side but three on the same side as the Danish ships. This was very awkward! While all the ships were stranded, the Danes attacked the crews of the three and there they killed some of the King's chief men. Worse still – when the tide came up again, it reached the Danish ships first, so that they rowed safely out to sea, while the English raged with fury on the mudbanks.

Perhaps the Danes cocked a snook at them as they sailed by. Alfred's grand new ships were not, after all, a great success. It was not just the size that counted, but skill in managing the ships and knowledge of winds and tides.

In the year 896 Alfred must have been thankful, and yet, perhaps, very sad. In spite of raids like the one just described, he knew the big Danish danger was gone. Yet, in the last few years, so many of his faithful bishops, ealdormen and thegns had died – some of old age, but many in battle, and some just worn out by the struggle. He knew very well that without these men he would never have beaten the Danes; their hard, faithful service had brought the victory, and now that the work was done, it was sad that they were no longer there. Alfred himself was probably very tired by this time and we do not hear of anything special that he did in the next three years.

Years before, when the first great fight with the Danes was on, Alfred had made his will. With great care, trying to be fair to all, he had divided out his villages, houses and lands between his wife, his children and his brother's sons. He left them each a sum of money too. Then he thought of his faithful bishops, ealdormen and thegns – those that might be left – and provided a sum of money to be divided among them. He also wished money to go to priests and poor men, if there was enough left. Finally, he begged his children not to be unkind to any of his servants who had been specially bound to him, but to let them go free if they wished.

In the year 900 King Alfred died. Perhaps he had already told the chroniclers not to write a long piece about him, for this is all the 'Anglo-Saxon Chronicle' says:

> In this year Alfred the son of Ethelwulf died, six days before All Saint's Day. He was king over the whole English people except for that part which was under Danish rule, and he had held the kingdom for one and half years less than thirty; and then his son Edward succeeded to the kingdom.

Alfred liked deeds better than words. Once, when he was translating one of the Latin books, he stopped to think about how he would like to be remembered, and he wrote:

> I desired to live worthily as long as I lived, and to leave after my life, to the men who should come after, my memory in good works.

This was better than a grand tombstone or a long *epitaph*. Actually, nearly one thousand years later, men did put up a statute to Alfred in Wantage where he was born. On it they wrote this long epitaph in praise of Alfred:

> Alfred found learning dead, and he restored it. Education neglected, and he revived it. The laws powerless, and he gave them force. The church debased, and he raised it. The land ravaged by a fearful enemy, from which he delivered it. Alfred's name will live as long as mankind shall respect the past.

But I like better the words in which Bishop Asser praised King Alfred:

> He was especially and wonderfully kindly towards all men, and very merry. And to the searching out of things not known did he apply himself with all his heart.

9 *Two problems connected with King Alfred*

THE ALFRED JEWEL

One day, nearly 300 years ago, some men dug up a beautiful jewel near the Isle of Athelney. It had a richly-patterned gold frame and, in the centre, an enamel picture of a man holding a flower in each hand. At the bottom was a golden boar's head ending in a socket-hole where once there had been a wooden or ivory handle (now rotted away). All round the rim in golden letters were the Anglo-Saxon words:

AELFRED ME HEHT GEWYRCAN

These words mean 'Alfred ordered me to be made'. There is a picture of the jewel on the next page.

This jewel is a great unsolved problem. Indeed, there are three puzzles: Did it belong to King Alfred? What was it used for? Why was it lost at Athelney? The words do not say *King* Alfred, which is strange if it really was the King's, and there were plenty more Alfreds who might have had it made. But still, such a rich jewel would be most likely to belong to a king, so many people think it really was King Alfred's. Then was it a jewel from his crown? Perhaps it was. The crown would fit round his helmet, and so, perhaps in the time of great danger when Alfred fled to Athelney, he buried the jewel so that no sparkle of flashing light from it might betray him to the Danes. Or perhaps he dropped it as he fled.

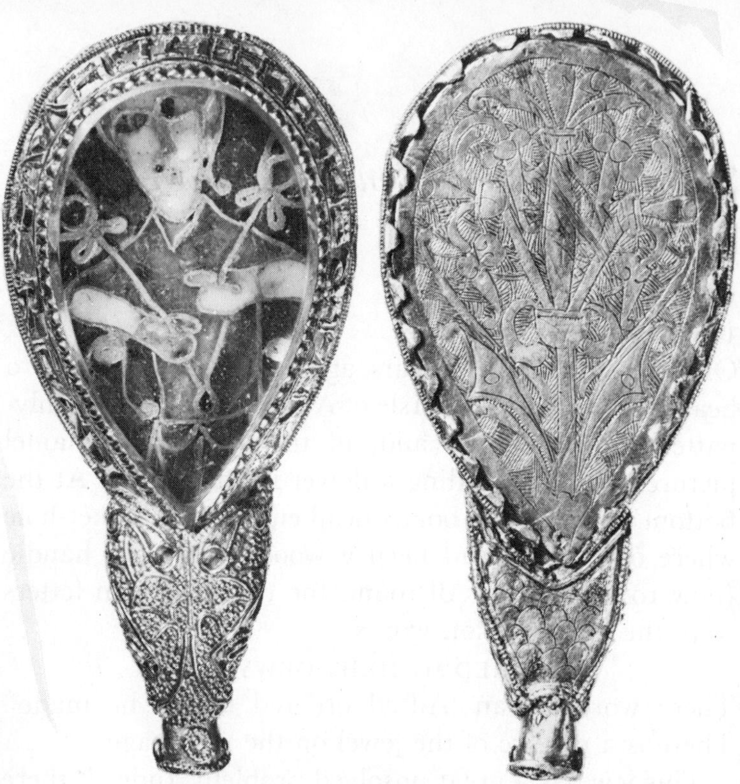

Some people, however, think it was not a crown-jewel but the head of a special pointer which Alfred gave to the monks at Athelney to point the place in one of the books he gave them. So perhaps it was not Alfred who buried or lost it but the monks of Athelney.

We cannot solve the puzzle yet, but one day we may find another clue which will tell us the jewel's secret. If it was really made and lost in Alfred's time, it lay in the earth 800 years before it was found. Today you can see it for yourself in the Ashmolean Museum at Oxford.

ALFRED'S WHITE HORSE

On the hillside near where we think Alfred fought the battle of Ethandun, there is a large white horse cut out in the chalk. You can see it from the train if you are travelling from London to Weymouth or the West Country.

Many people think Alfred had it made to mark his great victory over the Danes. But the horse we see today was certainly not cut out by Alfred's men for we know it was cut in this modern shape in the year 1778. Before that, however, there was an odd, comic-looking horse there, and what we should so much like to know is if this one was Alfred's.

This is a problem like the Alfred Jewel. It looks very old. In fact some people think that it was there long before Alfred – like the one above Wantage. They believe that Alfred took it as a lucky mascot and perhaps recut it when he won the battle of Ethandun. But the puzzle is that for hundreds of years after Alfred nobody seems to have noticed the white horse at all. If it was really there, do you think *nobody* would write something about it? That is so unlikely that many people think it was not there in those days and that King Alfred had nothing to do with it. They think it was cut much later by some people who purposely made it look old in order to fool everyone else coming afterwards. What do you think about that?

The Westbury White Horse today

10 Later stories told about King Alfred

After great men are dead people often make up stories about them. They are not content with the truth but want to add something to it, or even invent quite new stories of what they think their hero ought to have done. We call these stories *myths* or legends. There are myths about Alexander the Great, Charlemagne, Richard the Lionheart and many more modern people. Do you know any of these? Probably in a hundred years' time people will be telling myths about Sir Winston Churchill.

We do not know how soon after his death people started making myths about King Alfred. There certainly were stories going round, told by one man to another, but it was not until about two hundred years after Alfred's death that men began to write down these legends in the chronicles which we can still read today.

ALFRED AND THE CAKES

This is the most famous story about Alfred and here is how a chronicler in the twelfth century tells it:

> When King Alfred heard that the army of the Danes was so strong and so near, he straightway for fear took to flight and forsook all his warriors and all his people, treasure and treasure-chests. He went skulking by hedge and lane, by wood and field, till by God's guidance he came safely to Athelney and

took refuge in a swineherd's hut and obeyed him and his evil wife very willingly. It chanced on a day that the swineherd's wife heated her oven and the King sat by it, warming himself at the fire, for they knew not that he was the King. Then the evil wife waxed wroth of a sudden, and said to the King in anger: 'Turn the loaf so that it does not burn; I see every day what a lusty eater thou art and thou wilt be glad enough to eat it all hot.' He straightway obeyed the evil wife as needs he must.

In what ways does the story you know differ from this one? Later on other writers added bits to the story and turned it into verse. This is how a sixteenth-century ballad-maker told the end of the story:

Where lying on the hearth to bake
By chance the cake did burn:
'What! Canst thou not, thou lout,' quoth she,
'Take pains the same to turn?

But serve me such another trick,
I'll thwack thee on the snout',
Which made the patient king, good man,
Of her to stand in doubt.

ALFRED IN THE CAMP OF THE DANES

This story is told by a twelfth-century monk named William of Malmesbury:

While Alfred was in Athelney, he wished to find out the plans of the Danish army. So he disguised himself like a wandering minstrel and juggler and went boldly into their camp. He was able to get right into the innermost place where the Danish leaders were holding a council of war. There, playing his harp in a dark corner, he listened and looked as hard as he could and found out all their most secret plans. He stayed in the camp several days until he was satisfied that he knew everything. Then he stole back to Athelney, gathered together all his own leaders and explained to them how easily they could beat the Danes. All leapt to the task and they fell on the barbarians, defeating them with great slaughter.

OTHER STORIES ABOUT ALFRED

Many other stories were told. One of these makes Alfred the founder of Oxford University. In another he discovers, when out hunting, a beautiful fairy child named Nestingus. The child is dressed in purple with gold bracelets on its arms and is found in an eagle's nest at the top of a tree. Alfred brings it down and carries it back to his court to be cared for and educated.

Here are some lines from an Anglo-Saxon poem about Alfred:

England's shepherd,
England's darling
In England he was king.
A very strong and lovesome thing,
He was king and clerk,
Full well he loved God's work,
He was wise in his word,
And wary in his work,
He was the wisest man
That was in England.

How do we know?

You will understand now that it is difficult to find the real Alfred because he is often hidden behind legends. In trying to find the truth we can only trust what was written at the time Alfred lived (we call these contemporary sources) and sometimes it is hard to know what really was contemporary.

The main sources which people think contemporary are:

1. Alfred's laws and land-books which gave gifts of land.
2. Alfred's translations from Latin into Anglo-Saxon. We cannot be sure how much Alfred wrote himself, but we can pick out the bits of his own writing which he put in.
3. Alfred's Will.
4. 'The Anglo-Saxon Chronicle.' We are fairly sure that this was started by King Alfred, as you read on page 55. If this is so, we can trust the Chronicle on events which happened in Alfred's time and after, but we must remember that when writing about earlier times the chroniclers were only telling tales they had heard.
5. Asser's 'Life of Alfred'. This is our biggest problem in trying to decide the true sources for Alfred. There certainly was a real Bishop Asser who knew King Alfred, but the question is: Did he write the 'Life of Alfred' himself or was it made up by someone later who put Asser's name as author to make it seem true? If only we had the first *manuscript* in which the Life was written, we could probably tell if it was a forgery, but alas, the only manuscript known was burnt. So we only have left copies of the Life printed in the sixteenth century before the manuscript was burnt. The trouble is that Archbishop Parker, who had the book printed, put in a lot of legends. Many of these false pieces have been detected and most people think that what is left is the true Life written by Bishop Asser who knew Alfred. But some people still argue that the whole book is a collection of forgeries, one added to another. You can see that in history one of the great problems in how to distinguish the true from the false.

Things to do

1. Make a big map of the south of England and mark on it all Alfred's marches and battles against the Danes.
2. Write your own Chronicle of Alfred's doings between the years 871 and 878.
3. Paint a picture of the heathen Danes bursting in on the Christmas feasting at Chippenham in 877 (see page 25).
4. Discuss why Alfred found the Danes so difficult to defeat.
5. Make a model of a battle-scene between Alfred and the Danes, for example, the Battle of Ashdown (page 20) or Ethandun (page 27).
6. Discuss the laws on page 43. Do we make laws about the same sort of wrong-doings? Do you think it is right that a man whose dog bites someone to death pays 6 shillings while a man who cuts off someone's beard pays 20 shillings?
7. Write and act a scene in a law-court in King Alfred's day.
8. Did Alfred spend too much time and effort on books and schools and not enough on armies and ships? Hold a class debate on this subject.
9. Find out all you can about different inventions for telling the time. Ask you library for a book about clocks. Make models to show different ways of measuring time, including Alfred's.
10. Imagine you are one of Alfred's ealdormen. Tell the tale of the last fight with the Danes in 892 (see pages 61 to 67).
11. Make up a story about how the Alfred Jewel got lost.
12. Do you think the story of Alfred and the cakes (see page 73) could be true? Write down your reasons for thinking it *either* true *or* false.
13. Discuss some of the myths and legends you have heard about famous people. Try to distinguish the stories that are quite false from those that have some truth in them.

Glossary

Abbess, the head of a house, or abbey, of nuns
ancestor, a member of your family who lived before you
authentic genuine, true
to barricade, to build up barriers to prevent your enemy getting through
blood-feud, quarrel between two families in which each side swears to do murder for murder and injury for injury
bower, private room in which the king or nobleman and their families sleep
burh, fort or fortified town.
byrnie, coat of armour made of small metal rings, worn by Northmen
chrism, holy oil used in baptism
chronicle, history of important happenings
churl, peasant or man who works on the land
compensation, payment to make good damage or wrong done
Danelaw, part of England in which the Danes settled and lived
ealdorman, king's chief man who governed a shire and led its army
earl (*or jarl*), Danish word for a man like an ealdorman
ell, about 1.15 metres
epitaph, words (often carved on a tombstone) in memory of a dead person
falcon, bird of prey trained to pursue and strike down other birds
falconer, man who trains falcons and hunts with them
folk-moot, meeting of all the people in one district
forefather, same as ancestor
to forfeit, to lose
forge, workshop for heating and shaping metals
goad, spiked stick for driving oxen and other animals
 heathens, people who are not Christians

horse-whale, kind of whale found in the Arctic region
hostage, prisoner whose safety depends on his own side doing as the enemy asks
initial, first letter of the first word in a sentence (also first letter in any word)
kindred, family
kinsman, relation
legend, made-up story, generally about famous people, places or events in the past
locust, insect like a large grass-hopper which swarms in clouds, devouring every green leaf on the land and leaving a desert behind
manuscript, book written by hand
mead, strong drink brewed from honey, drunk by the Anglo-Saxons instead of beer
Mercians, people who lived in Mercia, a kingdom in the middle of England
minstrel, man who sings long story-poems to the music of the harp or other instrument
mitre, bishop's crown
monastery, house where men (monks) live a religious life
myth, same as legend
nunnery, house where women (nuns) live a religious life
ordeal, solemn test supposed to show whether an accused man was innocent or guilty
patriarch, important official in the Eastern Orthodox Church, higher in authority than an archbishop
pitcher, large jug
plague, a serious infectious disease which caused many deaths
prow, front of a ship
reeve, man who looks after the king's or a nobleman's property
shire, Anglo-Saxon word for county. Some counties (e.g. Hampshire, Wiltshire) still keep the Anglo-Saxon word
stark, very hard (on page 40 it means very cold)
thegn, an important servant of the king
tutor, private teacher
venison, deer's meat
wergild, price paid when a man was killed
witenagemot, meeting of the king's wise men

Index

Printed in Great Britain
by Amazon

38825027R00202

THE LOSS REPORT

Alex Breck

SEILACHAN
FORT

Published by Seilachan Fort

www.alexbreckbooks.com

ISBN: 978-0-9933887-4-3

For my family

Alex Breck

"This is certain, that a man that studieth revenge keeps
his wounds green,
which otherwise would heal and do well"
Francis Bacon

Prologue

He shivered in the dark shadows, more from fatigue and gnawing hunger than the unrelenting damp numbness that followed him like an unwanted dog. Life on the streets was proving to be a tough gig, for sure. But there were ways you could level up the odds. Hunting alone, but targeting larger groups of prey, seemed to yield better returns. He'd already established that fairly early on. He didn't care overly much about the reasons. But he guessed that maybe they felt the social pressure of not being too obviously hung up on the real reason they had congregated there. It was like on those natural history programs where the hyena pack would circle the young buffalo, momentarily distanced from the rest of the herd. That last person hurriedly leaving the table to catch up with the others. No-one wanted to be seen as 'that guy' who was more interested in finishing his double-cheeseburger with maple-syrup bacon strips than crowding around some screeching nobody, pointlessly trying to keep up with the latest memes from the scrum of cubicles of their software development office across the road.

Then there could be the added *faux pas* of acting like a tight-fisted bastard. He'd already observed some victims being ridiculously profligate with their leftovers when they'd become tied into an obligatory staff-kitty situation. The compounding

effect of inebriation also vastly improved his hit rate, but that couldn't be part of any successful strategy at this time of day. He winced as stomach cramps gripped him in a vice once again, forcing him to double over in pain and he looked around to see if anyone had noticed, fighting to retain some semblance of normality, a last vestige of self-respect. He didn't need anything like that to mess up his plans, right now. Normality. Shit. He thought he could vaguely remember being like them, somewhere in the past, in his dreams, when he'd had the opportunity to enjoy a glass of wine or the luxury of eating for pleasure, rather than survival.

A little bird fluttered somewhere close, above his head. He looked upwards, trying to locate the source of the insistent *chit-chit* distinct above the white noise of the city. There it was. A robin, smaller than the omnipresent pigeons, his little blushing chest puffed up with lusty bravado. For some reason, the man took this as an omen of good fortune. He squinted his eyes, unused to the early afternoon sunshine which bounced off the highly polished glass of the terraced courtyard. That's when he saw it. A half-eaten carvery special. All you could eat. And he knew he could eat a fair bit, given the chance. Moving ever closer, out of the shadows now, he could smell the outdoor barbeque and his guts did another premature foxtrot. He fixed his eyes on the prize.

Looked like several untouched slabs of meat. He could see some turkey, beef, roast chicken and wait a minute, was that honey-roast ham? Wiping his nose with the back of his hand, he decided he could taste the sweet aroma of the sauce, even from out there in the filth of the gutter.

It was time to go in for the kill. He coughed to clear his throat and forced himself to smile as if he meant it. He stepped forward.

'Excuse me, pal, do you think you're going to finish that plate of cold meat? I haven't eaten today.'

The lad put down his phone and sneered at him. No more than eighteen, the man decided and zero chance he'd survive unscathed on the streets on his own, even for one night. As he waited for the inevitable response, the man thought about the façade of civilisation that cocooned this lad who would never have imagined a circumstance that would lead to him have to live like this, in this primitive other-world. The teenager spat at him. 'Fuck off you hobo twat.'

Wanting so much to lean forward and grab the guy by the throat, to tear at the soft white flesh with his bare hands, instead, the man stepped quickly backwards, before any staff members noticed the stand-off. He pulled himself deeper into the protective gloom and waited for another chance. But that was the third time today. Time to try

something different. He had to do something about his look.

Checking his appearance in a shop window earlier, he couldn't tell anymore if he could do much about the way he looked or not. His face was always a mess of dried blood and dirt. A quarry-like hole in his mouth told him he must have lost a couple of teeth and it felt painful enough for him to think it must have happened recently. He knew he smelt terrible and he didn't like to dwell on what was causing the irritating itching underneath his many layers of clothing.

He didn't know how long he'd been like this. He couldn't remember his name, where he was from, or how he had ended up on the streets. It felt like it couldn't have been long, but that was only a hunch based on the fact that he couldn't remember anything about his 'street-life' further back than a week at most and it was staggering how quickly he'd deteriorated even in that short time. If it had been much longer, he guessed he'd have been dead by now. He'd been forced to adapt. He'd learned to steal. But the fights hadn't helped. He'd lost his watch and his shoes during that awful first night. Well, the first one he could remember. And with no coat, it got fucking cold after dark, even here in the middle of this huge city.

Where was he? Although he felt lost, confused and alienated, he recognised the more famous landmarks, crazily enough, although in his current state he thought much of the city centre looked more like location shoot for some post-apocalyptic movie. And why were there roads blocked off and people wearing surgical masks all over the place? At least he could understand the language even though he was pretty sure he wasn't from around these parts. He tried not to speak unless he had to because there was something about the way he spoke which seemed to antagonise people. They called him a *sweaty sock*, which he learned was street slang for 'Scottish,' but the crumpled scraps of paper in his torn jeans were in many other languages and he instinctively felt his bruised and aching body had covered a lot of miles in the recent past. But where had he been headed for? Who was he running from?

He *was* running, that much he understood. From whom or exactly why he had no idea. At first, he'd had that sickening feeling as if he'd woken up on some lounge carpet after a wild party, with little recollection of how he'd got there. But much more than that and weird as it sounded, deep inside he felt he'd been betrayed by someone. He knew he couldn't speak to anyone about that. Last night's miserable attempt at procuring some food had sparked a snarl of

recognition and frantic pointing at television monitors, followed by his madcap escape from two startled policemen who'd been too busy shouting into their comms units instead of running after him. Evading them had been an instinctive response. He didn't feel fit and he knew he couldn't be in the best of health but he had easily outrun them. Maybe he'd been a famous cat-burglar seeing as he'd scaled up that drainpipe so professionally. Or did he belong in a circus? Something about that rang a bell. His life was certainly a bad joke right now and he cringed as he remembered he still hadn't even managed to steal a newspaper to see what he'd done to make himself newsworthy. Too tired to think, he allowed himself to sink back down into the squalid shadows, becoming once again a wraithlike phantom lurking in the dark, waiting to pounce.

Chapter 1

EIGHT WEEKS AGO

Despite being half-cut as usual, the man felt his face flush with embarrassment. But he shuffled a little to his right to make room for the broad-shouldered guy, momentarily off-balance and now feeling suffocatingly warm under the bright casino lighting of the Bellagio Las Vegas. He raised a small pink hand to order another drink and the unwelcome intrusion would normally have been quickly forgotten as he turned his attention back to the craps table. He was helplessly mired in every Sin City vice all the way up to his scrawny neck, but good old-fashioned gambling would always be the charge galvanising him into action each and every evening.

But then the guy nudged him harder and this time Gerry spilt his new drink. He turned angrily and found himself looking up at a grey statue. The guy had no neck and his square face reminded Gerry of those blocks of granite hewn from the mountains of Mourne that his brother-in-law had favoured for his undertaker business. For gravestones. Come to think of it, he couldn't remember when he'd last seen skin as translucent white on a body still the right way up. Gerry quickly chose to take the easy way out and ignore the insult. There'd be no point trying to reason with this bloodless monster who he guessed must be wired to the moon. *Time to move*, he decided. Too late.

‘Sorry there, wee man, let me get you another of those, will ye. An’ am I not right in thinking it’s the beautiful Liffey water yer more used to drinking?’

Gerry stopped dead in his tracks, unable to think. He’d been reasonably successful in concocting his new persona over here, but recently, he’d kept having the distinct feeling he was being followed. At first, he thought he was imagining things and then perhaps it might have been old Brenda checking up on him. But she’d more or less dumped him now after his one too many furtive assignations with cheap tarts younger enough to be his daughter. She seemed happy enough with the Palm Springs condo, the pool guy and not forgetting, the money. What was left of it, anyway.

Cast adrift in the neon swamp of Las Vegas, more often than not, he’d wash up in a low-life joint off-Strip, where after too many Rusty Nails, he’d start blathering about the old country. His ex-colleagues back home would have called that ‘ill-advised.’

Gerry blinked fast. The last thing he wanted to do was start reminiscing with this body-double from some Bela Lugosi reboot. But then he noticed the enormous hand waving in front of his face, crisscrossed with scars and with fingers like fat sausages. Scratch that, he thought. The last thing he wanted to do was annoy the owner of that hand.

He allowed big Robert to buy him several drinks and then the pair of them abandoned the gaming tables and set about having a good old bevvy

session. Unencumbered by the restraining influence of their wives, the two men did what all ex-pat's do when abroad, they fabricated a fantasy-version of their home country and bemoaned the awfulness of the place they now resided in.

'Apart from the women!' Gerry slurred and the two men clinked glasses in a time-worn tradition. 'And the weather,' he added.

His huge companion had warmed up by that point and his pudgy cheeks had turned from white to maybe alabaster at best. He joined in the toasting with more restrained enthusiasm. 'And the whiskey, thanks be to Jesus!'

Gerry listened to the big guy in awe as Robert explained how he'd cracked a tooth falling down the hotel stairs several days ago. Not having availed himself of any travel insurance, he'd opted instead to pull the tooth out himself.

'I wrapped it with a length of string, right, like me old da' had taught me. Tied the other end to the hotel room door, right? Kicked the feckin' door hard as I could, no problem there, right?'

Gerry nodded.

'But instead of me tooth coming out, the bastarding door handle broke off and now the jaw is worse than ever! The only thing that works is the whiskey!'

Gerry looked in horror as Robert's face showed what he guessed to be a rare demonstration of emotion as it broke into a massive grin, exposing a

bloodied and sparsely-toothed mouth. Gerry was reminded of a graveyard for a second time. He didn't like to think what the door handle situation must be like back in Belfast. Completing the bizarre picture, in addition to his deathly complexion, the man possessed a streak of white through his otherwise black hair that gave him the look of a mad scientist. With alcohol short-circuiting his brain-mouth connection, Gerry heard himself speak before he could do anything about it.

'What happened to your hair then? S'pose that was another accident?'

Robert stopped smiling. 'Now then, that was no accident. That was an act of God, so it was. My friends call me Brock. Have done since I was a wee lad.' Gerry's face must have given away his confusion as he wondered if the guy had ever been 'wee'.

The other man growled, 'Brock, ye know, as in *Badger*... only now they call me Brock the butcher. Take another drink?'

Chapter 2

FOUR WEEKS AGO

Ridge Walker ducked as another round screamed past him, obliterating a clump of rock and heather above his right ear.

He cursed under his breath. *Why the hell I'm whispering I'll never know*, he thought angrily. It was true. The raw wind up there was savage even on a beautiful summer day like today. Down below him on the west side of the hill, the waves pounded into the rocks thereby rendering anything he might want to shout to be utterly indecipherable.

If he peered around the rock carefully, he could see the midday sunlight glinting off the wet seaweed, winking teasingly at him like bright-eyed sirens luring sailors onto the rocks with their seductive bird-song. That wasn't all he could see from his lofty perch amidst the alarmed cries of the gulls. He was trapped on this exposed cliff, there was a posse of men with guns intent on killing him and there wasn't a damned thing he could do about it.

Ridge leant his head against the sun-warmed granite and closed his eyes for a moment, breathing in the comforting aroma of the peaty heather crowning the hundred-foot stack he'd scaled dozens of times since childhood. Generations of his family had been buried in that same peat, only a couple of miles from here. His own mother would still be warm in her final sanctuary, laid to rest alongside his father

only weeks ago, sheltered in the lea of the hazel woods. Despite his predicament, Ridge gave a wry smile as he thought how both his parents would be spinning in their graves if they could see him right now.

He'd made a solemn promise to his ailing mother, that his wild adventures were behind him and how he would never again put himself or his family deliberately in the path of danger. Yet here he was, hanging from a cliff, dodging bullets. His beautiful wife Orla, and their two kids would be coming over the rise soon and unless he could get down from this crag, they would be walking straight into a killing field.

Wait a minute. He carefully switched his handhold and shielded his eyes from the blinding sun. He swallowed and frantically began shouting and waving his right arm like a madman. It was Orla, the August sunshine making her outrageous red hair shine with an even stronger intensity. She'd seen him already, he saw with relief, and tears came unbidden as he saw little Alex in her arms and his big sister hanging on to the other hand.

It was time to move, and fast.

Closer now, Ridge could see a line of men in tweed jackets and hats standing awkwardly amongst the bracken as Orla waved her arms at them, pointing angrily at the sky and back towards him as he scrambled down the cliff as fast as he could.

By the time he'd bounded over the few hundred yards, Orla had the tartan rug spread out and the sandwiches were being ransacked by the kids.

'Now, Mr Walker, we couldn't have picked a dafter day to do this than August the twelfth, sure we couldn't,' Orla's green eyes were gleaming with mischief as he knelt heavily beside her, breathing hard. He kissed her forehead and then ruffled the children's hair before standing back up again.

'Here, I've got a wee refreshment in the bag for you too, hun. Where you after going to now?'

Ridge grinned for a second and then set his mouth into a grim mask. 'I'll only be a minute, love. I need a wee word with these *gentlemen*. It won't take long, trust me.'

Orla shook her head and turned her attention to the food preparations. Ridge knew she must have been at least as angry as him back then, but now, as the eldest surviving member of his clan on Sorsay, it was incumbent on him to keep things right.

He strode up over the rise which acted as the spine of the large field. Any idiot with more than a basic understanding of rural life would have known that you wouldn't find grouse on this exposed stretch of land and their 'drive' had been headed in the completely wrong direction. It was all too common these days, for groups of people to book a trip online and arrive on the island without the permission or assistance of any local gamekeeper or other folk

experienced in Highland ways and then proceed to get themselves into all kinds of trouble.

It had only been the week before when half the island had been up all night searching for a lone kayaker who'd gone off to sea without any headgear and got sunstroke. Lost and confused, he'd eventually been found miles from where he had intended, his kayak upside down in the water and him with severe hypothermia, even in August.

The men were bickering with each other and obviously still smarting from whatever barrage of invective they'd endured from Orla. The nearest man, resplendent in a tweed deer-stalker and plus-fours was cradling his shotgun which was cocked and presumably ready to fire. *That's your second mistake pal*, Ridge growled to himself.

The man swung around and attempted a friendly smile before clocking the look on Ridge's face.

'I say old chap, I'm dreadfully-'

Ridge pulled the gun roughly from the man's arms and hissed furiously at him.

'Whoa, steady pal! What the fuck are you doing?'

He snapped open the weapon and emptied both cartridges before turning it back towards the red-faced man, butt first.

'Never, repeat never, carry your gun loaded and cocked. And *never* point it in the direction of me or my family!'

Ridge glared at the other men, his flint eyes blazing with a raw intensity. Every one of the men backed away and lowered their guns, some of them trying to quietly remove their shot without being noticed. One younger lad placed his weapon gingerly on the grass and backed away slowly as if his gun would spontaneously explode at any moment.

The deer-stalker guy didn't seem too happy about being spoken to like that in front of the others and he lifted his chin in what he doubtless had been taught was an authoritative manner.

'Do you know who we are? FYI this is the 'glorious twelfth' and we've paid a lot of money to come over here for a day of grouse shooting and you have no-'

For the second time in as many minutes, the man had his gun snatched from his hands as Ridge struggled to hold himself together.

'-Just shut it, pal! *F-Y-fucking-I*, this is MY land! There are no grouse in this field and if you don't get out of my sight I'll stick this up your arse!'

'Listen here you common little-'

Ridge snapped. He flicked the barrel back into lock and prodded the butt of the gun hard into the man's face. His nose instantly erupted with an impressive fountain of bright red blood. As the polished hardwood connected for a second then a third time, Ridge heard the small bones of his nose splintering and the man's hands went to his face as he dropped to his knees.

Ridge surveyed the others and snarled. 'Anyone else got something to say? No? Well get out of my sight and don't come *anywhere* near here again. Got that?'

The ashen-faced men nodded nervously and Ridge threw the bloodied weapon at their feet and turned away. He fought hard to hold back a smile. Fuck me, he thought, *I'm turning into a right mad old bastard...*

He'd decided two years ago, after witnessing a close friend being brutally murdered and then having his brother-in-law being apparently blown to smithereens by a car bomb, that there would be no more 'Mr Nice Guy.' But this was the first time since then he'd had to put it to the test.

He walked back towards the family picnic and grinned to himself. *That's better. It'll all be fine now.* The timing of this temper tantrum was a funny thing. Their upcoming holiday over in Chile, which they'd been looking forward to, excitedly counting down the days on the kitchen calendar, was evidently much-needed. Ridge had splashed a little of his recent inheritance on the trip, mainly to see Orla's big brother, who, as it turned out, hadn't been blown up after all. A trait that seemed to run in the family.

Chapter 3

TWO WEEKS AGO

It wasn't the cheapest, she was well aware of that. And despite the over-the-top gondolas, she had to admit to absolutely loving the god-awful cheesiness of the Venetian. Sure, Gerry would be shocked at the cost if he found out, but a funny feeling in the pit of her stomach told her that Gerry wouldn't be figuring much in her life from now on. She still didn't understand what she'd got herself into and she hadn't had time to figure out if it was what she wanted.

But right now, she wanted to party. Party like she'd spent the better part of her life living, if that's what you could call it, in a drab, grey, depressing Northern Ireland. A miserable dank corner of a backward primitive island where, in her prime years, most people's idea of a rare old time had been to throw a petrol bomb through a lounge window. A place where you could be spat on getting your shopping simply because your man worked for the police.

Brenda looked around at the sheer opulence of the Tangerine Lounge, drinking in the gold furnishings and the glamorous finery. It was a million miles from grey old Ulster. And now it was payback time.

She'd spent a fortune already since she arrived in Vegas only the week before. She quickly learnt that

the probability of finding the perfect nightclub offered the same cruel odds as roulette, but the Treasure Island's Tangerine Lounge fitted her like a diamante glove. Always quick on the uptake, she soon learnt to only pick up the dice with one hand and if the dealer puts money down in front of you, you pick it up, no question. She never wanted to leave, ever.

Their Palm Springs house had been a lovely escape when they first came over from the old country. Deliciously warm and dry, the pair of them had spent months lying by their pool lapping up the heat, like two contented fireside cats.

But then the money had begun to eat away at Gerry. It was no longer enough just to check his balance every day. He wanted to spend it, to show everyone how affluent he was. Sadly, Brenda quickly realised that moving 5,000 miles away had done nothing to improve the mindset of the pathetic excuse of a man she'd married all those years ago. Childless and emotionally barren, she could now see how their marriage had been like a prison sentence for both of them. And now they had the means to fulfil every longed-for sensation. At first, Gerry had been fairly discreet about his wee tarts. Then he lost weight, stopped eating, and soon he was rutting like an alley-cat. It was as if he had something to prove all the time. Brenda had found it disgusting. Bad enough he would drink himself stupid, and even the drugs she could

almost forgive, as it seemed as if everybody popped a pill these days.

They began frequenting the Vegas Strip more and more often and Gerry seemed to mistake the affectionate nickname for a subliminal instruction. She'd never been a likely candidate to be nominated for sainthood, but when his gambling and whoring began to burn more in a weekend than they'd budgeted for a month, she had had enough.

That was why the whirlwind of the last few weeks had been so refreshing. Meeting Angelo, her beautiful smooth-skinned boy, had been a physical and emotional awakening for her. She'd discovered feelings she couldn't have imagined only a few months back. Relishing recent memories with a warm flush rippling up her body despite the ice-cold air-conditioning, Brenda looked at her watch and smiled. He'd be finished his bath by now and she thought she might pop back up to the room and let him make love to her all over again.

That little fellow Jimmy had promised to meet her for a coffee before he flew back to drab Belfast and she was surprised he hadn't showed. A more unlikely man to bump into in Las Vegas you'd be pushed to find, she thought. He didn't drink and hated gambling but he did seem fascinated in the line of work her Gerry had been in and he certainly hadn't been tight with his money last night.

Brenda picked up the pile of chips from the green felt table and smiled. You called them checks

over here, not chips. And from the $20,000 Jimmy had let her have last night, she'd already bumped that up by over five grand. She'd never thought there would be much of a call for office photocopiers these days, but Jimmy promised her he made a killing. She wasn't too keen on the other guy, the big quiet one with the dodgy hairdo, but she reckoned he'd be fair handy if there was any heavy lifting to be done.

Chapter 4

ONE WEEK AGO

'Jeez! Will ye *look* at that.' Orla leant back in her seat to let him get a glimpse of the snow-topped crags below. Ridge blinked. The wings of the plane looked like they were only metres above the jagged teeth of the Andes Mountains. He fired off a few photos with their prized new camera and settled back into his seat for the imminent descent. He used to love everything about flying but for some reason, his ears didn't like the landings anymore. He found himself nervously fingering the disfiguring dark lines that wound their way around the otherwise pale skin of his neck. He knew exactly what the reason was. Same reason he would never wear a tie again.

He squeezed Orla's hand gently.

'Glad to see you're finally awake love. I thought I was going to have to leave you here,' he laughed.

They were both glad to be on the last stage of the longest flight they'd ever experienced. Close to fifteen hours, non-stop from Heathrow to Santiago, Chile. Ridge had no real complaints though. It had been his idea to choose this brand-new direct route and they both understood how important it was that they had as few stops as possible especially on the US continent. Every take-off and landing was another chance for their fake passports to be discovered or

their faces to trigger some new automatic face-recognition software.

He'd occupied himself by eating his body weight in food and watching more films than he'd seen in the previous year. But, his beautiful wife, Orla, had slept – the entire flight.

Neither of them had ever flown business class before. Not even when they'd attended a state funeral in Washington DC a couple of years before. That time they'd met the President of the United States who'd made a cheap joke about their not turning up to a medal ceremony which his predecessor had personally invited them to a year or two before that. Orla had shown him photos of their two young children, citing the eldest as her excuse for being unable to come. The President had laughingly agreed and, back home on Sorsay, both baby Alex and his sister Isla had a signed photo of '*Potus*' on their bedroom wall.

The flight had been an unusual extravagance and Ridge had not felt fully comfortable with the idea. As with all travel plans, the budget had grown arms and legs and it shocked him a little to think that the last fifteen to twenty hours had cost him as much as the annual salary of the first post-university job he'd ever had.

He swallowed as he felt the Boeing 787 Dreamliner dip imperceptibly and glanced over to his wife. Orla had been videoing out the window and sensing his discomfort, she turned and quickly

scrabbled in her bag for some sweets for him. He smiled his thanks.

The seats were luxurious and there had been plenty of space to move around the cabin too. But for poor exhausted Orla, it must have looked like one huge comfortable bed. Ridge knew she'd been running around like a blue-arsed fly before they'd left and with their normal 'built-in' babysitter no longer around, the last few days had been pandemonium with the kids. They'd had an enormous stroke of luck, however, with the timely arrival of Valentina.

Ridge had decided to rent out his mum's cottage rather than have it sitting empty. Both of them had felt it would help them get over the loss of both of Ridge's parents in two short years if they 'made the break' with the house. Financially it didn't seem like a bad idea either. Orla's writing career had stalled slightly due to the two kids and Ridge had been too focussed on recovering from his ordeal in Tokyo and rebuilding their bullet-ridden cottage to do any IT consultancy work whatsoever.

This holiday was going to be their 'last hurrah' for a long while and they decided renting out the other house would set a precedent for their new lives as a sensible and modest-living 'thirty-something' couple.

It was only after a couple of weeks with their fiery Spanish tenant who Ridge re-named as '*Volcanic Tina*,' that they discovered Valentina had been an au pair for the previous summer in Alicante.

They'd no time to check the truth of her claims and no reason to doubt the capable if tempestuous, young woman. Django, their enormous beast of a dog, had taken an instant dislike to her, but Seamus, the island ferryman, and Ridge's oldest friend had been more than happy to take the Labrador and German Shepherd cross, citing the fact that the black wolf would be company for him. In what felt like no-time, they'd agreed to let Valentina look after the kids, booked their flights and soon they were hastily exchanged toddler toileting tips for Spanish language tips and packing the two kids off a few hundred yards from home. Two days later their excited parents embarked on this latest adventure 7,000 miles away on the other side of the world.

Ridge gripped Orla's hand more tightly as the enormous aircraft gently sank towards the runway. Despite this trip being purely for pleasure and familial obligation, as opposed to anything more sinister, he still felt relieved to have her alongside him. Plus, he knew she needed a proper holiday even more than he did and he vowed to do his damndest to make it a memorable one.

*

The airport was compact, modern and efficient and before they knew where they were, Ridge and Orla found themselves standing out on the pavement rubbing their eyes in the bright sunshine. Ridge laughed as he stood holding Orla's sunglasses, as she stripped off two entire layers of clothing to

reveal her freckled shoulders and still firm physique despite two children in rapid succession.

'Bleedin Nora! I thought Colm said it was their winter over here! What's it after being like in the height of summer? A sauna?'

They had meekly followed a line of fellow passengers through the air-conditioned foyer and on to the street. An enormous man stood alongside them brandishing a folded map and he muttered something under his breath about a taxi. Ridge glanced up at the tall signpost nearby and nudged Orla.

'See? That's a taxi rank there. Let's find out if they go to Valparaiso eh? It'll save us all that faff about transferring to the bus station.'

The pair of them had tried to plan their trip as independently as possible, bearing in mind Colm was not the type of man who'd allow anyone in his family to 'wing it,' as was the infamous M.O. of his brother-in-law. Although Colm had insisted on booking them a hotel in Valparaiso which was around sixty miles from Santiago and on the coast, they'd been allowed to make their own arrangements to get there. Even Colm had agreed that with their flight arriving early in the morning, the two of them could surely travel that short distance before the hotel room check-in time of 4 pm.

Between a little guesswork and surreptitious eavesdropping, Ridge worked out there were plenty of taxis' and they decided to ditch their luggage and go explore the city for a few hours. Orla had seen a

huge skyscraper which dominated the city and so they had planned to make that their main focus.

‘But I’ve got to get something to eat first hun, me stomach thinks me throat’s been cut, so it does.’ Orla complained.

‘We’re not going back in there. Come on let’s get that bus and see where it takes us eh? The cost of any grub at the airport would probably pay for our taxi to the hotel.’

Ridge grabbed his protesting wife and bundled her onto the air-conditioned bus. ‘Tightwad!’ she spat at him playfully. Ridge laughed. ‘It’s not my fault you slept through every meal on the flight!’

From the airport, the city looked like a weird amalgam of unattractive Seventies’ style buildings, which reminded Ridge of the concrete monstrosities that had blighted areas of Central Scotland, optimistically called ‘New Towns’ by the town planners, and huge gleaming ultra-modern glass offices. The overall ambience seemed to improve the further away they travelled from the airport and Ridge hoped the centre was going to be more appealing as he could see Orla looking less than impressed. Spotting some artisan food shops he quickly jumped up and pressed the stop button. ‘Come on,’ he shouted. ‘Let’s get you some food!’

They stuffed themselves with two large Cornish pasty-type affairs which Orla had recognised from a guidebook. *Empanadas* they were called and

suitably hefty, even for a fierce Irish woman with a hunger to match.

An hour later, they were atop the Sky Costanera which they'd discovered was the highest point in all of Latin America. The 360-degree view was magnificent and Orla even managed to get lunch despite the protestations of her still too-full husband. The elevator had only taken seconds to travel the 300 metres from ground to roof and Ridge had almost left the contents of his stomach behind as they stumbled out into the stunning sunshine of the glass-enclosed deck. He consoled himself with an interesting looking cocktail instead. Orla had told him it was called a *Terremoto* which she said meant 'Earthquake.'

'Are you sure that's what it's called?' Ridge had asked dubiously.

'Tink so, love,' Orla had mumbled between mouthfuls of avocado salad. 'But me Spanish doesn't seem to work as well over here. Been practising an' all, so I have. It's not like in Spain, I knew that, but it's not like it was up in Mexico either. Don't know what they're after sayin' to me, half the time!'

Ridge looked down to the ant-like people below and wished he was back down there with them. He'd thought the building looked like a glass crocus bulb waiting to unfold, only uglier.

Instead, he looked out beyond the city which didn't seem that big, being completely dwarfed by the majestic mountain range. He'd much rather have been over there and despite a little smog lingering over the

city-centre, he reckoned the colder air over towards the mountains was even clearer than back home and he longed to play with his expensive binoculars which had served him well over in Japan.

After a whirlwind tour of the city, they took an ultra-modern people-carrier taxi in plenty of time to get them to Valparaiso. Ridge was surprised to notice one of their fellow passengers was the same big guy who'd stumbled out of the airport with them that morning. He never forgot a face and certainly not one as ugly as that.

The only others in the taxi were a nervous-looking young Canadian couple and an older business-woman who never once looked up from her laptop. Ridge instantly nick-named the big guy as Lurch. His face was a clammy chalk-white and he made the edgy tourists look tranquilised in comparison. Fumbling for a particular page, Lurch dropped his pocket-sized phrasebook and it fell by Ridge's foot. He instinctively reached down and handed it back to the man. 'There you go, pal,' he said and was taken aback when the man smiled and said, 'Cheers, laddie.'

Ridge instantly felt Orla tense up alongside him and he knew why. Lurch had spoken with an unmistakable Ulster accent. Over there you could tell a lot about a man by the way he spoke. Ridge knew those two words would be enough to tell Orla if he was a Protestant or not and if pushed he guessed she'd

be able to tell him which part of the North he had grown up in.

The pair of them exchanged glances and their unspoken conversation didn't need to be said out loud. What were the chances of a man from Northern Ireland being with them in this small taxi by accident?

Ridge tried to look calm as Orla glared at him, her left hand squeezing his right. By the look in her eyes, he imagined she'd prefer to be squeezing some other part of his anatomy right then. Of course, he shouldn't have spoken to the guy and even if he had, he should've adopted a neutral accent. They'd gone over all of this stuff carefully before they left Scotland. It was a schoolboy error and he felt annoyed with himself. He'd knew he'd have felt less relaxed if he'd been travelling on his own, but here with Orla, he ought to be acting twice as careful as he'd twice as much to lose.

Ridge spent the next ten minutes trying to convince himself that coincidences *do* happen from time to time and he felt comforted that Orla had relaxed her vice-like grip on his hand. The aura of apparent tranquillity didn't last for long. He felt like kicking himself shortly after as their taxi swung right off the motorway to join the back of a long queue for some official-looking security check-point.

Lurch immediately leant forward and began to mutter inaudibly to the driver. Then Ridge and Orla watched in horror as he pulled out a thick wad of paper money and waved it in front of the bewildered

man. But the language of hard cash spoke more eloquently than Lurch ever could with his little phrase-book and seconds later the taxi pulled back out into the stream of traffic and sped hell-for-leather towards the overhead signs for the Valparaiso city limit.

Ridge winced inadvertently as the vice tightened once again, but he couldn't help catching the big guy's eye. Lurch returned the look with a thin smile, pointed a meaty finger at his watch and shrugged his enormous shoulders. Despite the probable idiocy of doing so, Ridge found himself on the verge of opening his mouth to say something of a thank-you when the grip on his hand became too intense to think coherently. He took this as a direct command and the remaining twenty minutes of the taxi ride was spent in an uncomfortable and, for Ridge, painful silence.

Chapter 5

TODAY

The tall angular man would have stood out in a crowd even without his crown of unruly red hair, greying ever so slightly at the sides. Despite never being particularly soft or remotely overweight, Colm knew he'd lost several pounds since he took on the vineyard.

The women who worked for him would often gather and comment on his bony frame and make helpful culinary suggestions to the man's wife but always in a careful way because they knew what a fierce temper she had. It was often said amongst the vineyard workers that it should've been Juanita who had the red hair, *pelo rojo*, or sometimes they called it *pelo de Diablo's*, 'Devil's hair,' in her case. This was as much a criticism of Colm as it was Juanita, even though both were universally loved amongst everyone in the valley.

But Colm's insistence that the blood-red products of the vineyard be named '*Sangre De Demonios*' or 'Devils' Blood,' had not gone down particularly well with the predominantly Catholic workforce, to begin with, and consequently, many of them had left around the time he had bought the business. Happily, for Colm, their numbers had swollen to twice that size since then, due to the unparalleled success of the vineyard and his firm, but fair, management and significant investment.

*

Colm stood up and stretched his aching back, looking down from the highest point of his 40-acre estate. He would never tire of this view. Leaning on a wooden rail that ran a hundred metres downwards and supported the youngest vines, he gazed up at the unbroken blue sky and the contrast with the piercing white of the snowy mountains. Then his eyes surveyed lower down to his own wee piece of heaven, the translucent green of the immature vine leaves with their little veins clearly visible under the constant spotlight of the late August sunshine.

He'd known precious little about the wine business when he bought the ailing vineyard. He'd never even been a huge drinker, of any form of alcohol. He knew how many people in his former profession had met an untimely end because of it.

Back then he'd have called it winemaking but now he was wise enough to know wine wasn't made, it was grown. And after a lifetime of death and destruction, much of it raining down on others at his behest, it suited him to live quietly under the sun with his beautiful Mexican wife and gently shepherd each harvest to fruition.

Colm wiped the sweat from his brow and smelt the earth on his hands. He loved this place. This sanctuary. He was wealthy enough to live anywhere in the world. He had investment properties in every continent but he chose to live here. He had no history in this place, but the plan was for a long future.

A huge Andean Condor drifted on thermals high above him, scanning the terrain for prey. Colm watched him with both affinity and admiration. The air was so still and silent, he almost felt he could talk to the giant bird.

He had hardly registered the sound of grumbling gravel as a vehicle drove fast through the main gate below him. But for some reason, he lifted a hand to shield his eyes and scanned the lower reaches of his estate and towards the house. As far as he was aware, the vineyard wasn't expecting any lorry deliveries that afternoon but as his wife handled much of the day-to-day administration of the business and he had little involvement in her rapidly growing organic fruit and vegetable farm, he couldn't rule it out completely.

But he could see this was a black saloon car and it had parked some ways from the main house and office. Two thickly-set men got out and walked away from the main hub of the vineyard and roughly in his direction. Perhaps they'd already been to the house and he hadn't noticed? One man appeared to be on a cell phone. Then Colm saw they were in police uniform. Something didn't look right and he felt his gut instinct kick hard.

Colm peeled around to the right and leapt nimbly as a cat into the shade of his young vine bushes while at the same time whipping out his phone. He called Juanita.

'Did you see the black car come in? They didn't come to the door? *You sure*? Okay, get to the safe room NOW! Don't open it for anyone until I get back to you. Sure it's likely nothing at all and I'm after being jumpy, but still, you know the drill, move quick my love. Bye.'

Before his phone was back in his pocket, Colm had already sprinted twenty yards back up the hill, towards an innocuous-looking green wooden box fixed around head height to a fence post. He didn't have half of the security procedures that he'd insisted Ridge and Orla had to have installed at their little Highland cottage, but there was one of these boxes located every hundred yards on the estate.

The boxes weren't made of wood either. They were made of a composite material that looked like wood. Wood as tough as tempered steel, bomb-proof and carefully designed to throw off overly inquisitive eyes that would see them as odd-looking bird-boxes and another European quirk to add to an already long list. But few bird-boxes had thumb-print access.

Colm grabbed his military-grade binoculars and a small Sig-Sauer automatic pistol which he quickly slid into the back of his jeans. Police or not, he wasn't taking any chances and he'd had dealings with enough corrupt law officials to know that a uniform meant precious little if enough money was involved.

He walked quickly down the rough hillside to be in a better position, feeling like the Condor now

and wondering if the huge bird still had his back, high above.

Soon he was walking down the main boulevard of the vineyard, although still at the steepest section. Tall trees arched over from each side offering a little dappled shade and giving the workers a temporary sanctuary from the ever-present sun. At this time of day, the sun seemed to pour in from the lower end, the eastern slopes, giving the boulevard an eerie tunnel-like feeling.

The two men probably thought this gave them an advantage as the light was behind them and directly in the eyes of anyone they would come upon. But Colm knew they would be perfectly silhouetted in the cool country air, defined as sharply as the black centres of the thousands of targets he'd pierced so precisely over the years.

Colm didn't try to conceal himself and he walked slowly down the centre of the road. At first, he thought he'd been a tad paranoid. But never more than at that moment did the juxtaposition of his old and new lives become more jarring. For here, in this green and verdant vineyard, this organic cradle of life, had come an aura of death.

These guys are definitely not police, he decided. Only a second later he caught one of the men nodding almost imperceptibly to his comrade and the first guy unholstered his handgun and began to raise his arms.

Before the second man had removed his weapon, Colm had dropped and spun completely around. His gun spat twice and the two men fell, as one, to their knees, each with a neat hole in the middle of his forehead.

Colm lowered his gun and stood for a moment, savouring the silence and what he understood could only be a temporary victory. He looked up to the sky but the Condor had vanished. Clouds were appearing out of nowhere. He knew it would happen one day. He'd brought the Ulster rain to this sun-drenched valley.

He felt his phone vibrate and pulled it out of his pocket without taking his eyes off the two kneeling men.

'Colm? Thank God. It's me and Orla. I think we might have a wee problem.'

Chapter 6

The past week had been such a hoot for all of them that Ridge had felt faintly ridiculous even calling Colm.

He and Orla had enjoyed an idyllic few days at the vineyard. Meeting Juanita again had not been the awkward experience he had envisaged, their brief 'holiday romance' being consigned to the realms of ancient history. He could see how Juanita had blossomed alongside her marvellous farm produce and any fool could see how much in love she and Colm were.

After all the worry and grieving for his brother-in-law, following their misadventures in Tokyo, when they had all believed he'd been killed, Ridge had thought he would never have seen Juanita again. At the time, he'd had nothing reassuring to say to her or anyone. Colm had seemingly given up his life for him and Orla, to safeguard their little piece of heaven that had been cruelly violated. Thankfully, it had been just one more of The Piper's many lives that Colm had used up. For Ridge, it had been wonderful to see Colm, not only alive but vigorous and well and obviously proud of his gorgeous wife and their new life in South America.

But that morning, he'd suggested the pair of them do a little holidaying on their own to give Colm and Juanita a chance to catch up on their vineyard

duties and let everyone have a breather from familial duty.

Valparaiso had proven to be a jewel of a city and Orla had laughed as her island boy had made a bee-line for the busy port. But he saw Orla had been even more impressed than he by the colour and energy of the bohemian atmosphere with its unique bars and restaurants. She'd been snapping away at the vibrant murals and graffiti and had already picked one to be the cover of her next paperback, although Ridge hadn't been convinced.

But he loved the fact that Valparaiso wasn't your average Western city with the usual chain stores and generic atmosphere. He soaked up the backpacker vibe and happily accompanied Orla through the various little back-street shops and cafes.

They'd taken refuge from the unrelenting sun with a spectacular lunch at a quirky restaurant with a large awning covering an outdoor seating area. It seemed to specialise in towering burgers and they'd considered themselves fortunate to find a table. Close enough to the cobbled street that they could smell the two-stroke oil from the little scooters racing past like demented hair-dryers, they were protected from the ensuing dust by a gorgeous hand-made stained-glass partition.

Orla had been standing up taking a couple of close-ups of the art-work and that's when she said she'd first noticed the odd-looking guy staring at her. With her flame-red hair, it couldn't be helped in a

predominantly dark-haired continent and Ridge hadn't been unduly concerned until she sat back down and dug him in the ribs.

'Ridge, hun, it's not me he's bleedin' starin' at, it's *you*!'

'Away and fuck off,' had been his disparaging retort with his attention far more applied to the quivering plate of charcoaled meat in front of him. All the same, he inched himself a little higher as he bit into his juicy triple burger and tried to see who Orla had been talking about. It wasn't too hard as it turned out. He spotted the guy immediately and swallowed his entire mouthful of beef without chewing it, wincing in pain as the lump travelled down his tightening throat.

Ridge's first thought was the guy hadn't made the slightest effort to blend in. Despite being with a group of three or four other guys he seemed to be apart from them, somehow distinct and separate. The fact that he looked like a flamboyant Westerner and the others seemed more indigenous might have helped, but it was more than that. It wasn't that his Trump-style peroxide blonde hair was long and effeminate, partially covering one eye and which he constantly flicked back off his face with an exaggerated flourish. Nor was it his shirt which had to be the brightest neon-pink polo this side of San Francisco.

What made this guy unforgettable was his face, or more specifically, his eyes. Huge brown eyes

with long tinted eye-lashes that stared at you, cold and unblinking. They reminded Ridge of the dead eyes of diseased cattle on Tullich Farm, back on the island. He remembered as a boy, how their faithful family Labrador could stare for Scotland, a different experience altogether, as his warm understanding eyes would speak to your innermost soul and then promptly ask you for a biscuit.

He had no inkling what these eyes were asking for. Hooded and saggy, they continued to bore into Ridge who, completely unnerved, had stopped eating and turned back towards his wife. 'Jeezo, Orla... you're right enough. What the fuck's he staring at me like that for?' 'Fancies you, obviously,' was the unhelpful reply, but Ridge could tell by that peculiar little furrow in her forehead, in the space between her eyes, that she wasn't unconcerned.

Ridge took a long draft of his beer and used the raised glass to snatch another quick look at his strange admirer. He sensed strong homo-erotic overtones, yet in a colder and more predatory sense, quite unlike anything he'd ever noticed from visiting some of his friend Thad's gay haunts, all those years ago in San Fran. Tilting his head slightly and pretending to be interested in Orla's food, he first noticed he could hear the guy's voice. Although he seemed to be actively speaking to his companions, he wasn't deviating for a split-second from his surveillance and his nasal voice cut through the general hubbub like a surgeon's scalpel. Ridge

recognised a transatlantic accent and, if pushed, would have said the guy came from New York.

Orla stood up and flashed a startled waiter one of her killer smiles. She whispered down to Ridge. 'Keep eating will you, I'm going to try and get a photo of this guy, in case me brother has seen him around.' Ridge watched in admiration as his wife expertly drew the waiter in with a smile and a tilt of her head. Barely seventeen and with a long pony-tail and wispy beard, the lad allowed himself to be cuddled by the pretty older tourist lady and wheeled around into the exact position she had picked for her photo. With one arm around the boy and her phone on the selfie selection and held high, Orla held her finger for more than a second with the camera on burst mode and capturing a stream of images.

Ridge was still trying to hear what the guy was talking about but there was too much interference. He got the feeling his 'friend' didn't know the people he was with and he guessed the others were speaking Spanish. If someone had told him the other men had been paid to sit there then he wouldn't have been surprised such was the sense of forced bonhomie between them.

Despite the heat of the afternoon, Ridge shivered. 'You get a decent shot of him?' Orla nodded, her eyes fixed on her phone and her thumb flicking madly. 'Okay then, you fire them over to Colm and I'll give him a quick bell or he'll wonder what we've been smoking!'

Chapter 7

In all honesty, Ridge expected his brother-in-law to laugh and tell him to man up and grow a couple. During their visit, Colm had been much looser and more relaxed than he'd ever seen him and Ridge felt more than a little silly. But Orla still had her serious furrow going on and he had to bow to her greater experience in such matters. There was absolutely nothing to make the pair of them think the guy was anything more than a creepy nutcase, but Ridge couldn't argue with the notion that he'd feel a whole lot happier to be told the guy was a well-known eccentric around the tourist haunts.

When Colm replied as tersely as it was possible to be, Ridge got a genuine fright.

'Don't move okay. Call you back.'

Ridge swallowed hard and looked at his wife. 'All images sent,' she whispered and smiled like a naughty schoolgirl peering past him to see if the guy was still there. He was and he obviously hadn't stopped staring either. Ridge saw her face go white, then set hard.

'Shite,' she said. 'The bastard's only gone and given me a thumbs up.'

'What? Maybe he's a friend of Colm. This could well be a wind-up, you know!'

'I hope you're right. Drink up will you, let's get a coffee somewhere else, I've lost me appetite somehow and-'

'-Can't love. He told us to stay put...sounded different to this morning. Should be okay, shouldn't it? Remember how funny he thought we were when we told him about that big Irish lump, Lurch?'

'Aww yeah, it'll be fine! We're in Valparaiso for Pete's sake, nothing happens here does it? When have you ever heard anything about Chile in the news these days apart from wine or salmon farms? But if we stay here any longer love, I'm going to confront him, so I am.'

Orla stood up and Ridge gulped, thinking it was all about to kick off. She saw his face and laughed. 'Going to powder my nose – if that's allowed?'

Orla had no sooner vanished into the restaurant when her cell phone started vibrating on the table. Ridge grabbed it.

'Hello? Oh, hi Colm. What? No, she's gone for a pee. I *know* what you said. Yes, we're still here in the same place. Hold on...' Ridge grabbed a menu and stood up, craning his neck to see the corner sign-posts. 'Yeah, that's right... the corner of *Gonzalez* and *Toco*- yep, uh-huh, that's the one. No, we'll wait. I'll get her to call you when she-'

Ridge looked at the phone in frustration, as if it could provide him with all the answers. Colm had been brutally short with him. Ridge felt as if he'd done something wrong. His brother-in-law had only wanted to talk with Orla and for some reason, he was in a hurry.

The afternoon sun had moved since they first arrived and Ridge was now exposed to the blistering heat. He'd just stood up when he saw his stunning wife weave her way through the tables and he smiled. What did he have to complain about, honestly?

'We off then?' Orla smiled.

'Eh, no love. Colm rang. He's in a foul mood and wanted us to stay put until he spoke to you. D'ye want a drink here?'

Orla frowned. 'Maybe. Let me see what the *craic* is first, alright?' She continued to stand and looked around as she put her phone up to her ear.

'Colm? What's up? Away and *shite*. You're not feckin' serious?'

Orla sank into her chair, elbows onto the table and put her head into her free hand.

Ridge had a horrible feeling in his stomach, one that he hadn't had for two years. Orla nodded uselessly and spoke into the phone quickly and quietly.

'You sure? A *Paul Simon*? I can sort of remember, but do we- What? Oh *fuck*. When? Okay then but how long?'

She flicked her wrist to check the time. 'I've got fourteen-ten. Okay. Got that. South down *Inez*. Seriously, in thirty minutes? Okay, *twenty-five* then. It'll take us two minutes max. The place is mobbed, so it is. Promise? Okay. See you.'

Orla looked at him and Ridge tried to read her expression. Right there and then she looked too much

like her big brother for his liking. She relayed the gist of her call with Colm and Ridge spent the following twenty minutes trying not to be sick.

Chapter 8

They made a theatrical exit from the restaurant flourishing the waiter with effusive thanks and a sizeable tip before making sure they left by the front steps thereby having to walk right past their odd-looking watcher.

Ridge knew a little of what was about to go down but the exact details he wasn't too clued up on and there wasn't a single bit of it he liked. But he'd long ago given up trying to second guess his shadowy brother-in-law and if he understood one thing it was that when you're backed into a corner there is no-one on earth better qualified to get you out again safely.

He saw the taxi rank two hundred metres ahead on the right-hand side of the potholed road. Orla had told him not to get into one before she did, as they needed a particular driver who'd been given instructions to pick them up and then drive them out of town like Ayrton Senna.

They found themselves having to elbow their way through the busy streets until the throngs of people quickly thinned out and when Ridge glanced backwards he saw the reason why. Behind them, the air was filled with an explosion of banknotes. There were hundreds if not thousands of twenty-thousand-peso notes swirling in the air like paradoxical wedding confetti. It looked as if someone had thrown a shopping bag full of money from an apartment window, which Orla confirmed had been the case.

Ridge had been told not to look back but he couldn't resist and his reward was to see their friend struggling to get down the steps of the restaurant such was the melee caused by the financial bonanza. Their eyes met for a fleeting moment through the confusion and then for a second it was like there was only the two of them, the hunter and the hunted. Ridge didn't hear the mayhem around them, he was only aware of those cold dead eyes tracking him and he turned and bolted after his wife.

Ahead of them, the sidewalk was empty and as they crossed quickly into the street a young woman with a baby-buggy began to cross opposite them. As they met in the middle, Orla nodded and made a hand signal which Ridge couldn't decipher, before she grabbed his hand and began to power walk across to the right-hand sidewalk.

Glancing backwards, Ridge saw a wheel had fallen off the buggy on the poorly surfaced road and the woman had bent down to make a quick repair. Then, only seconds later, as they reached the taxis, he felt the rush of warm air as a car flew past his shoulder at breakneck speed. Ridge caught the flushed features of the same woman who'd had the buggy, before Orla pushed him into their car. With his door barely closed, the taxi tyres squealed and Ridge was thrown backwards. He hauled himself up in time to see the bright yellow flash of an explosion rip through the last few taxis in the line and as they sped off all he could see in their wake was smoke, dust and flames.

Chapter 9

Darkness wrapped itself around the many windows of the ranch-style kitchen and as Ridge slumped over the enormous wooden table he had an uncanny feeling of déjà vu. Another Cabinet of War. But weren't they supposed to be on holiday? His face couldn't conceal his confusion and Colm nodded in an unspoken recognition as he sat down opposite and placed his hands out in front of him as if to offer his surrender. He drew himself up for a moment and let out a huge breath. Ridge couldn't remember him ever looking so tired and, well, *old*.

'Okay. We appear to be having a situation, so we do,' he began cautiously.

'*Sit-u-ation*?' Orla went off like a firework, as both men had anticipated. 'I think it's a wee bit more than a bleedin' situation, don't you? How many people were killed or injured back there? Innocent wee souls out for a-'

'-Okay!' Colm slammed his hand hard on the table, hard enough for Ridge to feel the impatient vibration through his elbows and into his skull. 'Would you prefer it to have been the pair of you? Where would THAT have left yer wee babies back on Sorsay? Answer me that Orla!'

Ridge saw her eyes welling up and he knew he had to intervene. He was no match for either of them in the aggressive interrogation stakes but his loyalty to Orla was incontestable.

'That's enough Colm! We've had a tough day alright. Jeezo, give her a break.'

But Orla had stood up and she clearly wasn't finished yet. Her face had gone that scary purple colour which always forecasted rough weather and this time Ridge could tell she was fomenting a powerful storm front headed Colm's way.

'You *promised*! You said those days were over, so ye did! And what about *her*?'

Orla pointed accusingly at poor Juanita who'd come into the room, carrying a large tray of snacks, glasses and a decanter of rich red wine. She stood as if paralysed, her face chalk-white and Ridge could see she'd obviously been crying only moments before.

Now it was Colm's turn to jump up and he towered over the others. But he spoke more softly than before. Ridge knew he was trying hard to be conciliatory although he doubted it would last too much longer.

'We're ALL in this together Orla, now will you please sit down and listen for a minute?'

They sat at the table and Ridge poured each of them a healthy measure of wine. He reckoned it was going to be a long night and the blood of Jesus had never failed him yet.

'Those days of violence *are* over, I promise you, and my wife here will back me up on that one-hundred-per cent.' Juanita nodded meekly but Ridge thought it was hardly a show-stopping affirmation. Colm continued.

‘Our whole lives are poured into that red stuff you’re drinking now, Orla. We’ve little energy left for anything else, honestly.’

‘But-’

‘-Aye! I know what you’re after thinking Sis, but I’d be a right fool to think that after a lifetime of killing and deception, I mightn’t need a wee bit of back-up every now and then, now don’t you think?’

‘Every now and then?’ Orla spluttered.

‘Fair point lass. But believe it or not, this has been the first time anything has happened since we came here.’

A cold dread wrapped itself around Ridge’s heart. ‘Do you think it’s got anything to do with our arrival? I mean... with that guy at the airport and-’

‘-Not at all, Ridge. I can see why you’d think like that and it’s good you *are* thinking.’ Colm smiled and raised his hand. ‘But I do have a few things to say and it’s true, we will all need to put our thinking caps on if we’re gonna sort out this once and for all.

So listen up, will you?

You know back when you were attacked on the island, an’ yer wee sanctuary ruined? Well, I made a promise that I’d never allow that to happen again.’

Colm took a theatrical break to scoop some wine down his throat and Ridge felt himself being drawn back into that murky but enthralling world.

‘I went back over to that swamp and I cleared up as many loose ends as I could. It’s no game. I made sure that no-one would ever know those eedjits had

been anywhere near Sorsay and to do that I had to eliminate good people along with bad. A great deal of money was flashed and in the end, I had to, as you know, fake my own death.'

'I've got a right bastard for a brother, so I have,' Orla muttered over to Juanita, but she was smirking as she said it. They all knew she'd done exactly the same thing a few years before and the petite Mexican girl sitting right there had been one of the few happy consequences of that tumultuous time.

Colm smiled briefly before his face set into a hard mask once more. 'Unfortunately, one of the people I paid off to help me fabricate my death in the car-bombing has ratted me out, so he has. I was only recently made aware of that. And I've been expecting some fall-out for a few weeks now, but to be honest, I never expected it to happen all the way down here in Chile. Literally, no-one knows I'm here and I have taken a great deal of trouble to ensure that's the case. I'll tell you a wee bit about yer man in a minute but I have to warn you that we're possibly not out of the woods yet and we should be seriously thinking about getting the fuck out of here in the next twenty-four hours or so. I'd sorely like to stay and defend this place, which is *our* sanctuary, Orla, but it might make sense to follow the old 'attack is the best form of defence' strategy.

I need to tell you that less than an hour before you called with your wee admirer problem, I had two local thugs here at the vineyard. It was a weird one,

to be honest, because they never hit the house and there were only two of them. Now anyone who knows anything about me, in my professional capacity, would know that two hired monkeys would never be able to take me down.'

'So where are they?' Ridge knew what the answer would be more or less before he'd finished mouthing the first word. But when it was Juanita who piped up, he was reminded never to underestimate the strength of his pint-sized friend. She gave a thin-lipped smile and nodded her head towards the part of the estate which had been turned over for her organic farms. 'Let's just say, we've got a fresh supply of organic protein for the pigs...'

Ridge gulped. This was no game like Colm had said. People had been killed in the city and also here on the vineyard. A terrible thought came to him.

'Do you think the creepy guy in the restaurant and the two guys here were part of the same team? Was it a timed thing, you know what they call it? A simultaneous operation?'

Colm placed his hands on the table again and Ridge felt strangely calmed by that. 'It's possible Ridge, but this guy you encountered today is in a different league in every respect from the two who came to the farm. That's one of the reasons we had to put such an elaborate plan into place.'

Orla lifted her head, her eyes shining. 'Did you know about the two guys before we called you?'

Colm nodded. ‘I had only put them down a couple of minutes before Ridge called.’ ‘So it’s likely then? Ridge ventured.

‘Not sure yet, he might have been there on some other business entirely or it could have been a reconnaissance mission which again made it necessary to use extreme measures.’

Ridge winced at the image of the explosion in his head. ‘Do you think we got him with the explosion Colm? He’d have had to be pretty close wouldn’t he?’

‘Impossible to tell at the moment. I have yet to hear from my people at the scene, but Juanita was listening to news broadcasts on the radio and according to that there were no fatalities and the media are painting it as a fiesta stunt gone wrong.

It was only meant to be a diversion and escape operation. To have killed Sten Hellström would have been a coup indeed.’

Ridge stopped trying to balance one guacamole and cheese nacho on top of another and waved a hand vaguely at Colm. ‘Yeah, I’m dying to find out. Who the fuck is this guy and how do you happen to know who he is.’

Colm didn’t smile. His face was deadly serious.

‘Well. No-one really knows who he is. You say you’re *dying* to find out? Most people who come into contact with him do end up dying. He’s Scandinavian but that’s about the most we know. He’s a top international assassin, one of the best in the

world. I know about him because he’s been recruited by the same people as have employed me in the past, including the CIA and other American customers.’

Orla spoke. ‘So, he’s good, then?’

‘Exceptional, Sis. His name is almost definitely fake. Hallström is Norwegian and so most people think it’s a made-up surname and a play on Hell Storm. Like a lot of these guys, there’s a huge amount of folklore and mythology about him.’

‘Pot, kettle and black...’ Orla delivered her line with a deadpan voice and only Ridge found it amusing.

Colm coughed quietly and continued. His first name Sten, is reputedly false too and I’ve heard people say he’s more dangerous than a Sten gun.

The most infamous story about him is that he chose the name *Sten* because it’s *Nets* in reverse. He allegedly likes to despatch his victims, once he’s tortured all the information he requires out of them, by wrapping them in fishing nets, tying the net to the back of his car and then driving fast over suitably rough roads until there’s nothing left of them. A particularly horrible way to die and also an efficient one for the killer with little or no mess to clean up afterwards and precious little forensic evidence.’

‘Holy fuck.’ Ridge thought back to this cold fish eyes and he knew what they reminded of him of now. A killer shark.

Colm brought a flask of black coffee over the table and Ridge looked outside, shocked at how quickly the sky had become dark.

Each of the four of them instinctively pulled their chairs closer to the big table and the others leaned in as Colm began to speak once more.

'The big worry is what the hell he's after doing in a sleepy place like this. Assuming he's here to kill me, we first need to find out if he's still alive and I would bet that he is. Then we have to know who's paying him and then I'll see if I can use my contacts to either buy him off or 'persuade him' to go and fuck himself.

I may as well tell you that I've already messaged Thaddeus and put some feelers out to the Diamond Dogs too. Not only could they be handy if we get into any more bother, but they might be implicated too. Especially if this is all coming from where I think it is.'

'What do you mean?' Ridge asked, only just realising that he was feeling exhilarated by the thought of seeing Thad and DJ and the others, despite the dangerous situation they might be in.

'I don't want to say any more right now if you don't mind Ridge, until I find out more. I've got eight men patrolling the grounds.'

'Are they all-'

'-No Orla, they're not properly trained but they *can* shoot and the people around here are naturally tough. They know that if anything happened

to me this place would quickly dry up and their jobs too, which means we've got ourselves a loyal wee army if needed. Help yourselves to a side-arm from the drawer over there and I suggest we try and get some sleep and all being well, we'll know better exactly what we're dealing with by morning.'

Minutes later, Ridge and Orla bade Juanita goodnight. Last to make his way towards the impressive hardwood staircase, Ridge saw Colm come out of a hidden hall-way door. Dressed head to toe in jet black, Ridge guessed he wasn't planning an early night. He wondered who else might be out there in the darkness tonight wishing them harm. He shuddered and with it went all ideas of a good night's sleep.

He needn't have worried. After two hours of broken sleep, the pair of them jumped out of their skins when Colm crept into their room with a little pencil torch.

'Come on! Grab some clothes and whatever you need for a night away, I'm taking you to a hotel. It's not safe for you here anymore!'

Orla wasn't having any of it. Even in the semi-darkness, Ridge felt the worry and reluctance in her voice. 'What about you? If it's after being too dangerous for us what the feck are you-'

A prodding finger from Colm stopped her dead in her tracks. His reply was a bleak hiss. 'No arguments. There's a black pick-up out the back and I want the pair of you in it in two minutes and it's up

to you whether you want to be unconscious with a bag over your head or not...'

Chapter 10

The fat man stood aside for a brief moment and indicated with a sigh of frustration towards the hotel door. His equally large companion squeezed carefully past in the narrow corridor and bent his knees to gently drop the luggage and insert the card into the reader with one hand before using his other to twist the handle and open the bedroom door for his boss.

Maximiliano grunted his approval and seconds later he slumped gratefully onto the impressive king-size bed and massaged the ugly stump where his right hand should have been. He was trying hard not to be a grumpy and immature prick like his old chief had been.

He'd seen how well that had gone.

But his arm still ached from where he'd thumped someone a little too energetically the day before. The tech was getting better every year but he was yet to see the day when prosthetic hands would be designed for punching a man in the face hard enough that his nose splintered.

Max took a deep breath and tried to let his irritation flow out of him. He slipped off his bullet-proof vest and looked around the lavishly decorated suite. But the anger couldn't be assuaged as easily as that. *You try opening a hotel room with one fucking hand*, he muttered to himself.

No, the only thing that was going to help him get over his annoying predicament was the death,

preferably slow and agonizingly painful, of the man who'd brought about the situation in the first place. The man or the ghost? No-one could ever be too sure these days. Not true, he corrected himself. According to his associates in Europe, it didn't matter if you called him *The Phantom* or *El Gaitero, The Piper*, it was one and the same man. Yet, there were still too many unanswered questions for Max to be able to sleep comfortably at night. He'd been warned by strong and resourceful men, each of them leaders of their own little fiefdoms, not to pursue his current plan of action. Their words still rang in his ears.

'Leave *El Gaitero* alone. Awakening him would be a mistake.'

'You already know full well the *bicho* who was responsible for your unfortunate situation.'

'You've seen his charred remains, haven't you? *Madre de Dios*! It's a different master that the snake Xavier will have had to answer to.'

Most were unsympathetic and unwilling to assist him for fear of the myths and folklore around the mysterious phenomenon that wiped out the mighty Ramon and almost all of the major Central American drug cartel leaders almost a decade ago.

As the time had passed inexorably by, so had the memories of that cataclysmic event and like prairie grass, the cartels had grown new leaders, each one more vicious and conniving than the one before him.

But none tougher than Maximiliano, and he congratulated himself with that thought. He'd stayed true to his vow to never stray off the path as Ramon had so spectacularly done. He didn't do drugs himself. He'd never violated the young women who were regularly offered up to him and often used by his contemporaries as bargaining chips, in hostage or blackmail negotiations or as sweeteners when a deal had gone particularly well.

With his daily phone calls to his loyal lieutenants completed, Max ran a bath and contemplated the likely success of his plans. He was comforted by how well he'd fought his way back to the top after what had happened. Most who'd found themselves in the dilemma that faced him off the West Coast of Mexico would have perished there and then. His reputation as a hard man was legendary throughout Central America. The brutal fact that he'd sawn off his own hand with a rusty piece of chicken wire and then swam ten miles back to shore was an enduring testament to his physical and mental toughness.

But no matter how tough he could be with his enemies, he could never shake off the feeling that there was a man out there who'd got the better of him, whether indirectly or not. A man, who had kicked him when he was down and used him as a dispensable pawn in a vicious game he'd not been considered worthy enough to be invited to participate in.

How strong a message would it give out to his peers far and wide, if he could be the man who eliminated, once and for all, the apocryphal Phantom? His enemies would know he had dominion over that spectre of death who had rained terror with impunity across the globe. Max sank deeper into the relaxing bath and almost closed his eyes before a moment of panic made him jump up with a start.

Images flooded into his head of circling crocodiles waiting to pull him down into a death roll. There would be many who couldn't wait to see the Phantom claim another trophy. And what of his family? He was already comfortable and in an assured position of power. Was it right that he should risk their lives for his personal vendetta? But it was already too late for any private qualms. He'd entered into a duel with the Devil himself, hadn't he? That's what some were saying.

He forced himself to close his eyes and he allowed his head to sink back under the water. But he alone knew the truth. There was no Devil. He wasn't fighting a ghost either. Maximiliano would prevail because he knew the truth about The Piper.

Chapter 11

Colm stood in the darkness, almost invisible in his black battle fatigues with only his trade-mark red hair giving away his identity. He was genuinely vexed. For many years he'd manoeuvred through his dark and murky world utterly alone. He'd lied and deceived friends and family, suffered mental and often physical pain in his quest to keep them safe from harm. Ignorance is bliss, he would tell himself as he missed a family wedding or shrugged off a stab wound as a bad case of indigestion.

Then circumstances changed and he found himself elected as the leader of a rag-tag bunch of professionals and amateurs. A small but deadly effective group of men and women who operated under a different code from that of their enemies. They didn't risk life and limb for riches. Power interested them not one whit. They did what they did for love. And Colm had to admit, the uncompromising power of love was a force to reckon with.

Yet, as always happens in war, there were casualties. At first, it would be those on the periphery. But the vortex of death and destruction always speeds up as it nears the centre. Two years ago they'd lost the group's de-facto father, a man once as powerful as The Piper himself, who'd been cruelly executed amongst the dark trees of the Suicide Forest under the shadow of Mount Fuji.

And now, the maelstrom was spinning closer still. He knew he couldn't stop what was about to happen. The forces now ranged against them had grown too powerful whilst he'd been tending his vines. He had thought that he might have found a sanctuary and a way out. Sickened by the life he'd led and the things he'd seen and done, he thought he'd turned his back on violence and that had been his single biggest mistake. Men like him had to be vigilant at all times and he understood finally that he could never escape the path he'd been trained to follow all those years ago. He would never find a safe refuge for The Piper and those close to him.

Unless.

He had a plan. Granted it was a hastily constructed plan, rough at the edges and supremely confident in scope. In a way, he had already embarked on it even before the events of that day. But it would be difficult, if not impossible to fully carry out and he would need to revert to his preferred mode of operation for it to work successfully. That wasn't the toughest part, however. To make this work, once and for all, he must risk the lives of those he loved most. Then he would make the ultimate sacrifice. Only then would his family be safe.

But first, he had to establish who and what he was up against. He placed the cheap burner cell-phone onto the cobbled street and stomped his heel down hard, obliterating it. He then picked out the SIM card and snapped it in two.

The reason he'd vented his anger so uncharacteristically on the innocent phone was that he had received confusing and contradictory intelligence. It wasn't the first phone he'd used and destroyed that evening either. News that the Mexican drug cartels were still after him wasn't particularly surprising given the radical pruning he'd given their organisational chart a few years before. He'd hoped the fresh wave of management would have been more forward-looking and he hadn't known until recently that the fat slug Maximiliano had even survived. He'd be easy. But Colm already knew he wasn't operating on his own. His bed-fellows were far more of a worry.

But even the broad array of malevolence which had seemingly coagulated into a cohesive force against him, didn't worry Colm too much. He was used to that. They'd often thought might was right before he won the fight. They still hadn't seen the light.

No. What troubled him more than anything was the patchy but reliable information concerning precisely who these bastards were trying to kill. For the first time in his life, Colm had learnt that his carefully constructed magical spell-weaving stories had conspired to turn his legend on its head. Instead of building up his fearsome reputation and scaring off possible foes, it now seemed that the idiots had become so ridiculously confused about 'The Piper' that they thought he was someone else completely.

Tonight, he had been told that the target of Maximiliano's ire was a mysterious Scotsman. A man who they blamed for the death of Ramon and to whom they'd awarded the dubious title of the best freelance assassin in the world. His brother-in-law, Ridge Walker.

Chapter 12

The best freelance assassin in the world awoke with a start. It was the smell that did it, an unwelcome double-act on top of the claustrophobic heat. He patted the other side of the bed and feeling it cold, sat up and rubbed the sleep from his eyes. He didn't know why they called it 'sleep' because you only seemed to get it on nights like he'd just had where they'd had practically zero. He reminded himself to congratulate Colm for his splendid choice of hotel.

At first, they'd thought he might have been taking the piss when they'd arrived at the O'Higgins Plaza Hotel in what had felt like the middle of the night. Now they knew for certain. A wedding disco which only got into the swing of things at around 3 am had continued all the way through the Sinatra repertoire until six o'clock.

Ridge looked around the spacious but dark bedroom. The old furniture made him feel at home and he would have been lying if he said the damp musty smell was a new experience to him. But at least back on Sorsay, the air was fit to breathe. Their 'air-conditioning' had undoubtedly passed away before Sinatra, although it did manage to emanate a continuous bronchitic wheeze which helped to drown out the cacophony from downstairs.

Orla crept in with two cardboard cups in her hands. The aroma of ground coffee hit Ridge like a train and he felt his stomach rumble like one too.

‘Hey, lover boy! Thought you’d be needin’ this, so I did. Was that the night from hell or what?’

She handed him a pastry deftly whipped from her pocket and he devoured it without a word. But Orla was on great form despite her lack of sleep.

‘You’ll never believe me, sure you won’t,’ she laughed. ‘But that bastard brother of mine was telling the truth about this place. It’s really called the ‘O’Higgins’ hotel, honest to God. It’s named after some dead famous Irish fella, Bernardo O’Higgins-’

Orla caught the incredulous look on his face.

‘I swear! They’ve got posters about him downstairs! He was one of the first rulers of Chile when they split from the Spanish. The Chilean War of Independence it was called, worse than the bleedin’ Scots so they were!’

‘Must’ve been when they built this place,’ he muttered.

Orla jumped back on her feet and Ridge saw that she’d already gathered up all her stuff and her bag was at the door.

‘Come on let’s get out of here hun, I don’t like the feel of things, all joking apart. I tried calling Colm but it only rings out and I’m wonderin’ what the sense was in packing us off like that. If there’s trouble back at the ranch he’d have been better with me, I mean us, there with him, wouldn’t you say?’

Ridge felt irritated. Both at her insinuation that he’d have been no use in a fire-fight and at being rushed this soon after waking up.

‘Don’t ask me, Orla. I mean you’re the expert after all aren’t you?’

He couldn’t be angry for more than a second though, they had too much going on to be falling out over his petty insecurities. He skelped her playfully on her rump and quickly threw his toiletry bag into her rucksack.

‘But it’s pretty obvious to me. He wanted us safely out of the way so he could present himself as bait. I hope his troops are up to the job but I know what I’m going to do – let’s find a bar with decent wi-fi and I’ll get hold of that big poofter, Thaddeus.’

Ridge stopped for a second in the doorway as they both turned to survey the room. He had stopped smiling.

‘Then you can fart around here as much as you want my love, but I for one am going straight back to fight alongside your brother whether he likes it or not...’

Chapter 13

He hadn't seen a girl as pretty as her in many a long year, Liam decided. When he pointed her out to the rest of the gang it was the only thing they'd agreed on all day. For him, it was one of the few downsides about their extended South American adventure. The dearth of good-looking red-heads. And the sunburn. 'Jesus is it getting hot already or what,' he muttered and pulled his bar seat back under the protective canopy. The other men broke off from their bad-tempered discussion and laughed. 'It's not the sunshine that's getting you all hot under the collar you dirty old bastard,' one of them said. Liam flashed him the bird and settled himself back into a comfortable viewing position.

He fully accepted that he might look like a grey-haired old git these days but he could still remember back in the day when his head had an unruly crown of rich red hair almost as bright as the young woman sitting a few yards down in the middle of the stone-floored courtyard.

The lads had already been sitting there for three hours and the sun was hardly past its highest point. He'd given up listening to their moaning and gripes. He could've joined in but he chose to keep his regrets to himself and much preferred to admire the scenery and reminisce about the happier days, before they had been forced to live this half-life, exiled thousands of miles from the land of their birth.

It wasn't too awful mind you, he had to admit, as John Lee Hooker sang *Boom, boom, boom, boom* over the heads of the busy bar. They always played great music here, lots of seventies and eighties guitar bands and his personal favourite, the blues. Back in Boston, Liam had been a singer in a band. They'd never amounted to much more than a warm-up support act, but they did once get onto the lower reaches of a Springsteen gig.

The boys were half-way through their annual week-long get-together and it was normally around this point when they all started to bicker and the alcohol would ignite simmering tensions. But then they'd all go back to their individual little pieces of paradise and start looking forward to the next year. He knew that underneath the petty squabbles, each one of the three men would give their life for him and he would do the same.

He took a long draught from his glass and watched the young couple more closely. He might be out of touch with modern dating methods, but to Liam, it seemed the pair of them didn't communicate well with each other. Maybe they hadn't got to know each other yet? The skinny white-faced guy looked nervous enough for it to be a first date. Plus he always seemed to be on his bloody cell-phone. He felt sure if he had been fortunate to have a gorgeous lady like her on his arm he would have pierced his heart with a thorn before he ignored her the way that guy was doing.

The music changed abruptly and Liam grimaced as one of those monotonous rap tunes came on. That wasn't the only thing that didn't seem right all of a sudden. Her young beau might not have been paying the red-head much attention, but she was definitely getting some serious heat from a group of local types. Only they weren't local. Liam edged his chair sideways towards his comrades and placed a heavy left paw onto the table slowly but with enough force to make them all stop talking and pay attention.

'Boys...' was all Liam needed to say.

Each of the men turned to look in the direction Liam had indicated with his eyes. They each saw a gaggle of men moving in close around the small table with the hot red-head. Liam, Charlie and the guys had been drinking there for years and they could spot a cartel thug at a thousand paces. Liam touched his right hand to the far side of his heart and they all saw what he meant. Either these men had been extremely well paid in cash or they were carrying hand-guns.

One of the men leant over the girl and said something and Liam immediately saw her face crumble. A hot wind blew dust through the courtyard as the couple jumped to their feet in terror.

Then everything went a little crazy in that slow-motion way that reminded Liam of those big-budget US action movies he still liked to go and see when he got the chance.

He tipped their table upwards with as much strength as he possessed sending their bottles and

glasses flying towards the startled young couple. Charlie, who was the closest, launched himself through the air like the star Louisiana football player he used to be, hitting one of the guys in a flying shoulder charge while delivering a neck-breaking kick to one of his companions. Danny followed close behind him and roared like a demented bear so loudly that one of the assailants simply froze in fear giving Danny time to snatch his gun out of its holster and smash it across his skull with a sickening crunch.

Liam by this time had hoisted a metal chair and proceeded to crash it over another guy's head trapping him by the arms as the seat of the chair disintegrated. Liam broke his nose with a spectacular head-butt sending bright red blood over a brawling confusion of bodies on the slate floor.

Seconds later there was a loud scream as a huge black pick up smashed through the now-empty restaurant tables and Liam closed his eyes with the certain knowledge that their mad adventure was now over as he had always known it would one day be.

But he heard an Irish accent shouting and he opened his eyes to see, not a Valparaiso policeman, but a beautiful freckled face and the bonniest smile a man could ask for. 'Are you after coming or not?' she asked and he felt himself being hauled to his feet before other strong arms lifted him into the back of the truck seconds before it screeched off through the cobbles at high speed.

Chapter 14

Colm pulled over on the outskirts of the town. He smiled grimly at his sister who sat inside the cab, still shaking. He nodded towards the motley crew out on the flatbed. 'Where did *Neil Young and Crazy Horse* come from?'

Orla looked back through the narrow window and Colm could see she had to force herself to say something. 'To be honest, I've not a notion what happened back there but there's one thing I am sure of an' it's that without those guys, I wouldn't be sitting here now, sure I wouldn't. They saved our lives Colm!'

He nodded and placed a hand on her knee. 'Okay, that's good enough for me. But this isn't over yet and I need to give them the chance to bail, okay? Then we're back to the vineyard, pronto.'

'Okay but I'm coming out with you.'

It was party central out on the roadside. Colm couldn't stop himself laughing as the men whooped and hollered and swapped versions of the recent action, the stories becoming exaggerated with every passing second. The only quiet person was Ridge and he was even paler than usual. Colm knew he'd have to have a quiet chat with him later, but now wasn't the time.

The men slowly lost their effervescence as each of them noticed the tall man with the lovely

young woman, her arm wrapped tightly around his waist.

It was Liam who spoke first. ‘Brother and sister, right?’

Orla nodded meekly.

Liam brightened up. ‘Does that mean that you-’

‘-Nope. Husband.’

Orla pointed at Ridge who blushed as he always did in those situations.

‘Thought so.’ Liam lied unconvincingly and everyone laughed.

Colm clapped his hands together and got everyone’s attention. He didn’t know who these guys were but he trusted them enough to be fairly honest with them. The fact that not one of them had registered the smallest complaint about what had happened, spoke volumes for Colm. He had a need for men like these.

‘Okay guys, my name is Colm and this here is my bonnie wee sister Orla and her man Ridge. But I see you’ve already met.’ The men all laughed again.

‘I want to thank you from the bottom of my heart for what you were after doing back there! It’s not every day you meet people of your calibre, we appreciate that you didn’t have to help us out like that..

Now, I don’t know what plans you have for the rest of the day, but I am the lucky owner of a vineyard a few miles down the road here and if you’re

up for a party and I'm after thinking you might be, then you're more than welcome to come over. We've plenty of food and wine and there's a bunkhouse where you can get cleaned up and stick around for as long as you want. Now I have-'

'-Any beer at this vineyard?' Liam interjected. The men all laughed again. One of the others poked him hard in the ribs and muttered theatrically, 'I've only got three words for you, Liam. Gift. Horse. Mouth.'

Another taller, slimmer, man wasn't smiling. He caught Colm's attention with a look and Colm instantly recognised him to be their leader.

'Danny here. What's the catch? The kinda party you're talking 'bout ain't over yet, I'm thinking.'

Colm smiled, glad to be able to talk openly with a man who understood what they might be dealing with.

'I was just going to say, Danny. You will have seen that my sister here had a wee bit of a situation with some unwelcome advances and-'

'-Bullshit. If you'll pardon my language missy.' Danny spoke with an unmistakable Southern drawl and he bowed his head imperceptibly towards Orla who glared at her brother. Colm smiled more genuinely this time. The guy had passed the test.

'Good. Okay, I can see you're the sort of men I need on my side right now. You want the truth here it is, but it's not pretty. These thugs were trying to get

to me through my family who are only over here on holiday from Europe. I have had a long-running disagreement with a local drug cartel and it's only now come to the boil.

You are right, Danny, in your suggestion that this won't have been resolved by today's stramash. In fact, it may only have exacerbated matters and I'm expecting the vineyard to be next on their hit list. I would like to invite your help on this matter and let me add that, being ex-Army myself, I have a sizeable armoury and a small local force of between ten and twenty men already in place. I would anticipate being attacked by far fewer men than that although they may have a greater selection of weaponry.

Oh! One further thing I should say. Neither I, nor my family, wish to be brought to the attention of the authorities and if you choose to help my sister and me, you can name your price and it will be paid to any bank account in the world.

What do you say?'

Liam immediately put his hand up. 'So, you didn't specify what type of beer you had.'

Danny cuffed the back of his head and scanned his companions who were all beaming like naughty schoolboys. He turned back to Colm, smiling himself and extended his hand.

'We don't believe a freakin' word of what you said, however...,' Danny paused for effect, 'we share your aversion to officialdom and being military

retirees' ourselves, we do have a fondness for money. You can count us in!'

Minutes later they were bumping down the road replete with a massive supply of cheap domestic beer and a box of cigars. Colm felt reasonably pleased with himself until he caught that questioning look on Ridge's face. You couldn't win them all.

Chapter 15

The man slipped the phone gently into the breast pocket of his shiny new jacket and sat down slowly on to his mother's kitchen chair, careful to pull the trousers up a little at the knees to maintain their razor-sharp creases. He stared out of the window at a view he knew better than any other. He'd been forced to waste far too many years of his life looking out of windows, he reflected. It was only now becoming light, but as the grey fingers of dawn crawled menacingly across the plastic table-top, he could already tell it was going to be another bleak Ulster morning.

His thoughts returned to the conversation he'd just had and he groaned with a frustration bordering on out and out fury. He pounded the crudely tattooed fist of one hand into the palm of the other, unconsciously mimicking what he'd like to be doing to the face of the man he'd been speaking to. It was no use. He had to get outside. A freedom of sorts.

Brendan felt the damp cling to him in a death-grip that had despatched countless others of his kind to an early grave. He coughed and pulled up the collar of his suit and trudged across the yard to the same familiar spot where he'd vented his rage many times before. He thought of events across the ocean and his right foot kicked the indestructible old wall hard, again and again. He'd seen his old 'da do exactly the same thing four decades previously. He remembered

with pride telling his school-pals how that was what real men did instead of bashing their women-folk on a Friday night. Then in case, he'd be thought of as a poofter, he'd repeat word-for-word what his father had taught him about what they'd do to any bastard Brit squaddie from the Divis Flats who made the mistake of turning down the wrong road on a dark Belfast night.

He kicked the wall one last time as bitter memories flooded into his head and he felt the familiar acid regret burn his insides. He'd been languishing down there in Portlaoise Prison when his father had died and because of some earlier bad behaviour, he'd been refused permission to attend the funeral. Brendan's response to that had been to initiate a prison riot to cover an attempted escape. He'd almost escaped too, but in the process, he'd battered a guard half to death which only resulted in the bastards tacking another 5 years onto his sentence.

With age comes wisdom, he thought despondently. When his wee brother Sean disappeared a couple of years ago, outwardly he'd never so much as batted an eyelid. Sure, his heart was bleeding and he'd been raging that he was still banged up and unable to do anything about it. He'd not bought the story about Sean being 'lost at sea' for one second. But he had known better to draw attention to himself. He had kept his head down, biding his time kicking walls and now he was out. He'd a fair notion who was responsible for what happened to Sean and

with a wee bit of international co-operation, he'd soon be exacting his revenge.

Brendan turned to face the grey vista with an unseeing gaze and struggled to picture his head-strong brother. He felt strongly that he was in some subterranean place, maybe he was at the bottom of the sea, or more likely buried deep in a woodland grave. His first instinct on getting out of jail had been to start searching for Sean. But it soon became obvious that he wouldn't find any answers from traipsing the familiar streets of this rain-swept town. He might never find out what happened. There had been some cataclysmic event for sure, some had called it a cleansing of sorts and maybe his wee brother had been in the wrong place at the wrong time with the wrong people. Brendan had spoken to almost a dozen heart-broken mothers and wives and the unspoken knowledge in those large watchful eyes told him more than words ever could.

He knew now that a beast had been awakened from the murky depths of history. A monster that ought to have been left well alone. Clenching his jaws hard, Brendan closed his eyes and saw his brother being pulled down into the green waters, the air being sucked from his lungs. The image of those frightened eyes staring from a luminous face, becoming fainter by the second, had haunted his dreams every night since his release.

Brendan might be free to stand outside now and breathe the cold fresh Ulster air, but his wee

brother had been left stupidly unprotected and exposed, never to feel the anaemic sunlight on his face again. And so, while there was a single breath left in his body, it would be his mission to exact a final retribution on those responsible. *I might've given myself a different brand of life sentence*, he muttered, as he glared up at the unpromising pallid sky.

Chapter 16

Colm pointed the men towards the bunkhouse and told them they'd find suitable clean clothes laid out for them and after a hot shower to come over for a meal to the main house. Danny helped him unload some of the gear from the pickup and he sounded suitably impressed with the six well-armed men at the makeshift security barrier.

'I reckon some of those weapons might be as old as me but hell, I couldn't help admiring the belt and braces way in which your men stopped us like that. They had the pickup surrounded within seconds.'

Colm acknowledged him with a nod. 'We don't get a lot of trouble around here but the men have been well trained in case of bandits who sometimes target isolated estates like these, thinking us to be easy pickings.'

Liam staggered behind them carrying most of the beer. 'I'd hate to see what they'd be like with a vehicle they hadn't recognised. But someone could steal this top box off of me for sure,' he grunted.

Standing at the impressive dark oak main door of the *casa grande,* Ridge saw Juanita waiting for them, still anxious and deathly pale. He knew something didn't feel right about all of this and he could tell her smile was forced. He gave her the briefest of hugs before she ushered the pair of them inside while glancing worriedly back towards her

husband and the others. 'Ridge wait up, will you,' she whispered but he'd not picked up on what she'd said and he blundered right into the kitchen before he saw that something was indeed seriously wrong.

Confronting him with that impassive granite face was the creepy giant from the airport and this time he had a pistol in his hands. Ridge instinctively ducked and wheeled around furiously yelling, 'Orla! Run!' He saw the panic on her face match his own confusion and he tried frantically to push her back through the doorway before they were both shot dead. With no time to react, Orla tumbled backwards as her husband fell on top of her and it was a laughing Colm who pulled him roughly to his feet.

'What the fu-'

'-Steady! He's with us, Ridge! It's okay, honest.'

The pair of them brushed themselves down awkwardly as they gathered around the vast kitchen table where it seemed the guy had been cleaning his automatic pistol. Ridge wasn't an expert but even he could tell it was a professional tool and he saw what he guessed to be a silencer nestled next to it, partly wrapped in a soft cloth.

His darling wife could never be accused of being shy in coming forward and true to form she took the initiative, thrusting out her hand more as an aggressive gesture than a means of facilitating international friendship.

'Me name's Orla and this is Ridge, me husband, but I'm after thinking you already know that, yeah?' She spoke loudly with a barely concealed anger and Ridge guessed he would have been the only one who noted a nervous timbre to her voice.

The man nodded without smiling and carefully placed the pistol on the table next to its companion. He looked like he was about to speak when Colm butted in with a cheesy bonhomie.

'And this here is Bob. He's here to help an-'

Bob lifted an enormous hand to silence Colm and Ridge thought he saw a flicker of anger cross the man's face.

'-No. It's not *Bob*. It's Robert, so it is now.'

They stood for a few moments of awkward silence before the man ran his hand through his thick mane of oiled hair and parted his thin lips in an attempt to show what he possibly considered to be his warmest of smiles. With a hand now aimed at Orla, he spoke directly to the pair of them while Colm seemed to be the recipient of a cold and reproachful glare.

'Sure, my old 'da is called Robert and I'm still way too young to be taking his place at the table. But my real friends call me Brock and I'd be honoured if the both of you'd call me that. Forgive me if I gave you a start there, but I'd only got in ahead of ye and I'm hearing it doesn't hurt to be too careful these days.' He nodded at Colm, 'so I'm takin' it that the trap's sprung then?'

Ridge launched himself across the table, his outstretched arms reaching for Colm's neck.

Chapter 17

Colm saw his brother-in-law go a deathly pale for a second or two before his face flushed a deep scarlet and he knew what would be coming next. He loved the lad more than any other man left on the planet but he could be a right pain in the arse at times.

'You BASTARD Colm!'

As Ridge roared at him and clambered over the solid kitchen table, Colm leant back a few inches, but enough. The angry face in front of him screamed obscenities and Colm felt hot spittle splatter his cheek as Ridge attempted to throttle him. He reacted by instinct, bringing his hands together as if he was about to pray and then he simply pushed them up and out before quickly spinning Ridge around and pinning his hands behind his back. With his mouth close to Ridge's right ear he tried to whisper calming words.

Then he heard a theatrical cough and he looked up to see a gun in his face. He should have known who the most dangerous person in this kitchen would always be.

Brock stood looking as helpless as an oversized schoolboy as Orla waved him back, flicking what had only seconds before been his gun but now somehow in her hands. She glared at Colm and then with the pistol indicated towards the gun's owner.

'Let Ridge go and tell me what's going on here or God help me, I'll blow what's left of your

man's brains all over this lovely kitchen here! You've set us up, haven't you?'

Colm swallowed and released his grip on a wriggling Ridge who didn't forget to dig him sharply in the ribs before turning to stand alongside his furious wife.

He blinked and then the gun was his. The others hadn't even had time to react. But this wasn't the time for showboating and Colm quickly placed it onto the table and held up his hands in mock surrender.

'Okay, okay! I get it, Sis, honestly, I do. Will ye just calm down and we'll sort this all out? You know I wouldn't willingly put you in harm's way!'

He pointed towards the huge panelled dining room and as they began moving through, he glanced around for a friendly face. Juanita was already making preparations for coffee and Colm wasn't surprised to see his brother-in-law liberating a bottle of red from a countertop. He saw Ridge wink at Juanita and he knew it would all be okay in five minutes. He loved these people and he could kick himself for causing them even the smallest of pain. But unfortunately, they were mired in the pain business for a wee while longer and it was up to him, as always, to attempt to make the best of an increasingly bad situation.

They all knew this was yet another Council of War before a single word was uttered and somehow

the thirty-foot oak dining table made a fitting location as the darkness enveloped the rest of the house.

Orla was still fizzing like an unexploded firework and Colm knew the first item on his agenda had to be getting her and Ridge properly on-side again.

'I can see how it looks Orla, but-'

'-Sure you can! So can we, we're not complete eedjits you know!'

Colm raised his hand but would give no sign of surrender this time.

'Fine! But will ye shut up for a minute and give me time to explain what's been going on here. We're in the shite up to our necks here and there's no time for any more drama alright?'

Brock coughed quietly and muttered, 'Our ears, Boss.'

Colm glared at him. 'What?'

'Our *ears*, we're in it up to our ears. There's more stuff I need to tell you, an' it's not good.'

Colm looked up at the ceiling and let out a long and frustrated sigh.

'Okay, let's take it one step at a time, will we? Does anyone have a problem with me trying to get a feckin' word in or should I leave it all to youse experts?'

Ridge drained a tumbler of wine in a single gulp and slammed it down on the table.

'Start talking, pal.'

Chapter 18

Colm paced around the kitchen table and Ridge was convinced that this was to make it harder for Orla or himself to catch his eye. To verify if he was telling the truth.

'Okay! Jaysus…! It's true. I did use you as bait, kind of. But I honestly had no idea we were up against anyone like Sten Hellström. I just-'

'-You just what?' Orla stood up to confront him, her cheeks blazing. 'You thought you'd risk the lives of your own family, an' us with wee bairns at home, so-'

'-Orla will you please let me explain?' Colm looked for help towards Ridge but he must have found little comfort from the steely composure Ridge was working hard to maintain. Still, Ridge took Orla's hand and gently pulled her down to sit next to him. He wanted the answers as much as she did but still, he refused to return the brief nod from his brother-in-law.

'Thank you. Now Bob, I mean Brock here, had found out that one of the police forensics guys who'd swapped some DNA evidence from my car-bombing, had been turned over, up in the States. Apparently, he'd blown half of the money that I'd paid him and he was mouthing off to anyone who'd listen that he was some big-time secret agent who was on the run from the FBI or whatever. It didn't take too

long for the Ulster boys to hear about it and Brock and a colleague had been despatched to interrogate him.

Unfortunately for us, the other guy had been heavily involved in our wee drugs cartel altercation back in the day when you three first got involved in all of this nonsense.' Colm smiled towards his wife who had joined the group minutes before.

'When we destroyed the main hierarchy of the cartels, we also did a good wee job for the US and European authorities by stemming the flow of weapons into Central America in exchange for drugs coming into Europe. And-'

'-We did, did we? Or are you sure you don't mean *you*?' Orla growled.

'Okay yes! I was doing a job for the good guys while I was being a help to my family. Where's the harm in that? I keep telling you this is a complicated business and I used to often work with opposing sides, but I have only ever worked for the good of the world for the last ten years. There's no point in turning down a side job if it can be done, now is there?'

'No. Harm. Whatsoever.' Ridge said flatly, for effect.

Colm held his hands up.

'Jeez, okay! I get it. I fucked up! But let me finish and then we can decide what to do about it, will you?

Good. Anyways, as I was *trying* to tell you. We, or I, was responsible for the taking out of two

operatives from the Real IRA who'd come over to Mexico around the time we were embroiled with Ramon and his gang. They'd been sent over by this guy Mickey who was working with Brock's recent pal. We cleverly infiltrated their group and Brock was able to accompany the guy over to the States and assist with the interrogation.

Once Brock and this wee guy, Jimmy, had got everything they needed, which wasn't a lot, to be honest.' The Irish giant nodded glumly. 'Then it was the logical thing to eliminate the lot of them. Cold and harsh but also clean and effective.'

Brock lifted his head and stared at each of them, daring them to question his actions. 'No more Jimmy, no more Gerry...'

Ridge swallowed and reached for the red wine. 'Alright, what exactly do we have here, Colm?'

Colm smiled and sat back down at the table.

'Well, that's after being the weird part, Ridge. And the reason for our wee bait-setting.'

Ridge found himself leaning in and noticed the others had done the same.

'Apparently, there is a belief back over in Ireland, stoked by gossip and rumour up there in Mexico too, that the real power behind the overthrow of Ramon was a man called *The Piper* and-'

'-No shit, Colm, we all know *that*!' Ridge slammed his glass down angrily, feeling like they were about to be sold a line they'd already heard a hundred times.

‘Would ye let me finish? Jeez! But for some god known reason, they think this person is not who you all think it might be. I had been thinking it was me who was the target.’

Orla looked carefully at everyone and then spoke slowly and quietly. ‘So what you’re after saying Colm, is that it’s me they’re chasing? They somehow know I’m not dead from that explosion over at the Scottish Parliament?’

‘No Sis, that’s *not* what I’m saying.’

Ridge sighed loudly. He was beginning to lose patience with all of this cloak and dagger theatrical stuff.

‘Okay then, what *are* you saying? Who’s the big bad wolf then…?

Colm poured himself some wine, took a slow draught and then swilled the glass for a second, appraising the contents, before replying quietly.

‘It’s *you*, Ridge. They all think you’re The Piper!’

Chapter 19

As the entire table sat stunned at what Colm had said, one man stood up, apparently unaffected by this bombshell.

‘It’s a lot worse than that Boss. Have a heart and find me some whiskey will ye? My jaw is grieving me worse than when Elvis passed away, so it is, and I’ve a fair bit of conversation to do myself.’

As Juanita scrambled through their drinks cabinet for some Jamieson’s whiskey, Ridge sat dumbfounded. Why would anyone think he was a professional assassin? Yes, he’d killed a fair few men, but half the time it’d been accidental. He looked first at Colm and then Brock as if he’d find the answer on their faces. Instead, he was met with the same impassive canvas as if they’d been trained not to give away the smallest hint of humanity.

Brock sat back down and poured a wine glass full of whiskey. He took a small sip, placing it back down with a gentleness that belied both his profession and his enormous hands.

‘As I was after saying, Boss. It’s a lot worse than you could know. Firstly, can I tell you that *most* of what you said is true. The majority of the eedjits seem to have bought into this idea that yer man here is the prime instigator in the Ramon cartel downfall but to be honest I think that’s because most of them have no stomach for this fight and they definitely don’t want to be confronting the real Piper, whoever

he might be…' He nodded deliberately over to Colm which made Ridge want to laugh out loud.

Brock then gave his best attempt at a grim smile in Orla's direction and continued. 'But sadly this isn't the main problem we still have. One of the men who tried to kill you over on your wee island, had a big brother. This guy was in prison at that point and he only got out recently. That's where the impetus for this has come from. He simply wants revenge for his wee brother. He doesn't give a fuck about the cartel and he is a far more dangerous animal than the rest of them put together because he is a clever man as well as being a hard man. From what I hear, he's spent every waking minute of the last two years, planning how to find the people responsible for his brother's death. Think about that for a moment, before I tell you the worst bit, which is on a whole different level completely.'

Ridge had that horrible dizzy feeling like his chair was falling fast through the ground. He would have argued that nothing could shock him further at that point until Brock picked up his glass and downed the rest of his whiskey in one long swallow. He watched as the man tipped the rest of the bottle into his glass and began talking again.

'It's fair to say we can rest easy that the North American leak has been eliminated and any fallout from that will fall back on our Irish jailbird friend, which won't do us any harm at all. But be under no illusion, he will not give up until we are dead or he is

dead and he will work with anyone who can help him achieve his goals. That includes both the US and the British governments.'

'Sure we're used to that.' Colm said quietly but Ridge sensed a worry in his voice.

'I still haven't got to the best part yet, Boss.

You moved to Chile for some sort of sanctuary, right?'

Colm nodded quickly but already Ridge could see the colour draining from his face.

Brock looked at their faces again. 'Well I'm sorry to be the one to tell you, but you couldn't have picked a more dangerous place in the world. Do you know a man called Ricardo Perez?'

Colm looked blankly at him.

'Maybe he used a different name, he has several aliases and not all Latino, if you catch my drift. Do you remember doing some work for a guy in the nineties, I think it was? What I heard was that this guy says you did the dirty on him and he's vowed to pay you back?'

Colm smacked his forehead hard.

'Oh Jaysus no! Not that? When will they leave me alone!'

Ridge hadn't seen his brother-in-law look as shocked in a long time. Orla looked equally surprised. 'What's going on Colm, who's he talking about?'

Colm took Juanita's hand and squeezed it gently before trying to smile but only worrying the rest of them even more.

'It's a long story and not pretty. After I'd given my notice to the Brits that I wasn't going to do their dirty work any longer and the 'peace process' was well underway, I had cast my nets wider and was doing wee jobs all over the world, so I was. Some of what I did I will never talk about, but even back then I had my limits. There was this one guy, I never knew his real name, but he gave me a contract to take someone out, and I can't tell you who. I didn't like the smell of it from the start and although the money was better than anything I'd ever been offered, I started to do a little digging. It was something I didn't normally do because, in that game, being overly inquisitive meant an instant death sentence.

Anyways, to cut a long story short, I found out that my client was the close relative of a Nazi war criminal who'd been hiding out in South America, it was in Argentina, I'd thought. I instantly cancelled my contract and returned the deposit that I'd been paid. It was all kept purely business-like. I didn't say anything about why and, as far as I knew, he didn't know me, and he certainly wasn't aware that I knew him.

Next thing that happens is that he sends a goon to kill me. It was an amateur effort and I took care of it easily. I found a letter which was to be attached to my body saying that I had been retired due to professional malpractice and that no-one cancels a contract with people like him. More wine anyone?'

Ridge shot out his empty glass.

‘I tried to go through the usual channels, offering to apologize and what have you, but the only response was another assassin. Since then there’s been a steady stream of eedjits trying to kill me, but they’d slowed down and eventually dried up about ten years ago and to be honest, I’d forgotten all about it. I think there have been eleven hitmen in total and I’m guessing Hellström will be making up the dirty dozen.’

Orla stared at her brother. ‘You’re after telling us that’s what all this is about? Some loony-tune old Nazi trying to prove he’s got a bigger willy than you?’ Colm nodded but Ridge was also looking at him intently and he saw Colm’s eyes flicker briefly towards the other man in that classic of all evasive giveaways. ‘Bollocks!’ He stormed outside for a cigarette even though he’d given up over a year back.

When he returned to the dark kitchen they were all sitting silently, each looking deep in thought. The only person who had a head up was Brock and Ridge took this to signify he still had more information to bring to the table. He also intuitively knew that Colm didn’t want this fresh intelligence to be brought out into the open, which made it all the more interesting. He gave the big Irishman one of his most direct arched-eyebrows questioning glares.

The big man smiled quickly and took the hint.

‘There’s more yet, Boss. D’ye want to hear it? About the wee painting?’

Orla slammed her hand on the table. 'Never mind *him*! We want to hear it, it's our bleedin' lives that he's been risking. Tell us the whole story or so help me I'll wring it out of you with my bare hands!'

Colm laughed at this which Ridge thought ill-advised at best but at the same time, it took a lot of the tension from the group. For some reason, he felt that the worst was over. He couldn't imagine what could top the fact that a steady stream of the world's top hitmen was on their tail, possibly for the rest of their lives.

'Okay, Robert. I'll take it from here. This is all my fault, again, but hear me out, will you? I had almost forgotten where the painting came from, honestly, I had!

After these people had sent five or six killers to my door over a couple of years, I was understandably pissed off. So, I paid someone to pretend to be an underworld art dealer at an exclusive, invite-only, or in other words highly illegal, sale. We knew our 'loony-tune' was selling a painting that I quite fancied and so I bought it!'

'Wait a minute!' Ridge was confused. How much wine had he had? 'You're saying this guy is extra angry because you bought one of his paintings? You paid him good money after everything he'd done to you?'

Colm smiled. 'Not *exactly*. My fake dealer sold him a couple of genuinely valuable artworks for a similar amount for which we were paid, fairly and

squarely. But with my payment to him for the single painting, I used another friend to send the money on a complicated and untraceable trip around the globe several hundred times before it returned safely to my bank account. By which time, I had physical custody of the picture. It's down in the basement somewhere wrapped up against the mice. That's why we've got the cats. I have half a dozen other art investments down there, and it's fire-proof too!'

Ridge had to laugh at this, despite the predicament they were in. 'How much are we talking about then, must be a few thousand like, eh?'

'Something like that.' Colm's eyes glinted in the candlelight.

'Is it a famous artist?' Orla had also sensed something big was going on. Ridge knew she had a far greater knowledge about art than he did and she'd taken him to most of the top art galleries in Europe when they'd first met.

'Cezanne.'

'Jeez, Louise! Which one?'

'It's called *Card Players* or something like that.

I always liked the roguish look of it, I don't know why.'

Ridge sat up in his chair. 'Okay, how much did you pay for it then?

'About three hundred and fifty or thereabouts.'

Ridge looked at Orla in shock. 'Your brother's telling us he's got a picture down there worth 350 grand!'

Orla looked quizzically at her brother who nodded in answer.

'Not 350 thousand, Ridge love. Million…'

Chapter 20

The rest of the evening was spent looking at the artwork in the basement and then watching Orla spin around the ranch spouting ridiculous figures as to how much Colm had relieved their friend of.

After consulting the internet, Orla reckoned the painting could be worth $500 million in today's money.

Brock had gone to bed seemingly uninterested in the whole thing, but his parting comments were that he'd heard it said the source of their troubles had valued his losses in the whole sorry matter to one billion dollars.

Colm told them he'd converted a huge amount of the stolen money into land across the world and also into gold which he had thought was appropriate seeing what the Nazi's had done during the war. He had also gifted one hundred million dollars anonymously to the Simon Wiesenthal Centre in the States.

After establishing that Colm couldn't afford to repay the man a billion dollars, not that he would ever want to, the four of them had sat up for hours trying to work out how to counter an enemy who was prepared to spend up to a billion dollars to get even with them. Frantic calls to locate the Diamond Dogs had proved fruitless and they waited to hear from Thad. In the meantime, they drew up their battle plans.

Colm was convinced that the smiling assassin would still be alive and that meant a strike would take place soon, if not the next day. He also advised that if possible, they should split up and get as far away from the ranch as possible. Colm had pulled some strings so that Ridge and Orla could hide out, over on the Falkland Islands for a few weeks assuming they could make the next flight on Saturday. The time difference between them and home meant they could check on the kids within a couple of hours. Ridge decided to let Seamus the ferryman in on their situation seeing as he had been previously embroiled in the horrible attack and its aftermath on Sorsay which had led to the death of the Ulster jailbird's brother and added to their current headaches.

Ridge and Orla were shown a map of the estate and where all the emergency weapon boxes were located. He disabled the fingerprint access so they could all use them.

'The main gate is stronger than it looks and we've got a couple of Stingers to throw across the road if needed. The vineyard workers can all stay off work over the next couple of days apart from the ones who can shoot. It'll be on a purely voluntary basis but I'm guessing we'll have at least fifteen or twenty and these guys are pretty tough. Then we've got our crazy crew from earlier, which means we're looking at a garrison force of twenty.'

Orla had her business face on now.

‘Will that be enough? We’re maybe facing a billion-dollar army here? What other weapons do we have?’

Colm was already pulling back a beautiful old Indian rug which ran the length of the converted eating area, to reveal a huge oak-panelled hatch.

‘Not much to be honest. A dozen MP4 assault rifles, two RPG’s, a box of grenades and a few flash-bangs to disorientate the wee buggers.’

Ridge and Orla looked at each other. ‘Not much?’ Ridge croaked, his throat having gone dry as sandpaper. ‘That’s enough for a small war!’

Colm nodded his head and smiled. ‘And war is what we’re going to get, methinks.’

Chapter 21

As the first umber tones of dawn seeped across the oak table, there were two tired women sitting alongside each other, each one cradling a mug of coffee to ward off the morning chill.

Orla had thought she'd have been the only one awake and she'd been surprised to have found Juanita sobbing quietly in the empty kitchen. And when she'd innocently asked what everyone asks when they find someone crying, that's when the floodgates opened in earnest. Although they'd never spent a great deal of time together, Orla felt a strong bond with the diminutive girl. They both had a great deal in common, and she knew Juanita was a young woman who was a lot stronger than most people would have given her credit for. They'd both overcome adversity against the odds and the fact that Juanita had once shared a bed with Ridge had all but been forgotten about and these days, Juanita was more like the sister she'd never had.

Orla sat down next to her, gently shoulder-barging the smaller woman.

'Sure, we've been in worse scrapes than this, Juanita.'

The girl sniffed and blew her nose noisily in reply. Orla continued with her well-worn line of reasoned thought, the same argument she'd used on herself a hundred times before.

‘It always seems bad at this point, what with all the waiting and uncertainty and-’

‘-That’s what I mean!’ Juanita lifted her head and for the first time, Orla could see her eyes and how angry she was.

‘You said it, *amiga*. That word - *always*. It’s always going to be like this. It’ll never end until he’s dead or we’re all dead along with him. If we survive this one, there’ll always be another killer to take their place and on and on it goes. And the worst of it is, I think he likes-’

‘-No! That’s not true! Maybe at one time but not anymore. That man loves you more than anything, so he does.’

Orla squeezed the girl’s hand and felt herself drifting upwards as if she was looking down on the two of them like a ghost might do. She’d often felt the anguish shared by hundreds of Irish women throughout the Troubles who had borne the emotional brunt of the incessant killing and bitter betrayals. The poor wives, mothers and sisters who had endured the bleak years alone after their men had been cruelly taken. The phone calls, the knock on the door on a dark night, the regrets and the long lines of mourners on another wet funeral morning.

She understood how Juanita felt. She knew of many girls who had never married, their boyfriends having been shot outside the backs of pubs on a busy Saturday night whilst they’d been pulling pints inside. The killers had would often have walked through the

packed public bars and yet mysteriously, no-one had seen anything. These girls, who had to suffer the agonies of knowing that it might have been the local butcher or the lad who repairs the family washing-machine who had put a gun to the head of their young lover. She'd seen these women standing in the rain clutching their empty insides as they talked to the gravestones about the children they'd never have. She'd also known women who'd been left with seven hungry kids to bring up, who'd married again, not for love, they'd tell her after one too many vodkas, but out of necessity.

Yet Orla knew she'd become part of that cycle of violence herself. But only because she'd had the power to do something about it. She had refused to meekly accept the deal she'd been given and both she and her brother had tried to make the world a better and safer place. She had to get Juanita to believe that, even if she struggled with some of it herself.

'But Orla, it's my fault these people are here. If I hadn't left Ramon and met Ridge then these people wouldn't be trying to kill you.'

'I think the last remnants of that lot up in Mexico are the least of our troubles, to be honest, me girl! You're after forgetting the billion-dollar army are you not?'

Juanita glared up at her.

'See! It'll never end then, will it? Unless I do something! We'll be following Colm around the world hiding from these people-'

‘-S’cuse me, missy.’

Orla jumped. She’d not noticed the man come into the kitchen, wrapped up as she was in their conversation. It was Charlie, one of the new guys from the café. Juanita had nick-named him Harry Connick Jr because she’d said he was ‘New Orleans cool’ and he talked in that same smooth way.

‘I am sorry if I startled y’all just there.’ Charlie smiled and even in the early morning gloom, his gleaming teeth and easy charm brightened up the room. Orla felt both of them melt a little as if they’d been somehow been cosseted in a warm blanket. He continued in the same slow Southern drawl. ‘But if you’re talkin’ about who I think your talkin’ about, then I’d like to say that me an’ the boys, well, we’d follow that guy, Colm, to the end of the world. Now point me in the direction of that coffee, will you?’

*

Brock seemed to be the only person who wasn’t running around in a panic. It was only 7 am but Ridge and the rest of them had been up for ages, any thoughts about getting some sleep having proved to be a complete waste of time when their adrenaline levels were in the red zone. The big Irishman sat quietly at the wooden table, drinking his coffee and cleaning his pistol in such a calm manner, you’d be forgiven for thinking he was finishing off the Sunday crossword.

Ridge sat down next to him and started fixing some make-shift petrol bombs using the plentiful

supply of wine bottles. He tried to break the ice. '*Devils' Blood* right enough eh?'

Brock tilted his head a little.

'You'd be wanting to make that a wee bit longer, I'd say. Unless you can run like yer man Bolt, anyways.'

Ridge pulled the cotton rags further out and smiled.

'Tell me, Ridge. Who's this bunch you keep trying to get hold of, the *Diamond Dogs*? What type of outfit are we talkin' about? I can't get a word out of yer man Colm. They're something to do with you, aren't they?'

For a brief moment, Ridge was sorely tempted to simple tap his nose and tell the big guy that it was strictly on a 'need to know basis,' but then he decided he didn't want a Molotov cocktail up his arse.

'Brock, you wouldn't believe me if I told you what they were wearing the first time I met them, but apart from all that nonsense, they're an extraordinarily deadly team of uber-mercenaries who happen to have become part of the family.'

The Irishman looked more animated. 'And are they going to be assisting us with this wee bit of trouble?'

Ridge glanced around for his brother-in-law, unsure about exactly how much to give away. 'No sadly, they are too far away, I think. They're always working and they won't be able to make it down here in time. That's all I know to be honest and there's

nobody who wouldn't be happier to see them than me, that's for sure.' He stopped what he was doing for a second and it hit him for the first time how true that statement was. He wondered if he and Orla would get out of this one. They'd been fortunate in the past but they'd always had the Dogs' backing them up at some stage. An image of the children flashed through his mind and he stood up abruptly.

After a few minutes searching, he found Orla busy over towards the frontal section of the main area, checking out the narrow trenches which circled the estate and which had just been installed with some barbarous looking razor wire. For some reason, he tried to hide his anxiety and kept his voice as relaxed as he could muster.

'Hi love, did you get hold of Valentina yet?'

Orla, pliers between her teeth, growled in reply. 'Nope, it was after being their sleepy time, I thought I'd wait a wee bit.' She swivelled around and presented Ridge with her bottom. 'Phone's in me pocket 'hun. Can you get it? These bleedin' gloves took me ages to get off last time and I'm after trying to finish this last stretch. You'll get better reception back over at the ranch, so you will.'

The phone rang out. Ridge called again, determined to leave a message at least but this time it answered on the first ring.

'Hullo…' The voice was muffled but it certainly wasn't the Spanish girl.

'Who's that?'

‘Huh, Ridge? It’s me ye daft prick! *Seamus*. What’s the big panic, pal? Run out of stamps over there, I’m guessing, that’s why we’ve no postcards.

And you’d be cheaper wi’ the Skype, wouldn’t you?

The landline’s been going all morning so it has! Chile, Chile, Chile… must be costing you a fortune!’

Ridge stubbed a toe hard into the red dust, confused.

‘Wait, what? Never mind that, what are *you* doing there, isn’t it a wee bit early for socialising?’

‘Ah…, well now. You see, me an’ Valentina, we’re… uh-’

‘-Seamus!’

Despite everything, Ridge had to laugh. ‘You’re telling me that you’re *shagging* our kid’s nanny?’

‘Aye, well, I wouldn’t have put it as prosaically as that but why not eh? She’s even grumpier than your own dear wife in the mornings but there’s not a lot of action around here as you know and she gives a really magic-’

‘-Stop right there Seamus. Are Isla and wee Alex in the room? Where’s Valentina?’

‘Ah, right. Naw, she’s taken them for a wee bit of fresh air, it’s been pouring for two days and that’s it only stopped the now. Is everything okay, you sound a wee bit funny like?’

Ridge swallowed. ‘No, we’re all fine over here. It’s just that we might not be able to call for a while, the reception’s even worse than Sorsay. Tell Valentina to give them a wee hug from us and we’ll try again in a couple of days. Got to go Seamus, cheers.’

He deliberately hadn’t given his friend any chance to interrupt. He wanted to say more but it wouldn’t have been fair. Besides, what could the ferryman do? The best thing was that he remained oblivious and that he helped look after the children. Maybe for a lot longer than he’d anticipated.

Ridge had been standing outside, about one hundred yards from the glass-covered rear of the ranch house and as he turned to go back in he barely noticed a black shadow flit across the flagstones in front of him and then up and over the huge expanse of glass. Then the sky went dark for a second like a huge cloud had descended out of nowhere and then the windows exploded into a million pieces. He ran. Through the falling glass, he saw Brock enveloping the diminutive Juanita in his generous arms and pulling her down and under the safety of the kitchen table. That’s when the second blast hit.

Chapter 22

He leant against the rough-hewn stone doorway of their overnight accommodation, smoking contentedly. It was shaping up to be a gorgeous morning and despite his raging sore head, Liam had been forced to agree with the others about this latest adventure being exactly what they had all been needing. Before this, he'd been the only member of their gang who'd been voicing concern that their annual get-togethers had lost their attraction and that he'd likely be giving it a miss next year. It hadn't been a popular notion. He knew the others were at least pretending to be blissfully happy with their 'new' wives and unwilling to rock the boat in any way that could jeopardise their safety in what were still foreign lands. But he also knew they shared the view that if they weren't able to meet up and be their true selves one week out of every fifty-two, they'd lose their minds.

What Liam hadn't yet got around to saying this year, was that he intended on going back to the US and taking his chances. He'd never taken a woman down here, not on a permanent basis anyway. He still missed his wife back in Boston and his nights had become plagued with nightmarish thoughts about her and his son Michael who'd be in his late twenties by now and who he reckoned would doubtless be getting a wife of his own. Even the thought of a few

years gaol-time didn't put him off as much as it used to do.

The whole thing had got out of hand. Part of him felt like they'd all been trapped in some form of group psychosis, a collective madness brought on by their shared predicament. At first, it was only supposed to have been a temporary solution, until they worked out how best to return home. But they had never been the best of friends, even before their foolhardy adventure.

Danny and Charlie were from Louisiana and the three of them had pitched up together in Iraq as part of the US Army 2nd Infantry Regiment during the infamous second battle of Fallujah back in 2004. Having acquitted themselves well during some of the bloodiest fighting of that entire conflict, they found themselves medalled and grouped together in a specialised Task Force. Disillusioned by subsequent army failures and a series of horrible suicide bombings, they didn't hesitate when they were offered a way out through a shadowy private security operation called Blackwater. Soon after, when Blackwater was given a contract to protect key Government assets back home in the aftermath of Hurricane Katrina, the boys jumped at the chance.

But with the prospect of being shipped back to Iraq a couple of years later, Liam found himself being talked into joining the other pair in the Louisiana Fire Service as if it wasn't already too damn hot for a

Boston boy. It was there they'd hatched their ridiculous plan.

Liam stubbed his cigarette out with a swivel of his boot, the tiny filter becoming instantly lost in the red dust. Feeling a vibration through his feet, he cocked his head for a second, thinking he'd heard something above the cacophony of noise around him as the ranch workers prepared for a possible attack. With the sounds of Danny and Charlie playfighting their way down the narrow stairs of their bunkhouse and crashing through the door, Liam turned towards them and remembered how easy their plan had seemed.

It had only been a week after they'd learnt of the tragic killing of Blackwater contemporaries in a desert ambush in Yemen and then back home they'd narrowly avoided being incinerated in an explosion at a New Orleans petrochemical plant. The following day had been full of easy and safe call-outs, but the boys had still been reeling from their brush with death.

'Way too old for this kinda shit,' was all Charlie had said as they were walking into a bank to investigate a faulty alarm. But it was Danny, always their de-facto leader, who had remarked on the fact that no-one ever questioned their credentials when they appeared at high-security installations. Nor did they quibble about switching off their internal systems, providing passes and generally being super-helpful in allowing the boys to roam freely

throughout their normally impregnable buildings. Obviously, it had much to do with their firefighter uniforms, but Danny reckoned it also had a lot to do with their military bearing and perceived authority, no matter where they were.

It only took them a couple of hours that night and a considerable number of beers before they committed to robbing a recently opened bank. The publicity surrounding the bank had been impressive and the Fire Service had been closely involved with the interior set-up, with Danny, Liam and Charlie on first-name terms with half of the security staff. The bank stored high-value gemstones and this was to be their target. It was a simple matter to charter a private jet for Mexico City, respond to a non-existent setting off of the security alarms at the bank on a layoff day and walk out with over a million dollars in cash and as much again each in diamonds.

Rich beyond their imagination, yet terrified of the inevitable consequences of their robbery, they'd embarked on a drug and alcohol-crazed spending spree of fast cars, even faster women and wild parties. They'd been like a bunch of high school friends whose parents had all skipped town for a week leaving behind their wallets, car keys and a fully stocked drinks cabinet.

It didn't take long before they realised they weren't cut out for the high life, their money wouldn't last forever and the shelf-life of their friendship was rapidly nearing a best-before date. That was around

the point when they began to miss their old life back home and that's when the bickering intensified. They'd also been drawing a little too much attention to themselves and Liam had suggested they split up for a while, which quickly became a permanent situation apart from their annual drunken reunions. Danny and Charlie had opted for the beaches of Brazil whereas Liam had plumped for the less glamorous solitude of Belize where at least he could speak English most of the time. Each year they would rendezvous in Chile and every time the recriminations and bitterness would emerge more quickly than the year before.

Liam laughed as Danny barrelled through the door with Charlie in a tight head-lock. He had to agree they'd not got on so well in years and he was grateful to their strange new friends for helping them find common ground again. At first, he hardly heard the first explosions behind their bunkhouse as his two companions were making such a ruckus around him.

Liam turned as he felt he ground judder.

'What in the Sam Hill is that?' said Charlie, standing tall enough for a large-calibre round to pierce his skull and cause his head to burst like a watermelon.

Chapter 23

Ridge was caught out in the open and he was defenceless. The second missile had hit the main house dead centre. He lifted his arms off his head, brushing aside masonry, glass and burning debris. Straight ahead he saw the wooden table still unscathed with his two friends hiding underneath, not moving. Then to his horror, he saw the ten petrol bombs still lined up neatly where he'd left them only a couple of feet above where they crouched.

He swallowed down his panic and tried to think rationally. Granted, it had been a hell of a long time, but it wasn't the first occasion where he'd been under fire and terrified for his life. But this reoccurrence had happened too quickly. He didn't feel ready, but then, had he ever been prepared for this type of thing? The biggest worry jangling frantically in his head was it would all be over all too soon anyway, unless they started to fight back. He had to take his chances and run full speed for the house. If he couldn't get Juanita and Brock out of the kitchen soon, they would surely be engulfed in a burning inferno. Ridge gulped a huge breath and glanced overhead. The air was rent with the sound of gunfire and he knew the helicopter couldn't be far above him, the noise of the rotors drowning out anything else and making rational thought impossible. Where was Colm? Was he still alive?

He leapt to his feet and ran. Only a few feet to go, he had almost made cover when the ground shuddered and he felt that awful hot wind, one he knew only too well. Seconds later the air was a maelstrom of broken glass and swirling objects. Flat out on the stone courtyard, the unmistakable smell of petrol wafted over him and Ridge couldn't bring himself to lift his head to see where his friends must have perished. How could it all have gone pear-shaped so quickly? The dust coated his face and he struggled to wipe the dirt from his eyes. This time, he guessed his luck had finally run out. He tried to think where Orla would have been when the first rocket struck the house. Then he heard the staccato rapping of gunfire which meant two things. The battle wasn't over yet which meant there was still a chance they could overcome the enemy but it also told him the helicopter couldn't have been the only attack. Of course! The main forces would be coming through from the front of the estate, exactly where his wife would be.

He imagined he could hear her voice cutting through the chaos and smoke and he knew he must be hallucinating. Then he felt an enormous hand lift him by the waistband of his jeans and he fought to get upright. It was Brock! And there in the ruins of the kitchen, standing right next to the ten green bottles and equally unscathed he saw his gorgeous wife and a soot-covered Juanita, her huge eyes shining through the gloom.

*

Colm had put the Molotov's away safely and they all sat around the table as if, in a parallel universe, nothing had ever happened.

Ridge uncorked a dusty bottle of wine as Colm coughed to get their attention.

'Okay, that was round one to us. Thanks be to Jesus that we had those RPG's, although it would have been a lot better if I hadn't missed the first time!'

He explained how his men had seen the helicopter from a long way off and he'd grabbed the rocket launchers when the first attack came in. When the downed chopper had exploded it had caused almost as much damage as the first missile strike.

'The two Humvees which tried to get through our front door were only a tester. They now know we've got helicopter-killing potential although they won't know we only had two rockets and they're both spent.'

'So, they won't send any more choppers?' Ridge tried to keep the hope out of his voice.

'Correct. They would only have had the one, I'd say. Why would they have thought they'd need a second one, I'd be surprised if they do. But they nearly succeeded with the iron gate and if they'd hit that from the helicopter instead of the house then I think we'd have had a much tougher fight on our hands.'

Colm looked at them all gravely.

‘My best guess is that they’ll return as soon as they can with a lot more ground assault capability. They aren’t based too close to here or we’d know about it and even when they do come back we’ll have plenty warning, so my thoughts are that we all arm ourselves to the teeth, get as many grenades, petrol bombs as we can carry to the front perimeter and only leave a small force back here at the house.’ Colm looked directly at his wife and she nodded.

‘The good news is that we didn’t lose a single man during that attack, whereas they sustained heavy casualties. The next-’

‘-*Wrong*!’

They all turned and shrank back in horror at the sight of Liam staggering towards them, his entire upper body drenched in blood, white eyes glaring manically from a red-splattered face.

‘They got Charlie. Blew his goddamn head clean off! I’m fixin’ to help make damn sure it don’t happen to anyone else…’

Ridge saw Colm open his mouth to speak but stop as Juanita wailed in anguish and pushed abruptly past him and out of the kitchen, howling like an injured animal. He also noticed a strange look on Colm’s face as his eyes followed his wife’s retreating departure and continued to stare for a few more interminable seconds.

‘Liam, we are all devastated to hear that. Charlie was a good man. But you’re in the right place to stop anyone else getting hurt. Ridge, I want you to

come with Liam and me and let's see if we can salvage anything useful from the two vehicles, either weapons or intel about who, what or where. Okay?'

Ridge stood up and ruffled Orla's dust-covered head.

Colm punched him on the shoulder.

'The rest of you, start moving out and prepare for the next assault. It'll be brief, I can tell you that, be ready for a fast and vigorous battle. Don't be holding anything back, alright?'

*

The next few hours were spent in a frenzy of preparation and nervous activity. Ridge felt a hot wave of nausea course through him as his fingers stuck to the already blackening gloop slathered all over the door handle of one of the attack vehicles. Vineyard workers had already begun the grim task of dragging the bodies across the red dust and into a small bothy-cum-guardhouse adjacent to the main gates. They had killed seven men, three had perished in the chopper at a guess and another had died in one of the vehicle crashes. None of the men appeared to have been blonde-haired, which either meant the assassin had got away clean or he was directing operations from afar.

'I doubt he's doing all this by remote.' Colm shook his head in answer to Ridge's questioning.

'For a start, it's nigh on impossible to do it right and more importantly, this guy is a psycho loner-'

‘-what, like most professional hitmen?’ Ridge interrupted.

Colm glared at him and then continued. ‘He’ll prefer to work on his own and when he can’t, like in this case, he’ll definitely want to be in the thick of the action because he won’t trust anyone else to do the job properly.

The last thing someone in his position wants is to report back that the contract has been fulfilled, only for the mark to pop up again as right as rain.

Here, stick one of these on, will ye? We stick out like spare pricks at a hoor’s wedding, so we do!’

Ridge caught one of the black balaclavas which Colm had appropriated from the enemy vehicles and reluctantly pulled it over his encrusted hair which admittedly was the only non-black hair on the estate apart from Colm and Orla’s flaming locks. It was unbearably hot and the itchy wool made his already-aggravated skin crawl. Colm did likewise and the pair of them muttered to the gods.

Colm grabbed Ridge’s arm as he went to yank it off again.

‘Here! Do you prefer your head to be air-cooled instead?’

Ridge felt a strong finger poking hard between his eyes and an unbidden image surfaced of his beautiful wee friend Jakia, a neat bullet hole in the centre of her tiny forehead. He still found that gig a tough one to stomach, the knowledge that his brother-in-law’s finger had pulled the trigger that ended her

short life. He never would fully understand the cruel circumstances that caused her to die in that dark vortex of half-truths and betrayals which had engulfed them all amongst the suffocating heat of Northern Pakistan.

Grunting his unwilling acquiescence, Ridge nodded and turned away towards darkening skies. He'd never forgive Colm either, despite their bond, closer than mere family. A tie stronger than blood, but mired waist-deep in the stuff, nevertheless.

Ridge saw men running towards them, their heads kept low, the leader brandishing a radio phone. He pulled up in a flurry of dust.

'Boss, we got company. Three more trucks inbound less than a click from here, reports are they're moving fast.'

Colm picked up an assault rifle and nodded to Ridge before thrusting it into his arms. Ridge was about to ask him where he should station himself when he heard a piercing scream that cut through the hubbub like a gunshot in a library. Orla!

Chapter 24

The man urged his pilot to go lower and even faster still. The pilot had been growling continuously, but the man leant forward and pressed harder. He knew his gun must be digging hard into the pilot's side and the guy had just seen what happened when people annoyed him. He knew he wouldn't get any serious trouble and once they were done, he'd kill this fool and make his way back overland.

Flying had never suited him. Too many problems and not only from the conventional dangers. In his profession, anonymity was everything and to have to present himself to people, complete with expensively sourced false identification, every time he needed to cover large distances fast, for him was too much of an unnecessary risk. Risk made him nervous.

He pulled the pistol back for a moment to wipe the sweat and grime from his eyes. The skin on his arm was cooler but equally soaked. Everything seemed to make him nervous. Especially at night. And it was much worse here in this heat, the oppressive suffocating heat. He vowed to try and get some sleep later, once this was over.

The sky was too dark now for him to see where they were going and he snarled at the pilot to speed up in a bid to cover his worry that he didn't have complete control anymore. He trusted that the guy could navigate accurately with the impressive

array of twinkling lights laid out before him. It hadn’t been part of the plan to take the chopper and the pilot hadn’t had more than a few seconds warning. But when the first helicopter had been within touching distance of completing the mission, he’d kicked himself for not having had a back-up. It could all have been so easy. After they’d fled the first miserable debacle, he’d found the small private airfield almost by accident and when they stumbled upon the tiny helicopter replete with a pilot literally polishing the windscreen, it was too good an opportunity to pass up, unplanned or otherwise.

He wasn’t one of the most highly paid assassins in the world for nothing. He understood the ranch was acutely vulnerable and timing was as critical to his success as any weapons or subterfuge. He’d never get back there quickly enough by road and this helicopter was manna from heaven. But the naïve young pilot hadn’t looked on the job offer as a suitable career promotion however and after a cursory check that his bodyguard here could actually fly the thing, Hellström had deftly wrapped an arm around the startled airman’s neck and snapped it as cleanly and efficiently as he’d done a hundred times before. It had felt good and helped cool his rage for a few moments.

Now they were only minutes away from the ranch with their tiny chopper loaded ankle-deep in weapons. With a large ground force close behind, somewhere down amidst the darkness and in constant

contact, he felt a little more confident about this most difficult of missions. It wasn't just because it was going to be his last. He had promised himself several times before that some particular mission or another was going to be the final job. But despite the jangling nerves, sleepless nights and the terrifying silence that engulfed him in the dark, he always came back for more. Of course, it didn't help when each new mission promised greater rewards than ever before, as each fresh success helped to consolidate his reputation.

But this time he had to stop. Careless mistakes had been made and he had always been a stickler for detail. He often thought he should have been an accountant; such was his penchant for spreadsheets and planning. Perhaps he should have been one of those hatchet-men who were sent in to carve up ailing businesses, amputating various limbs to stem the haemorrhaging of the body corporate. He'd have been good at that. Cold, calculating and merciless.

The sweat trickled between his eyes and he blinked furiously, the patchwork of lights blurring like the oncoming headlights in a rainstorm. The bandolier of bullets around his neck was heavy and irritating. He didn't feel as cold and calculating these days. The complete opposite. He felt hot, tired, hungry. Why was he hungry all the time? It must be his nerves and the lack of sleep. Night after night, walking alone, street after street, each one as empty as the last. Sometimes he thought it might be his guilt,

stalking him through the hot rain each night like a vengeful panther. He knew he'd gone too far and too often. He didn't ever want to think about the things he'd done. In a world where you eat everything that moves, his appetite had been impossible to satisfy. He'd been a bloodthirsty beast and yet now he knew he'd had enough of killing. His once neatly-ordered mind which had been a sanctuary of calmness was now more akin to a basket of bees. And the only thing that scared him more than the claustrophobic night silence was when it was replaced by the inevitable buzzing swarm that swirled around his tormented brain making it impossible to think.

Chapter 25

She appraised her naked body in the full-length hall mirror for a few moments longer and nodded her head in self-satisfied appreciation. Her long legs, still honey-brown despite the weather, were certainly her best feature she decided, although she knew from experience that the men were mostly interested in her ample bottom and still-firm breasts. She doubted there would be many young women within a hundred miles of her, who'd have the confidence to walk about their house like this, exposed for all the world to see.

Cradling the phone in her right hand, she continued to gaze at her reflection and allowed her other hand to gently explore below her navel. Her skin still had a vague sheen of moisture across it from their recent lovemaking, yet she remained distinctly unsatisfied. He was enthusiastic, she had to give him credit for that and she smiled at herself as she thought back to the activities of the last half-hour. But he was hopelessly inexperienced for a man of his age and he'd none of the class and style of the sort of men she usually allowed to strip her and fuck her in broad daylight.

A cold draught played across her skin and it shook her from her reverie. She glanced across the large open-plan living area, relieved to see the baby still asleep. There was business to be done. Urgent business too, if only she could get anyone to answer their phone. She held the mobile in both hands now

and unthinkingly at first, she found she was slowly rubbing it between her legs as if this would somehow relieve her twin frustrations. When the phone began to ring and the vibration sent a wave of arousal tingling through her body, she thought at first she might still be fantasising.

She swallowed, hoping it wasn't him.

He'd been phoning all the time and he'd become angrier with each call. She flinched and any thoughts of another innocent seduction scene later that afternoon evaporated as she remembered her only meeting with him, her rigid body gripped by cold fingers as she had reluctantly allowed him to have his brief moment with her. The phone continued to ring and when she glanced at the screen, she saw a number she knew well. Clearing her throat, she hefted the 9mm pistol with one hand and brought the phone up to her ear, vaguely aware of her damp and shaking fingers.

'Hello, Valentina speaking…'

Chapter 26

Orla couldn't see Ridge anywhere and she had given up looking for the time being. People were running everywhere with hastily prepared sandbags, boxes of ammunition and trenching tools. Under her careful supervision and with lightning-fast translation services provided by Juanita, the little women of the vineyard had worked quickly and effectively to string razor wire all across the estate. Meanwhile, their men-folk had dug a series of parabolic trenches, each one deeper than the last so if any of the attacking vehicles managed to penetrate the outer fortifications, they would be quickly be brought to a juddering halt as they fell into ever deeper craters.

She knew the next attack was imminent and if she was going to do it, she'd have to act fast. But she'd have preferred Ridge to have been with her, to say a few words to them, in case they couldn't get in touch for a while or at worst, would never get another chance. Theirs was the only number in her contacts list and after scanning the area for the hundredth time, she took a deep breath and pressed the green button.

The call was answered almost immediately and Orla felt a wave of emotion wash over her.

'Hello…?

Hey Valentina? It's Orla here, how are you? Have you been trying to call us… I see there have been some missed calls from you, are the kids alright?'

There was a second or two of silence and Orla was starting to think they'd been disconnected before she heard the girl speak, although it was in a voice she would never have recognised.

'Hello, Valentina speaking. You are still alive then…?'

Orla pressed the cell phone harder to her ear and bent her body over in a bid to cut out some of the background noise. Despite the mayhem around her, she could hear the icy tone in the other woman's voice and she knew instinctively that this wasn't a jokey rhetorical question like her old Mam might try and pull off when Orla had been poor at keeping in touch. More than that, she heard none of the customary lisps of Castilian Spanish which didn't make any sense at all.

''Course we're still alive, we're on our holidays! What're you on about? Are the kids there with you, can I speak to Isla?'

'Isla is with your recently-arrived mother for the moment and young Alex is fast asleep right beside me. They could have been dead by now as far as you are concerned. I have been trying to contact you urgently for more than 24 hours-'

'-What's wrong Valentina?' Orla could hear something else in the other woman's voice. She couldn't make up her mind between anger or fear.

'What's *wrong*, Orla… is that you never answered my calls.

What’s wrong is that you have put the life of your little boy at risk.

What’s wrong is that I have a Glock 9mm pistol pointed at his sleeping head. If you don’t put down your weapons and surrender yourselves immediately, I am going to put a bullet through his brain and then I am going to walk for four minutes to the house of your husband’s mother. There I will kill your mother and then your daughter. Then I will set each house on fire and you will n-’

Orla thought the call must have gone dead as a tremendous bang reverberated out of the tiny speaker and left her reeling. She held the phone at arm’s length and stared at it in complete horror. It had been a gunshot, she was sure of it! Had Valentina gone insane and killed her baby boy?

Orla lifted her eyes to the darkening skies and screamed.

But she couldn’t stop herself putting the phone back to her ear. Clutching it to her head with both hands she fell to her knees and prayed to a God she no longer believed in that her child was safe. Nausea engulfed her as she sank into the dirt and surrounded by noise and mayhem, she heard nothing but an ominous silence at the other end. Orla looked again at the phone to see if the connection was there and seeing that it was, she pressed it harder to her ear as if that would make a difference. Oblivious to the increasingly frantic melee of people around her, she

failed to see the man in army fatigues running towards her, his face disguised by a weird-looking mask.

She shouted above the noise.

‘Valentina? Valentina you fucking bitch! Can you hear me?’

‘*Orla*? Is that you? It’s Seamus here. I don’t-’

Orla couldn’t believe it! It was alright, a dropped phone maybe. Jesus, she was getting dramatic in her old age!

‘-Seamus, you dirty bastard, that wasn’t funny, neither it was! Ridge was after tellin’ me you-’

‘-You’d better stop right there with all that, Orla.’

Looking up, Orla saw the man too late to do anything about it. He had an MP4 pointed at her and he’d jumped a five-foot-high strand of razor wire as if he’d been on PCP. Distracted by her joy at hearing Seamus the ferryman but at the same time thinking he didn’t sound much like himself either and she’d better stop reading things into the distorting effects of the international phone connection, she’d already drop-kicked the guy in the balls before he had time to pull off his balaclava and curse her as only her husband could.

But she had bigger fish to fry right then. As Ridge rolled in the ground in agony she put her hand out straight in front of her to keep him away, her eyes telling him there was still something amiss back home.

'Eh, I don't know how I'm gonna say this Orla, but you know you spent a ton of time and money doing up the place after the 'last time'...? Well, you're definitely going to want to re-do the living room.'

Orla had heard enough nonsense for one day. She helped pull Ridge up as she quickly mouthed 'It's Seamus,' and growled back into the phone.

'Seamus, what the bejesus are you on about?

Where's Valentina and what was all that-'

'-That's yer problem right there, Orla. Valentina, or at least Valentina from the shoulders up, is all over the back wall of the room. Her brains, as if she had any, are running down into yer fish tank. Real sorry an' that, but the shotgun was all I had. I'd been rabbiting earlier, and it wasn't as if I was expecting this kinda shite to be going on. I had just walked into the room, bollock-naked by the way, and saw her with the gun and heard what she'd said. There's been calls from Chile all night and I knew in a second something bad was going down. I mean she was way out ma league from the start, wasn't she? I should have known right away that only a homicidal Spanish sociopath was gonna want to shag me with a body like hers, shouldn't ah? It's going to take a wee bit of-'

Orla felt her head spinning and she gripped Ridge hard. She knew from experience that after the shock he'd had, the ferryman wouldn't be able to understand anything complicated and she kept it brief and as simple as she could.

‘-Seamus never mind that. Get me Mam and the kids and get off the island right *now*. Grab their passports and some money, there are fakes in a wee box along with a pistol and lots of-’

‘-I know where it is Orla.’

‘You know? How do-’

‘-Ridge told me. He told me about the guns and all that, just in case. I have the PIN code in my back pocket here.’

Orla kissed her husband, laughing at his surprise and then looked serious again.

‘Good man, Seamus. Go to London. Book into the most expensive hotel you can find and don’t move until you hear from us.’

Orla grabbed Ridge and hugged him as hard as she could, speaking fast into his armpit.

‘Jaysus, you’ll never believe what’s happened an’ you were right about that *wagon* Valentina! She’s been in with these bastards from the start, so she has! A bleedin’ spy in our own home, an’ there our Seamus has gone an’ blown her head off with a shotgun!’

Her feelings of relief quickly returned to panic as she felt herself being pulled abruptly to the ground and then smothered as Ridge shouted across to the others.

‘Quick, get down! Look, another chopper.’

The words were hardly out of his mouth before Orla saw the advancing machine over his

shoulder, bursting through a cloud of black smoke and then she saw the missile streaking towards them.

She screamed again.

Chapter 27

They were almost directly over the site now and Hellström had instructed his man to take them up higher so as not to be heard. He was disappointed not to be able to see anything of use tactically from that height due to the darkness and the thick black smoke which shrouded the whole area. It seemed to emanate from the vineyard itself. He clenched his teeth in annoyance but at the same time, he had to give them credit. The smoke attracted attention to the place, but it also made it impossible to pinpoint any target.

His frustration levels had reached boiling point when the girl's phone had been engaged once again and when he started to wonder if anything would go to plan with this operation, he'd received confirmation that the vehicles had arrived and the second attack wave was on.

Nudging the alarmed-looking pilot with the tip of an RPG, he pointed to the ground and the other man nodded glumly.

'Down! Down more!'

The helicopter descended fast into the thick black smoke and as the pilot pulled up out of the dive the downdraft of the rotors cleared a path ahead and Hellström couldn't believe his luck. There right in front of him was the main ranch house and little people scuttling to each side like ants. He fired and the chopper rocked slightly. The missile raced ahead and the last thing they saw before the smoke obscured

their vision was an enormous explosion. *Target acquired*, he said smugly, more to himself than anything and gestured the pilot to loop around for a second run.

For the first time that day, he started to believe the mission could be achieved and quickly too. They bore down once more and Hellström strafed the landscape with machine-gun fire, leaning out and chasing down helpless men as they vainly tried to outrun the vicious bullets ripping through the dust. The opportunity for action, to do anything to silence the insistent buzz of self-doubt, had him grinning from ear to ear. The ground troops would have to mop up the mess, but he reckoned another direct hit would complete the devastation of the main base then he could land and hunt down the elusive Piper assuming he hadn't been blown to oblivion. Part of him hoped he hadn't yet perished and he could fulfil the contract in the way he preferred, belly to belly, *mano e mano*, like two prize matadors duelling to the death.

Bullets were ricocheting off their machine now as the battle had begun on land as well as in the air. As the pilot zig-zagged through the smoke, Hellström constantly urged him lower. He reached down to the floor of the cockpit and began throwing as many grenades as he could get his hands on. The rocking of the helicopter wasn't helping and one grenade he tried to chuck across the pilot and out of his side hit the inside of the pilot's Perspex door opening and landed back on the horrified man's lap.

Both men froze in horror for a second before the pilot made a frantic grab at his crotch and threw the grenade past Hellström and out into the air. His arm gesture was so violent and panicked that in conjunction with his momentarily one-handed piloting, he smashed his boss in the face and almost sent him tumbling to his peril below.

Hanging half out of the tiny cockpit, Hellström screamed abuse at the other man, the spittle flecking his chalk-white face like a rabid dog.

But the furious pilot was having none of it, as the chopper bounced from side to side.

'What the fuck!' The man roared.

'You're gonna get us both killed! And you're gonna be bombing our own men down there, tossing them out like that. You fucking lost it man or what?'

The helicopter had increased height during their altercation and the pilot banked clumsily to bring her round. Hellström was convinced he'd done it on purpose and swung a second rocket launcher at him threateningly.

'You want a piece of this, you piece of shit? I'm the boss around-'

Both men jumped in terror as the missile launched in a huge burst of flame and despite wearing headphones, Hellström felt his eardrums sing. The flash blinded him momentarily but he guessed the RPG had somehow been activated by his knee and although it left the cockpit without hitting anything important, the shock of how close they'd been seemed

to end their debate. The assassin clung on desperately as the stunned pilot fought to regain control. As he clung on precariously with one hand he reached down to a wet feeling on his right thigh and brought up a hand dripping in blood. That was when the pain began to overcome the adrenaline and he realised he'd badly burned his leg. Furious, he struck out at the other man, the blood splatter cutting a jagged line across the man's shocked face. The pilot thumped him hard in return. 'Hey! Who do you think you're pushing around,' he growled, and Hellström could see there was no mileage in provoking him further. As if to answer that thought, the chopper lurched again to the left and he felt himself tumbling towards oblivion. He wrapped the seat belt around his left hand, as gravity attempted to tip him out the hole yet again. But there was no way he'd allow himself to fall out, he wouldn't give this guy the satisfaction.

Both legs were dangling in the air and he looked down to see burning vehicles, his crazy situation allowing him an unfettered view of the battle scene. He'd squandered their last missile but they'd still be able to cause mayhem with the rest of the stuff rolling around the floor of the helicopter. Still struggling to get back inside the cockpit and grabbing a grenade with his right arm, Hellström swung his arm back to get greater power behind his throw when a loud bang went off in his ear and he felt a hot liquid splash the side of his face. He turned his head and looked down in terror at what was left of his hand.

Bright red blood spurted out from the wrist and he felt his throat scream in a guttural fit of primitive anger. A bullet from below must have detonated the grenade. He would never be able to shoot a rifle again and as images of carbon prosthetics and painful operations flashed through his panicked mind, he surprised himself by laughing hysterically.

The pilot stared with huge fearful eyes and this empowered Hellström further. He hauled himself back into his seat and brandishing his bloody stump at the other man, he screamed at him to go lower and faster. He'd complete this mission no matter what the cost. He'd his reputation to consider. This would be his last act. He couldn't imagine living beyond this and he'd now become an unstoppable weapon. A man who was prepared to die to succeed.

'Down!' he screamed. 'Down I tell you! Straight down!'

Chapter 28

Liam and Danny found themselves in a decent-sized foxhole near to the front of the estate. Liam was still in total shock about Charlie's death and he somehow wanted to stay close to where he'd met his end. They were each crouching on one knee, precariously balanced between the vicious wooden spikes they'd helped to prepare only a few hours before. Before everything had changed. Swallowing hard, Liam realised deep down that he'd known this escapade was going to irrevocably change things.

It was what he'd wanted. *But not like this.*

Guilt began to seep into his blood like a black poison and he shook himself hard. He couldn't let himself take the blame for Charlie. It wasn't as if they were a bunch of wet-behind-the-ears kids anymore. They'd all seen action before, They'd each taken their chances and brushed with death, often daily. The realisation hit him that they'd possibly all been longing for a way to escape their self-imposed imprisonment in paradise. It had been like they were trapped inside that Eagles song, *Hotel California.* Maybe this would be the only way they could ever leave?

Looking across at a white-faced Danny, he could see his friend had been similarly affected and he'd not seen that intensity in his face since they'd clawed their way out of Fallujah. Danny had managed to acquire one of the few weapons that hadn't come

out of the Ark and Liam could see he had channelled his rage into deadly precise and controlled sniping. In the last twenty minutes, he'd taken out at least seven of the enemy. Liam slammed another magazine into his heavy wooden rifle and lifted it awkwardly as he instinctively sheltered from yet another attack from the swooping chopper. They had little enough fire-power on the ground and he knew enough not to attract its vicious attention by trying to bring it down with his too-slow weapon. He felt Danny kick him hard and that's when he began to hear something different about the noise of the engine this time. It was crashing. He tried to stand up but he was too slow and the last thing he saw before the noise and dust enveloped him was his last comrade sprinting left towards the only available shelter.

A wave of hot black smoke and debris tore at his skin for a few crazy seconds and Liam guessed the blast would only be a moment behind. He braced himself for what was to come, only to find the air clearing and sudden and absolute silence. He heard birds. An ominous shrieking of crows cut through the swirling smoke and there, right in front of him was the helicopter, virtually undamaged. He could see the pilot was obviously dead, his upper body had been pressed through a hole in the cockpit windscreen, too small for the purpose by far. Sitting in the co-pilot seat was a fair-haired man who turned towards him and smiled as if he had spotted an old friend in a crowd. Even from fifty feet, Liam could see his cold

dead eyes and he knew this man had to be the assassin-prick who had brought all of this down upon them. The man looked around him and Liam guessed the guy would be dazed, even more than he was. Flames had sprung up hungrily around the machine and Liam knew that raw animal survival would soon have the guy moving fast, no matter how bewildered or injured he might be. They wouldn't get a better chance than this. He glanced around for Danny and his stomach lurched as he saw his lanky friend spread-eagled face-down in the dust twenty feet away.

It was up to him now. He alone could avenge their deaths. Liam shouldered the rifle and let his breath out slowly and calmly, exactly as they had been trained, all those years ago. He was just about to squeeze the trigger when he saw the man explode. One second, his target was there and the next, he'd vanished. Liam was certain he hadn't fired a shot and he couldn't understand what the heck had happened. He felt something bounce against his shins and that was when he smelt petrol. Before he could react, the helicopter erupted in a fireball, lifting him off his feet and tumbling him through the air. He landed hard on his back, the air knocked out of him. When he made to sit up, he saw one of the wooden spikes sticking up between his legs and he felt another which has scraped his left armpit, but other than that he was completely unscathed.

He blinked a couple of times, not believing what he was seeing. Then he heard a familiar voice

and that's when he guessed why he hadn't felt any pain, because he must already be stone dead.

It was Danny. He looked as astonished as Liam felt. 'What the fuck, man? Look!'

Danny pointed and Liam looked down between his legs again. 'You got *wood*, amigo!'

Liam laughed and struggled to get up. He had to agree, the wooden spike did resemble a phallus. Then as he was about to attempt a humorous retort, he saw what was lying at Danny's feet and this time it was his turn to point incredulously.

'And *what the fuck* is that?'

'Oh yeah, that…' Danny muttered. 'I was going to ask you the same thing, bro.'

Chapter 29

The blistering heat from the burning house made it almost impossible to move, the downdraught of the helicopter somehow accentuating the effect, *like a bizarre fan-oven*, Ridge thought. It rolled across his back in fiery waves, the scorching air searching out the smallest tear or gap in his clothing and searing his flesh. He'd found himself in a tiny foxhole which afforded him minimal protection from the front, barely enough to stay alive. But he was completely open to the air and he felt hopelessly defenceless. If one of those lines of bullets tore down in his direction he would have to think fast. Orla must have been one thought ahead of him, he decided, as he glanced across to see she'd somehow managed to move twenty metres further away from the ranch than him, taking up a far more sensible and strategic position to his left and she was protected by a large sheet of tin which had been ripped off one of the buildings from Juanita's organic farm. He tried to attract her attention but the noise made it almost impossible and he could see she was fully occupied giving covering fire to the men at the front left side of the razor wire which, judging from the cacophony of gunfire, seemed to be where most of the action was taking place.

Ridge decided he'd be far more useful up there and as there was plenty room beside Orla, he'd make for her first and then try and see what he could do then. He smiled idiotically as he thought he'd

probably be best asking his wife what they should do next. He lifted his head but quickly thought better of it as the smoky air became more turbulent again and he guessed the chopper was coming in for another attack. That's when he saw the vineyard worker up ahead, trapped in the open, between him and Orla. She stared at him for a second and then buried her head. If they'd been on the wing, then she was playing centre-forward but from where Ridge was sitting, she didn't look like she was planning on scoring any time soon.

Tiny as she was, she still couldn't squeeze her small frame into the hollowed-out footprint she was trying to shelter in and even from that distance he had seen the terrified look on her face. Then, above the mayhem, he heard her baby wailing. Ridge shook his head quickly as if to clear his thoughts. It all made hellish sense now. That's why she seemed unable to hunker down, she was protecting her child with her own body. With theatrical timing, he heard the helicopter approaching and already he could see the ground way ahead becoming a ferocious pandemonium of bullets. He couldn't believe what he was seeing. Unless she moved, the woman was going to be directly in the cruel path of destruction. It was almost like the sick gunner was choosing his targets. He'd be next.

Ridge tried to see Orla's face for one last time before he rolled over onto his back and thrust his machine gun upwards. He tightened his finger hard

on the trigger and let off half a magazine straight up into the smoky air.

'Pick on someone your own size, ya bastard!' he roared.

He jumped to his feet and ran. Still firing over his left shoulder, the gun rattling against his ear, he sprinted over to the horrified woman and scooped her up around her waist and stumbled on towards Orla. Already guessing what he was doing Orla had taken up a direct defence position and a steady stream of automatic fire tore through the sky only feet from his head. They all fell into the shelter of the aluminium sheeting and waited for a hail of bullets to cut them into pieces. But nothing came. The woman hugged Orla and Ridge sat and stared at the three of them, shocked. He smiled inanely and felt the tears run down his face.

Thick black smoke had blanketed everything and it was impossible to see what was happening. Sounds took on a greater significance and even the ground seemed to be shaking more. Huddling back under the miraculous safety of the wriggly tin roof, Ridge and Orla looked into each other's eyes. Ridge thought he could see regret mixed with her usual defiance and he worried again that maybe this time they had chanced their luck once too often. Underneath them, everything dropped for a second. It reminded Ridge of that super-fast Costanera elevator when they'd first arrived in Chile, which now felt like a million years ago.

Orla grabbed him tightly as they felt the planet move sideways and they both knew what was coming next. Ridge managed to lift his arm over Orla's head as they all became engulfed in hot black dust as the explosion continued to reverberate across the estate. He guessed the ranch had been destroyed this time and, despite the ringing in his ears and the safety of their little bunker, he knew he had to find out what had happened. With Orla pulling him back and the acrid smoke burning his eyes, he pulled himself up and leant out. He swallowed and at the same time, the warning bells in his ears stopped. In fact, he could hardly hear any sounds at all apart from the crackling of a burning vehicle nearby, which proved he hadn't gone deaf. Questions rattled through his brain. Had they lost the fight? Where was Colm?

He couldn't see the ranch house through the smoke but he felt sure it would be gone. Did that mean the workers had surrendered? What would happen next? But where was that evil helicopter? The fact that he couldn't hear the distinctive engine or any vicious bullets tearing up the ground must mean it had landed. But there was no gunfire either. The battle must be over. Colm would never willingly acquiesce, Ridge knew that, deep down in the pit of his stomach and acid bile began to rise inside him. His job now would be to safeguard Orla, as best he could, and somehow get free from this mess and find their way back to Sorsay, whatever it took. Ridge imagined he could hear the gulls, high on the cliffs overlooking the

Anvil and he wished they could all be back there now. He stared up into the black smoke, his attention drawn by something more than desperate longing.

There! He heard it and his heart sank. As the first sounds of the chopper cut through the black murk and he felt the air become more turbulent, he fell to his knees. His head dropped to his chest and in that single moment, he was a broken man. They had a second helicopter. Yet there was something different about that engine, it sounded more like a whine rather than a roar. For a brief second, he clung on to the hope that maybe one of his bullets had almost taken it out. Maybe it was about to crash, but would it spiral down on top of them all? The high-pitched sound grew louder and Ridge lifted his head now, seeing Orla emerge, with the smaller woman by her side. He could see tears streaming down her grimy face, but then he saw the sparkle return to her eyes as she broke out into a huge smile.

Ridge turned back around quickly to see a tall dark man leap nimbly out of the helicopter only moments before it landed softly in the dust. Jumping to his feet and hardly believing his eyes, he found himself waving madly at the still-hunched figure in black battle-fatigues who was running underneath the spinning rotors, directly towards them. He still couldn't process what he was seeing. Could that really be Thaddeus?

Chapter 30

Ridge stared at the slender man standing before him, smiling his familiar toothy grin, but in a face that somehow didn't fit anymore. Was that a wig? *Of course,* it'd be a wig, this was his big gender-bending pal Thad after all!

'Thad! What the hell are you doing here? How'd you find us?'

The other man smiled meekly and prepared to receive the bounding Orla. Smothered by her arms he pushed her gently off and tried to speak under a barrage of kisses.

'You know me, guys. Always gotta be your dark knight in shining armour, right? Gee, I'm, real sorry it took us this long to get here but I guess we did good with that chopper!'

Thad turned towards the other guy who had sprung out of the helicopter and was now striding towards them. He was smaller than the 6'4" Thaddeus which wasn't unusual, but there was something else about the man's gait, and then Ridge looked again at the snug-fitting black jumpsuit. He clicked only a second before the girl pulled off her helmet, setting free an enormous retro-style Afro hairdo and a beautifully dark-skinned and mischievous red-lipsticked face.

'Yeah!' The girl bounded towards Ridge. 'It would've been a lot easier if youse *cunts* hadn't been trying to shoot us down!'

Before Ridge could react, the girl reached a hand up behind his head and pulled him towards her and into a hard kiss. Taken by surprise, he tried to fend her off, but she didn't let him go until he'd felt her strong tongue probing the inside of his mouth.

Stepping backwards to take Thad's hand, she glared defiantly at the stunned couple and then unleashed a huge smile at her companion. 'Yeah, okay… I kinda get where you're coming from Thad, but I don't feel it, ya know, *here*,' she pointed at her crotch provocatively, before turning back to Ridge and Orla and self-consciously trying to adopt a less shameless countenance as if she'd been coached to do this before their arrival. 'Sorry guys…'

Predictably, Orla wasn't going to put up with any of these theatrics, no matter how pleased she was to see Thad. And there was something else weird about this woman.

'Hold it right there, ye *wagon*! Where are you after coming from that ye think ye can waltz up here bold as brass an' start snogging the face off my man?'

Ridge was flattered for a second and he loved the way her accent got so much stronger when she was fired up and that's when the lightbulb went off.

'You're Scottish?'

The girl bowed in a theatrical curtsey and Thad laughed, no doubt sensing that the time was right for some intervention tactics.

'May I introduce my good friend Roxy? And yes, you're right, Ridge. Half Scottish to be exact.

Now, any chance of a drink at this goddamn vineyard we've travelled all this way for? The welcome wasn't up to my usual standards and I'm hoping the rest of the hospitality will make up for it.'

They looked around at the slowly clearing air and Ridge saw that by some miracle, a large part of the ranch house seemed to be still standing although he couldn't vouch for it still having a roof. He couldn't hear any gunfire and many of the estate workers were beginning to appear, many of them looking traumatised and bewildered.

'Come on then,' Ridge volunteered. 'Let's see if we can take some shelter at the main house until we work out what to do next.'

As they traipsed slowly through the debris of shell casings and fallen masonry, Ridge spied his brother-in-law along with Brock and Liam in the distance. Colm look tired but he waved cheerily enough, giving Thad a thumbs-up sign before pointing to the house.

'I'll see you over there in a wee while,' he shouted. 'I'm just after checking on the others first. Have you seen Juanita?'

They walked the rest of the way in a tense silence. Ridge saw Thad take Roxy's arm in a way that he thought peculiar and he could see Orla glancing warily between Thad and Roxy and giving him one of her quizzical looks. Something was wrong here, he knew that, but exactly what, he couldn't fathom right there.

The ranch was badly damaged and they arrived to find a distraught-looking Juanita in the last stages of bandaging up a couple of estate workers in the blackened ruins of the roofless kitchen. The massive oak table had withstood the onslaught and they all made for the heavy chairs. Juanita brightened up for a few minutes when she saw Thaddeus and it was when he wrapped her in his long arms that Ridge noticed how much weight his friend had lost. Normally the diminutive girl would have been completely enveloped in his bulky frame seeing as Thad normally weighed twice as much as Juanita. But not now.

It was Orla, never one to shy away from speaking her mind, who broached the subject on everyone else's lips.

'Thad! I'm loving the wig and all that, but will ye tell me what's going on with you, you look like death warmed up?'

Juanita had already started crying and Ridge only now could see with horror that she had been devastated by the developments of the last few days and he guessed she was suffering from post-traumatic shock. He vowed to speak with Colm as soon as he got back. He looked at the now obviously gaunt features of his friend and braced himself for further bad news. He felt Orla's hand squeezing his and he shot her his bravest smile. He saw Thad give Roxy a look and she nodded back, and any traces of humour vanished in an instant. She reached down under the

table and brought up a small tightly packed black pack that no-one had even noticed. She began to unzip it carefully as Thad looked up at his friends and began to explain.

‘Yeah, I’m kinda in the middle a’ something right now. This trip is like a vacation for the two of us, to be honest. We’ve been through hell-fire the last few months and if it hadn’t been for this girl here who-’ Ridge couldn’t fail to notice the sharp kick delivered under the table followed by a fiery glare from Roxy.

‘Thaddeus, these people are your best friends, right? Do them a favour and get to the fucking point will you?

Thad raised a large hand in mock surrender and attempted a smile.

‘Okay, already!’ He placed both hands on the soot-covered table and as he spread out his long fingers, the bony joints told their own story.

‘I’ve got a rare type of cancer. There, I said it.’

Juanita stood up and walked away as if she was in a trance. Orla’s hand gripped Ridge’s hand hard enough that it felt like his bones would break but she didn’t let her any emotion show on her face. ‘Go on,’ she said evenly.

‘It’s called NHL, non-Hodgkin’s lymphoma. But it’s treatable and I ain’t gonna let it beat me, that’s for sure. And this girl here, she’s my-’

‘I’m his medical nurse…’ Roxy banged a small glass bottle on the table. She’d opened the pack and it was full of medication.

Ridge took a breath. ‘What stage are you at, Thad? How long have you been ill? Have you had a lot of treatment?’

Thad looked straight into his eyes and Ridge saw the pain there for the first time.

‘Near the end, buddy, near the end. We got anything to drink around here?’

He could see this was a show of bravado, an attempt to show him the old Thad was still there underneath this pale facsimile. He glanced at Roxy, who shrugged and nodded. Orla dropped his hand and went to see if there were any wine bottles not blown to smithereens.

Colm and Liam turned up. After Colm had nearly crushed Thad in an inappropriately manly gesture, Orla returned with an armful of red wine and told Colm to calm down and listen to what Thad was telling everyone. Ridge blew the dust out of some glasses and whispered to Colm that he’d better see Juanita and quickly.

‘I’ve just come from her,’ he announced, seemingly to the entire group.

‘She’s going to be fine, I promise you.

We’ve had some great news, so we have.

There’s not one of them left to bother us, for sure. We’re in the clear for now.’

Orla glared at him. 'Well that's grand, so it is! But Thaddeus here isn't in the clear, I'm after thinking, so will ye shut up and let him speak.'

As Colm looked on puzzled, Thad lifted his glass, looked at Roxy, then made to toast them all. 'Here's to you all, my best friends in all the world.'

'Go on Thad,' Orla implored.

'Okay, it ain't pretty. I got cancer, Colm. I've been kind outta sorts ever since my dad died and Ridge nearly hung himself. They say that I must' a been tired out and my immune system got too low after all the strain. Anyways, first off I got glandular fever. They thought it might be HIV for awhile and overall, I thought it might have been the lesser of two evils.

But the glandular fever only weakened me further. I was in D.C. doing some 'super-fly spy-guy' stuff that I'd kinda inherited from the old man and at that point I'd even wondered if I'd been poisoned by the Russians, like your *Novichok* guys over in England! I know now that I should' a been taking it easier but hey, you know me, right? I was having a ball in D.C. and that's when I met Roxy here and she's been looking after me ever since. I owe my life to this girl.'

'Thank you Roxy' said Orla and the other girl smiled and nodded.

'Then the glandular fever turned into this whole other ball-game. The non-Hodgkin's lymphoma means that my body is fighting itself. I

joked at first that it must be the gay part fighting with the straight part, as I could never make up my mind, right? But the joke ain't so funny now… Anyways, I got a ton of chemotherapy which nearly killed me on its own. Goddamn drugs. Gimme *good* drugs any day, but not those motherfuckers. Worse than basic training at Quantico!'

Thad put one hand behind his head and neatly lifted the ridiculous wig off to reveal a completely bald head. Ridge thought he'd never seen a head looking as beautifully smooth and shiny and it reminded him of burnished chestnuts back in his schooldays.

'Suits me, right? I'm still the same Thaddeus, guys. More elegant looking, a streamlined model these days, built for speed!

The worst is over, Doctor Roxy here tells me. We've just finished a long spell of treatment and that's why I look like shit. Basically, I ain't been eating much 'cause the drugs make me puke it all back up again. All we gotta do now is wait for some results to come through and then go back for a small amount of follow-up treatment to make sure.'

Orla reached out and took his hand and with her stronger looking hand next to Thad's, it made his look even thinner, the muscles standing out almost like an anatomical model.

'Thad, please tell me you're not after breaking off your treatment to come down here an' help us?'

Thad picked up her hand and cocooned it within his brown fingers before leaning over and giving it a gentle kiss. He didn't raise his head and Ridge looked at Roxy for some feedback. The girl didn't fail him.

'You're joking Orla. You know him better than that, I think. He was bored shitless with me and the hospital. Yes, of course, he should still be there, from a *medical* point of view but this is Thaddeus we're talking about here. And it's only a wee bit of nip and tuck left to be honest. It should be a walk in the park for this eedjit.'

Roxy dug him playfully in the ribs and right on cue, he lifted his head, fully composed as usual.

'Man, I was glad of the excuse to have an adventure! And anyhow, what's the point of fighting cancer if I haven't got you motherfuckers to hang out with afterwards 'cos I let some slimeball Nazi massacre you in a hissy fit over a few fuckin' paintings?

'You promise us that's it?' Ridge felt his voice cracking with emotion and he took a gulp of dusty wine to mask his fears.

'Kinda, Ridge. That's it or that's not it… And if not, then I rightly am a goner, no doubt about it.'

Chapter 31

Colm got wearily to his feet and came around the table to stand behind Thad. He massaged his shoulders as if he was kneading bread and Thad yelped uncharacteristically.

‘Easy soldier!’

Ridge could see this was all a macho bravado act of Colm’s to divert attention from his rapidly moistening eyes.

‘So Colm, what’s the next step? We can’t-’

‘- No, of course, we can’t stay here, Ridge. First thing, I got to see what’s going on with Juanita. Then, I suggest we all get the fuck out of Dodge.

We’ve made some important headway, but this place is no longer safe nor readily defendable. If they come at us again, we’ll be like sitting ducks. If we can commandeer you and your helicopter, that would be a huge help, Thad. I have a plan, of sorts but it’s going to take a bit of effort from all of you, but if you’re up for it then I think we… what the hell?’

Colm had been the only one standing and facing the main entranceway and the rest of them turned quickly to see what had startled him. It was Danny, looking tired and with a nasty cut down one side of his face. But that wasn’t what they were all staring at. Hanging from his right hand by a clump of unmistakably blonde hair was a bloodstained human head.

'This the fucker, you've been lookin' for...?' Danny growled as he swung his arm back and sent the head rolling across the tiled floor like some grotesque bowling ball. At that moment, Juanita came through into the room from the other door and she squealed in terror as the head slithered past her feet, the cold eyes staring up at her accusingly. She turned to the rest of them with eyes like saucers and screamed, 'You...! *Basta*! You are just like *them*!' She turned and ran and Ridge could hear her screaming all the way through what was left of the ranch house.

Danny stood stock still, aware he'd made a bad situation even worse. 'Aww shit! It's fixin' to get dark out there pretty soon and I didn't want to lose the fucker. Sorry guys, I kinda figured it would be a good thing... didn't Liam tell ya?'

Colm nodded, his face ashen white. 'He did Danny, that he did. But I was going to wait until the right moment before I told everyone, you know what I mean?'

'And I don't need to be frickin' Einstein to guess that this was a world away from the right moment, yeah?'

'Correct Danny, that was after being an entire universe away from the right moment.'

Chapter 32

The dark sky twinkled silently as they re-convened a couple of hours later, shivering despite the still air. Colm had forbidden any fires until they had left, the estate workers having been given their strict instructions about what to do. Ridge couldn't remember seeing him as blunt and cold for a long time and he decided to keep quiet and see what would unfold. He had complete faith in his brother-in-law and when Colm clapped his hands, he listened attentively, as did the others.

'Okay, let's keep this short and to the point guys, we've got a lot to do and time isn't on our side, neither it is.

We've got to get away from here before there's any chance of them coming back. My instinct tells me that, with Hellström dead, the people behind this will ultimately decide to take matters into their own hands.

That's what I would do.'

Ridge ventured to raise a forefinger. 'Can we ask questions, Colm?'

Colm sighed and then as if deciding on the spot, nodded and flourished his hand theatrically, giving Ridge the floor. 'Okay but keep it brief.'

'I was only going to ask if you think we have the advantage now?'

'Fair point. But no. We have no advantage against the likely power of this enemy. Our only

saving grace is we have lots of experience, enough money as we could ever need and contacts around the world who can help us when required. And we can also kick ass with the best of them. But that also means they'll have the same, if not more.

With that in mind. Thad, can you ferry me sister and this eedjit to Santiago please, as quickly as possible? Tomorrow's a Saturday and I've arranged seats for a flight to the Falkland Islands, so I have and-'

'The Falklands!' Orla shrieked. 'That feckin' bastion of Brit imperialism! Jeezo, Colm, you'll be booking us a room at Buckingham Palace next. Do we *have* to go there?'

Ridge couldn't help himself. 'You got another of your 'quaint' Irish hotels over there too, have you?

He saw Colm struggling to keep a straight face.

'Alright, less of that will ye! And Ridge, you got off lucky, I could've put you both in the 'Robinson Crusoe Inn' so I could've!

The Falkland Islands is a safe haven, which is what you need right now. And from there I can get you a military transport flight back to the UK under the radar with no questions asked. Okay? And here's me thinking yer man here would be overjoyed at seeing some sheep again!'

Roxy, do you have enough fuel to get to Santiago tonight? The flight to Stanley is only once a

week and it's mission-critical that you can get them there by tomorrow morning?'

Thad and Roxy looked at each other and then nodded back to Colm. Thad raised his hand. 'What's your plans for us after that, buddy?'

'I'd like you to go straight back to DC, Thad, you've already helped enough. But I'm after thinking that's a forlorn hope. If you can get back here and help me tidy up things then we will have some serious shit to sort out if we're ever going to beat these guys.'

He glanced over to Danny and Liam. 'And you two are permanently on the payroll if you choose to stay. We guessed you'd be looking to avenge Charlie's death and we'd surely love to help you if you'll let us.'

Danny spoke for the first time in hours. 'Ten-four on that.'

Chapter 33

Captain Juan Perez smiled as he eased his F-16 Viper down from Mach 2, the bright red, white and blue flag of the Chilean Air Force disappearing from the bright sun for a few seconds as she powered through the cloud layer towards his target. The old joke that '*you don't fly an F-16; it flies you*,' was perfectly true, which meant that, even at 800mph, he only had a few moments available after he disabled the APG-68 radar system before questions would be asked.

He radioed in that the aircraft was having guidance issues and for safety reasons, he may have to eject over the empty and open lands east of Valparaiso. Then slowing the plane as his target appeared on a tiny screen, he launched his two Maverick air-to-ground missiles. He held his breath for half a second, as he always did, as twin streaks of grey-blue smoke scorched through the cool air at twice the speed of his aircraft. He watched the display carefully. It was a direct hit. Captain Perez felt grateful that they wouldn't have even known a thing about it, yet he still circled as instructed. *Leave no witnesses*. He glanced down, horrified to see a long line of enemy fighters running for the safety of nearby trees. Clenching his teeth, he let go a brief volley from the M61 Vulcan cannons. There would be no need to revisit a third time.

Informing control that he'd alleviated the problem and saved the aircraft by jettisoning

armaments, he felt himself being pushed hard into his seat as he pointed the nose of his powerful fighter upwards, confident of imminent sunshine and a long and lavish retirement.

Chapter 34

Three days after their hurried departure from the ranch and a painful separation from Thad, Ridge and Orla found themselves in the surreal serenity of the Falkland Islands after a short hop from Punta Arenas and a long trek down the Chilean coast from Santiago.

After establishing that Seamus had got the kids safely to London, the pair of them had slept for 18 hours straight. And now, if truth were told, Ridge had to accept Colm's joke comments about this place. As he peered through the cracked and moss-ridden glass of their tiny bedroom window, he couldn't help agreeing that he did find this windswept and inhospitable island to be a comfort. With the barren outlook and spartan accommodation, it wasn't a million miles away from Sorsay even if it was on the other side of the world.

But as he fiddled with the primitive cooker which gasped like a pensioner on forty fags a day, he heard himself growling in frustration at almost everything else Colm had said before they left. His mood had been as black as last night's sky ever since the vineyard battle and he still hadn't forgiven Colm for allowing them all to be used as bait, even if it had been the most logical tactic. He'd long since grown tired and cynical about the shady methods of his brother-in-law and the way in which he could coldly compartmentalise his emotions, almost like a

machine. A killing machine, he muttered as the archaic stove finally began to warm up.

Orla had been out for ages and he suspected the lure of even more photographic opportunities had waylaid her simple plans for the purchase of basic comestibles for their breakfast. Reaching for his cut-price cigarettes, he stood in the doorway and gazed out past the rows of tiny prefab houses and across the bright aquamarine water. Drawing the smoke deep into his lungs he savoured the warm feeling before exhaling slowly like any other man who'd gone back to the demon habit after years of abstinence.

Guns and cigarettes hadn't been on the vacation-planner agenda, yet here he was, back in the thick of it again. He flicked the stub into the wind and watched as it sparked brightly for a moment before fizzling out on the damp grass. He fervently hoped that the fighting would also fizzle out now that they had all dispersed and the horrible little assassin had been eliminated in such a graphic manner. He shuddered at the memory of Colm's comment. 'Sure, I'm going to stick his feckin' head on a spike and leave it here as a warning to any other wee fucker who's thinking of earning his stripes by collaring me.' The image floated in Ridge's mind and it brought back dark visions of another beheading, this time of a dear friend, a tragic event that he was unable to prevent and during which he'd been perilously close to losing his own life.

He hoped that Colm had only been joking but part of him wasn't too sure. Orla had told him of her chat with Juanita and he had to agree with the wee lassie. This situation was unlikely to be the last of its kind. Yet, she had known what she was getting into with Colm right from the start and it wasn't as if her previous 'beau' would ever have been described as your ideal match, with him being one of the most notorious drug cartel leaders of modern times. Perhaps when the pair of them arrived over in the next few days, they could all have a period of peace and reconciliation before they worked out what to do next. Orla wanted to get back to Sorsay as soon as possible, but as the family were safe and the prospect of a decomposing Valentina in their lounge awaited their homecoming, Ridge was of a mind to stay a week and salvage something from their trip, if nothing else.

Yet, even as the thoughts of a relaxing break entered his mind, he knew it would be an unlikely event. Talking to his brother-in-law on the phone hadn't helped to put his mind at rest either. Colm had been uncharacteristically gloomy. The thought of abandoning his vineyard sanctuary hadn't sat well with him and Ridge could sympathise with that. His and Orla's wee hideaway on Sorsay was a non-negotiable part of their new lives and despite the events of the past and this recent tragedy, he was determined that they should be able to continue to live there, safely, for many years to come. He grimaced as he looked across the water. Of course, it was partly

Colm's determination to re-establish Sorsay as his sister's sanctuary that had led to him taking such drastic action over in Ulster which in turn had led to their current predicament. Maybe Juanita was right. This would never end. Ridge turned his back on the panoramic vista and slammed the door hard against the cold wind.

The water had boiled and he poured it into a huge tin teapot to wait for it to steep. Ridge absentmindedly piled white sugar into the enamel mugs and tried to make some sense of where they were and what they should do next. What Colm had said before he and Orla had left, had confused him at the time and still, two days later, it danced around inside his weary brain and didn't seem to make any more sense than it did back then. According to some of his sources, it wasn't only a billion-dollar army funded by a lunatic Nazi they had to worry about. It wasn't only a Mexican drug lord or a rabid Ulster paramilitary hardman, each with personal vendettas that threatened to consume them until all parties were deceased. No, it seemed they also had the might of the CIA on their case too.

Thad had flatly denied this of course, but in the same laboured breath, he'd had to admit that he had been out of the loop for a while due to his cancer treatment. However, it was inconceivable that the Yanks would go against Colm after everything he and the rest of the gang had done for the Americans. Admittedly, their relationship with the latest

President was poor compared with his predecessor, but they had been given medals in the White House for Pete's sake. Colm and Thad's dad had worked together at the highest level on operations spanning the entire globe. Obviously, Colm himself had never met the President and he never would. His identity was his most precious asset and his protection against circumstances like the one they were facing right now.

Ridge scratched his head. What had gone wrong? What had changed? Thad no longer had the same influence with the US spooks, that much was obvious. Yet his father had been a legend, he even had a building named after him at Quantico. Nothing could ever besmirch his reputation and his legacy, his only son's inheritance, must surely mean Thad's continued safety. But did that shield extend as far as Colm and the pair of us, Ridge wondered? The new regime in the White House had certainly shaken the apple cart and so maybe all deals were off?

The door flew open and Orla burst in like an explosion in a firework factory, her cheeks raw and her eyes gleaming.

'Sure, it's a cold wind out there! But it's gorgeous all the same. I'm after getting some amazing shots, so I am. Think I'll send them into a photographic competition, I mean, where will I get the chance to be in a place like this ever again?'

Ridge smiled and handed her a mug of tea.

‘Thanks, love, that’s grand. I got some sausages here and you wouldn’t believe but they actually have soda bread!

Jeez, that tea’s wee bit sweet, did you put it in twice maybe? Is this you trying-’

Orla jumped as a new burner phone jumped on the eighties-styled plastic wood table in front of them. Ridge made to reach for it but Orla was closer.

‘That’ll be Colm’ she said and put the mobile to her ear, her breath still heavy after her walk against the wind. Ridge saw the colour drain from her cheeks in a second and he swallowed nervously. What had gone wrong now?

‘You’re in where? *Miami*? What the-?

So you’re *not* coming to-? But we’re not-?

What? Oh, *Jaysus*… Ridge’s going to love that!

But what about? Oh! Okay then. Bye…!’

Orla took his hand and squeezed it hard. She looked in shock and she stared at the phone in her other hand as if she expected it to talk. Ridge wanted her to talk and he growled.

‘Tell me, what am I not going to like then…?

Are you planning to let me know anytime soon?’

Orla jumped for a second as if she’d been rebooted.

‘Oh Jeez, me love! When’s the last time we had a skiing holiday?

We’re after going to Antarctica, *tonight*!’

Chapter 35

His hands shaking, the man placed the phone carefully back into the docking station and stood up. Looking out across his beloved city, undisturbed by the benevolent ringing of the huge and venerable Great Bell for another year at least, he found it hard to comprehend the chaos and venom that had poured from the correspondingly tiny device he'd held to his ear only moments before. The library-like tranquillity of his peaceful existence had been shattered by the two pieces of bad news he'd just received.

'You promised us success, this time' the first voice had rasped.

The robotic accusation continued; mid-Atlantic vowels strangulated by voice-altering software.

'But once again, your friend *El Gaitero* has fled. We have wasted considerable resources chasing this shadowy nuisance and your fool's errand has caused us to lose face with important and dangerous people.'

The man had been taken by surprise, he conceded to himself as he watched the blue sky being rent in two by a large airliner, barely visible wings glinting as it banked away towards the Continent. It hadn't been fair at all, just not cricket, to get two such devastating calls at the same time, out of nowhere. He'd been deep in thought when his secretary had put the first call through. With only two unsolved clues

remaining from that morning's Times crossword, he'd been thinking that this was going to be a red-letter day for sure.

He replayed the rest of the first, rather one-sided conversation in his mind, annoyed and embarrassed to realise he'd been standing there wishing he'd been on that damned plane.

'And not only have we lost The Piper once again, but the assets you were instructed to retrieve have also been incinerated-'

'But he told me he had a fire-proo-' the man stuttered.

'Please do not interrupt me again!

Maybe he had, maybe he hadn't? I question whether you have the requisite skill to navigate the treacherous swamps favoured by our Phantom. But I ask you, did this mopping-up exercise truly warrant bombing from the Air Force?'

'I thought it would be quick and clean.'

'Quick and clean?

This affair was never going to be quick nor clean. My conclusion from this sorry arrangement must be that maybe you are too fond of staying clean and you do not have the *cojones* to be of any further use to me.

I can even smell your fear from here.

And you would do well to fear me. With the paintings destroyed, all that's left is the mission, the man and his book. I don't believe he would have left

without it and therefore all you have to do is find me The Piper and your life will be spared.

But be under no misapprehension as you sit in that comfortable office of yours, growing ever fatter from the generous stipend my patronage allows. You are not as safe as you think.

Bring me that book.

If it happens to be drenched in the still-warm blood of our elusive Piper, then so much the better. Fail me in this task and I will spill your plentiful blood without a moment's thought.'

The man had swallowed hard on hearing this and then jumped as his secretary came through on the other line.

'Not now!' he hissed.

'But you said, if they used the code, *you know*, that I was to alert you, *no matter what*!'

The man sprang from his chair displacing his newspaper and knocking over an empty coffee mug.

'What? It's *him*…? Right! Gosh, give me two secs will you, please tell him I'm just coming.'

The man cleared his throat as he settled back into his plush leather chair and flipped a switch.

'Sorry about that old chap, and yes I fully understand the gravity of the situation. It so happens that my team have located our man and if you will permit me to end this delightful chat, I can proceed with my mission as planned.'

Chapter 36

The young woman eyed him up and down appraisingly and smiled, a faint blush visible through the heavily applied mask of beauty products. Colm had been fast asleep before the last of the passengers had even boarded and he folded back his long lean frame as the girl poked his shoulder. Feeling instantly exhausted and in need of a long shower, he scratched his bollocks through his grubby black jeans without a trace of embarrassment.

'Hello, as you seem to be the only passenger in this extra-legroom row, sir, will you be happy to help us out in the event of an emergency landing over water and take the responsibility for opening this door here and-'

'Pull this bit here!' Colm correctly identified the relevant handle and did his best to smile despite his bad mood. 'Sure I will and I've been through this a fair few times, so you're fine, thanks.'

'Oh, that's grand,' she said, her Irish brogue escaping for a second. 'You're a keen one! We don't get many like yourself.' And with that, the woman was away attending to the myriad tasks that needed to be taken care off before take-off.

Colm settled himself back to try and sleep but as the smell of their first onboard meal began to waft malevolently down the aisle, he knew instantly it wasn't going to happen. He decided she was most likely to be correct in her assumption that there

weren't many like him on their overnight flight to London.

He doubted that any of the other passengers would be on a fake passport or would have bought and paid for the entire row to avoid being disturbed on the slim chance they did manage to catch some shut-eye.

He was equally sure none of the others would know how to construct a lethal garrotte out of the ridiculous yellow and white plastic masks, the correct use of which the stewards were currently giving a synchronised demonstration of, each one of them giving the automatic pilot in the cockpit a run for its money. Jeez, he was certain he would be the only passenger who had experience of using a plastic pen to both save and take a human life. He winced as he acknowledged to his internal commentator that he'd only ever saved one life that way but had used a pen to kill someone on three separate occasions.

There were a few people he'd like to kill right now and with the way he was feeling, he wouldn't need any weapons whatsoever. Maybe it was true what Juanita had said. That he was as bad as the people he was tasked with eliminating and that with people like him, the vortex of death would continue for as long as he lived, until both he and everyone close to him, was dead. The fact that he'd made his beautiful brown-eyed girl blue, was one of the main reasons he felt like tearing the head off the overweight man in the seat in front, who continually bounced in

his seat as he attempted to get the attention of a steward. Colm thumped the back of the man's headrest hard with the heel of his hand. The movement stopped. He had no clear idea what had happened to Juanita apart from the news that she hadn't returned to the ranch after fleeing the night before he'd also had to leave. He had originally figured she would have stayed locally, got the whole thing off her chest to a sympathetic ear and then returned.

By the time he had left for Miami, he knew that scenario to be unlikely and he feared she might have returned to her family up in Mexico. There weren't many of them left after the vengeance of Ramon's cartel had run it's course and despite Colm paying for their security for over a year now, he had to face up to being unable to locate their whereabouts or contact any of them which worried him greatly.

His list of worries was long and grievous, and a lesser man would have required a written list in order not to forget.

That thought made him sit up sharply. Most men *would* have had a list of what to do next. Most men would have kept a list of who he worked with, who he had killed and why. Most men would have kept a book. A black book of death.

Colm heard himself growl, sounding like his hapless brother-in-law Ridge Walker. Poor Ridge had been left thinking he was somehow the reason all this mayhem had befallen them. Even Colm had been

fooled into thinking that the not insignificant matter of a billion dollars had been the main thrust of their problem. He took the tray of food and smiled his thanks, settling the food onto his tiny fold-down table and wondering which part of it would be the least offensive to his tired taste buds.

Of course, the money had been a factor. Stealing from a billionaire Nazi could never be considered a clever move.

His wiping out an entire layer of the management tree of most of the Central American drug cartels had also been a factor.

Twenty years of death and deception at the behest of Her Majesty's Intelligence services and then the CIA had been a factor.

A career at the pinnacle of the international assassin business had been a factor.

His ability to somehow weave in and out of those shadowy worlds without ever becoming a part of them, always maintaining his mysterious aliases, never allowing his guard to come down, *that* had been a factor.

Colm pointed to the little bottles of red wine, holding up four fingers and throwing the young man his most winning smile while holding his stare in a who-blinks-first contest. Victorious, he wrenched off the cap on the first bottle and took a long drink. This might be the only red wine he'd be seeing after his two years of loving toil in the supposed sanctuary of his vineyard.

But in the end, it had all come down to one thing. He had been too good at his job and consequently had lived for too long. And that meant he knew too much.

So, if it existed, what would The Piper's book supposedly contain?

It could be a true and *bone fide* record, a detailed exposé of all the dirty deeds and Machiavellian politics throughout the years of The Troubles and afterwards. The Brits would kill to stop that being published.

His book could be a list of the world's top assassins, arms dealers, embargo-breakers, high-tech surveillance experts, forgers, money-launderers, government agents, logistics, recruitment and procurement specialists, torturers and clean-up squads – a blood-stained Rolodex of death at your fingertips. Colm knew the Yanks would kill to be the first to get their hands on that.

A lot had changed within the cold and calculating world he'd inhabited over the last couple of decades. But much had stayed the same. The breed of men who bestrode this world would never change. Political systems could appear to rise and wane, but it would be the same people who pulled the strings. Much like the shadowy and powerful elite that controlled the world's banks and stock markets, the people who made capital out of the endless cycles of boom and bust, these cynical masters took a longer view of world events. They would analyse a situation

like an accountant would scrutinise a set of financial reports. Balance sheets. Profit and loss accounts. Win or lose. Live or die. Elimination. Survival. There would be scant profits to read about in his book, if he'd written one. He dealt more in taking away rather than the adding back. Colm decided his book, to these men, would simply be another Loss Report.

Or his book could instead be an honest confession. An admission of guilt. An absolution even? The Piper had a lot of blood on his hands. Could he wash off some of that with his book? There'd be numerous authorities across the world who'd love to clear off a substantial backlog of unsolved murders and unexplained death cases for which he'd been responsible for.

Maybe in some crazy and twisted biblical re-interpretation, there were some in authority who viewed his book as a Book of Revelation. A tool to bring righteousness to the world.

The worrying rumour he'd heard was if the book didn't exist already, and most believed that it did, someone had recently offered to ghost write the book for The Piper. The name mooted had been that of his own sister, Orla. Now *that* he knew to be nonsense, even though Orla was a great writer and she of all people knew more about his secret life than anybody. But was it? Had someone else asked her? Would she have told him even if she had been approached?

He ripped the cap off the second bottle and drank. The cruel irony in all of this, of course, was that all Colm wanted to do was to retire, to turn his back on violence and to live out the rest of his life peacefully, maybe starting a family and nurturing them alongside his vines.

But he'd unintentionally brought these diverse and dangerous elements to his vineyard. He'd summoned the rats to Chile for one last showdown like some bizarre Pied Piper in reverse. Colm drained the bottle of wine, grimacing at the bitter flavour as he attempted to process the latest news he'd received just before boarding.

He knew the ranch had been hit again and hard. It hadn't been a total surprise. After all, that's why he'd fled and why he'd sent Orla, Ridge and Thaddeus away the day before him. But it was the scale of the attack that had surprised him and that was something that didn't happen too often. He would never have thought a private individual could have been able to command that level of firepower. The poor man who'd spoken to Colm, one of his most loyal men who only lived a couple of miles away, had described a jet louder, he'd said, than the worst monsoon thunderstorm. He'd said it had unleashed a vengeance more deadly than any lightning storm he'd ever experienced. The man told Colm there was a crater big enough to hide a hundred horses and the bullets which had torn through his friends and

relatives had been bigger than the teats on his oldest cow.

He knew Juanita hadn't been among the dead which was a huge blessing. Liam and Danny had been up North on another mission and had been unharmed. But for any of his innocent vineyard workers to have been killed was a painful wound in Colm's side. Normally he was unmoved by death as it affected only those who had chosen to become a part of the vicious theatre of hate which he'd watched being played out across the globe. He crushed the empty wine bottle in his fist and reached for the last one.

He had wanted to retire. That had been the honest truth of it. He had wanted to turn his back on violence. But as the fury gripped him, a shadow crossed his face and he once again became the menacing creature many had feared over the years. This time, this final time, they would all play to his tune and it would be a dance to the death.

For the only way to end the cycle of death was for him to raise the stakes. He would avenge his vineyard workers and bring a level of vengeful destruction and retribution on his enemies that would have the world talking about The Piper long after the man had been laid to rest. This time he was playing for keeps.

Chapter 37

‘Patience my father, patience… our time will come!’

Ricardo lifted the gold paperweight, enjoying again the heft of the large eagle in his hand. He’d briefly considered throwing it through the plate glass window of his bright modern apartment office but, as always, the weight of history that dwelt within the object he held, calmed him.

He quietly admonished himself for his impetuous thoughts. After all, he had waited his entire life to be in the position he was in right now, and it would be childish and naïve to assume that everything would go exactly to plan. Of course, there were going to be what the brash Americans would call ‘speedbumps’ on the road ahead. He should be grateful that the changes happening around the world had coincided with his time on earth, unlike his unfortunate father, who had gone to his grave railing against the *Lügenpresse*, the lying press, who he said had pushed his demoralised German people into their mania for commemoration.

The final straw had been the 2,711 stone slabs that had been installed as a Holocaust memorial in Berlin when his father had made his fateful last visit to the Fatherland a few short years back. Of course, he could never have anticipated the meteoric rise of the right once again. It had been a cruel irony that progress had begun soon after his early death. Ricardo remembered the strain etched on his father’s washed-

out face, heavy dark bags weighing down his tired grey-blue eyes. They had stood for what seemed like forever, the two of them alone in the rain, Ricardo holding his frail father's arm, looking at the concrete abomination in horror. The words his father had spoken had burned into his soul and served as a relentless stick that prodded his side whenever he felt like giving in.

'My son, you must avenge our people.

Why are we the only ones who have planted a memorial of shame to pierce the heart of our capital? We seem to want to commemorate everyone else; the fucking Jews, of course, the gipsies and the queers – why not acknowledge the outstanding patriotism of your grandfather's glorious *Wehrmacht*?'

Ricardo grimaced as he wondered what his dad would have made of their beleaguered multi-cultural nation today. On his recent visit, he had struggled to find true representatives of their once-proud *völkisch*, their pure German race, anywhere he walked on the streets. He had read recently that Germany had been infested by more than ten million foreigners since the crisis in Syria, thanks to that bitch Merkel.

It was ironic that the enemy his men were unsuccessfully hunting down, had called himself 'The Piper,' when in reality it was the German Government itself that had acted like a demented Pied Piper, inviting these rats to come into their nation. Those vermin who had been given free housing, food,

education and even healthcare. He slammed the eagle hard on the table. And how have the ungrateful swine repaid us? With hundreds of killings, murders and rapes.

But enough was enough. World events had at last begun to turn in Ricardo's favour. The rise of the DAfT party after the ridiculous EU bailout of Greece, although a slow burn during his father's last years, had taken on a meteoric success of late, buoyed by similar political gains by other right-minded parties throughout Europe. Soon they would be restored to power and Germany's borders would be permanently controlled with, if necessary, the authority to shoot migrants as they sought to enter the country illegally. It was time to put an end to the Islamisation of Germany.

He smiled up at his office wall. In between a favourite photo of his father and a carefully ironed original German Deutschmark, sat an old copy of the front page of a German newspaper similarly ironed and encased within a polished glass frame. Der Spiegel had published an article decrying the mainstream fascination with punishing its citizens with painful reminders of the Nazi era. Ricardo had learnt some of the text off by heart.

"*If the Germans were once the greatest sinners, they now apparently want to be the greatest penitents.*"

That time would soon be over. Ricardo looked forward to the day he could walk past the Reichstag

with his head high. The day he could be christened with his real name, his German name, the name of his grandfather, Herr Rauff. Then he could begin the resurrection of the German population, a nation in his view who had become a brutally defeated people. The new order in Germany would take the re-education of the country on a complete 180-degree turn. Instead of teaching about the Holocaust, they would remind the German people about their previously renowned philosophers, musicians and inventors who more than any other country had shaped the modern world.

He looked out across the bustling late afternoon city and took a deep breath. There was no doubt the momentum was with them now. Momentum and timing. He understood from his successful career in business that if you had those two weapons in your arsenal then you could be unstoppable. And they had allies around the globe, even if some of the parties concerned were oblivious to their complicity. The Americans were pulling most of their troops out of Germany. That fat and fake-tanned old goose, Trump, had greatly helped fan the flames of old-school populism and then their old enemy, England had inadvertently done the German far-right cause a massive favour with their Brexit fiasco. Even down here in South America, the once-imperious British Parliament had become a laughing stock.

Now all they needed was a little injection of party funds then they could take their message to the

people with greater force and it would be the turn of his people to take back his country and their proud history.

Ricardo glanced at his watch. He had important international calls to make. People to talk to. People to kill. He'd wait until his office staff had gone for the evening, you could never be too careful, his father had taught him that. He took a drink of his cold coffee, savouring the bitter black liquid. Yes, he thought, if the British could be proud of Lord Nelson and Winston Churchill and the socialist French, their Napoleon Bonaparte, then Germany had the right to celebrate the achievements of the German soldier in both World Wars. One day they would even learn to be proud of the Nazi party and men like his grandfather.

He picked up the phone and smiled.

Chapter 38

It was unbelievable. He allowed the lifeless body to drop silently onto the rough ground below and as far as Danny could gauge, their presence had still gone undetected. He turned and nodded to Liam, out towards the right, on point, as they'd practised many hundreds of times together in another lifetime. So far so good. Incredibly, everything was still under control. Yet the river of sweat running down his spine told another story. It had been a long time since Danny had killed a man with his bare hands and until the recent fracas in the courtyard of the Valparaiso restaurant, he had doubted if he would ever have the nerve to do it again.

Why were they here? This wasn't for America, for the Stars and Stripes. His home country would have him incarcerated for the rest of his days if they caught him here, only an hour of fast driving from the New Mexico border. Danny spat into the red dust and glanced across the darkened estate grounds. Everyone drove fast around here.

They'd both felt it, the night before. They were tantalisingly close to being back home in the land of their birth. Danny knew Liam's thoughts on going back. The idea had crossed his own mind more than once since Charlie's death last week. The events of the last 10 days had brought their South American exile to a violently sudden but, in retrospect, not such a premature conclusion. Danny saw that now. He

knew that even if the red-headed bombshell had never entered their lives, their annual reunions would not have lasted another year and also that if Liam had returned to Boston to face the music, it wouldn't have been much longer before they'd have come after him too and all three of them would have shared the same fate.

But things had changed of late. In a big way. Liam had stopped talking about giving himself up. Even this close to the States, he hadn't faltered. For they had a purpose now. A mission of sorts. They had more money than they could ever have imagined, and more than that, they had a job to do. Not the sort of job you'd want to have bandied about in the bar or at your kid's football game, but still a job, nonetheless.

When Colm had sat the pair of them down and outlined his position and what he wanted them to do for him and what he could do for them in return, they jumped at the offer. Colm had said he would allow them the entire evening to mull it over yet they'd both grabbed his hand and shaken on the deal within the first ten minutes. It had felt good, real good. No longer directionless and in hiding, now they had a powerful force alongside them. Danny didn't want to know the full story behind the calm Irishman and his crazy sister. But he felt an instant camaraderie with the pair of them and there was something else too that had swung the deal for him. A feeling about Ridge Walker that Danny couldn't put his finger on. Liam had mentioned it too after they'd agreed to the whole

thing, once they'd crossed the Rubicon, the point of no return. The young Scot had a strangely comforting aura around him. It was either completely effortless on his part or more likely, as the two of them suspected, an elaborate cover fabricated to disguise one of the most professional international killers on the planet. Neither Danny nor Liam could make up their minds who the hell the real 'Piper' was, but to them, it didn't matter. They pledged their allegiance to Colm and the team. To follow 'The Piper' until death.

*

Liam whispered through the comms and Danny ducked down low. Death was a likely outcome for them that night unless they were both careful and lucky at the same time. Their mission for this trip up north had been stark and brutal in its simplicity. Find the leader of the Sinaloa drug cartel, a man by the name of Maximiliano and terminate him with extreme prejudice.

The first part had been easy.

Most of the drug cartels operated almost with impunity, their control of the two main levers of power being both their incredible wealth and the accompanying threat of devastating violence towards anyone stupid enough to cross them. Their offer of *plata* or *plomo*, silver or lead, seemed to be enough to virtually guarantee their licence to print money. But, although they were not confined to the shadows as were their North Americans counterparts, they still

preferred to maintain a pretence of being distinct from the normal population, keeping the locations of their headquarters a 'secret' and heavily defended with a large security cordon over several city blocks.

But Maximiliano's organisation was not 'most of them.' Larger than the rest of the groups combined and with many of the clans inherited from the ravaged debris of Ramon's once imperious cartel, the man seemed to be impregnable. When Danny had reconnoitred the location of his northern base, where they'd been reliably informed he could be found, he'd at first thought they had been fed dummy intel. The Sinaloa cartel practically had information signs on the adobe walls of the town and as Danny drew closer he half expected to find an illustrated tourist map with a 'You Are Here' dot and then a ''Drug Cartel' castle logo further down.

He'd shaken his head in disbelief at the ease in which he carried out his detailed surveillance. The main security installations would have been obvious to an 8th-grade schoolkid. Heavy concrete bollards had been installed along all the main roads which headed inwards to the base, like spokes in a wheel. The lumps of concrete had been positioned diagonally opposite each other to create speed-reducing chicanes. The narrowing effect would also preclude the authorities from bringing any tanks or heavy artillery anywhere near the hub. Danny guessed the cartel must have a separate location close by where they would be storing their own large items of plant

and equipment and he made a mental note to find out exactly where before they made their actual raid on the base. In the same way, but only obvious to a trained sniper like Danny, the cartel had situated tiny pillboxes along the same routes on the highest of the buildings available. Danny could see immediately that these were still unsuitably low in most cases, there not being a huge amount of tall buildings to choose from, and he reckoned the ‘kill zones’ were small and sporadic with several good entry points of close-to-zero visibility for the right size of team.

That was how they had managed to get near to the main hub with ease. Liam on a second surveillance at night had noted a far sparser detail of men on the rooftops so naturally they’d carried out the mission under cover of darkness. With Danny taking one side of the road and Liam the other, they’d traversed the rooftops quickly and quietly and despatched all of the snipers without firing a single shot, each hapless man looking outwards or downwards towards the perceived threats of the road and not thinking for a second that anyone would be foolish enough to jump from building to building.

It had been all too easy until this exact point, Danny thought. The sniper he’d despatched had been a tad faster than his colleagues and Danny was forced into a brief but frenetic tussle. Rather than break the man’s neck from behind with one quick movement, he’d had to resort to a brawling street fight and the

man had fallen off the roof. His crumpled corpse now lay on the sidewalk in plain view.

And that had been the reason for Liam's terse message. They'd been rumbled.

Chapter 39

With the element of surprise now gone, Liam knew they'd have to move fast before the entire area would be swarming with enemy goons and, from what Colm had told them about his old foe, more than a few highly-trained *sicario*. He peered over the lip of the building. A couple of men had hunched down next to the body, trying to work out if he was alive whilst a posse of old women harangued loudly them from a nearby doorway. It was when a taller shadow flitted across the road and gave the lifeless body a vicious kick that Liam knew they were in trouble. The man glanced up in Liam's direction but by the time his head had lifted high enough to see him, Liam had scampered onto a lower roof and made to rendezvous with Danny in the bowels of a disused engine repair shop. Danny was already in position, breathing heavily.

'We've gotta get outta here fast, Danny! I saw a guy back here, motherfucker was cool as a cucumber, like whaddaya call him The Man With No-'

'-Yeah, saw him,' Danny puffed and Liam heard the frustration and annoyance in his voice. 'Let's move. Stay close.'

Danny had ditched his shoulder bag and as he turned towards Liam for a brief nod of mutual understanding before his face set into a dark mask, Liam had to admit he looked every inch the highly

paid assassin that he'd recently become. Two Sig Sauer 9mm pistols stuck into the back of his black fatigues and he'd an army-issue knife in his right fist, the 5-inch black blade glinting dully in the half-light. Liam guessed that Danny wouldn't be allowing any more opponents to get away from him. He tiptoed behind the taller man, his own weapon upfront and ready to use. The Glock was chunkier, but it had always been his favourite and he'd thought it could have doubled up as a knock-out baton if silence or subterfuge had still been a viable option.

They glanced out across the darkness, the oppressive heat closing in on them like an invisible blanket, heavy and suffocating. All Liam could hear was his own heart beating a powerful bassline and, distracted for a moment, he hesitated for too long. Danny moved out into the street, towards the centre of the wheel and as he made himself more visible a black shape leapt silently out of the shadows and launched itself hard into Danny's torso. Danny turned quickly unable to stop himself from falling but long enough to twist around towards his attacker and turn the knife upwards and into the man's exposed throat. Seconds later, as Liam jumped onto the man's back to haul his head back it was obvious he'd already died, the hot blood still gushing across the startled Danny. Shocked, Liam extended a wet hand, slippery with blood and the pair of them staggered onwards, heads low and zig-zagging in and out of the shadows.

Pistols to the fore, they ran under an archway and rolled, Danny to the right, Liam to the left. The guards were not at their posts yet, despite the fracas and Liam guessed the guy with the raw throat must have been the football player he'd seen earlier and that he'd must've preferred to take care of the situation personally rather than raise the alarm. Liam remembered a lesson from basic training, '*leave your ego at the door*,' and he smiled grimly.

There! In the shadows, Liam caught sight of a man disentangle himself from a partially disrobed woman and grapple for his weapon. The guy didn't get halfway close, barely having time for a muttered '*Que mierda*!' before Liam slammed two rounds into his chest. The woman screamed for a second until, seeing Liam's placating hands, her eyes enormous and staring, she worked out pretty damn fast that he wasn't going to harm her and saw the sense in silence. As Liam moved quickly past, she was already raking through the guy's pockets. Not the sentimental type, Liam decided.

Speed would be the key to their mission, Colm had drilled into them. Remove the head of the beast and the body would be harmless. Once Maximiliano had been killed, the pecking order would be up for grabs and the chances were those who were still alive would probably start shooting at each other.

Now they were being fired upon from inside the citadel and Liam saw Danny make a movement with his hands. He knew what to do.

They both unclipped a pair of grenades and tossed them through the open spaces that doubled as windows, running fast enough to use the adobe walls as protection from the blasts. Liam felt the heat across the top of his head as he looked over to see Danny jumping up and charging through the acrid smoke of the main entrance space. Firing at anything that moved in the smoke and dust, the two men made quick work of the few stunned cartel men. Danny left a precision-timed explosive by the entrance set for five minutes. This would double as a warning to anyone else stupid enough to venture in but also as a cover for their escape, assuming they'd fulfilled their mission in that time.

Liam followed Danny as they pushed through a couple of empty, open-plan sitting areas, towards more private rooms at the back. Their target had to be there unless they'd been supplied with bad intel, which they'd known was always possible. Liam gritted his teeth and kept running. If Maximiliano wasn't here, they would be unlikely to survive. Not even for five minutes. He thought of his family, financially secure but never knowing where their windfall had come from or the true cost. Then up ahead, in the middle of the back wall, a large fake-oak door opened and one man appeared.

The guy was enormous and Liam gulped. He had to be at least 350 pounds. Liam glanced over at Danny and as their eyes met, he saw the confirmatory gleam in his partner's eye. This fucker was

Maximiliano. He'd chosen to face them himself rather than be cornered like a rat. To take a warrior's end. That's when Liam saw the Uzi sub-machine gun and he hit the ground fast.

The gun barked a staccato burst and Liam heard rounds bouncing into the dusty floor all around him. Expecting the next second to be his last, he frantically attempted to wriggle behind any available cover but he couldn't see how he was going to get out of this one. But the bullets stopped as violently as they'd begun and as Liam looked cautiously upwards, he saw the huge man staggering backwards and that's when the screaming started. Danny had seemingly recovered faster than him and as Liam cautiously moved forward he saw what had happened.

Maximiliano only had one hand. They'd known all about the story of him hacking off his hand to save himself from drowning off the coast of Acapulco. He'd been toting the Uzi on his 'bad' arm and it must've slipped off and he'd shot himself in the foot. Literally. Not only that but he'd massacred most of his left leg in the process and by the volume of blood that was gushing across the floor he'd likely ruptured his femoral artery.

The two men advanced carefully. But they saw the colour draining from Maximiliano's face and knew it was over for him. He'd stopped screaming and had slid down the wall, accepting of his fate. Liam thought the big guy looked almost embarrassed. He waved at the gun which was lying in a pool of

bright red blood and swore under his breath but made no attempt to pick it up and use it against them. Liam could see the exact moment when it was effectively over. The big man took a breath and his enormous tattooed shoulders rolled up and round before all the fight seemed to leave his body. He looked at them with a glassy-eyed expression. Liam thought he looked as if he was maybe glad it would soon be over. As Maximiliano turned towards Danny, he blinked before lifting his heavy chin upwards. Danny raised his arms and put two rounds into his forehead quickly and coolly. 'Let's get the fuck out of Dodge' he whispered to Liam and turned away. A brief image of Juanita crossed Liam's mind and whether this bloated monster had killed her and he wondered if his friend had also had the same thought as he was sure he could hear the emotion in his friend's throaty words. Job done. Now to escape this nest of vipers before all hell broke loose.

Chapter 40

Ridge stamped his numb feet in frustration. Orla slapped his head hard with the back of a hand.

'Hey! Would ye mind staying still?

It's not easy putting make-up on someone else's face, neither it is.'

He growled. 'Is it not finished yet? Can I see a mirror?'

'And I'll not be taking any back-chat either. A mirror?

Jaysus! For a clown? Like it or lump it, me love…'

Despite the inordinately long time his wife was taking to apply a little make-up to his face, Ridge had to admit that he was having a lot of fun. He breathed in gently, enjoying the physical intimacy as Orla leant over him and he tried to nestle further into the warmth of her body. His reward was another clout, this time from an elbow.

'Cut it out!'

He smiled as Orla stepped back from painting a red circle on each cheek, her bright green eyes sparkling with mischief.

'Would you stop moving your face! You'll end up with squinty cheeks!'

Ridge grinned inwardly and allowed his wife to continue. It was a welcome relief from the relentless chill outside and near-constant darkness. Of course, they'd known an Antarctic winter wasn't

going to be a walk in the park, especially as it was still the height of summer back home, but they'd been totally unprepared for what met them on their arrival at Rothera less than a week ago.

Back then, Ridge would have been happy to scamper into the mouth of Moby Dick, such had been his fear that their rickety old De Havilland Dash wouldn't make it across the sea from Mount Pleasant airport, which now seemed like a bustling metropolis in comparison with the British Atlantic Survey base. They'd been met on arrival by darkness and biting cold, but at least there had been the reassurance of solid ground under their feet and after all, he was a Scotsman. Bad weather was part of his DNA.

But they were hideously under-equipped and despite the base being half-empty, the indigenous boffins, who bizarrely referred to themselves as the *winterers*, hadn't been too keen on sharing out their warm-weather gear. One Dutch girl had likened it to allowing a student flatmate to share her best underwear, such was the importance they put onto their clothing in such an inhospitable climate. Ridge had thought her frostier than a snowman and he had retorted that she'd obviously had an entirely different university experience from him. He quickly decided that anyone who volunteered to maroon themselves in the gloom of Antarctica, thousands of miles from a decent boozer for five months at a time, had to be psychologically damaged.

They'd both been frozen, even indoors. All their aspirations for exploring the icy tundra, spotting wildlife or indulging in outdoor sporting activities soon evaporated quicker than the heat from their sleeping bags. Daylight had been fleeting but stunningly rewarding and Orla had taken hundreds of photos. In the darkness, she'd had plenty of opportunities to photograph the Aurora Borealis, directly above them, crystal clear and undiluted by the lights of civilization. That morning, Ridge had helped out for a few hours over in the garage workshop, fixing a broken caterpillar track on a vehicle, not unlike some of the estate ATV's back on Sorsay. In return, one of the mechanics had allowed Orla the use of a small drone camera and the two of them had recorded some incredible shots, catching the brief sunset in all its majestic splendour.

The unexpected isolation had given Ridge time to consider their predicament. Colm still hadn't been in touch and anyway, their cell phones had no connection outside of the immediate area. They'd spoken to Seamus from Port Stanley the day before they left and apart from the ferryman going stir-crazy in their London hotel, all was well and the kids and their gran seemed to be enjoying the bright lights of the city. When the research scientists found out the two of them had young kids, a couple of them had let slip that they could get the use of a satellite connection if they wanted but up until then Orla had been reluctant as she didn't know who to trust at

present. Obviously, for them to have had to scarper as quickly, something had got seriously fucked up at the Falklands end which had spooked the pair of them, especially his wife. It wasn't like Colm to send them into a danger zone unwittingly and Orla had confided to Ridge that as far as she was aware, no-one had ever breached Colm's carefully constructed security system. She'd reminded Ridge about the general idea Brock had given them about the uncompromising hand fate had dealt the ex-copper up in Vegas.

As he savoured the brief moments of daylight, Ridge couldn't help being impressed with the cruel majesty of the surroundings but at the same time, the unrelenting whiteness made him long for the lush green of the Scottish Highlands. Mixing with the wide variety of nationalities on the Station reminded him of the international complexities of the enemies that faced them. He'd picked up a couple of old newspapers out of boredom and read every single word of every page front to back and then all the way to the front again.

Normally, he wouldn't have paid much attention to the football pages, especially as most of the coverage was for the English teams. Football didn't register much on the radar of a tiny Scottish island when there were too few youngsters to play the game and when you had the far superior spectacle of a shinty match to replace it. But he desperately hoovered up every word on every page.

He decided that he could quite easily divide up the various elements that ranged against them into football teams of sorts.

Firstly, there was the good old-fashioned and traditional, the blue team versus the green and white striped team. Glasgow Rangers against Glasgow Celtic. Protestant against Catholic. It pained Ridge to think how little progress had been made in his own country to take the heat out of this ancient rivalry, where even today his university town would be riven several times a year by loyalist Protestant marches and then their Irish republican counterparts the following weekend. He'd been terrified by one of these confrontations as a lad and only this morning, twenty years later, he'd read a newspaper report about another ugly incident where police helicopters, riot squads and dogs had been used to quell violent sectarian attacks after a march. Vicious though these two paramilitary teams might be, Ridge understood them and was comfortable in the knowledge that Colm, more than most, had their measure.

Then there was a more unpredictable element and one which they had previously discounted until now. The team with the red and white flag. The English. Arrogant, superior and controlling for centuries, could there be, as Orla suspected, an MI5 or even MI6 angle to the situation? After all, Colm must have ruffled more than a few feathers in the corridors of Millbank over the years.

Ridge sighed as the sky blackened and he turned away to find a quiet corner to marshal his thoughts further. It would be crazy to rule out the Americans from all of this. Vulgar and audacious, with more dodges than a New Patriots running back, they had up until recently, always been considered a loyal friend to Colm and the rest of the gang. But with a new and impetuous President in the White House maybe all bets were off. Their most powerful ally in Washington had always been the incredible Tadashi, but since his cruel murder and now with his son seriously ill with cancer, maybe the American team had a new play in progress.

There had to be consideration paid to the Central American teams, the dirtiest of all the players and with home advantage until this recent snowy development. On the face of it, Ridge would have discounted the drug cartels as being the most dangerous, despite their fearsome reputation, due to their splintered and disorganised structure and lack of funds as compared to the vast wealth of the United States. Normally, given the slightest of encouragement, they could be relied upon to start fighting among themselves and of all the teams, they would be the ones most likely to start battling before they even made it out of the tunnel and onto the field. However, with the seemingly limitless funds of this Nazi spawn and his cohorts and the spectacular successes of the last weeks, again you would have to

agree that their championship group position had advanced significantly.

None of these teams cared who lived and who died, providing the desired result was achieved, which appeared to be the obliteration of The Piper and anyone connected to his legend.

Lastly, of course, was the true ‘home’ team of the tournament. A rag-tag mixture of amateurs and professionals, retired players and talented fresh recruits with valuable transfer potential. Colm, Orla, Ridge, Thaddeus and the Diamond Dogs had one unique advantage over the other teams. They weren’t motivated by avarice or by power, they were literally fighting for their lives and the love of each other.

Ridge looked up as Orla appeared at the door of the mess room. He’d been lost in his thoughts and hadn’t realised he was the only person there. The rest of the station had been buzzing about the ‘show’ they were putting on that night and they’d all gone off to get ready. He waved over at his wife and tried his best to fake a smile. The clown costume he was due to wear would have to work pretty hard tonight he thought and wondered if he still had time for a sneaky cigarette before all the nonsense started. He couldn’t shake the memory of the time when he’d played football for his very life in the oppressive humidity of a Central American jungle. Scary as that had been at the time, he knew this time he was in a different league altogether and he also had a lot more to lose.

Chapter 41

It was almost completely dark, with only the faintest wisps of salmon-pink light tiptoeing in with the sea breeze. The summer dawned early at that time of year and the old man guessed it must only have been about three o'clock in the morning when he first heard it. He never wore a watch, he normally had no need of such fripperies, but he knew it would be important later, to know the right time, when he told his story to the others' in the pub.

He'd been out rabbiting, and it had been another fine haul as the eight or nine dead animals tied around his waist by a piece of rough hessian string attested to. Donald MacDonald had always been good at hiding, lying low when it was called for, especially when he'd been in a bit of trouble with the missus. As the low throb of the engine grew louder, he crouched down a little further just in case.

Donald wasn't a fool. This was no tourist trip.

For starters, he'd never known any grouse-shooting party to have foregone the dubious pleasures of a Highland cooked-breakfast and there weren't any landladies that he knew of who'd have been happy to serve one in the wee small hours.

And he couldn't think what a rich holidaymaker would be wanting with a beast of the like he was expecting to catch a glimpse of any minute now, assuming the wind direction didn't change again. The only time he'd heard engines like

that had been when they'd still had the air show over the water at Macrihanish, when the jets and the bombers would scare the bejesus out of the women and make all the wee bairns greet.

That was his official story anyway.

Donald blinked and despite his initial worry about why they had come back again, he couldn't prevent the wry smile breaking across his craggy features. There it was! He strained his eyes to focus on the dark object, flying impossibly low across the breakers like the last time, nose-down, sniffing the contours like an enormous hungry dragon-fly. He quickly untied the rabbits, picked up his gun and started to run.

*

As he skilfully piloted the Bell Twin across the machair and over towards the LZ, Joey looked down at the wild bleak beauty of the landscape and wondered how anyone could live in a place as uncivilized. Then he snorted and decided civilization maybe wasn't such a hot ticket anymore, not from his recent experiences. He gestured over the noise of the massive Pratt & Whitney turboshaft engine and the man next to him nodded and smiled. They'd both seen the crouching figure close to the cottage, he was the only living thing for miles big enough to register as a red dot on their heat sensor.

Patrick pointed a stubby finger towards his mouth and a wide grin temporarily softened the block

of ebony that passed for a face. He laughed through the comms.

'Now listen up Joey! Don't you go givin' us an encore of that *Badman* shit and start all that tryin' to kiss the poor ol' motherfucker this time, okay?'

Joey 'Badman' Barbarossa or to use his stage name, Barbarella, giggled in return as he turned the chopper into the wind and began their careful descent.

'No problem, boss! I ain't in the mood none, anyways. Hey DJ? You good to go back there?'

A voice muttered from somewhere, deep in the bowels of the machine which the two other men took to be in the affirmative.

If truth were told, none of the trio were particularly overjoyed with this unofficial mission. If it hadn't been for Colm's insistence and the strong bond between the men, forged in battle and cemented by a timeless Marine Corps tradition of always looking out for a brother soldier, Joey doubted if they'd have taken the ridiculous chances they'd already taken to get to the West Highlands of Scotland that morning.

It wasn't as if they had been at a loose end. International assassins of their calibre were always in high demand and when you considered that each of them had the expertise gained from half a lifetime's service with the US Marine Corps, and then factored in their unusual 'hobby', then they were undeniably unique. Known throughout the industry as the 'Diamond Dogs,' for their lavish burlesque stage

show, the three of them were wealthy beyond most people's dreams and they didn't need to work for wages anymore. These days they tended to take a lot of adventurous vacations that required a great deal of imagination and even more expenditure.

When not on holiday, they were excessively picky about which contracts they would accept. The Dogs' were much more motivated by the 'why' when considering a new assignment and their principal rationale for accepting a job these days was karma. If they could right any perceived wrongs by their actions, even up the balance, or do something helpful that no-one else was able to do, then they were in. Even better when it involved an assignment requiring spectacularly dangerous or outright audacious manoeuvres, the crème de la crème being ones they'd never pulled off before.

Admittedly, today hadn't ticked many boxes for the men, but at the same time, they had taken great pride in successfully evading the attention of Spanish, French, British and Irish authorities as they took a seriously dangerous military chopper from their secret base in Andorra, over the Pyrenees, across the Bay of Biscay, up the western side of Ireland and then skirted back around and down to the tiny island of Sorsay.

DJ was particularly pleased as this had been the first proper test of their new anti-IR decals and camouflage paint. Way over-specced for the mission, nevertheless it was the ideal opportunity to test the

new kit without putting themselves in too much danger. DJ had spent the previous two days coating the helicopter with sheets of expensive and almost impossible to procure state-of-the-art decals which rendered the machine invisible to detection by radar and infra-red devices. Looking like normal camouflage which had become pixelated, the men had been nervous about its efficacy and they were genuinely pleased to have a non-combat job in which to test it as a stealth chopper.

The huge helicopter landed as close to the cottage as was feasible, the 48-foot rotors still spinning loudly. Slightly hidden behind the lea of the hill it would only be seen by someone who had watched it land, like old Donald who stood nearby, clutching his tweed cap to his face in awe. In addition to being the pilot for today's sortie, Joey was also the ordinance guy for the team and he grabbed a brace of M4 Carbines and some ammunition, just in case, while in the back of the machine he could hear big Patrick and DJ grumbling as they dug out the clean-up kit. This was going to be a mother of a morning for sure.

Exactly how bad, became all too clear to the guys as soon as the rotors stopped spinning and the full force of the awful stench hit them like a balled-up fist.

DJ was always the first to voice his opinions and, on this occasion, Joey wasn't too surprised by his reaction.

‘Holy shit! Dudes… you want me to go into that motherfuckin’ hellhole…?

He’d already seen the old man standing waiting for them, his hat still clenched tightly over his mouth and nose, and Patrick growled as they gathered up their equipment and began walking slowly towards the house.

‘Listen good, DJ. Shut the fuck up okay?

That *hellhole* to which you refer, is the domicile of our much-loved friends, Ridge and Orla and their two beautiful itty-bitty kids. We are the sorry motherfuckers who is gonna fix up the place which has been smitten by some seriously messed up and disgusting evil shit and you have voted yourself the job of throwing said shit outta the chopper before eleven hundred hours.

Now, what have we here? Is this Mr Donald I have the pleasure of meeting once again?’

The old man seemed shocked that they’d remembered his name and he stepped backwards out of the shadow of the three large black men.

‘Is it tae dae wi’ the house, ye’ve come about? The Walker faimly huv no been here for ages, like. There’s yon awful smell.’ Donald MacDonald gestured towards the cottage, only taking his cap away from his face for the minimum time required.

‘I didn’t ken whit tae dae aboot it. Naebody’s been in like, but. It smells like something died in there, a bit like old man MacPherson’s place a couple of years back…, it was weeks afore we knew he’d

died an' I was thinking o' ringing the Cooncil on the mainland an-'

Patrick had been scanning the landscape impatiently, allowing the old man the opportunity to state his concerns. But Joey knew they were pressed for time and he laughed inwardly as Patrick stopped the old man in mid-sentence, holding out his enormous hand and flashing him his most sincere stage-routine smile.

'-I wouldn't do that if I was you, my friend.

Mrs Walker is still on vacation overseas, but she telephoned us yesterday and seeing as we were in the neighbourhood, in a manner of speaking, and us being such *good friends* and all, she asked us to stop by and give the property a look-over before their return.

She mentioned something about a refrigerator door being faulty and she was worried, correctly as it appears, that some of that fine Scottish venison might have gone off.

And she also asked me to bring a case of 18-year-old Glenmorangie to say sorry for any inconvenience. If you would be so kind as to show my boys here the best place for a quick-burning fire and not breathe a word about our visit to *anyone*, especially our friends in the police department, then you'll find the whisky sitting in the chopper for you along with a special present from us to you. Think a fancy laser-sighted rifle will help you catch more

rabbits? Big Joey here will even help you fetch your whisky home.'

Chapter 42

Nursing a cold Styrofoam coffee, Colm sat and stared at the opaque windows, watching the fresh streaks of rain which, struggling without the home advantage, were gradually losing their fight to reach the bottom of the soot-encrusted glass. His filthy mood matched the grim afternoon. It had been a while since he'd ventured across to this part of the world and today, he remembered why. Even wearing the heavy black wig ensemble that he liked to call his 'Elvis gig,' the cold insistent damp seemed to get deep into his tired bones.

At last, the man came back to the dingy basement and gestured for him to accompany him upstairs into the operations room. Both men knew that if they were discovered, it would mean jail time for each of them but for Colm that would mean more than a few months of discomfort. If they caught him here, he'd never see real daylight ever again. A great deal of cash had already been exchanged to make this next hour, lunchtime for most people, profitable in more ways than one. For Colm, he knew he had to find a result here, but equally, he understood deep in his achingly empty gut that whatever happened next, it would be a lose-lose situation for him.

The extent of his predicament had been taxing his brain for several days and there were too many elements to the cluster-fuck of recent disasters that he couldn't square. For a man like him who liked to plan

his campaigns with a level of detail and precision bordering on the obsessive-compulsive, it twisted his melon that he couldn't see where the problems were originating.

In his spreadsheet-like analysis, there was something not quite right. A glitch in a formula. If there had been a Loss Report in reality, then on a page somewhere, there was an equation that didn't balance. And people were dying as a result. People close to him were in mortal danger and he didn't seem to be able to do much about altering that fact.

That he was up against a formidable array of foes was a given. But he'd beaten greater enemies in the past. Crushed their faces into the dirt. Yes, the vast wealth of the Chilean enemy made that side of the bargain much harder to negotiate, but at the end of the day, it took more than money to beat The Piper. Money, weapons, men… it was all numbers and things. 'All the gear – no idea,' they used to say back in the day.

Knowledge was still the key to this puzzle. With knowledge, he could overcome all the other shortfalls and still come out on top. When he broke everything down into what he knew, what other people knew, that's when his gut started to hurt.

He broke it down into smaller and more precise equations. What each player in the game could know and what they could not know. What the effect of this knowledge, player by player, could do to shape the outcome of the game. He drilled down

from strategy to tactics. Cause and effect. Action and reaction. When it hit him, when he eventually realised what had been staring him in the face for hours and he'd been trying to avoid admitting to himself, he had felt physically sick.

This was the sole reason he'd taken one of the most ridiculous risks of recent years to travel back to an Ulster which was already at boiling point over the political shenanigans at Westminster. What this man was about to show him would square the circle once and for all. But it meant he would have to do some killing. The difference this time was he'd be killing a man at the highest levels of government, with a legion of protectors. Even worse than that, he'd be killing a friend.

They sat down in front of an entire wall of computer screens, all blank.

'Alright,' Colm said without enthusiasm. 'Show me what you've got.'

'Sure now? Okay, you're the boss.'

The man hit a couple of switches and opened up what looked to Colm like twenty-five separate portals into hell. As each CCTV screen flickered into life, to reveal a bleak and grainy video, he swallowed hard and leant forwards, trying to make sense of what he was looking at. Luckily his friendly operator had been well-picked for this job and he'd done his homework. Colm was no expert in surveillance camera work, but he guessed this lad must've spent

more hours than was healthy staring at these tiny squares of pixelated intrusions.

'I did as ye asked. I used our new face-recognition software on yer man here,' he pointed up towards the top two rows of screens.

'Seeing as he doesn't go out much, mebbes a wee bit agoraphobic after being banged up for all those years, it wasn't so easy I can tell you. But you see there, the quality is grand, so it is, and there's no doubt it's him. Agreed?'

Colm nodded without taking his eyes off the pale looking man shown on the screens, his face remaining blank of expression, cold, calculating and purposeful, like a big cat stalking his unknowing prey.

'As you can tell he's not exactly a party animal either and almost all the image captures we've got on him, show him alone. That made the next part easier if you look at the middle row of screens, but before that, check the bottom two rows and confirm that you agree on who *this* guy is?'

Colm's only outward reaction was to blink faster than usual, but underneath his assassin's mask, his brain had begun to spin wildly out of control. It was only then, that he'd realised he had been half-hoping his recent analysis had been flawed and his mad conjectures to be wide of the mark.

Most of the footage on the lower screens showed a man in his office, sitting mostly, or showing him entering or leaving his place of work. He seemed

to be a gregarious man and he was rarely on his own apart from when he was making phone calls. Colm squinted his eyes and he noticed that in several of the screens, the man was making cell-phone calls whilst at his desk, his landline phone sitting idle beside him.

Colm barked at the man sitting alongside him.

'Ye've got audio on these mobile calls, right?'

'Of course! Clear as a bell an' all! Give me a minute.'

The fact was that the man in the office was exactly who he was expecting to see. It was Colm who'd paid for his office to be bugged after all, although at the time it had been only a routine precaution.

But when he dragged his eyes upward to the middle row of screens, that was where the real truth-bombs were located. He narrowed his eyes to focus on one image of two men shaking hands. It was the meeting of these two men, that proved his analysis was correct. There was no legitimate reason on God's earth for these two men to know each other and the fact that they were meeting in Ulster, on their own, only served to dig his friend an even deeper grave.

He thought back to how this man had saved his life in the past and the lives of others. He had always appeared as an avuncular buffoon. Obviously clever and well-educated but hopelessly impractical and never the sort of guy you would expect to betray you. But then, Colm had experienced betrayal many times and at every level of society, nothing ever

shocked him these days. He closed his eyes for a moment. What was that saying? *Absolute power corrupts absolutely*. What would it have been in this man's case? Money? Unlikely although he'd never rule it out. Power and status definitely could be the underlying impetus for his callous actions.

Then it came to him in a blinding flash. Sex! The guy was a misogynist as many of his class and generation had been brought up to be. His attitude towards women was terrible and like most little public-school boys he was probably terrified of them. Throw in a little insecurity and social ineptitude and you've got the classic blackmail material for the gutter press to whip their readers into a masturbatory frenzy over. Colm decided to dig a little deeper into this before he pronounced the final sentence on his foolish friend. Maybe his life could be spared. But not the other one.

He forced himself back into the room.

'Let me hear the phone calls then. And if you've got any for the meetings over by that would be grand. But let's be smartish or your bosses are going to be back from their lunchtime snooker game any minute.'

Chapter 43

Orla smiled to herself as she rearranged the few available coverings to try and hide her lithe body as decorously as she could manage. Her naked flesh shivered in the coolness of the room, or was it her seemingly unquenchable desire for that rapscallion husband of hers? By no stretch of the imagination could sleeping module B2 ever have resembled a boudoir, yet for two days solid, the pair of them had been like a pair of newlyweds working their way through the Kamasutra. She wasn't too sure if poor Ridge hadn't fallen asleep in the shower, he'd been away so long. She hoped he wouldn't succumb to sparking up a ciggie indoors, as he'd hinted he might do, sounding like some boasting schoolboy desperate to fulfil that age-old movie cliché. That comment had earned him a deft slap in a tender part of his anatomy. And each time he'd started to make a move to put some clothes on, Orla had mentally turned a fresh page in her book of ultimate seduction and switched the setting on her huge green eyes to hypnotic.

When they'd first arrived at Halley Six, she felt sure it had been a mistake, equally as foolish as their entire escape to the Antarctic had been. Looking like a location set for a budget sci-fi movie on the outside, inside it was even worse. Brightly coloured and modern, it had felt to Orla like they were in a hellish youth club or perhaps a minimum-security prison facility. And it might as well have been on

lock-down with the weather having taken a bad turn as soon as they arrived, the 30-knot winds sharp enough to slice you in half.

But staying at the main base at Rothera hadn't been an option. That they weren't welcome was the understatement of the year, but more than that, Orla knew she might have strangled that little bitch who'd been making doe-eyes at Ridge all the way through their pantomime. Of course, her eedjit husband hadn't exactly discouraged her, his leering grin made even more ridiculous by the clown make-up as, intoxicated by the rush of public performance, the girl had proceeded to wave her ample posterior in his face in full view of the whole audience, her thin nylon tights stretched to the point of invisibility and leaving little to the imagination.

As for the audience, they were treated to a whole new interpretation of the Greatest Showman musical as Ridge, resplendent in an acid-green Afro wig, was placed in the invidious position of holding at bay a simpering Tinkerbelle and a snarling Catwoman intent on tearing the other girl's head off.

Orla laughed quietly, hearing the door handle being turned and she had to concede reluctantly that for a while, he'd done a pretty good job of defusing the situation, seeing as he'd not had the benefit of her years of close-combat training. It wasn't until she'd noticed his enormous hard-on that everything had really kicked off.

Still, they were here now, in a world of their own and over the last 48 hours they had managed to release all of their pent-up sexual tensions, worries and general frustrations over their crazy situation. As the door slowly opened, Orla thought of the deep red sunsets of Autumn on Sorsay and gave her most seductive smile yet.

Ridge wasn't even looking. He was too busy keeping control of the tiny tray piled precariously with enough steaming breakfast comestibles to feed a football team.

He smiled.

'Here love, I thought we could do with replenishing our energy levels, eh? But watch will you, those tomatoes are bastarding hot!'

Orla allowed the fleecy blanket to fall away from her shoulders and, as she steeled herself not to pick up a piece of warm toast, she flicked a hand dismissively towards the outer reaches of their tiny cabin.

'Later… come here, will ye?'

And it was dark once again by the time the pair of them snuggled together and hand-fed each other the cold repast.

But by the following day, cabin-fever had truly set in and the pair of them had begun to explore the tiny station. Orla eased her aching body into a gentle workout in the compact but adequate gym while Ridge took a totally different tack altogether,

befriending one of the engineers and bartering a pack of cigarettes for the sharing of a spliff.

Ridge also discovered that there was only one way to communicate in or out of the station and unlike the larger Rothera base, the comms point was in a small and much more private location. His laid-back engineer friend arranged a suitable time and Ridge and Orla decided to use this rare opportunity to contact Colm. They'd had enough of the whole snowy solitude thing and between them, they had already made up their mind to talk Colm into letting them return to the UK. They couldn't help with anything while they were hidden down there and besides that, they hadn't seen the children for ages and they couldn't impose on poor Seamus and her long-suffering mam for any longer.

Orla would make the call. She had been pumping herself up for a fraught conversation but although they got what they'd wanted in a way, it didn't quite go as planned.

Colm was highly pleased to hear from them as it turned out.

'Jaysus! I didn't know what was going on Orla. Didn't you get any of my messages?'

Orla didn't feel like explaining what had been happening.

'Sure, we've been exploring,' she winked to a bemused Ridge. 'Exploring *all over* the place, so we have, an' we left the mobiles at Rothera 'cos you said they'd be useless anyway, an-'

‘-Alright then, never mind about that Orla, just listen quick will ye?’

Orla straightened up, sensing the change in his tone. ‘Go on, sure.’

‘Right, there’s been a development over here, so there has. I’ll not say any more than that for now, but basically, you’ve got to get out of there asap.’

Despite herself, Orla couldn’t disguise the happiness in her voice.

‘You mean we can come home, we can-’

‘-Not home Sis. Not yet anyway and listen carefully, you are both still in danger, far more than I had anticipated. It’s some handlin’ I’ll tell ye. But I’m cleaning it up as best I can but there’s little I can do to protect you when I’m as far away.

You’ve got to get to London as fast as you can, understand? Meet me there. The ‘phones will work once you get away from there.

You can use the other passports, you know?’

Orla nodded uselessly, then croaked her affirmation. Colm continued at a pace.

‘And you still have your gun, right?’

‘Yes, but-’

‘-And what about Ridge, does he have a weapon?’

Orla felt the blood drain from her face. This was no joke.

‘No, Colm, just his devastating personality and-’

‘-Alright, no worries, get on a plane as soon as possible but do NOT go via the Falklands this time. Use one of your Amex gold cards, you know?

Fly to Punto Arenas then grab whatever’s the fastest and most direct way back to London, okay? Go business class and don’t speak to a living soul about your plans.’

Orla shook herself and stood up, feeling claustrophobic and panicky in the tiny comms room.

‘Okay Colm, we’ll try and get back to the main base today and then try and find a way to get away.’

‘Orla. Catch yerself on, will ye? Listen to me, carefully. *No trying*. You have to get away fast.

Do *anything* you have to do to get out of there today, you hear me?

Anybody who tries to stop you, you go through them for a short-cut!

Understand? *Anything…*

Now go! Be safe and speak soon.’

They ran silently back to the little module and only then Orla relayed the conversation to Ridge as he quickly shoved on all the clothes he could find. The pair of them were buzzing from the call and Orla couldn’t help agreeing with Ridge that the whole situation seemed unreal, almost as if they were in a film set and any moment now they’d hear the snap of the clapperboard and they could all go home. They both felt uneasy about leaving the sanctuary of their

wee love nest and all their earlier claustrophobia had been replaced with a deep sense of foreboding.

As was often the case with her brother's dealings, Orla had more questions than answers. The kids were safe, Colm was obviously not in any immediate danger, so what had been going on? Why were they the ones who had to go on the run all over again?

Ridge was being brave; she could see it in his face. That pretend toughness that fooled everyone but her. He'd looked out and down the garish play-school corridor and was obviously nervous about the prospect of getting back to Rothera quickly and then the much more awkward task of persuading the Station Chief to allow them to leave for civilisation.

'You ready?' Ridge grabbed her hand and squeezed it.

'Always, my love' she replied, sounding more determined than she felt and wishing she'd not lied to her brother about bringing the gun with them.

She felt him pulling her back in through the narrow door.

'Wait' he said.

'Stop that, ye eedjit!' Orla hissed at Ridge thinking his timing for getting up to nonsense was lousy.

'No Orla. Get back in here, *now*! I have an idea.

Do you have any make-up with you?'

Orla let out a sharp breath of frustration. 'Make-up? Are you mad? I hardly wear any an' what would-'

Ridge threw up his hands.

'-Just listen for a minute, okay? You must have some of that white stuff, like when you did my face the other day and-'

Orla stabbed a finger hard into his chest.

'That was clown make-up, ye eedjit!'

Now it was Ridge who lost his temper.

'I *know* that Orla! Would you let me finish for fuck's sake?

If you have *any* sort of make-up that you could put on my face that might make me look like I had the fucking Black Death, then that would be a pretty good way for us to get off this mad space-ship, wouldn't it?'

Ridge spoke fast, his eyes gleaming.

'I mean…, you know, the main medical peeps are all over at Rothera. There are only five other people here right now and the last thing they'd need is for us to give them all the fucking lurgy, right? There's no way they'd stop us from going!'

Orla laughed. He was right. It was a typical flying-by-the-seat-of-your-pants idea that had somehow got Ridge out of a hundred dangerous situations and one of the reasons she loved him more than any other man on the planet.

She grabbed his face with both hands and kissed him hard.

‘Genius, so you are!’

Chapter 44

Getting back to the main base proved to be faster and easier than they could ever have hoped for and Orla decided that once they were finally allowed to hang up their adventuring spurs, she would push her man into the acting profession. His exploits over the last couple of hours had been genuinely Oscar-worthy and she would never have imagined that the gelid remnants of a fried breakfast could be re-purposed into a face as convincingly festering.

It was the next part of their plan, which was no more than a vague hope, which she knew would be far trickier.

Flushed with the success of Ridge's pasty-faced idea, they decided to stay with the theme for as long as feasible, which they both knew would last precisely two seconds, once the medical personnel became involved.

Orla played down their sudden return and her husband's peaky complexion so that they wouldn't be red-flagged too soon and as he made his way over towards the hangars, she rushed off to their accommodation block to grab what she could.

Her face had gone numb even before she'd completed her icy trek through the snow and she cursed her incompetence at forgetting her balaclava, especially after ripping the mick out of her husband for leaving his ultra-warm hat back at Halley. Still, the look on Ridge's ridiculously made-up face as she

burst into the relative warmth of the main hangar, told her that their mission had hit a stumbling block.

'Come on, man! The weather's clearing up, honest. Hey Orla, didn't we see blue sky heading from the West only a few minutes ago?'

Orla could hear the tension in his voice. Ridge was trying hard to be pleasant and reasonable with the guy, who she recognised as Martin, one of the stalwart European's who Ridge had befriended a few days earlier. He'd told her Martin had over-wintered for many seasons and she knew well that not only could he fly the plane, fix the heating systems and splint a broken limb, but he'd be one of the few personnel who'd know where the guns were stashed.

She flashed her best smile and tried to imagine how the conversation had gone up until that point.

'Jeez! He's not after looking too good, is he? Martin isn't it? I feckin' told him we shouldn't have been allowed to self-clear ourselves for travel.'

Ridge shot her a *what the fuck* look but weirdly she heard Martin speaking the words.

'I don't understand. Why do you want to leave this soon?'

Martin glanced between the two, still bemused, perhaps suspecting he might be the victim of a prank, being played by a kooky couple who'd got bored of being cooped-up quicker than the others. Orla slowly edged ever closer, her green eyes locked on to his, analysing every movement, down to the smallest tic.

Ridge guessed where this was going and took the initiative, bending over double with a bout of theatrical coughing. As Martin was momentarily distracted, Orla stepped forward, her gaze never leaving the other man's face. She was now in striking distance if it had to come to that.

Martin looked from one to the other, and as he picked up a clipboard and waved it randomly at them, Orla could see he was uncomfortable with confrontation.

'I get that you're ill, guy, but the protocol is that you go to medical. If you're infectious, then it's even more important that you get isolated fast before you give it to the entire station.'

Orla quickly scanned the area around the man. Three banks of screens, cameras monitoring every area of the base, all showing nothing but grey buildings half-submerged in snow. Three plastic workstations, three plastic filing cabinets, one smeared black with countless oily fingerprints. One small steel cabinet. She pulled off a glove and slammed a hand on the closest desk in genuine impatience, causing a couple of pens to roll off. Orla hoped he'd make a move to grab them, but he just jumped and his demeanour changed, any remnants of a smile evaporating faster than the steam from a coffee mug in this perishing climate.

Orla pointed an accusing finger at the man.

'Listen Martin. The truth of the matter is… and there's no easy way to say this, sure there isn't,

but we've not been completely *honest* with any of you here. Yer man here has been exposed to a highly dangerous nerve agent. There's a lab at Port Stanley, you won't ever have heard of it. It was the Argentinians, we discovered it way back in the eighties, after the war. There's a bunker a hundred metres down under the airport.

Ye didn't think all that fighting was over a few feckin' sheep now, did you?'

Ridge coughed again to great effect and Orla could tell he'd warmed up to the idea. As a steadily more worried-looking Martin glanced from one to the other, she let her husband add to the saga.

'She's right, man. It's supposed to be classified but there's no time left for following protocol.

We've been working for months on a vaccine and it's been going well. But then they started live-testing it for the Yanks, using some poor wee fuckers from Guantanamo! You know, the camp that's supposed to be empty now?'

Martin's face was now ashen.

Orla could sense they were at a decisive point in their strategy and went in for the checkmate.

'So Martin, that's when we decided we wanted out. We took a sample and left, intending to alert the world to what's going on there. For democracy!'

'And for science…' Ridge added limply.

‘But does that mean that I’m… that we’re all going to be-’

Orla moved closer still.

‘-No don’t be daft! We’re not after putting any of you lot in unnecessary danger. We’re scientists! Like everyone here. No, the virus is spread on contact.’

She gestured towards Ridge, partly to keep him quiet.

‘He got infected when we tried to help one of the test subjects to escape with us. Sadly, she didn’t make it to the plane. The ‘doc here would have to touch you, or cough on you and even then it takes 10 days to become fully virulent.

But now we know he’s infected, we have to get him away from here, back to the vaccine. Me too, there’s no chance for me either, unless we leave today.’

Orla nodded over towards the other end of the enormous hangar. ‘You’re lookin’ at two dead scientists unless we can get that plane in the air…’

With moisture now visible on his face, Martin began to panic and Orla saw him glancing at the steel cabinet every few seconds. ‘But I can’t fly in this weather, I *really* can’t. We’d have to get Jacob, the pilot who brought you in to do it and there’s no way he would leave the base without official clearance. You guys are going to have to, you know, self-isolate…’

Martin edged closer to the cabinet, his forehead glistening with sweat. ‘I mean, until we can get the vaccine flown over to you, that’s all.’

‘Martin that won’t work! They will only deny all knowledge and we will be left here to die. With you!’

Orla launched herself at the startled engineer and in two seconds she had his arm twisted around and up his back. He tried to wriggle out of it but she was too strong for him.

Ridge appeared to hardly move but somehow he was there, right up against Martin. He simply leant in towards the struggling man and slowly, deliberately, licked his face.

The effect could not have been more profound. Even Orla was shocked. She felt the man go limp in her arms like he’d had all the blood sucked from his body. She sat him down in his chair and turned to find Ridge crouched down at the lowest steel drawer. It opened, apparently unlocked. Inside was a small digital safe, the kind you get under someone’s bed. Just big enough for the family jewels, precious heirlooms, maybe a folded up will with a dark secret or two. And a handgun.

‘What’s the code, Martin?’ Ridge growled.

‘Uh…? I don’t have, I mean I don’t-’.

Ridge stood up and turned his body quickly, all pretence of a stoop or any physical affliction abruptly gone. He drove a fist hard into Martin’s solar plexus, lifting him out of his chair. Orla stepped back,

allowing him to fall to the ground. She stood motionless as Ridge pushed a chair over and made as if to be lining up a couple of hard penalty kicks into the guy's crotch.

'Wait! Wait a minute, will you! I might be able to find the code. I've never had any reason to use it but I think it might be in the drawer there.'

Orla leapt over the stricken man's legs and looked inside the steel drawer, letting her hands run along the inside. 'What, this?' she replied, trying hard to stifle a laugh. In her hand was a small fluorescent pink scrap of a post-it-note. On it, there were 6 large numbers crudely scrawled next to the word, *CODE*.

She punched the code and the subsequent bleep told them they'd struck lucky. Orla reached in and quickly retrieved the gun, tossing it up to Ridge who wasted no time in pointing it at Martin's head. She peered into the safe to see if there was any ammunition but it was empty and a small cough was enough to alert Ridge who checked the magazine while Orla helped Martin to his feet.

Ridge gave her a surreptitious thumbs-up as they got him settled once again. He brandished the weapon in the well-worn style of a bank robber before wiping the back of his hand across his stained face and glaring at his former buddy.

'Okay, Martin, no more games, okay? We need you to buzz Jacob now. Tell him whatever you want, but real calm and preferably missing out the bit

about the armed hijack. Enough to get him to come over here *muy pronto*, okay?'

Chapter 45

To say that he felt uncomfortable about this meeting would be an understatement. Yet, as he stared out at the unremitting rain, Brendan knew he had to follow this promising new lead, no matter how unusual it seemed.

Back in the day, he'd never have agreed to something as impromptu and maverick as what he was about to do that afternoon. But as he listened to the cheery clamour of the radio and smelt the 'new-ness' of his fancy taxi-cab, with all the digital dashboard and yer man's Bluetooth headset an' all, he understood only too well that times had moved on in Belfast. He had to operate in a different environment now, a faster-paced world than he was used to, where respect was rare, boundaries were blurred and he felt increasingly like a fish out of water. Adapt or die, always keep moving. Never truer than today.

He'd had contact from a supposed *friend*, but with none of the usual code-words given or any attempt at passwords or anything like that. Nothing to indicate the provenance of the individual. The old ways seemed to have been dispensed with in these modern times and his hard-earned rank cut no ice with the untrustworthy young men who ran the lucrative drug lines through the North. Brendan found the huge numbers on the financial side of the business to be mind-boggling compared to what he'd been used to,

before he'd been taken out of the picture for all those years.

But on the positive side of the trust ledger, this man *had* obtained his private mobile number, the one he only gave out to a small number of sources. He must have some close connection, precisely with who was a fact he'd be able to establish fairly easily. And to give him further credit, he did play by the proper rules by refusing to give any names over the phone, including his own. He also called twice, each call lasting less than thirty seconds, rather than making one longer call that might have been more easily tapped. Brendan liked that. That was old school.

What he liked, even more, were the few words the man had whispered to him, however brief.

'I know where young Sean's killer can be found, here in the city today.'

'Come alone, tell no-one. Meet me at Pirate's Inn - Room 220 1400 hours.'

That was why he'd agreed to come to this hotel, not far from The Falls distance-wise but hundreds of years apart in every other sense. This part of town he'd only ever have visited in his younger days if he was going to do some serious damage. He crossed the carpeted foyer, feeling unsettled by the bright and colourful interior and wondering why everything had to look like some kind of women's hairdressers these days, even the banks didn't look

like banks anymore. He'd still gladly put a bomb to most of it if he was being honest.

He took the stairs rather than the lift, a vow he'd made himself while still cooped up in prison; that he'd endeavour to always stay strong and fit, savour his ability to move physically and freely and never rely on technology. It staggered him to think how anyone could understand how to work these lifts and even more, those bleeding electronic room keys they all have now. At least he didn't have to worry about that today. Room 220. He took a deep breath and knocked.

The grey-haired man who opened the door was much older than Brendan had expected, but then their short conversation hadn't given him a lot to go on. The man gestured with his head to come on in and the expression on his face didn't say much more either. As he walked past the slightly shorter and heavier man, it struck Brendan that he hadn't formulated any sort of picture of what he might expect from this meeting, other than be given some up-to-date location and with any luck, the ID of the man he hoped to kill before the day was over. What he didn't expect to happen was when the man pulled out a gun and shot him point-blank in the face.

It only took him a second to realise his head was still connected to his body. He wasn't going to die, not just then at any rate and the stinging sensation in his neck told him he'd been shot with a tranquillizer

dart and at that point, he passed out into the arms of the other man.

Loud music woke him from the strangest dream and he found himself gagged and bound in a solid kitchen-type chair in front of the plasma screen television which was torturing his ear-drums with some disgusting rap garbage. He struggled to free himself while trying to see where the man had gone and that's when he noticed with horror the clear plastic sheeting that had been placed under his chair. The man was doing something behind him. He couldn't quite hear with all the noise from the TV but his eyesight was still good and Brendan could see his reflection off the large screen and bizarrely it looked like he was folding bath towels. Then he saw the selection of bright shiny metal implements neatly arranged on a white towel on the adjacent table. He felt his stomach rush up into his throat as he realised it wouldn't just be the feckin' music that would be torturing him that afternoon.

The man picked up the remote, flicking through the music channels and he turned the volume up even further before pulling the small glass table with the dentistry items closer. Brendan bucked and kicked in a hopeless attempt to free himself. The thick adhesive tape was too tight for him to get any meaningful words together and so far his assailant hadn't uttered a syllable himself. Brendan knew he didn't have much to bargain with but he could be a loyal lieutenant for the right leader and if he could

only get to talk to the guy, to bargain, jeez, to beg for his life.

Despite the cacophonous nightmare in front of him, Brendan was alerted to the TV remote falling to the ground at the left side perimeter of his vision. He glanced up at the screen just as he felt the room shake and the air move abruptly telling him the door had been kicked in. Praying this was some miraculous rescue but at the same time thinking *how could that be possible*, he shut his eyes and kicked out with all his might. If this was going to be his last few seconds on earth, he'd do his best to take one of these bastards with him.

The chair tipped over. He felt more able to move and opening his eyes, he was confronted with a tall apparition, momentarily blocking out the light. Bracing himself for death, instead, he yelped in pain as the man wrenched off the gaffer tape, taking half his face with it. Seconds later his hands were free and then he saw the man had knelt down to quickly slice the rope around his ankles. He looked across at Brendan and gave a thin smile. 'Come on! Let's get you out of here' he said and reached out his hand.

Brendan didn't need asking twice and he leapt up and out of the chair. Seeing the older man prostrate on the floor, still silent, he raised his foot to drop-kick the bastard in the face before he felt himself being pulled roughly backwards.

'Hey! No time for that, he's dead anyway. Quick… let's go.'

They ran down the stairs and out of the rear of the building without being noticed by anyone and then Brendan saw the guy had a car waiting, the engine already idling. Old school. Within two seconds they were away and heading towards the on-ramp for the A12 going North.

'Here…' the man said while looking all around them carefully as if they might have picked up a tail. 'Stick this on will ye, just for a couple of minutes!' He tossed a black canvas bag from the back seat, pointing at his head.

Brendan understood and again, he appreciated the time-honoured traditions being upheld. 'Sure, no problem, it's been a feckin' crazy enough day so it has!' He pulled the bag over his head and everything went as dark as a prison cell after lights out. He felt compelled to continue talking, high on the buzz of being still alive and keen to communicate his gratitude. 'And who do I have the honour of thanking for saving me from that gruesome wee fucker?'

'No names…' was the terse reply. 'We're not out of the woods yet. But ye can thank a Brit from over the water. You've got some friends in very high places, so you have.'

Initially, Brendan couldn't think who the guy was referring to, his mind racing as it was and busy combing through all of his numerous contacts in Ulster to work out who he'd be having to pay first for this obviously soon-to-be-costing-him-dearly top-quality favour. Then it clicked. It had to be him, but

straight away he doubted the veracity of this information given the context.

‘A *Brit* did ye say…? That narrows it down a wee bit, so it does.’

‘I’m after thinking that,’ the other voice said, sounding distracted or perhaps not particularly interested. Brendan wasn’t overly keen to keep this thread of conversation going, but he didn’t want to appear ungrateful, especially as he’d still no clue who he was dealing with. Luckily the silence was broken by his rescuer.

‘That’d normally be something ye’d be keeping to yerself around here, but then we’re living in different times so we are, eh?’

Brendan felt himself breathing out, relaxing almost, despite the odd situation and feeling a kindred spirit now in the safety of the car. ‘Ye can say that again! Where does the demon dentist fit in then? I’d had a wee tip-off on a personal matter, a bit of a *family* problem from way back and fuck-all to do with any business dealings, particularly with our friends over by.’

‘I’m sorry to hear that. There’s no respect these days. You’re safe with me. I’m not from around here an’ I’m only a foot-soldier, you understand, sent over from England to clean up some loose ends for our colonial friends. We’ve been watching that guy for weeks, so we have, wondering what the fuck he was about. There’s a lot of far more important things kicking off right now as you probably know, better

than me I'll wager, and they're not going to be very happy with your wee family tiffs getting mixed up with the other stuff. I'll be sending in my report soon as I've dropped you off. You'd best start thinking about getting your story straight, know what I'm saying?'

Swallowing fast and thankful his face was hidden under the bag, Brendan was experienced enough to understand when he was being given a last chance to put things right.

'Ah, yer fine so you are! This wasn't anything serious at all, I don't know where yer man back there fits in but I soon will, I promise. Did you know I had a wee brother?'

He found himself talking faster and faster, and it felt good to unburden himself with everything that he'd been up to, the progress that he'd made. There was something comforting about talking to a man whose face he couldn't see, almost like being at confession, although it had been several lifetimes since he'd last been to speak to a priest and he'd have to book the poor man for an entire week to get caught up on half the sins on his conscience.

'Sure, and everything else is going just grand, you can tell them that from me if you like. I agree America didn't go to plan, but you probably know that already and it's like you were saying, we live in different times now and you can't rely on anyone to do a decent job these days. But, we'll be keepin' up the Ulster end, don't you worry about that, an' that

fucker, *The Piper* or whatever the feck he calls himself these days will soon be dead and gone one way or another. You could be getting a wee bit more work yourself over the next week or two if you know what I mean. Tell yer Government man that our wee trap I was talkin' about is all set and I'd bet on most of the action to be happening over in London now anyways.'

Brendan felt the car slowing down and he realised he'd not been paying much attention to the journey, trusting that he was out of danger and feeling safe under the protection and assured smooth driving of this man. He'd have sworn they were on the motorway only a wee minute ago but now he felt sure they'd returned to heavier traffic which meant they'd still not left the city centre.

The booming echoes told him they were maybe in another underground car park and then the clicking of the handbrake confirmed to Brendan that finally, they'd reached their destination. He felt keen to meet his now-silent rescuer face to face and waited for the bag to be lifted off his head.

Instead, the car door was abruptly opened and he was bundled out. No worries, he thought, maybe there was a ways to walk first. He heard the driver get out and slam his door and then there was the unmistakable creak of a van door opening. So it seemed they hadn't finished yet. Maybe the vehicle swap was yet another security precaution and despite his awkward situation, Brendan felt a warm glow of

satisfaction in this confirmation that these guys were the real deal.

It came as a huge shock when he felt himself being roughly propelled forwards, bad enough that he nearly lost his footing. Then the hessian bag was ripped off his head, his relief being short-lived and quickly replaced with confusion as he found himself staring at the same man as they'd left for dead back at the other hotel. Standing by the opened door of an old Transit, the old bastard betrayed no greater emotion than before and it only took the now-worried Brendan a second longer to recognise that they were back at the same place they'd started from and to grasp the fact that he'd made a monumental error of judgement. He knew then he was a dead man walking and didn't make any pretence of fighting back as he felt a strong pair of hands grasp his head from behind and twist sharply.

Less than a minute later, with the corpse aboard the van and the rusty doors slammed shut, the two men shook hands. Then the taller one jumped back into his car and screeched out of the car park like he'd been called to a fire.

Chapter 46

Feeling too conspicuous in his over-large blue overalls, Ridge sank further in his seat, trying not to think about the number of hours they still had to go before they arrived back in London. At least he had an aisle, he told himself. Next to him, poor Orla had been virtually catatonic since they left Antarctica and the few words she'd spoken at Puerto Montt, had been to say she definitely did *not* want a window seat.

He didn't blame her.

It was Orla who'd bagged the window seat of the tiny aircraft that had laboured up into the unforgiving cold air and away from Rothera. She had been the one who'd had a clear and unfettered view of the carnage yesterday afternoon and an incredible three flights ago.

Ridge replayed the events of the last day in his mind.

It had started well.

The pilot Jacob, had swallowed the bait and joined them in the main hangar, as planned. Ridge had been relieved to see he was a small guy, wiry and fit looking, but no match for Orla and himself and of a meek disposition to boot. He was no idiot, however. Jacob had taken one look at Ridge's barnacled face and begun to laugh, no doubt believing that he'd fallen victim to a clever practical joke orchestrated by the two volatile newcomers who'd made such a scene

at the pantomime. Then he looked down and saw the gun.

While they'd been waiting nervously for the pilot to arrive, Ridge had made Martin prove to him that the De Havilland was fully-fuelled and to confirm that the flight across to the mainland would indeed be possible. The fact that another man was going to be arriving and effectively taking the pressure off Martin, seemed to have had an intoxicating effect on the young German who had now begun talking non-stop and promising them the earth. Orla had privately expressed her doubts as to the veracity of his information and she'd commandeered his laptop and had been typing furiously while the pair of them checked the aircraft over.

Orla had established that they had enough fuel to get them across to Tierra del Fuego and into a little airport outside the Argentinian city of Ushuaia. Martin had assured them that the Rothera station flew there often and they'd not be questioned. The plan was then to fly up to Puerto Montt and from there, masquerading as Scottish salmon-farm workers returning from an aquaculture conference, head for London via Miami. The US stop was the only worry for Orla but Colm had given them precise instructions about how to access a deposit box at the airport which contained fresh passports, so they could leave Miami with a different identity to the one they came in on. However, he'd explicitly instructed them to book

their flights into Miami online using their existing ID's but then re-book new flights once they had passed through the initial land-side security at Miami and on a different flight to the original one.

Faced with a mad Scotsman with a gun in his hand, Jacob had proceeded to do exactly as ordered, without question. He confirmed that he could fly them to Ushuaia and that the plane had the required fuel for the flight as long as the weather allowed them to take the shortest route. As they made their way over to the plane, Ridge had felt his gut instinct kick in hard and it hadn't been helped by Martin who'd begun talking at a rapid pace.

'So… you don't need me to come with you then and I'll stay and hold the fort here, right? We'll say that the plane has gone for a routine test flight to see if we can locate the electronic fault that's been plaguing us for weeks…I won't let anyone see the screen of course… and they won't know you've left the mainland…especially not that you're not heading back to Port Stanley… why anyone would want to go the other way I don't know and so-'

Ridge lifted the gun and pointed it at Martin, stopping them all in their tracks. He'd seen Jacob's mouth tighten and straightaway Ridge knew he was looking at no poker player. Something Martin had just said had been dangerous or stupid.

Orla, ever practical, had clicked immediately.

'Jacob. Tell me what the flight clearance code is, please?'

The man stammered. 'I forgot, sorry, you've got me so wound up, I normally write-'

Orla cut him off.

'-Is it on that screen over by?'

He nodded enthusiastically but his eyes had been directed elsewhere. She spun around to see Martin brandishing a length of scaffolding pole which was now spinning dangerously close to her head.

The noise of the gunshot was deafening as it echoed around the hangar.

They all stood shocked as the aluminium pole bounced onto the concrete with a discordant clamouring and Martin dropped to his knees, a large red circle quickly staining his right shoulder and chest.

Ridge levelled the gun at a quivering Jacob.

'Get on the fucking plane, now! Orla get the code.'

As Orla had sprinted over to the bank of computer screens, Martin looked up at Ridge, his tears rolling freely and his eyes imploring. If he had expected some degree of mercy then he must have been sorrier still when Orla ran back across with a scrap of paper in her hand and Ridge brought the butt of the gun down hard on his head rendering him unconscious.

The plane took off and immediately they were all made aware of the weather conditions not being ideal. There was no artifice in Jacob's face as he explained carefully that they'd need to fly a little

further inland to miss the winds and he'd make for the base at Halley before swinging back around for the southernmost tip of South America.

That was when things started to go crazy.

Chapter 47

They'd escaped the research station and a nervous Jacob had made the call back to his colleagues saying that a heavily-sedated Martin was with him on their impromptu flight as he'd had some vague sort of schizophrenic seizure and shot himself in the shoulder. He said that one of the newcomers had also been injured and her injuries had been too severe for the base medical team to handle and he was taking her and her partner to Port Stanley for emergency surgery.

Ridge and Orla had hurriedly whispered to each other that seeing as they had a long trek ahead of them, it made sense for one of them to get some rest and they'd continue to swap in 3-hour shifts until they'd got completely away and on a commercial flight home. Orla took first watch and she relieved Ridge of the handgun and moved up to sit next to the worried-looking pilot while Ridge grabbed some shut-eye in the body of the plane. Little did she know, she'd given up her last chance at some peaceful rest for the next 24 hours.

It all started with what seemed like careless chatter from other pilots. Orla could tell something was afoot by the increased communications and the look on Jacob's face. There was nothing but blue sky above and white snow below and she couldn't work out what there could be to get excited about.

'What's going on Jacob?'

The pilot eyed her handgun and swallowed.

'Not sure to be honest. I heard something about military aircraft in our airspace which is unlawful, but not unheard of. The Yanks, in particular, are prone to be testing stuff out down here because the airspace is empty in comparison with the rest of the world.'

Orla's mind had started racing at that point. Could it be anything to do with them? *Sure girl, you're after getting as crazy paranoid as that eedjit brother of yours...*

'So should I be worried?'

'How would I know?' he whimpered, 'I've no idea what's going on anymore. I've picked up something about an explosion or something. Reports of a mayday message and smoke drifting into the upper atmosphere. One of the guys at the base says he's got some weird readings from one of his balloons close to Halley.'

'What are Halley saying about it?'

'That's the funny thing. They can't raise them at the moment. But we'll be close in a few minutes and we can hail them easier from the plane.'

Orla peered down and couldn't see anything apart from endless whiteness. It took her a second to realise that most of what she was seeing was clouds reflecting the pure white brilliance back upwards.

'I'll take her down a couple of hundred feet,' said Jacob, as if reading her mind.

‘*Attention, this is November-niner-five-four-Delta-Lima calling Bravo-Alpha-Sierra Halley Research Station, do you copy, over*? Still nothing, I’ll try back to base and see if they- oh Jesus…!’

Jacob grabbed Orla’s gun arm and she looked at him in surprise, thinking he was somehow trying to disarm her. Then she saw the alarm on his face and peered down to see what he was looking at. There was no need even to look down. Out of the blue sky, thick black smoke quickly enveloped the plane and when Jacob banked right she saw exactly what the problem had been.

The base had been annihilated, she guessed by a bomb or missile. All that had been left was a smouldering ruin. She cried out in fright and reached around to thump Ridge who was still asleep and oblivious on the floor behind her, too disgusted by what she could see to even formulate any coherent words.

The sight of the pure white snow sullied by the bright red trail being left by a crawling torso was too horrific for her brain to comprehend and something Orla would take to her grave.

‘Turn around’ she ordered.

Jacob had looked at her in consternation. ‘I can’t do that! We’ve only enough fuel to-’

Orla cocked the handgun and pointed it at his head. ‘Turn the plane NOW!’

Ridge was fully awake now and Orla guessed the sight of her gun inches from the pilot’s right

temple would be enough to get his full attention even before the plane lurched abruptly to the right and he'd be able to see the grotesque scene below them. Several bodies lay scattered in the wreckage of the once futuristic-looking pods but only one was still moving, albeit pitifully slowly.

Jacob took the plane as low as he dared and it was only then the true extent of the bloodbath had become apparent. Bodies, which had been real people whom Orla had shared jokes with earlier the same day, had been ripped to pieces. The wretched creature crawling away from the smoking buildings had lost both legs and one arm in the explosion, red blood still oozing into the pristine whiteness.

'Land the plane Jacob,' Orla whispered. 'We can't leave that poor bastard like that!'

'Honestly, I can't do that! Even if I wanted to, if we land there, we'll use too much fuel taking back off again, we'll never make land at the other end. It'd be suicide for all of us!'

Ridge grabbed his wife by the shoulders.

'Listen, love, he's got a point. But more pressing is that this only *just* happened. That blood is still fresh, I don't care how fucking cold it is out there, this didn't happen too long ago. We can't be sure that whoever did this, won't come back again. They could be here any minute.'

Ridge turned to the pilot.

'But there are a couple of things we have to do before we leave. Jacob, can you please take us back

over the base again, as slow and as low as humanly possible, okay?

Orla, take your camera and get as many close-ups as you can of-'

'What?' she shrieked. 'Are you sicker than-'

'-Evidence!' Ridge replied angrily. 'We need to find out *who* the fuck did this and we can't do that without some back-up evidence, right?

Here, Jacob, we can open these fucking windows a wee bit, right? Without being sucked the fuck out, eh?'

The pilot nodded and began to turn the plane, gently angling it downwards.

'Orla love, lean out and get that fucking zoom working big-time okay?

And here give me the gun.

I'm going to take a different sort of shot.

We need to put that poor bastard out of his or her misery. Any objections?'

Orla shook her head, already preparing their expensive camera equipment for the saddest pictures she would ever take in her life.

Chapter 48

He glanced over at his sleeping wife. Orla had been having a bad time dealing with the tragedy at Halley. Not because she had grown softer, as they both had, but more for the unmistakable signs that the whole thing had a bad smell about it, a stench that seemed to follow them wherever they went. It wasn't death she found hard to bear. Like her brother, she could take it and also deal it out with the best of them. It was when the death of innocent lives were chalked up to their ledger once again. These young scientists had died, simply down to the fact she and her husband had decided to visit their secluded 'sanctuary' for a couple of days of unbridled passion.

Ridge sighed, wishing he too were asleep. It always worked for Orla, no matter where they were, if she got enough sleep, she could deal with anything. And although neither of them had been relaxed enough to sleep for nearly three days now, he still couldn't allow himself to drift off. He tried to analyse their situation, to be more like his brother-in-law, or even sleeping beauty alongside him here. The danger was surely over at this point. Unless their adversaries were prepared to down a passenger airliner to get them, they were safe until they reached London. And they would be with Colm after that. Something about that made Ridge feel safer already.

Banishing all thoughts about the Lockerbie air-disaster out of his mind, he wondered what would

be happening once they got back. It would be wonderful to see the kids but they'd already vowed to wait a day or two to be sure no-one was on their trail before they endangered young Alex and Isla and their long-suffering grandmother.

The flight to Ushuaia had been uneventful after the horrific drama over Halley. Ridge had killed the injured scientist with a clean shot to the head. No doubt that would come back to haunt him at some point, but it had been patently obvious the person would never have recovered and they must have been in horrific pain. Ridge would have wanted the same mercy shown to him.

In the end, Jacob had been a sterling help to them and he'd been instrumental in getting them through any potential obstacles before they waved him goodbye for their short hop to Punta Arenas. Ridge had joked grimly that the poor bugger must have wondered if he too was going to receive a mercy bullet to the forehead. That was how the pair of them had felt throughout the entire flight and even after they'd taken their next flight to Puerto Montt, they still half expected a strong hand on the shoulder at the least.

In Puerto Montt, they'd managed to procure some authentic fish-farming garb in an airport clothing store, plus some leaflets and other paraphernalia from a stand advertising an upcoming event, before boarding for the Miami leg of their last flight home. Ridge had even been able to coax a

tremulous laugh from Orla when he insisted on smearing a little sauce from his sushi snack into the inside lining of their overalls at the ankle to give the couple that authentic fishy tang. Whatever, it had worked and they were ushered through security with the minimum of delay.

Worried that they'd be picked up as soon as they arrived in the States, Orla bought a cheap burner phone in Puerto Montt and during the flight, she managed to contact Colm by SMS and upload the crash site photos to him. It was a one-way communication as she had feared and they wouldn't know anything further until their arrival back in the UK.

Safely in Miami, they found the location of their new passports plus a little spending money and they had a quick meal at a nearby restaurant before arriving back through airport security under new ID's.

Now all they had to do was sit it out. Ridge thought about the ghastly scene they'd witnessed at the Halley Station. The vision of intense white snow newly crossed with fresh red blood, indelibly printed into his memory, reminded him of his earlier thoughts about the serried ranks of their enemies being like national soccer teams. The Halley site had been like an English Flag. Red lines on a white background. But surely it couldn't be Colm and Orla's old paymasters at Special Branch and MI5 who'd been

behind the appalling attack? And how did *anyone* know where they'd be, assuming it was them who'd been the target. It seemed too big a leap of imagination to think that there could be any other possible rationale for the attack. They'd brought death to Antarctica as surely as they had done in Chile only a short time before.

Ridge drifted off into a tortured half-sleep, trying to understand why it had been the Halley site that had been attacked and not Rothera, where they'd been staying for considerably longer and more publicly. He reviewed every conversation and analysed each situation, looking for hidden meanings or missed clues, as Colm would have expected him to. Was the farcical stramash with the lassie from the pantomime all one big set-up? Maybe it had been. But even allowing for that, it didn't automatically follow that he and Orla would have elected to spend the next few days at Halley. They could equally have stayed put, or even chosen to return to the Falklands. The Falklands… something was annoying him about that, but he couldn't get a bead on it.

He knew they'd both be interrogated on their return and an attack like that, on a UK government-sponsored base with international connections wouldn't be something that Westminster could keep a lid on, even if they had wanted to. His last thoughts were concerning the person he'd shot and if he'd done the right thing… and he heard his brother-in-law whispering somewhere in the distance about dirty

wars, where nothing was black and white, a world where good people sometimes did bad things and bad people did good things. He was right, the world wasn’t black and white anymore, it was crimson red and white…

Chapter 49

Saturday midday May 2nd.

Considering they weren't exactly decked out in feather boas or coral pink mini-skirts or anything, the three of them were still drawing a lot of attention as they strutted their way down Oxford Street, each of them carrying an armful of designer-label shopping bags and wearing enough sumptuous leather to cover a Chesterfield.

It was Orla who spotted them first, nudging Ridge excitedly and pointing. Surprisingly, she saw big Patrick before she noticed the other two, despite the fact he was the only one without a wig. If Ridge had been describing Pat to someone who'd never met him before, the comparison to the famous sofa brand would have been wholly appropriate. He was a huge man, broad and heavy and his shaved head resembled an enormous iron block, nailed onto wide shoulders without the apparent need for a neck.

As several thousand pounds of designer clothing hit the pavement, Ridge and Orla were both hoisted into the air amid a cacophony of screams and laughter.

'Well look at you two!' Joey spun them around as easily as if they were little children, their feet narrowly avoiding decapitating some less than amused passers-by. DJ stepped backwards, placing his hands on his hips with a theatrical flourish and pouting his lips in mock disapproval.

'Oh, my Joey! I see it, but I don't believe it… we got two muther-fuckin' *church* mice here, that's what we got…!'

Ridge dusted himself down and glanced at his still-beautiful wife. But it was true, the pair of them looked even more out of place than the extrovert trio. Orla's crumpled monochrome coloured clothes were the same ones she'd left Miami in. The fresh streaks of gold-sparkled lipstick, courtesy of DJ's affectionate welcome, only served to accentuate her tired and washed out face. The pair of them hadn't seen any proper daylight for days until they'd found themselves deposited from an airport taxi onto the London streets an hour ago. Both had been too tired to think, beyond calling Seamus. They'd wept with bittersweet relief at hearing the kids on the other end, knowing they were only a few minutes away yet also wary of breaking their safety resolution about not risking a get-together.

There had been no holding back with the Diamond Dogs, however. Minutes after dropping their luggage in a nearby hotel and just as the pair of them were debating whether or not to go to bed, their Colm-issued burner phone had pinged insistently. But instead of his brother-in-law, it had been a persuasive Patrick who'd invited them for a late morning coffee. Although to a weary Ridge, it felt more like an order than a request.

‘And let me tell you now, it is you who is gonna be payin’ for the profiteroles, know what I’m saying…? You owe us, you owe us big time…!’

Shortly afterwards, they found themselves escorted to a restaurant named *Crunch* which looked more like a florists as it was bedecked from top to bottom in summer flowers and which Ridge guessed was the gayest looking joint that Pat and the boys could find this early in the day. He was pleased to see them again, as always, but memories of previous escapades hit him hard, like how he imagined an ageing boxer must feel when he sees a highlight reel of his most noteworthy battles.

The three tall Americans instantly took over the small eating area. They displayed their newly purchased treasures across several tiny tables, for inspection by a bemused Orla, who seemed unusually stuck for words. Joey’s head, even with him seated, was encircled by a hanging floral display which looked like pastel dreadlocks and which wouldn’t have looked out of place in a renaissance painting. Unsurprisingly, the staff were ecstatic and buzzed around the group attentively and having eschewed the potential delights of the varied pastries on offer, Ridge found himself cradling his mug of latte while drooling over the gorgeous pancake stacks of the others. Orla had allowed herself to be swayed by the other three and thankfully he was able to pinch a few strawberries and blueberries from her plate.

But the air of frivolity evaporated faster than the heat from Ridge's over-priced coffee and he could sense something more serious was about to happen as Patrick eased himself out of his chair and loped over to the counter. Ridge couldn't see exactly how much money Pat fished out of his pocket but the wad of notes was over an inch thick and he knew it would be enough and a little more, to buy them time and anonymity. The instant blush that rose up the girl's neck and face made him wonder if he hadn't pulled something else out at the same time. Pat pointed over at the door and then at the flower-head clock on the wall, smiling all the time and counting out the banknotes, one after another. By this time, the rest of the staff had gathered behind her and they stood looking at the money, mesmerised. As Patrick sauntered back to the group, Ridge saw the girl stuff the money under the counter while another younger girl quickly skipped across to the main door and pulled the blind down halfway, turning the sign to 'CLOSED' before glancing over to them with a guilty smirk.

The wigs were off now and Ridge took Orla's hand under the table. Patrick gave DJ a look and the other man quickly moved the plates and debris over to the counter, the nervous-looking staff only too happy to help the towering figure in the gorgeous plum leather stockman coat.

Patrick cleared his throat and smiled.

‘Okay guys, we was never here, their CCTV cameras have developed amnesia and we got thirty minutes before they open the doors again. We got a lot to discuss. Joey, you wanna give them the good news first?’

Joey’s eyes widened for a second. ‘The *good* news? Hell, there ain’t no motherfucking good news today, that’s for sure, but I got the less-bad news if that’s how you wanna play it?’

Patrick placed his enormous hands flat on the table and took a deep breath.

‘Yes, Joey…that’s exactly how I wanna play it, go on an’ give them the less-bad news, but please hurry the fuck up, we ain’t got all day, bitch.’

For the next five minutes, a shocked Orla and Ridge sat open-mouthed as Joey explained, in graphic detail, how they had cleaned up the cottage on Sorsay and disposed of the naughty nanny.

‘Hell, I’m guessing you gonna love the new look we gave it. Real instant karma guys. You know, tranquil as a motherfucking Sunday morning, know what I’m saying?’

Ridge nodded, noticing the look on his wife’s face. He made a mental note to suggest to Joey that he never takes up a career as an interior decorator and specifically to suggest that perhaps when describing the ‘new look’ paint colour he chose for the main living room, not to mention to the client that the duck-egg blue was chosen because it matched the exact hue of the brain material that had been liberally spattered

across the walls, in case any of it started to seep back through again.

Patrick raised a stubby finger and brought the first part of the conversation to a close. He looked carefully at Ridge and Orla, his black eyes glinting with a deep searching intensity and brought his voice down to a low rumble, making Ridge think they must be near an Underground line.

'Now listen real carefully you two.

You done good to get this far, your *Mr Serendipity* did his 'thang once again, that's for motherfucking sure.

But now I need you to think hard. We got a bug in the system and hell, Ridge, ain't you supposed to be a goddamn shit-hot IT guy?'

Ridge didn't understand what had just been said and he was thankful that Orla spoke his thoughts for him.

'What do you mean Pat?

Are you saying that someone we know is part of this whole plot or whatever it is? That they're after trying to kill us?'

Patrick nodded and shot a glance at Joey.

'What we're saying Orla,' Joey reached out and took a hand of each of them, making Ridge feel like he was in a weird séance. He continued quietly, 'It's hard to believe, but what we're sure about now, from talking with your brother, is that the attack on the base was deliberately targeted to kill you both.

Now as the Ordnance Bitch of this here detail, I have studied the photos you sent to Colm and I can say almost 100 per cent that the attack was carried out by an MQ-9 Reaper drone. The Reaper-'

'-But who could' Orla blurted out before Pat stopped her with one finger.

'Hold up, Orla. Let the man do his thing.'

'Thanks, boss. The Reaper carries a huge payload and can fly almost undetected even when fully loaded at 30,000 feet. My best guess is that the station was hit by two GBU-12 laser-targeted 500-pound bombs.'

Ridge felt sick and made a silent vow of thanks that he'd not eaten any pancakes. There were still too many questions in his head.

'Okay, this isn't solely some loony-tune Nazi then? You're saying this has to be a government thing? We've got entire bloody nations after us now, is that it?'

This time it was Patrick who spoke and he had his most reassuring voice working overtime.

'Close, but no cigar, Ridge. It's gotta be either the Brits or the US, no doubts about that. They both have Reaper drone capability.

But you gotta ask yourself, Ridge, why would they want you dead? What are you to them, these days? Our intel is pretty good here and I'm not sayin' we got all the answers but we are pretty sure this operation was clandestine at best and it ain't at the highest levels of government. You ain't *that*

important, no offence you understand.' Patrick permitted himself a wry smile.

'However, as I'm sure Joey will explain, like that English dude says in *Game of Thrones*, you don't simply walk into a motherfucking Walmart and purchase a Reaper drone. This smells like a lot of money changed hands.'

'And that ain't all,' said Joey. 'These drones are guided by advanced satellite communication systems with full infrared capability and all that good shit. But they couldn't find you two specifically without some outside assistance.'

'That means we got other players involved here. Someone who has the ability to track you.' Patrick saw the look in Ridge's face and growled in annoyance. 'And before you say it, I know about the tooth, Ridge. Colm and me, we been through that one already. Me? I'd get that mother pulled out, but hey that's cool!'

Orla slammed her hand on the table in frustration. 'How are they after tracking us then?'

Patrick smiled. 'Now *that's* the motherfuckin' question. And we got exactly fourteen minutes to find the answer.'

Ridge knew something was eating away at him. He'd already worked out the main base should have been the more obvious target if someone wanted to bomb them. How did they know the pair of them had skipped off for some peace and quiet?

'Pat, do you think it was someone at the base?'

'Unlikely' said Patrick. They'd be signing their own death warrant if you'd stayed at the main base at Rothera. They had no way of knowing you would go to Halley.'

It was DJ, their comms guy, who stated what they were all thinking. 'If it's not something in you, then it has to be something on you…'

Joey took it up from there. 'Think carefully, guys, did anyone give-'

The instant Joey spoke, it hit Ridge like a locomotive train.

'*Jesus* fuck. It's my ski hat! I left it at Rothera by mistake. It must have some sort of homing beacon in it.'

Patrick smiled but there was no warmth in his voice. 'Okay, *now* we're getting somewhere. Tell me, Ridge, where and when did you acquire the goddamn ski hat? Did you buy the motherfucker in a store or am I right in thinking someone must've given you it?'

Ridge knew exactly how he'd come by the hat. It played out in his mind like a clip from a home movie. He realised that this is what had been irking him for so long. He'd half-remembered what had happened but hadn't been able to put it all together.

Like always with these things, it had all been down to clever timing.

'It was at Port Stanley. At the airport.

We were about to take off when one of the office guys gave me his. We'd been joking about how cold the weather was going to be and how Orla here

had been the better prepared, as always. This guy, he chucked his hat at me, practically as we got on the plane.'

'No shit, he threw it at you! That was a motherfuckin' time-bomb he tossed you,' DJ was shaking his head in awe.

Patrick was laser focussed on Ridge. 'Good work, Ridge, now think carefully. Can you remember who initiated that last conversation, was it you or did he-'

Orla slapped her head. 'It was him! The guy. He started making a joke about it. I remember thinking how nice he'd been as he'd chased out after us wearing only a thin shirt and I thought it was funny to be wearing such a top-quality hat but no coat!'

'Name?' Patrick was fishing out a cheap-looking phone. Ridge guessed it would be a burner. By the tone of his voice, Ridge realised big Pat was already mentally allocating this man a grave. 'Did… you… know… his… name?'

'No.' volunteered Ridge. 'But by his accent, he was definitely from the UK and he'd been in the office with us before when we were waiting to get clearance. He knew where we'd come from and where we were going. He didn't know our identity, that I'm sure'

Patrick glared at him. 'You sure? How fuckin' sure?

Sure enough to bet this pretty girl's life? No... I didn't think so.

Hey man-'

Ridge felt the tears running down his face as he realised what the guy was saying. He stood up and turned away, angry at himself for two reasons. Then Orla's hand slipped into his and she squeezed hard. They both sat back down as Ridge and Patrick, who was already on a call, exchanged a brief nod.

'No, listen. Yeah, that's what I said. I want a complete manifest of every motherfucker who came and went from that airport in the two weeks prior to our package being delivered. Send it to our friend. Copy that.'

*

The meeting had broken up almost immediately after, but not before Ridge had detected a whiff of something else going on in the background. All three of the Diamond Dogs had adopted a more serious face, despite the make-up and their outlandish garb. Later on back at the hotel, Orla said it had been like the three of them had been simply enjoying a city mini-break until the pair of them had arrived but now it was as if they were having to go back to work.

And Ridge understood only too well what line of work these guys specialised in. Even the wigs and the make-up, it was all part of their disguise, to make them look less like the most highly paid assassins in the business. They took it in turns to wear different wigs and head-gear to outfox the facial-recognition cameras and if anyone cared to notice, they rarely lifted their heads when out on the street. If they were

in London, it wasn't to have pancakes with himself and Orla, despite the incredibly important breakthrough they'd made.

Someone was going to die.

The arrangements had been made to catch up later by phone and DJ had already given them a fresh burner phone and snapped their other one clean in half as if it had been a KitKat. When Orla had asked them if they'd heard anything from her brother, they had all looked at each other.

'He's in the air, we think,' volunteered Patrick less than convincingly.

'He's racking up more air miles than your dude, Branson. But we expect to see him tomorrow along with you guys. My suggestion is that you stay off of the sidewalks, get back to the hotel and stay there until then. Get some rest and be prepared for a tough couple of days before this is all over.'

Orla had bristled at this.

'All *what*, Pat? We were hoping to collect our wee children and take them back home, to safety. You're obviously thinking they're not safe yet, aren't you? But then neither are we, right?'

The rumble of an underground train emanated from within his enormous frame as Patrick looked to the others for some back-up. But despite being world-class international assassins, neither DJ nor Joey appeared to want to go up against Orla at that moment. Ridge didn't blame them. But he had home

advantage, plus he wanted to know what the hell was going on as much as she did.

'Pat. No offence pal, but we're not moving from this table until you tell us what the fuck is going on. I'm tired of this shit and my wife is too. We haven't seen our children for weeks now. Since then someone has tried to shoot them in their own house, with the subsequent carnage possibly psychologically scarring them for the rest of their days. Meanwhile, we've been chased, shot at, attacked by soldiers, strafed by helicopter gunships and then hunted by military drones. It's been more than *a tough couple of days*, wouldn't you say?'

Despite his anger, Ridge noticed the faintest curl of a smile on the other man's face and he knew Patrick understood the reasons for his outburst. The two men had formed a close bond over the years, a friendship forged in battle. It was time for the cards to be put on the table.

'Okay, okay amigo. Let's keep it *muy tranquilo.* We hear ya. But there ain't too much we can say for sure right now. Me and the boys here, we been out of the loop for most of this game-play. All I can tell you is that we are doing everything we can to resolve the situation.'

Patrick looked at the clock on the wall and over towards the gaggle of women standing expectantly at the counter. He saw they had hit their allotted half-hour and gave them a reassuring smile, indicating they'd been finished soon.

He continued in a low voice, as close to a whisper, as a man of his enormous lung capacity could muster.

'You are correct Ridge. You've been through some shit. But it is also true to say that it sure as hell ain't over yet. Here's how I see it playing out over the next few days, bearing in mind that a good plan never survives contact with the enemy.

First off, we have to confirm which motherfucking agency is on your case, CIA or the Brits here.

Next, we have to negotiate with the said agency as to where they got their goddamn wires crossed in connection with you two innocent civilians.

Meanwhile, Colm already has his game in play and he tells us he already has a good idea of the main individuals who've been fucking up your vacation and your interior décor.

Tomorrow afternoon, there is a large demonstration planned here in the centre of London, protesting against the upcoming visit by our esteemed *El Presidente*. We are going to utilise the mayhem caused by having that many people in one place to forward our mission, which is totally fucking classified beyond me, Joey and DJ here.'

Patrick smiled and laid his spade-like fingers on the table signalling that this conversation was coming to an end. 'Then all being well, the whole sorry-ass affair will be closed for good.'

Chapter 50

Saturday 1640 hours May 2nd.

The sun-tanned man snapped shut his expensive phone and glanced around at the other well-heeled patrons who were also enjoying the warmth of the late afternoon sunshine, flooding through the wide street entrance of the exclusive continental-style brasserie. He loved Paris and when he found himself in Europe on business, as he did several times a year and also increasingly these days when he was over on the *other* matter, he much preferred to soak up the ambience of that city more than any other. It was one of his guilty little secrets. Despite his ideological allegiance to the Fatherland, his avowed patriotism only took him to Berlin with the greatest reluctance and he would succumb to his visceral love affair with Paris whenever he could.

But this was London.

It would do, for now, Ricardo thought smugly. He'd recently spoken to his Irish contact, a man who'd proven to be an utterly reliable and efficient foot-soldier despite initial complications further afield. What had begun to look like a costly shambles and an abject failure of leadership on his part, was now starting to coalesce into what would surely be a magnificent conclusion. He found himself unable to contain his joy at what he'd been told and he beamed at a bemused waiter who had brought him a celebratory glass of champagne. Yes, it was a

thoroughly appropriate refreshment for this moment, a statement of intent and a recognition that his epic, although admittedly extravagant, and almost out-of-control, global operation was proceeding to its orchestral finale.

Chapter 51

Saturday 1635 hours May 2nd.

He always felt better after exercise. Even on a cruel day like this when he'd felt more dead than alive.

Colm had spent the last forty minutes of his second transatlantic flight in as many days with a phone glued to his ear. First Danny and then Thaddeus and finally Patrick.

Danny and Liam had proved to be worthwhile recruits to the team more than once already. Colm had been impressed with their capable elimination of Maximiliano, a formidable enemy who would plague them no longer. At the same time, he was no more than another name to be crossed out on his so-called black book, or as he preferred to think of it, his *Loss Report*.

But he'd been less impressed with their failure to extract any useful intel about the whereabouts of his missing wife, Juanita. Like the loyal and resourceful lieutenants they'd become, Danny and Liam had absorbed his tirade and channelled it into positive action, unbidden and under the radar. They had returned to Mexico, kidnapped one of Max's remaining foot-soldiers and forced him to lead them to a woman who had information on Juanita. They discovered she had indeed returned to her family home after leaving Chile but had then taken her

family to another location, naively thinking it to be more remote and therefore safer from harm.

Under duress, the woman had confessed that she'd accompanied Max and several of his top *sicarios* to the hill-top village where she watched as they had wiped out every man, woman and child. Before Colm had even asked him, Danny volunteered that he and Liam had travelled to this village themselves, and they'd found many fresh graves, several of which had remained unmarked. Knowing that Colm would want to know beyond any doubt, the two men had planned to dig each one up but had discovered the tiny body of his wife in the first one they went to. Danny then called an undertaker from the nearest city to recover the body and take care of it until Colm could decide what to do.

*

This had been the first devastating call Colm had taken earlier that day, as his plane circled London. He'd told Danny he could never repay the debt for their help but that if there was anything in the world they desired, then he would make it happen. What Danny had said next would stay in his mind for a long time.

'Sure boss, much appreciated. But what I want most in the world right now, is for you to not ask me what else I found out about Juanita.'

Of course, Colm could not let that one go and he forced poor Danny into telling him what else the woman had said.

‘She was a *puta*, boss. Just an animal, more vicious than a cornered coyote, you know what I’m saying. She must ‘a guessed we were going to kill her and she tried to come on to me and Liam. When that didn’t work, she opened her filthy mouth and let the poison flow. It don’t mean nothin’ boss.’

But Colm already knew, in the pit of his stomach. Her behaviour at the ranch, after the first attack, the things she’d said. *He should have known.*

‘Danny… tell me exactly what the woman said.’

And Colm had listened as he heard the confirmation of his worst fears. That Juanita, no doubt driven half-crazy with the incessant violence and death that surrounded them, had given in to the constant temptation of securing her family’s safety and security that must have been eating away at her for years. She had made the fatal mistake in believing they would be safe for ever more in return for giving up his location and ending the reign of The Phantom.

Arriving at his hotel physically and emotionally exhausted, the prolonged travel and cramped conditions had squeezed his tired brain as much as his body, but there was no time to waste. Thirty minutes of vigorous stretching and a mixture of Tai Chi and yoga movements had allowed him to close the door on his mournful thoughts and instead, focus on what needed to be done. He’d become the hard-hearted warrior once more. A man able to carry

out gruesome acts without any of the remorse that would plague your average citizen. Back in the day, his misdeeds had been strictly on the orders of his overlords. Then the tables were turned and he inflicted retribution upon them so monstrous, he'd become a metaphor for everything evil. Yet he'd somehow turned his back on all of that. He'd proved, to himself as much as to his legions of detractors, that there was light amongst the darkness of his soul.

Yes. It was true, he'd despatched many souls since then, but now he had become a force for good, a cleansing of sorts, brutal and unpleasant to the taste for sure, but extremely effective. Like a powerful medicine – once you had become well again, you didn't grudge the methodology that had saved you. And now, it was time to dispense some bad medicine.

Colm dressed quickly, covering a lithe yet scarred body with his preferred black clothing, his cloak of anonymity, before taking a long draught of cold water. He gargled for a few seconds then practised changing the shape of his mouth and the position of his tongue.

He had to get the accent exactly right.

Closing his eyes, he replayed the conversation in the car a few days previously, listening for any verbal ticks that he could employ, to give his performance added authenticity. He wasn't worried in the least. The man he was about to impersonate had lived his entire life within the blast range of his family home and Colm had taught himself to become a

master at accents, even those from across the pond. Getting the recipient of his telephone call to believe he was talking to someone else wouldn't be the difficult part. The tricky bit would be wheedling out the information he needed without making it too obvious, bearing in mind he had only a couple of muffled telephone recordings to base his posture on. If he got it wrong and the man realised what was happening then it would be a messier outcome and potentially dangerous.

Colm coughed to clear his throat and thought for a moment about who this man was, what he'd done and whether or not he might have ordered the death of his beautiful brown-eyed sweetheart.

The phone was dialling.

'*Hello there*! It's me so it is, do you have a wee minute?

Oh, you do, that's grand then! Would this be a suitable moment to update you?

You're in London so you are?

Well, I'll tell ye, that's after being an amazing wee bit o' luck, for sure.

Aye, I have some fantastic news for you, but I need to meet with ye, face to face. I know it's against protocol, but I don't think I should say over the phone, you never know who's listening and if you're over here anyways, then that's perfect, so it is.

Can I give you a clue?

Sure, I can do better than that, meet me in the morning an' I'll give ye that *Piper* fellow on a plate…'

Chapter 52

Sunday 0930 hours May 3rd.

Rubbing his tired eyes and instantly regretting it, Ridge forced himself to stand at the roadside for a moment longer to try and come to before risking life and limb with the strangely-busy Sunday morning traffic. Then he remembered there was going to be a march through the city in a few hours and these guys would be tearing through in a last-minute dash before the roads were all closed off. Wondering if he was up to the task that lay ahead, he found himself counting on his fingers just how few hours' sleep he'd had. It only took one hand. He wished Orla had come with him but the orders had been explicit, he was to do this on his own. Besides which, he doubted Orla could have been prised from their hotel with a crowbar after their surprise of the previous evening.

They'd had visitors. Visitors with guns. Guns and tiny children!

*

When Joey and the boys had knocked on their hotel door at 7 pm, Orla and Ridge were unsurprised as they knew there would have to be a 'Strategy Meeting' about the following day's activities. Ridge hadn't felt particularly energised to jump up and open the door, but when he was met with a theatrical 'DA-DA…' from the exuberant trio in the stylish way only they could pull off, he guessed something was in the offing.

It was Orla who saw them first and her screams must have been heard across London as the three mercenaries peeled off to the side to reveal young Alex and Isla alongside their beaming granny and a sheepish-looking Seamus.

The next few minutes were chaos as the wee children were picked up and hugged and spun around and hugged some more.

'Look how you've both grown so *big*!' Orla exclaimed, her wet eyes gleaming with maternal pride.

Seamus had taken Ridge aside and looked relieved to finally be able to tell him what had happened back on Sorsay.

Ridge punched him on the shoulder and joked about his lack of success with women and Seamus admitted that he'd taken a vow of chastity from now on, as long as he could live out his days in the safety and sanctuary of the island.

'This place is mental, Ridge! There are too many people and they never speak to each other. We've got to get away I'm telling you… there's folk cutting aboot in masks and talk of a virus from China an' that. It's no safe, honestly, I've been nearly greetin' thinking of being stuck here any longer wi' your weans, so I huv.'

Ridge glanced over the shoulder of his friend and caught the subtle head shake from Patrick. 'Don't blame you, Seamus, we're the same… can't wait to get home… but we're going to have to stay here for a

few more days yet amigo, until we can be sure it's safe. At least the cottage has been cleaned up eh?'

Seamus laughed despite his obvious discomfort at the situation. 'Aye, these guys have made it abundantly clear that I owe them big time! I'm taking them stalking later in the summer, although I'm shitting masel' at what calibre of guns they'll be bringing!'

It was late into the night before Ridge and Orla could get the kids to settle down and eventually go to sleep, each one holding on to a parental pinkie as if they thought they'd disappear as soon as they closed their eyes.

That was when Patrick had gestured to Joey, who then fished a Sig Sauer automatic pistol, complete with silencer, out of an inoffensive-looking supermarket bag of kids' clothing. Death delivered in a Bag for Life.

Pat looked across to make sure the kids were asleep.

'Ridge, I want you to take this tomorrow. We will also be in town but you'll be on your own for your meeting and we ain't takin' any more chances, you feel me…?'

Confused and thinking out loud, Ridge couldn't see why he needed a gun.

'But, I'm only going to see an old friend, right? What do I need a-'

'-Yeah, I git where you're coming from…we ain't had time to talk about that yet. I guess that time

is now. Orla, you need to hear this too, girl and it might not be to your liking.'

Patrick had everyone's attention.

'Colm is seriously worried about our colonial adventurer friend, Mr Logan Ross.

He sure has elevated his position since our escapades in Pakistan.'

Orla put down a tray of coffees, ordered from room service along with enough whisky to float home on, which she had suggested might have been Seamus's game-plan. They left him to it and he'd nodded off before the three Dogs got to the juicy stuff.

'Sure and he deserves his success! It was Logan saved me husband here from being kidnapped by feckin' terrorists, and he saved Colm's life too! And anyways, what's *he* got to do with any of this stuff?'

Patrick smiled. 'That's what we need to ascertain tomorrow Orla.'

Ridge wasn't convinced. He picked up his glass of Islay malt and savoured the peaty flavour as it burned the back of his throat.

'You still haven't answered my question. Honestly, you guys are getting as bad as her brother. What the fuck do I need a gun like this for if all I'm doing is going to see an old pal like Logan?'

It was Joey who sat closest to Ridge and he poked him with a single innocuous-looking finger. The force was enough to knock Ridge, who was sitting on his haunches on the floor, clean onto his

back. ‘Whoa, what the fuck!’ He scrambled back up glaring at the others.

Patrick interceded, his large hand raised ominously and nobody moved a muscle.

‘Hey Joey, cut out the Bruce Lee crap okay, we is *not* impressed. Now Ridge listen up and listen good okay? We have serious intel that the guy who gave you the motherfuckin’ ski-hat is connected to some dude at the FCO here in London.’

It was Joey who saw the question in Ridge’s eyes and presumably trying to make back up with everyone, he smiled at Ridge and explained. ‘Foreign and Commonwealth Office. Your friend Logan is now a director in their ‘Global Government Partnering’ division with a specific brief for business intelligence and contracts. This-’

Patrick cut in. ‘-Which in and of itself isn’t a problem and doesn’t damn the dude ‘cept we’ve picked up intel that he’s on the way to work for SIS and on the way he’s been lining his pockets with illegal deals before he takes his new position and finds himself under a level scrutiny that would make a preacher nervous, know what I’m saying?

And it would be fair to say that Logan ain’t *ever* been pure as the driven snow. That story he told you about, Ridge? Well… he’s been caught with his John Thomas where it ain’t supposed to be on too many occasions now and we reckon the dude’s being blackmailed into participating in this particular shit-storm.’

Ridge looked at Orla and he could see the obvious doubt in her eyes. He wanted to believe in Logan's innocence too but when he thought back to that drunken night in the hills above Islamabad, even through the mists of too much alcohol, he remembered feeling slightly queasy at his friend's attitude towards the female gender. One thing was confusing him, however.

'This SIS crowd, I take it that's something to do with our friends in the security services, yeah?'

Patrick saluted him. 'Give the man a cigar! The Secret Intelligence Service is otherwise known as MI6 and no friend to any of us in this room. These dudes will have files on each of us for sure and they'll be working hand in glove with MI5 here in London. We wouldn't be surprised if his sharing data about us wasn't one of the reasons he's been offered a job with the sons of bitches.'

Ridge cleared his throat and went for the kill.

'Pat, are you saying that Logan knew about the tracking beacon in the ski hat and that means he was complicit in the attack on Halley?'

Patrick looked at the pair of them and the slight nod of his head was enough.

Chapter 53

Sunday 1000 hours May 3rd.

The following morning, a weary and hungover Ridge Walker found himself going into battle again, unprepared and scared as hell. *Just for a change*, he had muttered while narrowly avoiding being run down by a hackney cab.

Ridge looked up and across the dark frontage of the beautiful but imposing building for a moment, appreciating it's haughty grandeur despite his nervousness. Set apart from the continuous terrace of the others by a narrow lane on each side, it was smaller too, although still casting a vast black shadow across the pavement. He squinted his eyes and took in the grotesque hawk-like gargoyles, their lascivious tongues and talons flicking downwards as if to catch unwary pedestrians. It was a structure designed to intimidate, he decided, grumbling a few choice swear words under his breath and momentarily alarming the security guard at the first door. Ridge remembered being back at school in the '80s when his Computing teacher had enthralled them all with photos of a Darth Vader gargoyle which had been one of the winning entries for a competition to choose contemporary themes for part of the restoration of the Washington National Cathedral in D.C.

He flashed his fake passport at the second guard and silently mouthed *the Force is with me, I am one with the Force*, as he entered the main foyer with

its huge vaulted ceiling constructed of the same solid marble as the vast smoothness of the floor. Wishing he'd brushed his teeth a second time, he swallowed nervously and ran his fingers through his unruly hair before approaching the main desks.

Ridge felt a little like he'd once done many years before when he'd been 'to see the Manager' at the local bank on the mainland when he was looking for a business loan to help him set up his computer business. The man's name had been Gregor Morrison but the ridiculously large three-sided and faux-leather nameplate on his enormous wooden desk only said *Mr Morrison* in thick gold lettering. In those days, they didn't want to even pretend to be your friend. The guy had half-listened to young Richard Walker's business plan and then only asked him two quick questions. Did he think personal computers, by which he meant laptops, would ever catch on and secondly, did he have any collateral? Needless to say, the old bugger turned him down and he obtained a far better rate from a more modern bank in Glasgow a couple of weeks later.

There are two important differences between the man he was then and the one standing here today, he told himself. The second being the fact that he had a gun tucked into the belt of his jeans. He took a breath and announced himself with the broadest smile he could muster.

'Good morning! Busy place for a Sunday, isn't it?

I have an appointment with Mr Logan Ross at ten o'clock and I was told to ask for a Vivien Pringle.'

Chapter 54

Sunday 1045 hours May 3rd.

It was almost an hour later when Ridge saw a heavily-built older woman traverse her way across the acreage of marble in his general direction. Stuffed into a tweed suit of dubious vintage, her gait was laboured and her pallid face indicated that she might collapse at any point. Anxious to get his meeting with Logan Ross concluded as soon as possible, Ridge had jumped out of his leather sofa too many times already in the last hour, in the mistaken belief that he was being summoned by one person or another. In this case, he was more concerned that this woman was going to expire in front of him and he certainly didn't need that attention. He picked on a particularly interesting swirl of avocado-coloured marble at his feet and was quickly lost in his thoughts.

This meeting was going to be fraught with difficulty for him, he'd known that from the first moment the idea was mooted. Unable to compartmentalise his emotions like his brother-in-law, he'd argued against the plan, citing his emotional conflict, general weariness and overall horror at the thought their friend, who'd previously transformed from zero to hero in a manner worthy of a Marvel franchise, might be one of the bad guys in this big-budget globe-trotting sequel. Even his savvier, and tougher-by-half, wife had expressed her incredulity that in true Agatha Christie style, the killer had to be

someone within their tiny 'social professional' circle. 'You'll be tellin' us next, it was after being in the Library an' with the bleeding candlestick' she had said archly.

However, Patrick and the other two men, would not permit the rationale for the mission, as they put it, to be up for debate. Ridge and Orla had both felt the absence of Colm that evening. Normally, before going into a dangerous situation the next day, he'd have sat them down over a large table and plied them with copious amounts of strong drink until they fell under a dark spell of such horrific yet beautiful necromancy that they would've signed an oath written in their own blood if he'd asked them.

With the three mercenaries, the conversation had been brief and to the point. 'It is what it is,' Patrick had said. Unexpectedly it had been the normally upbeat and more care-free Joey who had shown them a glimpse of his 'Badman' Barbarossa persona when he suggested they look at his downloaded list of dead and injured from the attacks on the ranch and at Halley.

'It's all there, in forensic detail and I got the upgrade VIP membership version in glorious motherfuckin' technicolour just for you!'

He'd gestured with a large thumb towards the other room where Alex and Isla were blissfully sleeping and with his eyes flashing, he'd growled, 'and unless we end this thing now, it will be *their*

brain fragments you be washing off the furniture, that's for damn sure…'

*

Ridge heard an impatient cough and he started, pulled momentarily from what had felt like one bad dream and now here he was, straight into another. He looked up, into the obviously irritated face of the woman he'd noticed a few minutes ago. She glared at him and managed to pull off a tight-lipped smile without exhibiting the slightest trace of humanity. Words leaked out from somewhere despite her mouth appearing closed.

'My name is Ms Vivien Pringle, Mr Ross will see you now. Please follow me.'

Eyeing the straining tweed-covered buttons warily, Ridge stood up and made to shake the woman's hand. However, she'd already turned around and instead he flicked her the bird and followed a few feet behind. Walking alongside Ms Pringle, he'd found she was a tiny woman, small and rotund, reminding Ridge of the overly-plump baby birds back on Sorsay. Unfortunately, she didn't possess any of their enthusiasm and joie de vivre.

'I love that Scottish name,' he ventured. 'You wouldn't get many offices open on a Sunday back home, that's for sure, have you lived in London for long?'

'I was born here. This is government, not some office. We are always open.'

They entered a tiny wood-panelled elevator and Ridge felt his stomach lurch as it rattled its way upwards, seemingly encountering numerous obstacles on the way, each time shaking the small compartment with loud bangs and other disconcerting sounds. He tried one last time for some humanity and to take his mind off the thought of vomiting over her tweed jacket.

'Big Brother, eh? Always watching, never sleeps, right?'

There was no reply. Somehow he knew she was grimacing at what he'd said, even from looking down at the tight bun grafted onto the top of her head. The elevator jerked its way to a standstill and the doors opened into a large open area of office space surrounded by tall wooden and glass partitions which Ridge reckoned led into another area of smaller waiting rooms. He wasn't mistaken and Ms Pringle pointed to a row of ancient wooden chairs and told him to wait. Ridge did as he was instructed and looked askance at his surroundings. He couldn't shake off the impression he'd stumbled onto the set of some geriatric TV show like that one about the rural vet, *All Creatures Great And Small*.

Far from worrying that he'd be subjected to all kinds of high-tech electronic surveillance and have his gun confiscated, he now wished he'd thought to use his phone to record the conversation as Orla had suggested. As her face flashed up in his mind and then the two kids whom he'd earlier kissed on the forehead

as they slept, he hoped he wasn't about to be castrated or put to sleep any time soon and he strained his eyes to peer through the thick wavy glass of the kind he'd last seen in a Glasgow public toilet. Difficult as it was, he could see a larger, darker shape silhouetted in the morning sunshine and that told him at least the head veterinarian was in attendance. Ridge clenched his teeth and thought of the poor woman he'd had to put out of her misery. Yes, now he knew her name even. She'd been 27 years old. Could the man he was about to meet be responsible for all of that? It seemed too incredible for Ridge to believe, even now.

The adjoining door creaked open and an unsmiling face told him he could finally enter. The office was larger than he'd anticipated and it also had a further door on the far side, perhaps leading to the next poor bastard in the chain of command. Rings within rings, he thought archly as he manufactured his best fake smile and strode towards his old friend and ally, Logan Ross.

'Logan! It's been a while eh? How the hell are you?'

He glanced around to see the less-than-vivacious-Vivien had retreated before adding, 'Jesus, you picked a cracker there! Not exactly brimming with the milk of human kindness is she?'

Logan reached a meaty hand across his desk and squeezed hard and with the utmost sincerity in his eyes. *Teach them that at public school*, Ridge decided, already thinking that he didn't like the

changes his friend had undergone over the last few years. Logan had practically doubled in weight and what might have been passed off as avuncular and big-boned, now looked morbidly obese. He thought about the woman who'd brought him in and decided the mid-morning tea-trolley in this joint must be something to behold.

'I am doing spectacularly well Ridge Walker, or whatever you're calling yourself these days, eh?' He winked and then ran his hands outwards with a theatrical flourish.

'As you can clearly see, I have well and truly blossomed since joining the Foreign Office. In fact, you could say a seed was planted back in Islamabad and from there, it grew into this!

And you may well cast aspersions towards my valiant secretary, but she is the most loyal and conscientious helper that a man could ask for.'

'And not too distracting either' Ridge added, with a smirk.

'*Pre…cisely*, old bean!

Now I have an extremely tight schedule I'm afraid and I feel I must dispense with any reminiscences about old times for another day and press you about what is it that I can do for you?'

Ridge swallowed and reached behind his back.

'What you can do is start telling me the truth about what happened last week in Antarctica. And unlike you, I have got all day, *old bean…*'

He placed the automatic pistol gently on the desk and sat back, pleasantly surprised by the look of complete horror on the other man’s face.

Chapter 55

Sunday 1130 hours May 3 rd.

The crowds had begun to gather from early in the morning and posing as a photographic journalist, Colm had paid a couple of art students to keep him regularly updated as to where the vast majority of the people were along the well-publicised route. The muster point had been a chilly mist-blanketed Battersea Park, yet the crowd was already several thousand strong by the time they set off, exactly on schedule. He'd been sent photos as requested and he was confident the planned march would successfully fulfil an altogether different purpose from that intended by those involved. He looked forward to a chaotic and well-attended cavalcade of colourful and noisy floats, banners, Samba bands and other assorted tribes of protestors young and old, disparate in many ways but aligned for their one common aim, a clarion call against the imminent visit of the unpopular and divisive US president.

Already, Colm had undertaken a covert surveillance operation in Westminster which was only ten minutes north of Battersea by cab. Satisfied that everything was in place, he'd donned his second disguise of the morning before making the slower journey further north. He'd travelled by motorbike this time, forced to take a circuitous route as the centre of London had become increasingly awkward to navigate. It seemed that with each passing minute,

the UK and American police and security services were ramping up their unbreakable ring-fencing of the Presidential motorcade. It hadn't escaped Colm's realisation, that should he find himself becoming ensnared by the authorities on this particular day and at this location, he'd immediately be suspected as being on a contract to take out the Pres.

He hid the bike in a hastily-acquired and hideously expensive underground garage. Maybe he'd take out the larcenous estate agent who'd extorted six months rent for what would be no more than 24 hours usage. But in this game, location was everything. And this place was two minutes on foot from his rendezvous. He checked his weapons and tested his other kit in a routine he'd followed a hundred times in a hundred dark places like this one. Wrapping a black bandanna emblazoned with a large anarchist symbol over his newly shaved head, he was walking now and almost at his destination. Colm nodded towards a distant roof, relieved that he couldn't see anyone there, but grateful to hear verbal communication in his right ear that he had been clocked entering Trafalgar Square and still a minute ahead of the plan.

Predictably, the place was jumping with students and young people earnestly putting the finishing touches to their placards. He watched several of them tearing an American flag into pieces. He admired their enthusiasm and envied their naïve idealism. Which nation's colours should take

responsibility for the atrocities inflicted on him and his friends over the last few weeks? That was what he was here to find out on this beautiful morning. He already had a strong case and as he stood there, motionless amidst the hubbub, he vowed that before the day was out, the alliance against him would fall like a house of cards. Colm had called his next meeting here precisely because it was thronged with people, mostly innocent civilians but also with a healthy mix of armed police officers. The seriously dangerous close-protection guys wouldn't be there until the Motorcade was closer, but he'd still bet a gallon of Guinness that half of the dread-locked, but still too-squeaky-clean, protestors were on the payroll of the CIA.

He tried to find a quieter spot for a moment. 'You hear my audio okay? Over.' The reply was instant. '*Lima Charlie. Loud and clear. Over.*'

It wasn't overly dramatic to say that this meeting was about as risky as it was possible to get, in many ways, but staging a confrontation with the man he was about to meet whilst amongst this nest of vipers, was equally dangerous for his adversary and bearing in mind the considerable financial resources at the other's disposal, it wouldn't have been safe to meet in a quiet hotel suite. It wouldn't have been unlikely for his adversary to have booked an entire hotel in order to kill one man. He'd done precisely the same thing once in Singapore.

There was another crackle in his ear.

'Good to go at two o'clock. Over.'

Colm saw the man. 'Copy that' he replied quickly turning away as he did so, pleased to see his target was considerably older-looking in the flesh although his oiled hair was still black. He was more slightly built than he'd appeared in any of the photos they'd studied the previous day, although many of them had been years old and dating back to their earlier jousting sessions when Colm had relieved the guy of an enormous amount of money. Thankfully, they'd never met in person. It was him, however, he was certain of that. He began his approach, knowing that if his counterpart had also been doing his homework, then this could be a brief and possibly deadly encounter.

'Know where I'd find a decent drink around here?' Colm proffered cautiously.

'That would be a Guinness I would expect,' said the other man, removing his dark sunglasses and eyeing him up and down without a trace of embarrassment.

'I'm more of a *Beamish* man, to be honest.'

As Ricardo Perez nodded and smiled, signifying he was happy with this opening gambit, he gestured towards a low wall enclosing the fountain. 'Shall we?'

It was as good a spot as any and the area of water would at least remain unoccupied and therefore free of any unwanted eavesdropping. The two men sat a couple of feet apart and made it appear they were

not together and far more interested in watching the frenzied and comical activity of the youngsters hurriedly strapping on their marching drums in front of them. Colm took the initiative.

'A lucky coincidence then…you and me both being over in London at the same time?'

'I don't subscribe to chance. My business affairs take me all over the world and London is a major hub after all. Tell me, what additional information do you have that couldn't be imparted over the telephone?' Senor Perez fixed his dark eyes on Colm and any trace of warmth had vanished.

'No worries! I've got photographic evidence an' everything, so I have, thanks to yer man *Ross*, to be fair. He's been a grand help an' the two of them, him an' yon Piper himself, they've been as thick as thieves for the last few weeks.'

'Really? I have no idea who you are talking about. Ross? Who is he?'

Colm smiled and waved off a young student who'd almost taken his eye out with a ten-foot length of bamboo cane, thankful for a moment to marshal his thoughts.

'You know fine well who he is!

He's a friend for life as far as I'm concerned after he helped me out wi' a wee bit o' bother over by. He's in the picture I have here, with yer man.

You don't have to be coy with me!

They were snapped in his office, for the love of Jesus. But the eedjit Ross hasn't a notion that he's with this Piper fella!'

Perez smiled like a patient father waiting for his errant son to confess to taking his car without consent and scratching the paintwork. He leaned in closer, the sun highlighting a patch of thinning hair and Colm could see the hair was naturally grey. But he could also hear the irritation creeping into the little man's voice, no matter how hard he tried to mask it.

'Yes, yes, that's fine.

I can see that you are a thorough professional. But can I see the photos now?'

Colm had taken a mobile phone out of his black combat jacket and he held it aloft. 'Ah, you mean these?' Perez made a sudden grab for the phone but Colm was quicker.

'Ah ah…! Not yet boss! You're correct in saying I am a professional. Ross told me about the missile attack that missed the Piper completely. At least back in my old bombing days, if we were gonna blow someone up with a rocket, we'd never have bleedin' missed them, know what I'm saying?

The one's on here are only the grainy rough-cuts, I'd call them. I've got some gorgeous originals back at the hotel, real *works of art* so they are! And they're all yours – once we agree our wee bargain here. I mean how do I know you won't stiff me with a few quid and then bung yer man 'blind Logan' the rest? I only want what's due me after all!'

Perez looked around him in obvious frustration. A couple of the drummers had begun hesitantly beating out a slow rhythm, with the others adding in additional layers of complexity, their faces shining with emotion as they gathered confidence from each other

'Yes! Okay, how much extra do you want? Just let me see the pictures!'

'That's better. Fifty thou sounds about right, wouldn't you say?'

Perez nodded and reached out his hand but Colm pulled his away once again.

'Mind! I'm only going to let you see the one, right now… until I get the money transfer. Then you'll get the rest, okay?'

The Chilean nodded, his teeth clenched, as Colm opened up the photo on his tiny burner phone. He handed it to Perez who held it close to his squinting face, his weak eyes scanning it eagerly.

Colm stood up as if to stretch and give the other man some privacy to study the picture. This was the crunch moment and despite his practised nonchalance, he was on high alert. The last thing he expected Perez to do was to laugh.

'Ha! Nice picture!'

'Sure now isn't it just' Colm ventured suspiciously.

Perez threw the phone back at Colm angrily.

'And taken within *the last hour* I would say, wouldn't you, *Brendan*?

I may not know much about your Irish way of life, but I do know that I'd be unlikely to cultivate a suntan like either of ours, living in the shadow of Portlaoise Prison.

And let me tell you, if that truly is the Piper sitting there in that tiny photograph, then he has reached the final explosive chapter of his much sought-after book at long last!'

Both men were standing now and whilst Colm had been momentarily distracted catching the phone, he saw Perez had slipped a small Beretta out of his pocket. He smiled at Colm.

'Killing him will be a pleasant distraction for my men this beautiful morning.

But then we both know who the real Piper is don't we?'

A barrage of sound from the Brazilian drummers ricocheted across the busy Square, repeating fast staccato phrases like machine-gun fire assaulting the ears. Colm was momentarily paralysed. The gun didn't worry him. He could disarm a dozen men like him without breaking a sweat. What was jangling around his brain was something else.

He'd underestimated this guy.

Of *course,* he would have Logan's office under surveillance. If Colm could do it, why couldn't Perez? He had to get to Ridge and fast. It only took a single second to make his decision.

Colm looked up and into the sunlight and pulled at his left ear once before stepping backwards

sharply. Immediately, a trigger was pulled on a high-velocity rifle almost a quarter of a mile away from Trafalgar Square and less than half a second later a tiny hole appeared in the forehead of Ricardo Perez and he fell back silently into the water, unnoticed in the pandemonium around them.

The Piper had already turned away, removed his black bandanna and continued to walk, slowly but in a straight line. He turned his black coat inside out to become yet another non-descript denim-jacketed student in a red baseball cap, staring downwards at a mobile phone to become quickly absorbed into the vast melee of protestors. Seconds later, the drumming stopped abruptly and the first awful screams could be heard echoing across the Square.

Chapter 56

Sunday 1135 hours May 3 rd.

Standing on the circular balcony of South Africa House, the elegantly dressed young woman grasped the sun-warmed granite with one hand while she used to the other to scan and re-scan the same small area of Trafalgar Square. It was hard to see properly even though her binoculars were the finest money could buy. Salty tears drenched her face and she blinked hard and squinted against the bright sunshine. Moments before, the woman had witnessed what she knew had been a life-ending act and the obliteration of a long-held obsession. The man she'd been watching so intently, imagining what his lips had been saying in his always eloquent fashion, had been cruelly silenced with a bullet to the head. She watched with a macabre fascination as the crowds first bunched up and then quickly fanned outwards, flowing away from the centre of her focus like a multi-coloured viscous soup.

There! She again caught a momentary glimpse of the body. Someone had jumped into the bloodied water and lifted the man out. There had been a few seconds of frenzied efforts to resuscitate him until they'd presumably noticed the bullet wound. The woman was experienced enough to know that with an assassination at this level, there might only be a pinprick of an entry wound, but at the other side, it would leave a gaping hole the size of a man's fist.

Josefa had known in an instant that the man wouldn't have survived. And in that same second of cold dread, she understood fully, for the first time in her privileged life, what role she had yet to play. She gave up on trying to locate the killer. He'd vanished into the crowds like the anonymous contract-killer he was and she knew he'd never be found. Men like him could make themselves invisible when they chose to and he would go on to kill many others, until one day he'd meet the same fate as this man had today.

She allowed the binoculars to fall around her neck and gripped on to the balcony with both hands, for fear that her shaking legs would be unable to support her slender frame. As she stared down in horror at the brushed-aluminium briefcase between her feet, she noticed her manicured and tanned fingers had become as grey as the stone she clung to. Josefa cursed the gods under her breath. It was time to make her heart into stone also. Time to use this innocuous-looking case to extract the ultimate payment from the people responsible for this outrage today.

They had been her father's last words to her and at the time she'd prayed that she would never have to obey them. '*This is what you must do…*'

Chapter 57

Sunday 1140 hours May 3 rd.

He walked fast, pushing through the crowds, growling at those who were too slow to notice the aggressive-looking man in a hurry. Colm was far angrier at himself for his many mistakes over the last few weeks. Perhaps he was getting too old for this sort of thing? Or had he allowed his personal feelings to cloud his judgement? That was *Assassin Rule Number One* for Pete's sake.

His current predicament was it appeared the authorities had been quicker off the mark than he'd anticipated and they'd blocked cell-phone reception in the Trafalgar Square area. He guessed that the Americans had insisted on this as a security measure no doubt suspecting the killing of Perez had some connection with the Presidential visit. As he strode ever faster now away from the square, it hit him that they would also be tracking every cell-phone that had been active around the kill zone and particularly one that was moving fast and purposefully, rather than milling around in a panic like most of the bewildered and frightened protestors would be doing at that point.

Ridge's life was in jeopardy and Colm felt unusually vulnerable too. He was only a short distance from his brother-in-law, who had put himself in mortal danger reluctantly and only at his firm bequest and yet he was unable to do anything to help him. The comms in his ear had gone cold as soon as

Joey had pulled the trigger and he trusted that the experienced mercenary would have followed protocol and evacuated the scene. Right now he was on his own. *That used to be the way you liked it*, his internal commentator taunted.

Thinking fast, he threw his phone onto the street and watched with grim satisfaction as it was crushed under the wheels of a red London bus. He cursed his decision to leave his new blockchain phone back at the motorbike on the basis it was too bulky to carry. At least it would be serviceable in a few minutes unless the Yanks had taken out every communication satellite over central London. Colm checked his watch. It had been ten minutes since Perez had been killed. With any luck, his own men won't even be aware of anything having gone wrong. Then he mentally slapped himself. *There you go again*, underestimating this guy.

Ten minutes could be plenty time for Perez to have a hit squad attack the FCO building although they'd need to be pretty damn good to get through the front door without alerting the British security services. Something was worrying him about Perez's use of the word 'explosive' and he wondered if he was being a tad paranoid bearing in mind one of the more exotic plans he and the Dog's had formulated over the last week or so during their London sightseeing vacation. Whatever he'd meant, Colm had to get hold of Ridge fast!

He approached the underground car park and surveyed the entrance carefully. Straight away, alarm bells began to ring. The two men standing on either side were dressed in almost identical 'civilian' clothing and Colm could see they were both wearing sidearms under their blouson jackets. Shit! He had to get to that bike. Think, man!

Quickly, a working plan formulated in his head, like the old days. Why did he need that phone? It was encrypted with military-grade software. There was no way they'd get anything useful from it this side of Christmas. He'd not left any other incriminating evidence short of his DNA which they'll have accumulated a bucket of by now, over the years. Looking around him, he saw a mid-twenties guy talking away into his reasonably up-to-date looking iPhone and he would be passing a dark entrance-way in a few seconds. Colm sped up for a brief moment until he was right behind the guy who was still oblivious to his presence despite the fact he had a man in lockstep inches behind him. Colm took a quick step to the man's right and grabbed his arms at the same time using the momentum of his movement to swing the guy around and headfirst into the ornate but solid copper security grating. The guy went out like a light and Colm lowered him gently to the ground without even checking to see if he was still breathing, his attention focussed on the phone and whether or not he could prise it from the man's hand without losing connection.

Two seconds later he was ringing his brother-in-law, desperately hoping he'd memorised the number correctly. It rang out. He tried Patrick next. If what he feared was about to go down, then their audacious plans for the rest of the afternoon's entertainment would have to be radically altered. No answer…

With communications proving awkward, he would have to get himself to Westminster instead and he wracked his brain to retrieve the details of the protest march road closures while he looked up and down for an appropriately quiet street. Less than a hundred yards ahead he saw a heavily built Asian man standing at the open door of his car. Leaning on the roof and talking on a microphone, as if to himself, the guy never knew what hit him. Colm thumped the back of his head hard enough to leave a dent in the roof of the dusty black Nissan. The man's nose exploded in a fountain of bright red blood and he passed out. Checking no-one had noticed, Colm dragged the man along a few feet and laid him down into the litter-strewn gutter alongside the car behind. After rendering two men unconscious within two minutes, this time he took a few seconds to put the guy in the recovery position in case he drowned in his own vomit. Then he pulled the man's blood-soaked jogging trousers down to his knees. He knew from experience that a man with his trousers down and a large hairy arse in the air was half as likely to be offered assistance and thus would buy Colm the vital

few minutes that could get him safely to Westminster. The keys were in the ignition and he jumped in and slammed the car into gear and threw it into a U-turn before gunning the engine as fast as he thought he'd get away with.

Chapter 58

Sunday 1155 hours May 3 rd.

It didn't take Logan Ross long to recover his poise. Ridge wondered if he'd got it wrong when he'd imagined seeing horror in his face and he decided in own his defence that he was going to have some difficulty reading the other man's thoughts, this man he'd got to know well during that bizarre episode in the humidity and dust of Pakistan. Logan's face had swollen to grotesque proportions over the intervening years, to turn his eyes into dark narrow slits and his complexion was now so florid, it would be impossible to tell if he was blushing or not.

There was always the voice. Ridge had become accustomed to making vital decisions on the hoof and he was a huge fan of listening to how people were saying things as much as to what they were saying. And there was nothing in Logan's calm demeanour that gave Ridge any comfort. He hoped Patrick and the others were also listening in to their conversation.

'Well! You've managed to sneak a gun into my office. What a clever chap. Is it even loaded? You must know that there's an alarm button located under this beautiful but utterly fake leather-topped desk and it would only take a couple of minutes before our doughty security operatives had your face pressed into this gorgeous Georgian stud-work and your right arm into a Half Nelson.'

Ridge leant forward and picked up the gun, just in case.

'But I wouldn't need two minutes pal, remember that, okay.' He cradled the weapon in his hands.

'Let's recap shall we. You were about to tell me a wee story about why you've gone over to the dark side after being such a useful big bastard. And you can ease that chair backwards too, that way I don't have to hit you across the back of the head with this.'

As Logan smiled and did as he was told and pushed himself away from any furniture, Ridge stood up, anxious he wasn't pressing any buttons.

'As you wish old chap, but I fear I have no idea what you're talking about.'

Feeling unexpectedly awkward and disloyal in front of an old friend, Ridge sat on the edge of the desk and placed his burner phone in front of him, more for moral support or back-up than anything else. He wasn't anticipating any calls. He saw it was switched off and quickly remedied that, feeling even more foolish than before, as he decided what the hell to say next. But then images of a blood-stained cross on virgin snow flashed across his brain and he steeled himself to be strong for the massacre of innocent lives lost on his account.

Logan still didn't seem too worried, and he certainly wasn't short of the verbiage. Ridge racked his memory banks to try and decide if this was the

sign of a confident Logan or a man about to piss in his pants.

'You were clever enough to switch your phone off downstairs, Ridge Walker, but look around you. There's a beady eye on every corner of these offices and unless I put in a good word for you with some friends 'in high places,' then I'm afraid you're going to be spending the rest of this year behind bars.'

Ridge had already clocked the small, black, cup-shaped camera housings on each corner of Logan's office. There had been two in the outer office and six on the way up, but strangely enough, he'd not noticed any downstairs. Too many invisible people coming in and out that wouldn't want to be identified, he guessed. A rush of adrenaline pricked at his armpits and he forced himself to remain in control. It was then, in a moment of cold clarity, that he knew he wasn't the happy-go-lucky adventurer this man remembered.

'It's you who's going to be in jail, Logan. Unless you co-operate fully.

I have friends too if you care to remember.

The cameras up here are not recording today although to the security team they will appear functional and anyway, I'm sure they have better things to do on a sunny Sunday afternoon than to peer too closely at a fat man behind a desk. But if they did, they'd perhaps notice that the weather out of that window looks more like the clouds of last Friday.'

Ridge smiled inwardly. Now *that* registered. Hit and sunk.

But Logan wouldn't lie down.

'That's all well and good. But I think you'll find that my friends out-rank your colourful bunch of desperados, old bean! And in any case, I have to inform you that, ultimately, we are all working for the same people, a sad fact perhaps, but one that I wish those noisy oiks outside would realise!'

'Is that how you justify your pathetic existence, Logan? Killing innocent people at the behest of some anonymous Americans? Is that what you call *Global Government Partnering* for fuck's sake? Ridge was shouting now, but he couldn't help himself and it seemed to be having an effect.

'Now listen here, wait just a minute will you,' Logan blustered. 'I had no idea about anybody getting hurt when I agreed to all of this, I only-'

'-Liar!' Ridge jumped up and started furiously pacing up and down the room.

'You knew it was Colm and the rest of us they were after! And Orla!

You were there with us all when Orla was about to pop. You're practically wee Isla's uncle, for the love of Jesus!

What do you think is going to happen when they catch us? They weren't exactly going to give Colm a government pension and call it quits. You do know who's behind all of this, don't you? A fucking

Nazi lunatic living in the last century and a bunch of crazed drug dealers with a grudge!'

Sweat was pouring from Logan's face, and his eyes appeared to be crying. He looked up at Ridge, less defiant perhaps but still determined to get his point across.

'No that's not true Ridge. I was only facilitating the diplomatic-'

'-*Stop* it, Logan!' Ridge snarled, jumping halfway across the desk, slamming his free hand hard and brandishing the gun in his other hand. Logan's voice was faltering and that meant Ridge must be getting closer to the truth. He heard a quiet buzzing and glanced down at Logan's desk in alarm. It was only his phone. He saw it light up momentarily with a SMS notification. Answering the phone was about the last thing on Ridge's mind at that moment but he knew it had to be one of only two people. Without moving from his position, leaning over the desk and eye-balling a visibly paling Logan like a madman, he stabbed at the button. The message was from Colm and customarily brief.

Where are you? Logan is the guy. Get away fast.

If there was ever a time to play his last ruthless card, it was now. Wishing he had a cigarette, Ridge blinked fast, swallowed hard and went for the jugular.

'Time to stop lying Logan. We know it was you. You called John Marwick in Port Stanley. We have a transcript of the call. You told him to give me

the ski-hat. You sentenced us to death. And you condemned those innocent scientists who had no involvement in any of this. All I want to know is why?'

To his utter astonishment and deepest regret, Ridge saw that his poker play had been on point. Logan visibly deflated in front of his eyes and he let go an enormous sigh.

'I'm sorry Ridge, with all my heart… but I had no choice. And it's you who is living in a bygone age. There's no place for mavericks like you and Colm in the twenty-first century. They will never allow you to rest, not after the things you've all done.'

'The things we've done? Hold on a wee minute here pal, any so-called maverick behaviour on my part was to stop people being hurt by the shadowy monsters who pull the strings in this fucked-up world. At least I can bloody well sleep at night. Can you say the same? Looking at the nick of you right now I think I already have my answer!'

'Sleep?' Logan whimpered. 'Maybe…perhaps, for a few precious moments, at the bottom of a gin bottle, before the nightmares begin.'

Now it was Ridge's turn to feel deflated and he sunk into the chair opposite, placing the pistol on the desk between them. He'd come here to try and find out if his former friend had been behind a plot to kill him and now he had his answer. He only now realised that he'd never believed it could be true and hadn't formulated a plan as to what he'd do next.

‘*Why* Logan? We trusted you. What happened?’

‘Blackmail, old bean. The universal currency around here.

You can guess the script, I would imagine. I was at an international convention in Washington. Too much to drink, *plus ca change*, a target painted on my back and, surprise surprise, a bright young filly who seemed only too eager to pop up to my suite. Beautiful, of course, jet black and legs like a thoroughbred… it turned out she was only fifteen and there was a 2-way mirror in the room. Classic sting operation, old as the hills. *Gotcha*… as the red-tops would say if ever they found out.’

Ridge was horrified that it had been that easy. It sounded like something from the sixties.

‘But it’s not too late to redeem yourself, Logan. You can still come clean and help us end this. These guys need to be brought to justice…this doesn’t only affect us, it’s a global thing. You can still do something good.’

But even as he mouthed the words, he knew it wouldn’t work. Come clean to whom? Logan likely understood better than he did that it would be virtually impossible to extricate himself from the tangled web he’d become enmeshed in. And Ridge also knew there was no chance that either he or Orla would be prepared to jeopardise their hard-fought secret identities to become officially involved. Logan would be on his own. He would be hung, drawn and

quartered in the media spotlight and every sordid detail of his life would be cast up and used against him. A lamb to the slaughter.

'No Ridge. Just not happening, old bean.

You can still escape all of this, no doubt. You have the skills and the contacts.

But it will never end for you, of course. They'll always be after you and Orla, to get to Colm and his blasted book. For me, I will-'

'-Wait a wee minute! What book? What on earth are you talking about?'

Logan let out a long and exasperated sigh.

'Colm's book! That's what they *all* want…!

They'll use the book as a weapon against other nation-states or agencies, or to hold as collateral for future international situations.

That's what all this horrible killing has been about!'

Ridge listened in horror to his former friend and the only part of it all that he fully understood was Logan's obvious desire to unburden himself to someone.

'I'm sorry, Ridge. I had no choice in any of this. You should understand better than anyone… it was you who started it, after all, that fateful night in the hotel bar. I don't resent you for any of it. I had thought my life to be effectively over before you walked down those stairs. Despite my appearance to the contrary, I discovered I am not the mild-mannered office-type after all. I enjoyed tremendously the

physicality of our encounter and all of that cloak and dagger stuff. No matter what happens next, I owe you a debt of gratitude and I apologise for my part in this sorry affair.'

Ridge growled impatiently. 'Get on with it Logan! You'll be telling me next that you are Clark Kent's bastard child, for fuck's sake.'

The other man blinked rapidly and carried on with his confession.

'Quite. Well, after the security services worked out my role in the rescue of that poor girl, it was open season on Logan Ross, old bean! They latched on to me faster than a sea louse on your Scottish salmon. I should have realised it sooner, of course; the way they promoted me and agreed to let me come back to good old Blighty, out of purdah at last.

It was only to get access to me more easily, to get their hooks into me. Helping you had dragged me, however unwittingly at first, out of the shadows. All my earlier misdemeanours and *peccadillos*, shall we say, were exposed to harsher scrutiny.'

Logan moved uncomfortably in his seat and Ridge could see the perspiration that had stained the front of his shirt in broad bands across the folds of fat. He leant in closer, sensing that Logan was finally getting to the meat of the matter.

'Not that they judged me for any of that. Far from it. But it was ammunition, you understand.' He looked at Ridge sorrowfully. 'It helped them to

wheedle information out of me about you, your family and your flamboyant friends.

To start with, my job was to find the location of the book, using Colm as bait with my personal knowledge and insight concerning you all and enabling his most powerful enemies, the one's who'd stand the best chance of success. Unsurprisingly, there's no shortage of people with a grudge to bear against a man like him.

But then I overstepped the mark. I began to see my new career in this place would have a short shelf-life and I began to market the book independently, looking to sell it to the highest bidder, even some of the monsters we'd been provoking to flush Colm out of hiding. I made a bad situation even worse. That's why I have to do this!'

And with a sudden movement that belied his enormous bulk, Logan dived for the desk, his hands frantically grasping for the hidden alarm button. Ridge was far too slow to respond and when he attempted to put himself in between Logan and the desk he found he was too late and much too light to be able to deflect the much larger man's path.

The next few moments were something that Ridge would replay in his mind time and time again, but still, they would never make sense.

Logan must have activated the alarm because immediately a siren began to wail and a flashing red light bounced off the hard surfaces in the room. As a shocked Ridge stood momentarily transfixed, Logan

pulled an old-style pistol out of a drawer and levelled it at Ridge. At that moment, a red-faced and panicked-looking Vivian Pringle opened the door, her mouth agape at the gun in Logan's hand.

Ridge grabbed her and pulled her in, slamming the door shut and on finding a key in the lock turning it quickly. He could hear Vivian asking what was going on and Logan telling him to stand still but all he could think of was stopping any more people coming through the door. He pulled at a filing cabinet to block the door but he had grabbed it too high up and it toppled over with an almighty crash.

'Stop Ridge!

I will use this gun if needs be. Vivian stand in the corner, PLEASE! This will all be over in two minutes if this fool will only listen.'

The cabinet was heavy and it dug itself into the carpet but Ridge still managed to push it sufficiently to impede the opening of the door. He turned to find a gun in his face.

Logan was backing away, his beefy arms outstretched, the gun held two-handed and pointing directly at Ridge. At that moment, Ridge noticed another door, a wooden door at the rear of the office, almost invisible in the dowdy office. He saw *Private* etched into the thick textured glass. He guessed it was more than an additional ante-room and Logan would have another way out.

'I'm sorry Ridge! I have to do this, there's no other way!' Logan raised his arms and Ridge sensed

he was going to pull the trigger. He was too far away from the desk to be able to use it as cover and his own gun sat there next to his phone, out of reach and useless. He closed his eyes and thought of Orla and the kids and also of his brother Gavin.

Then he heard an exclamation of surprise and a high-pitched scream from Vivian to his right. He opened his eyes to see the mysterious door opening and another man with a gun appearing. It was Colm.

But Colm was wearing a face he could hardly recognise. His eyes were black and his features betrayed no emotion.

'Put the gun down Logan. It's over. Don't be an-'

But Logan let out a tiny cry and swung his gun away from Ridge and towards Colm. It was only going to end one way. Ridge stood shocked as Colm's Browning pistol spat silently and Logan sunk to his knees, a neat bullet hole through his forehead and the back of his head splattered across the office window. Ridge held up his arms to protect Vivian Pringle, and as he did so, there was an enormous shuddering and the entire building seemed to sway for a second before everything started to collapse around him.

Chapter 59

Sunday 1230 hours May 3 rd.

Josefa tried not to look out of the hotel window and across the wide expanse of the Thames. She'd booked one of the most expensive suites in the city for what was supposed to be their victory celebration. They were to be toasting the end of a painful chapter in their quest to rid the world of a most annoying and costly vermin infestation. Looking forwards to a bright new dawn for the far-right in Europe and further afield, armed with a book of deadly and valuable secrets guaranteed to ensure no government nor politician would be stupid enough to stand in their path.

Instead, her father was lying in a British mortuary and their dreams of glory were torn to shreds. Josefa knew she didn't have the intestinal fortitude to carry on the fight without him. She wiped away the tears and took another long pull at her glass of warm champagne. It wasn't that she was a coward, far from it. She'd been brought up to be tougher than a wildcat, despite the expensive private schooling and the lavish monthly allowance. Then there was her genetic inheritance to consider. She had been born to rule.

But she wasn't interested in the political wrangling, the pacts and negotiations that her father had been singularly adept at. Throughout her young life, Josefa had exhibited a short attention span and

her energies could only be directed in one direction for so long before she would lose interest. If it hadn't been for her father, this project would have faltered many years ago.

Her father had understood this implicitly although he had never once criticised or chastised her for her many faults and weaknesses. Ricardo had never once told her how much he had wanted a son, even though she knew he had felt it with every wretched atom of his body.

He had given his wayward daughter specific instructions to follow in the event of his death. And she would carry out her duties to the letter as her lasting and final act of unconditional love to the man, to his vision and his mission.

If I don't return this morning, it will be because I have been betrayed. The English coyote will have sold me out to the highest bidder, as is his devious nature. Of course, I have foreseen this and planned my revenge, even from beyond the veil. This is what you must do.

From her vantage point, Josefa had a clear and uninterrupted view of the Foreign & Commonwealth building where the unscrupulous Logan Ross spent most of his waking hours. Had she possessed the same qualities as her father, particularly his forensic attention to the smallest of details, she might have noticed, through the alcoholic haze of her grief-stricken tears, that there had been an explosion of some kind and the building was in the midst of a small

dust cloud, not unlike the thick black smoke you'd see if there had been a vehicle fire.

Her attention, however, had been directed in a more inward direction, understandably, she would have argued, seeing as the next few minutes were going to be her last on Earth.

Josefa picked up the brushed steel automatic pistol for the hundredth time, admiring its lethal beauty and ruthless efficiency. She could be like that, she whispered to herself. They will remember her name in years to come. Statues will be erected to her, alongside her father, in the new Germany. Smiling, she raised her chin up proudly and allowed herself to dream for a brief moment, picturing herself as a brash and strident heroine, wondering if they would possibly adorn their new Reichsmarks with her face, always her best feature. She downed the last of her drink with a grimace of distaste and reached down to the small briefcase on the coffee table next to her.

There was only one way to do this. She lifted off the paper sheet of instructions and pressed the red button with the forefinger of her right hand and closed her eyes. A surge of primitive, almost sexual, adrenaline coursed up her spine as she thought about the havoc being created by the action of her finger just then. What only seemed like seconds later, she heard the wailing of police sirens and she smiled and made a prayer sign to the heavens. Then Josefa picked up the gun, enjoying the heft of it in her hand for a

moment before putting the tip of the warm metal barrel deep into her mouth and pulling the trigger.

Chapter 60

Sunday 1225 hours May 3 rd.

The floor felt as it was dropping downwards and Ridge had the same queasy feeling in his stomach as when they'd been in that ultra-fast elevator in the Costanera in Chile. But almost as soon as it started, it seemed to subside. There were chunks of plaster thumping down from ceilings, the lights had failed and he could hear alarms going off everywhere. He covered his mouth with a hand, coughing in the semi-darkness and tried to make sense of what little he could see. Little jets of water had sprung up all over the place, dampening down clouds of dust which were billowing everywhere. It was a scene of utter chaos but to Ridge, it felt like the actual building had settled back onto its haunches. Had it been an earthquake? In London?

A hand grabbed his arm and out of the shadows, the grubby face of Colm loomed menacingly. 'Quick! Come with me, I know a way out of here.' He looked across at the horrified secretary who stood transfixed, her vice-like grip of Ridge's shoulder indicating that she was having great difficulty processing the events around her. 'You too.'

Ridge was also having a few issues about the situation. 'What the fuck was that all about Colm? I mean, did you have to kill Logan for fuck's sake… and what just happened here? You don't get

earthquakes this bad in London, do you? Are we safe now?'

Colm pulled Ridge roughly and Vivian was now holding on tightly to his right arm and the three of them started to make their way across the now-devastated office and the prone body of Logan Ross.

'No, it wasn't an earthquake Ridge.' Colm spoke quietly but with the measured tones Ridge had only ever heard when they were in some perilous battle scenario and he kept a zipper on his mouth and tried to understand what the hell was happening.

'You have to understand. You were not to have been in the building when this happened. That's down to me. This was supposed to have been a message, *a symbol*, to the people who are trying to kill us. And I have a bad feeling that it isn't over yet. We have to get out of here now.'

Colm looked at Ridge in that direct way that always scared him half to death. 'Do you trust me?' Ridge nodded mutely and Vivian Pringle gave him a look that said *please get me out of here.*

'Okay then. We're taking the stairs and we're going down to the ground floor by the executive exit. Then we're after going a wee bit lower again.'

Without warning, Colm stopped. 'Shit!' Ridge braced himself for the bad news that he knew was coming.

'Ridge, can you take this lady down the stairs here and wait for me at the bottom.

Wait by an old painted-over door, really hard to see it, same feckin' magnolia colour as the stone walls. I'll only be a minute, I promise.

I need some proof about something and if it exists, then I know it'll be on yer man's hard drive so it will.' Colm proffered an SD card as a way of additional explanation before turning and heading back into the dusty office.

Ridge nodded like he had a choice and took Vivian's hand as if he had any more of a clue about what was happening than she did. The bewildered woman was in no position to argue and she grasped his hand as if he'd offered her the last lifebuoy on the Titanic. It was strangely quiet after the noise of a few minutes before and Ridge wondered for a second if he'd gone partially deaf. Lights had come back on as they started to stumble their way slowly down the stairs and Ridge felt reassured by the sounds of machinery re-starting and the gentle vibration of electricity. He was amazed at how little damage appeared to have been done by the blast or whatever it was. Had it been a bomb? Why would Colm have done such a thing? He turned to encourage the woman who clung on to him and as he was about to open his mouth, there was another deep rumbling sound. A secondary tremor? Ridge tried to think. It couldn't be! Colm had told them it hadn't been an earthquake.

But this time the sensation was entirely different.

A hot gust of foul-smelling air streamed onto them from above and he braced himself for more tremors. Hopelessly unprepared for what came next, Ridge felt immediately disorientated when a tumbling wave of debris engulfed them, accompanied by an ear-splitting explosion. He felt like he'd been spun by a washing-machine from hell and he couldn't stop himself staggering under the impact of the blast. The deafening bang that followed was so painfully loud he was convinced for a second that a jet-fighter had crash-landed on top of the building. After trying to look up through the storm of dust and fragments of building, but being unable to get his footing, Ridge felt himself fall uncontrollably backwards and he screamed as tiny slivers of flesh were ripped from his unprotected face.

Next, he heard the horrible screeching sound of steel girders being wrenched from concrete and then the floor disappeared from under his feet. As he plunged downwards, with his panicked legs cycling madly in a vain attempt to find solid ground, a brief hellish vision of 9/11 seared his terrified brain and he re-opened his eyes in time to see an enormous chunk of masonry spinning towards him out of the maelstrom before the lights went out again.

Chapter 61

It had been a full ten days now, but Orla refused to give up hope. Patrick and the boys had returned to their European base, with their tails between their legs, telling her they had another job scheduled. Orla didn't believe them. She knew they felt bad for what had happened. But no-one could have anticipated a second detonation within the same building within a few minutes of the first one. The authorities had initially suspected the cynical work of ISIS, who often set charges to blow shortly after an initial attack with the specific intention of killing or wounding those police, military or paramedics who had congregated around an attack to assist the first casualties.

Orla had been incandescent with rage when she had learnt of the original plan. And when Patrick had explained how it had actually worked exactly as intended, with zero casualties as far as they were aware, she told him to ask her brother and her husband what they thought of that ridiculous statement, telling him his next job should be a remake of *Dr Strangelove*.

Technically, Patrick had been correct. The building, which had been uniquely qualified for the job, being detached from the others, with one side facing the river and the physical structure of the design being such that it wouldn't fall in on itself, had performed exactly as in their computer-modelled

simulation. It had fallen vertically by ten feet, yet it maintained its structural integrity. Rendered functionally useless, it would have remained as a potent symbol of how vulnerable the British, and by inference, the Yanks, had been to the retribution of The Phantom whom they'd foolishly awoken.

And then there had been the final ace in the deck, which had been when the Diamond Dogs discovered the disused World War Two underground air-raid shelters which lay under the basement of the building and went deeper even than the original London Underground. These long tunnels had mostly been bricked-up and forgotten about, but Patrick and the boys had decided they would make a superb escape route from the 'show detonation.' If it hadn't been for the additional explosives, tightly-packed underneath Logan Ross's substantial desk, the plan would have worked.

Despite that, the saddened trio had taken personal responsibility for what they saw as the probable deaths of both Orla's husband and her brother. Thaddeus had been beside himself with grief and had insisted they try locating Ridge via satellite and the emergency beacon which Colm had instructed a dentist to implant in one of his rear molars, many years previously. But that had drawn a blank. There were several hundred tonnes of collapsed brickwork at the back of the beleaguered building and if Ridge had been caught under that then he was certainly dead. The old *Semper Fi* thing had bothered Patrick,

in particular, and his parting words to her had been bouncing around her weary brain ever since.

'Hell, I want Ridge to have made it through as much as you do, girl. But we can only take the *Serendipity* thang so far. I figure he'd plum used up the luck of ten men already. Be careful Orla. Best you focus on those beautiful kids and git as far away from this kinda life as you can.'

But Orla couldn't imagine life without Ridge by her side. They'd fought through too much, yet each time they had prevailed. She gritted her teeth as she navigated her way across the treacherous traffic, wanting to scream at the passing taxi-cabs. It wasn't the first time one of them had been missing, presumed dead.

She had stayed on in London, using any of her old contacts as best she could. But she had known she'd be quickly running out of road. There was one insurmountable problem about living with a false identity and having had your conventional and fully public funeral many years before. It meant that when you did die, there was no-one to tell. No-one to ask for help. You can't post a missing-person report for a husband already deceased.

Richard Walker had been a walking ghost long before he died a second time.

And Orla knew the authorities would not be interested in searching for a brother who didn't exist. Added to that problem, even for her to alert them to the fact that she, herself, was still alive, would be to

invite a twenty-year stretch at Her Majesty's Pleasure.

She was alone in her quest. In one of the largest cities in the world. *Almost alone*, she remembered, as the pale-faced figure in the distance waved across at her. She had Seamus. A simple Highland lad, who'd turned out to be the most loyal of friends. For him to have stayed behind, in this inhospitable and alien city, had been the one slender strand of hope that had kept her sane. And today, that hope had yielded her first piece of good news.

She hugged him briefly and allowed him to usher her towards a nearby café. He was clutching yet another of his paper street maps, already torn and folded, scored with pencil lines and thick question marks in red marker pen. It turned out that this man, who'd lived his entire life on an island without a single properly named street, had a photographic memory for city maps. In the last two weeks, Seamus had developed an encyclopaedic knowledge of the geography of central London.

His mission that day had been to try and make contact with as many of the many official and unofficial homeless organisations and street groups, while she made her, now daily, tour of the hospitals. It had been Seamus's inspired idea that perhaps Ridge could be lying injured somewhere and he'd maybe come to the attention of some of the vast legions of rough-sleepers who seemed to co-exist alongside the conventional population in a parallel universe which

he and Orla were only beginning to understand. 'You go first!' he said.

'Wait 'til I tell ye!' Trying to keep her voice low, Orla grabbed his right arm tightly and Seamus winced. 'Ouch! That nipped.'

'Shoosh! This is good news, Seamus,' Orla whispered. 'You know how the only body they were after recovering that wasn't vaporized by the second bomb was that cow-'

'-Vivian Pringle, Logan's secre-'

'-Well, you'll never guess what?' Orla's eyes were welling up as she spoke.

'I called in a wee favour or two with a woman who had access to the post-mortem records. She gave me a complete look at everything. It was ghastly, so it was. But there was this tooth, right? It was embedded in her left clavicle, you know… her collar bone.'

Orla saw Seamus nodding but she could tell he hadn't made the jump yet.

'I had a look at the DNA report on the tooth. They were trying to find out if it was Logan, so they were. But here's the thing Seamus… it wasn't Logan and it wasn't on any of their records, apart from one that was classified. So I offered her a year's wages, so I did, to let me have a wee copy of the DNA information. Then I sent it to Thaddeus in Washington, where he worked his magic on it, I don't know how… but listen. He said the tooth is 99%

guaranteed to belong to that handsome eedjit Ridge! Isn't that grand?'

Seamus looked blankly at her, then she saw the penny drop as he worked through the likely scenario. She continued. 'We know Ridge must've been beside the secretary when the second detonation went off, right, the one that caused the building to collapse?'

Orla grinned. 'And we know it was C4 that caused that second explosion, the one that we *didn't* cause… and it was located under the desk of yer man Logan. And they can't have been too close to the bomb, otherwise, they'd have been blown to smithereens like Logan?'

Now Seamus was smiling too and he had a tiny red circle growing ever larger on each of his plump cheeks. She knew he was dying to cut in but she couldn't stop herself and she wanted him to understand the breakthrough she'd just made.

'Okay Seamus… we know for a fact that no other body was found anywhere near where they found Vivien Pringle. We also know Ridge must've been beside her when the building collapsed, otherwise why would he have been biting her. Maybe her body somehow protected Ridge? Like a human shield..?'

Seamus raised his hand to speak.

'You're telling me that this all means Ridge is still alive!'

‘Yes!’ Orla whispered. ‘Now what have *you* got?’

She saw Seamus swallow, before looking carefully around the crowded café.

‘I think I know where he might be…!’

Chapter 62

The dog certainly helped, the man decided, after several hours of careful consideration. And she had been the first ray of light in what had been a dark few days.

'That's what I'm calling you,' he said, reaching over wearily to rub the dark-coloured mongrel's ears. 'Ray. Or maybe *Sugar Ray*, might be more appropriate eh? But just Ray to your friends…'

He lifted off his hat and ran his fingers over his battered skull for the hundredth time that day. It didn't feel any better than the last time. He was no boxer, that was for sure. But he was a fighter of sorts. And he'd won that particular round. Where had he learned to do that? It didn't matter, Ray was his now. And after the way he'd seen that junkie kicking into her before he had waded in with his spectacular rescue, he sensed the dog was as comfortable about the new arrangements as he was. Although if he'd received the sort of head injury he was worried about, it was going to be a one-night stand and he would be in the hospital by nightfall. He hoped it was just that things always felt bigger by touch than they were, particularly when you had no way of seeing them. Like a pimple on your leg, during the night always felt like a cleg bite. A *cleg*?

There it was again! Things were starting to come back to him today, faster than ever. Yesterday, he would have had no clue what a cleg was, but today

he could tell you it was a horsefly and a big bugger at that.

He also knew beyond any doubt that he had a dog. Back in the real world. He had owned a big black dog. Couldn't tell you what its name was or anything like that, but still, it was a real memory.

Like he knew he had once had a family. Kids. A wife who loved him.

Who *had* loved him would be more accurate. Then and now, he reminded himself. He was a walking cliché, like all the other street losers. Except that his fall from grace must have been particularly savage, otherwise why couldn't he remember anything about it. Drugs? He didn't think so. Drink then? Perhaps, he took a drink now, whenever he could, to numb the pain of another bleak night on the street. But how much does a man have to drink before he forgets his entire existence?

The dog wagged her tail at another passer-by and the man heard the comforting clink of yet more change landing in his old baked-bean tin. He pushed his hat gently back and lifted his head to take a look. Must be seven or eight pounds in there. On top of the few notes in his pocket, he would have enough to get them both something to eat tonight.

Maybe Ray had done him a favour in more ways than one. She was definitely a gold-mine, no doubt about that. That would have been the only reason those other drugged-up zombies would have tried to stop him from taking her away. But even with

one of them jumping up and down on his head, they couldn't coordinate their attack. He had killed one of them, he was sure about that. He was equally positive they'd be back after dark. This time there would be more of them, hunting him through the back-streets like a pack of wolves and they wouldn't be content only to kill the dog.

He *had* to remember more and quickly too.

He hoped having his skull pulverized against the pavement over and over again had maybe reset his brain. Whatever loose connection there had been had maybe fallen back into place. Images were flowing through his mind in ever-increasing amounts. Too fast to process, but welcome after the void of nothingness that he'd inhabited for as long as he had known. Places, faces, words, colours, sounds and smells. *Seagulls*. He had lived near the sea!

The man pulled his hat down low over his eyes and rested his head on his arms. It was happening. He was on the cusp of something amazing. He needed to let his brain absorb this new information. Then it would be time to get back on his feet and decipher these messages that were downloading into his mind before it was too late.

Another commuter had stopped and without lifting his head too far off his arms, the man looked warily at the shoes. Clean and practical Doc Martens, too well polished to belong to the type of people looking for him. Relieved, he was about to close his eyes, to resume his quest to understand what the heck

was happening to him, when the tin rattled a second time. But the shoes hadn't moved. He sensed that the owner of the shoes was probably tickling Ray's ear and he gave a silent thanks to the gods for bringing the dog into his miserable life, even if it would only be a transitory blessing.

But then he felt a gentle kick and his heart sank. He looked up quickly in alarm, temporarily blinded by the late afternoon sunshine. The man was a blurry silhouette. His voice seemed to reach all the way back into the darkest recesses of his memory.

'Jesus, you've got a *new* dog then? Bit of a wee runt is it not? And this is a hell of a way to try and get out of paying my folk's for the mountain of food that black wolf eats in a week, never mind those two hungry bairns of yours!'

'What?' He made to get up and he felt a hand grab his arm and pull him up strongly. That voice was familiar, but he couldn't place it. He tried to get a better look at the face but the guy had turned away and was shouting madly at someone else. Ray had begun barking furiously and now fully standing, the man panicked and tried to get away, but he was being held tight by hands far stronger than his own.

'I've found him! Over *here*…! Jesus, Ridge Walker you're a sight for sore eyes.'

And the man found himself being hugged by a man he knew. It was his friend from school. He had a boat. '*Seamus*…?'

‘Aye! Of course it’s me! Do you not know who I am, you daft bugger?

Orla! *He’s over here*!’

The man forced himself to turn his eyes away from his friend and then he saw her running towards him. Her eyes were glistening green and he remembered her beautiful face.

He remembered everything.

Ridge Walker grinned and fell into the arms of the only woman he had truly loved and then they hugged each other so tightly he thought his heart would burst.

THE END

ALSO BY ALEX BRECK

The Ridge Walker Adventure Series

He Who Pays The Piper
The Piper's Lament
The Piper's Promise

The Lachlan Maclean Thriller Series

The Devil You Know

www.alexbreckbooks.com